Judith Gould is the auth... ... MAKERS, both inter... ... blockbusters have been translated... ... foreign languages and have sold millions of copies worldwide. SINS was made into a major TV mini-series starring Joan Collins, which has aired around the world.

The author lives and writes in New York's celebrated Hotel Chelsea, and is currently working on a new novel.

Also by Judith Gould and published by Futura

SINS
THE LOVE MAKERS

JUDITH GOULD

The Love Makers: The Texas Years

Futura

A Futura Book

Typeset, printed and bound in Great Britain by
Hazell Watson & Viney Limited
Member of BPCC plc
Aylesbury, Bucks, England

Futura Publications
A Division of Macdonald & Co (Publishers) Ltd
Headway House
66–73 Shoe Lane
London
EC4P 4AP

A member of Maxwell Pergamon Publishing Corporation Plc

For ETTA BARRITT and GUY DOLEN,
mother and son.

With sincere gratitude and acknowledgment for the hours spent opening the book of your lives and letting me plot and twist and varnish it to the needs of fiction:

Because there really *was* a Good Eats Café in southwest Texas.

Because there really *was* an 'Auntie'.

But most of all, because every book needs a springboard, and your open-hearted tales provided it – after which a lot of artistic licence was taken by me.

Needless to say, the circus, any crimes committed, the Sextons, and a host of other ingredients are entirely the stuff of fiction and my imagination.

But even fiction finds its roots in the real world, and this background you have generously provided.

AUTHOR'S PREFACE

The Love Makers: THE TEXAS YEARS spans the period 1890 to 1928 and is what, these days, most people would probably refer to as a prequel since its parent, *The Love Makers*, was published first (in 1985). However, though this novel *is* a prequel in the broadest sense, it is also a story unto itself (as is the multi-generational *The Love Makers*, which covers the years 1928 to 1985).

Those readers who have already read the parent book will now find themselves journeying backwards through time to follow the early events which shaped Elizabeth-Anne Hale's destiny and which led to the building of her hotel empire. On the other hand, readers just embarking on *The Love Makers* saga can follow the exploits of the Hale family chronologically, by continuing with *The Love Makers*. But the story does not end there. One last book will comprise the *Love Makers* trilogy – *The Love Makers:* SECOND LOVE (which covers the period 1986 to 1990).

And here my apologies are due the reader who might want to tackle the entire three volumes without interruption. Two other books, *Dazzle* and another as yet untitled, both more timely with today's headlines, have shunted the order of the trilogy's appearance, but not, happily, its importance. I find myself returning to it constantly, like to friends long lost and found again.

That final and last book in this irregular sequence, is in the works right now. Hopefully, after reading *The Love Makers:* THE TEXAS YEARS and *The Love Makers*, you will feel as I do – and in the near future will enjoy reading *The Love Makers:* SECOND LOVE as much as I am enjoying writing it.

New York City
August, 1988

JUDITH GOULD

CONTENTS

CONTENTS

The Love Makes:
The Texas Years

PROLOGUE

1924

QUEBECK, TEXAS

1

Even before the first light of dawn appeared in the sky Elizabeth-Anne hitched Bessie, her ageing mare, to the buggy, climbed up on the wooden seat, and sat stiffly erect with that peculiar brand of dignity which was hers alone. With her pigskin-gloved hands, she pulled on the reins, and Bessie clip-clopped softly down Main Street, the dirt road that ran through the centre of Quebeck and led out through the fields. She turned around and glanced back at the receding Good Eats Café. The windows glowed softly from the lamplight and she could see shadows shifting on the walls inside. That meant her three children were already up and moving about. Getting things ready to serve the townsfolk breakfast.

She nodded to herself with satisfaction. Ever since she had been husbandless, the children had had to pitch in and help. Young though they were, they had done so without complaint. At least not to her face.

Expertly she flipped the reins, and Bessie dutifully picked up speed. The morning air was chilly and brisk, fresh against her face now that she was riding along at a swift trot.

She glanced up at the sky. The pock-marked moon was full and white, hovering low and bathing the town in an eerie, silvery glow. She loved the chill early air, had learned at a young age to appreciate it. Later, as the sun began to rise, the air would become dry and baked and gritty, making it difficult to breathe, but right now it was wonderfully refreshing. She took a

15

series of deep breaths, inhaling slowly, savouring the cold in her lungs.

To either side of her, Main Street was lined with creaky, gingerbread-fronted houses, hulking black shadows behind tiny, dusty front yards. She stayed off-centre on the dusty thoroughfare, avoiding the twin rails of the Quebeck Traction Company. If the wheels of her buggy hit the steel rails, they would skid and shimmy. She sighed to herself. Other towns had buses, but Quebeck still had its antiquated horse-drawn tram – a single, small-gauge railroad car, roofed but open on all sides. The traction ran from the railroad station down Main Street, and looped around the northern end of town. What use that was, Elizabeth-Anne did not know. The northern tip of town was where the wealthier people lived, in freshly painted houses with stained-glass windows and port-cochères – families which owned horses, buggies, and even motorcars. By all rights, the traction should have looped south, through Mexican Town; the Mexicans could ill afford to own even a scrawny mule and mean wagon. They *needed* the traction, not as a convenience, but a necessity. She herself had brought up the subject at numerous Town Meetings, but her efforts had fallen on deaf ears. Of course, not one Mexican had been present at the Town Meetings, or ever had been, for that matter. Quebeck proper and Mexican Town were treated as two separate entities coexisting in one small area, but with separate churches, shops, schools, customs, and laws. The people of Quebeck didn't care what went on in Mexican Town as long as its poor inhabitants didn't effect their lives – and the better-off whites wielded control. These injustices, and others like them, never ceased to rankle Elizabeth-Anne. It was a sad fact, but a true one: there was nothing that could be done. At least her efforts thus far had proved fruitless.

At the eastern end of town, Main Street petered out

16

into a single lane which led out across the fields, sparsely dotted with sage, and cactuses. Elizabeth-Anne snapped the reins again, urging Bessie to quicken her pace. She was in a hurry. She wanted to be at the construction site long before anyone else. She liked to be able to roam about, poking into the corners of her unfinished buildings in peace and quiet. For that, she had to get there very early. The Mexican labourers liked to start work at daybreak, long before it got hot, so they could enjoy a long siesta during the height of the noonday heat. Then, in the cooler, late afternoon, the work would once again continue until nightfall.

The dawn began to pale the blackness on the flat horizon, and the crystalline stars faded into the sky. By the time she neared the site, the sun was already starting to slide up from the east. She pulled on the reins and Bessie dutifully came to a standstill.

From her high perch, Elizabeth-Anne looked out across the countryside. Southeast lay the direction from which the new highway was slowly coming, two blue-black asphalt lanes being laid down from Brownsville, at the mouth of the Rio Grande. In another three weeks, it would reach as far as her property. Then it would continue on up northwest towards Laredo. She knew that it would be at least another year before it was entirely completed, but Elizabeth-Anne was a visionary and had learned to trust her instincts: cars had become commonplace, even in this sparsely populated patch of the southwest, and they would all soon be using this one new highway. Travellers journeying along it would need a comfortable, convenient place to stay the night.

Which was why she was building the first tourist court in southwest Texas.

Her aquamarine eyes narrowed as she nodded thoughtfully to herself. Then she permitted herself a rare smile. She was not a beautiful woman in the Dresden porcelain sense, but the smile gave her a radiance and beauty strangers might otherwise fail to see. She was a handsome woman, by necessity sturdy and strong. Her nose was thin and straight, and her waist-long, wheat-gold hair, though enviously fine and abundant, was not shown off to advantage. For efficiency's sake, she wore it tightly plaited and pinned up so that it wouldn't get in her way. Elizabeth-Anne Hale was, above all, a very proud, immensely practical, eminently capable, woman.

She felt a stirring within her belly, and she leaned forwards and looked down at herself. Her trim hourglass waist had always been as tiny and wasp-like as that of the most pampered, and a few months ago she had been able to span it with two hands. But that had been before she had become pregnant again. Now her belly was majestically swollen and her breasts had become heavy with milk, soon ready for the suckling of her newest young.

'Too bad your daddy couldn't have stayed around just a little bit longer,' she told her unborn child sadly.

She touched her belly in silent communion. The baby was due in a couple of months. She closed her eyes and smiled beatifically as she felt another movement within her womb. A series of kicks, lively and restless, let her know that all was well, that the child she was carrying was impatient to greet the world.

'Hey, settle down in there!' she jokingly chided the unborn child. Then she sighed softly. She had stalled long enough. She snapped the reins tight again and Bessie continued to trot on. The construction site was a full two miles from town, yet another quarter of a mile across the fields. Already, she could make out what was to be the tourist court, long and rambling, the rising skeletal timbers silhouetted against the sunrise like an ancient Greek ruin, and the sight of it filled her with an immeasurable sense of achievement and pride.

She glanced neither to the left nor the right, but

pressed her lips firmly together and kept her bright eyes focused straight ahead on the building which her ambition was driving her to erect. All the while, the gears of her mind turned and clicked as she thought of yet more ways to improve and expand that which she already had. In Quebeck, there were the Good Eats Café and the Hale Rooming House – no way to make a fortune, mind you, but with hard work, a decent enough living. And soon, out here where the highway would pass, would be the tourist court. That, she realized, could lead to other things. Bigger things. Even better things.

Yes, she had come a long way.

When she reached the site, she pulled in on the reins and climbed awkwardly down off the buggy, her full-length, grey calico skirt just brushing the ground. She tied Bessie to a scrub bush and reached into her pocket for a lump of sugar. She held it out in the palm of her hand. The horse gently nuzzled it from her, its nostrils flaring appreciatively. She patted its long muzzle and then began on her rounds.

Involved as she had been since the conception of her tourist court, she still couldn't help but feel impressed. Its very proportions dwarfed her. It was nearly two hundred feet long and fifteen wide. The walls weren't finished yet; the brick just went a third of the way up, and the rest was still the timber skeleton she had seen from far across the fields.

The manager's cabin was directly in the centre. It, too, was unfinished, but would consist of three rooms – an office flanked by a small bedroom and a kitchen. To either side of it were eight guest cabins – sixteen altogether. Each would boast a screened-in front porch and a private toilet with running water and a bathtub, and each cabin was separated from the next by a roofed parking space. These were virtually unheard of, but something she was certain cars necessitated. After all,

19

the Texas sun burned strongly nearly all year round here, and everyone with cars liked to park them in the shade, just like they would a horse. So shade she would provide. And . . . she had intentionally made them much larger than they had to be. With typical foresight, she had envisioned that in time not only would the reliability of cars increase, but their size as well.

In addition, her foresight had planned two billboards. Each would face the highway a quarter of a mile away in either direction of the tourist court. She could see them already. *Hale Tourist Court.* That was what the letters would spell, and to make certain that there was no mistaking the quality of the place, she would use a symbol – a gold crown – to assure weary travellers that the rooms were indeed fit for a king. Perhaps in time that crown would become as well-known in the area as the Coca-Cola script in the Quebeck General Store. She hoped so.

She strode about briskly in her sturdy black lace-up boots. She had just turned twenty-nine years old, and the fact that she was one of the first enterprising businesswomen in America had never even entered her mind. Work was nothing new to her – it was, quite simply, a way of life. If required, she gladly rolled up her sleeves and did the lowliest of chores herself. People wondered how a grass widow found the time to raise three children properly while running two flourishing businesses and starting yet a third. The secret, Elizabeth-Anne had discovered, lay in the management of time and priorities – the delegation of authority and putting the most pressing, immediate problems where they belonged – right in the forefront. Besides, what choice did she have? Her husband was gone, and the children were a living reality. The facts had stared her in the face when Zaccheus had gone off and left her, and she'd had to accept them – cruel as they were – right then and there. Someone had to run the rooming house and the café, and she couldn't afford to hire anyone other than the Mexican maid, Rosa. Besides, the bank loan for the Hale Tourist Court had already been made, and the construction begun. She couldn't stop in midstream, not if she wanted to repay the loan and be financially solvent. A woman on her own, no matter how young, wasn't left many choices, and certainly not in southwest Texas. She was just grateful that the businesses were there and doing well. Otherwise . . .

'. . . There's no time to contemplate any other tragedies that might happen!' she scolded herself harshly. 'This emotional rambling is one luxury you just can't afford to indulge in!' And with that, she resolutely swept the thoughts from her mind so that she could concentrate on the things for which she had driven out here.

Holding onto the two-by-fours, she stood on tiptoe and leaned over the waist-high brick walls to look into each of the unfinished rooms. Carefully she took note of the progress. She grasped the doorframes in her nimble hands and tugged and pushed on them with all her might to check their sturdiness. Then she clapped the dirt off her hands and stamped her feet on all sixteen of the wooden porch platforms, checking to make certain that they, too, were well-built and would hold up well. If you've got to build something, she opined, then why not build it to last?

Her inspection finished, she hiked up her skirt and pushed the twenty yards through the dry yellow-brown weeds to where the highway would pass. She found the surveyors' marker without any trouble. For a while she remained there, her body leaning slightly forwards, one hand held like a stiff salute against her forehead in order to shield her eyes from the glaring sun. Critically, she analysed the tourist court.

Yes, she reflected for the hundredth time, it was very symmetrical and pleasing to the eye. It looked like a comfortable rest stop – above all, there was a welcoming quality about it. She herself wouldn't mind coming across a place such as this one if she had spent long, tiring hours on the road.

Suddenly her eyes grew hard and her handsome features creased into a frown. Something was missing. The tourist court which seemed to have everything could use yet something else. But what? She searched her mind and then shook her head in frustration and sighed. It disturbed her when her instinct hinted at something she couldn't put her finger on. Well, in time it would come to her, she thought. Sooner or later, it always did.

2

Five minutes later, she heard the sound of an approaching horse. She turned around. Carlos Cortez had arrived on his old mare. He was the foreman she had hired, and he had turned out to be a good one, efficient and demanding, yet well-liked by the Mexican labourers.

Elizabeth-Anne knew that she had made a good choice in putting him in charge instead of a white man. The labourers didn't resent taking his orders. They considered him to be one of them, yet they looked upon him with admiration and respect. They felt that if anyone from Mexican Town made it across to the other side of the tracks, it would surely be Carlos. He had gone away and worked his way through a big university where he had studied engineering, and for this they were very proud of him. He was a feather in the Mexican community's cap, even if building projects where a Mexican engineer was welcome were few and far between.

He was young and handsome, too – perhaps too handsome for his own good, Elizabeth-Anne thought. He had the blue-black hair, dark glowing eyes, and bronze skin of the Mexicans, but his nose was surprisingly aquiline and his chin was square and determined. All the women in Mexican Town eyed him covetously, the young ones with open admiration, the older ones with hope and muttered prayers that one of their daughters would be blessed with the luck to be chosen as his bride. But for some reason known only to himself, he hadn't shown a preference for any particular girl yet.

Elizabeth-Anne watched as he dismounted and strode quickly towards her. After her, he was always the first to arrive on the site in the morning, and the last to leave at night.

When he reached her, he politely took off his straw hat and held it in front of him. 'Buenos días, Señora Hale,' he said formally.

'Buenos días, Señor Cortez,' Elizabeth-Anne returned politely.

Each time they met they greeted each other formally in Spanish before slipping into English. It had become a ritual of sorts. Still, Elizabeth-Anne couldn't overcome the feeling that his Spanish greetings and his formal 'Señoras', as well as the doffing of his hat, were not done without a hint of mockery. It was as if he were play-acting the part of the humble, subservient Mexican, and even the deliberateness of his English seemed somehow affected and mocking. But whenever she looked at him closely to determine if this was the case, she could never see beyond the guarded veil which dropped down over his eyes. There was something impenetrable about him, and although she was not frightened by him in the least, she did find the distance he deliberately placed between them a bit unsettling.

Now she looked around the tourist court and

23

nodded. 'The work is progressing well,' she said with satisfaction.

He nodded agreement. 'My men are good workers. In sixteen weeks it shall all be finished.'

Elizabeth-Anne shook her head and looked at him levelly. 'I was going to talk to you about that.' She lowered her head as if to inspect the scuffed tips of her boots, which peered out dustily from beneath her skirt. Then she looked back up at him. 'We must be ready to open for business in thirteen weeks,' she said softly. 'By then the highway will reach all the way to Rio Grande City, and there'll be a lot of traffic going by.'

He listened attentively, then he sighed and scratched his head as he squinted thoughtfully at the construction site. When he spoke his voice was quiet. 'The men already work like feverish ants eleven hours a day. We cannot demand more of them.'

'Then we must hire extra workers.'

'I'm afraid that is out of the question, Señora. These men are the best. They are trained and know what they are doing. Besides, the others are busy with ranch work or the crops. They cannot possibly leave their jobs.'

Elizabeth-Anne frowned. 'Then we must push the workday up. To fourteen hours a day.'

For a second, his coal-black eyes flared. 'But that means they will have to work through the noonday heat!' he protested. 'It's summer, and the temperature —'

'We raise their wages by twenty cents an hour,' she said firmly, 'and give them time-and-a-half for any hours they work beyond the usual eleven. For the extra money, they'll do it.'

He let out a deep breath and shook his head. 'I will put it to them, Señora, but I can make no promises. You understand?' He held her gaze.

She nodded. She herself would have preferred to speak outright to the men, but the Mexican men's

24

macho sense of pride was easily wounded, and, like most men she knew, they did not like taking orders from a woman. Women were supposed to stay home and cook and have babies was their consensus, not run businesses and putting up buildings. So she went through Carlos Cortez, who passed on everything she wanted to the men. It was a roundabout way of doing things, a method her headstrong nature rebelled against, but she was powerless to do otherwise – and smart enough to know when to compromise. She consoled herself with the fact that if anyone could persuade the men to do something, it was Carlos Cortez.

'I'll be by tomorrow with the payroll,' she said.

He nodded. Then he placed his hat on his head and reached into his shirt pocket. He took out some folded sheets of thin yellow paper. Wordlessly, he unfolded them and handed them over to her.

Even before she glanced at them she knew what they were. More bills from Coyote Building Suppliers. These were for yesterday afternoon's delivery.

She glanced at the first sheet. Then her brow furrowed and her lips creased into a frown. Hurriedly, she leafed through the rest, her eyes scanning the scrawled lists of items and prices. She stared at Carlos Cortez. 'There's got to be some mistake!' she exclaimed softly.

He shook his head sadly. 'No, there is no mistake, Señora. As soon as they arrived I immediately checked and demanded an explanation. "Rising costs". That is what I was told.'

There was the rustling of paper as she angrily slapped the sheets against her thigh. For a moment she closed her eyes and slowly twisted her head from side to side. Every week, the cost of building supplies went up. It was monstrous! No, not monstrous. Blackmail. That's what it amounted to. Ever since she had begun the tourist court it had been a constant drain on her finances, like a gluttonous monster that constantly had to be fed.

And what it gobbled up were precious dollars and cents. Already, it had cost her far more than it ever should have. And she knew that she wasn't to blame for going over budget.

It was the Sextons.

First, she'd had to get the loan for the land and construction costs from Quebeck Savings and Loan – a Sexton-owned bank, and Quebeck's *only* bank. Then she'd had to get all her supplies from Coyote Building Suppliers, which was also owned by the Sextons. The Sextons practically owned the whole county – their stores bought and sold the vegetable crops and all the beef, pork and poultry; their cotton mills processed the picked cotton, their freight cars shipped the citrus crops up north. As if that weren't enough, it was their land that produced nearly everything. And last but not least, their politicians sat in all the important seats of the local government. No matter which way you turned in this part of southwest Texas, you could always count on one thing: finding yourself face-to-face with a Sexton, or at least someone on the Sexton payroll.

Without exception, everyone had learned to hate the Sextons, and with good reason. They either owned you outright, or you were beholden to them in some way or other. Tex Sexton, the family patriarch, was a greedy, power-hungry egomaniac – and his young wife, Jennifer, was evil personified. While Tex was the undisputed 'king' of the county, his mean younger brother, Roy, had – until a tragic accident claimed his life – been in charge of the various hydra-headed branches of the family business. And since then, Tex and Jennifer had become more corrupt than ever.

Tex and Jennifer were rich beyond comprehension; they had more money, in fact, than they could keep track of. But somehow, they invariably managed to find the time to personally involve themselves in the pettiest of schemes. They milked everyone dry, and once there was nothing left to milk, they could be trusted to some-how squeeze yet another few drops of blood out of their victims. Long ago, Elizabeth-Anne had decided that the Sextons must be very unhappy people indeed.

But analysing the state of their happiness, Elizabeth-Anne realized, didn't do anyone a bit of good – herself least of all. Happy or unhappy, Tex and Jennifer were there, all-powerful and avaricious, sucking up the juices of the land and its people. For most of the time they had turned a blind eye towards her, but she had sus-pected that blindness to be only temporary and that her time would come. Now it had. They were going to take her for everything she had. They were going to milk her dry. Wasn't it enough that her beloved Zaccheus had run off because of them?

She felt suddenly weary. If only she didn't have to battle the Sextons' monopoly. If only she could buy her supplies elsewhere . . . But what choice did she have? she railed silently. Or, for that matter, what choice did anyone else have? Coyote Building Suppliers, with its twenty branches, was the only outlet of its kind within a radius of two hundred miles. There simply were no competitors to whom people could take their business; Tex had seen to that. He had neatly built himself a monopoly that covered any and all industries and busi-nesses that showed a decent profit. If anyone dared offer up competition, they were squashed as effortlessly as a beetle under a boot.

Cruelty was Tex's middle name. He was well-known to sit back and watch with amusement as potential com-petitors fought to gain a hard-earned foothold. Nothing gave him more pleasure than biding his time and waiting until the iron was hot before he struck. Now, out of the blue, he had lashed out in Elizabeth-Anne's direction, suddenly raising his already usurious prices. Why? Because Zaccheus had dared fight back?

It was a bad omen.

Tex frightened her. But Jennifer . . .

Elizabeth-Anne felt a sudden chill as she pictured Jennifer sitting in the enormous ranch house. Watching and waiting and scheming. Ever since they had been children, Jennifer had idled away her time plotting. But why strike *now*? Elizabeth-Anne knew she was in no way offering the Sextons competition.

Could it simply be because of Jennifer?

She tightened her lips determinedly. Well, she, for one, wasn't going to sit back and let Tex and Jennifer walk all over her! Not on her life! She would go to Coyote and see what she could do. If need be, she would seek out Tex himself and demand an explanation. Besides, what could he do to her other than make money off her hand over fist?

But Jennifer. Well, she thought, Jennifer was another story entirely. She could talk to Tex, but Jennifer would refuse even to see her.

Meanwhile, Elizabeth-Anne knew that she had no choice but to go ahead with the construction. Now, more than ever, she felt the desperate need for the revenues the Hale Tourist Court would bring in. It *had* to be open for business as soon as possible. No one but she knew the very precarious state her finances were in. The entire bank loan had already been eaten up. The Good Eats Café and the rooming house, along with six years of hard-earned savings, were paying the bills. If she couldn't open the tourist court within thirteen weeks . . . or earlier . . . and if she couldn't come to an agreement with the Sextons . . . or if they dared raise their prices yet *again* . . .

She looked at Carlos Cortez. 'I will see you tomorrow,' she told him briskly. 'Now I've got to head back to town.'

He followed her to the buggy and helped her up to the seat. In the distance, she could see the labourers' flat-bed truck arriving. The men were crowded in the

28

back, an indistinguishable mass of blue denim work-clothes and yellow straw hats.

Carlos followed her gaze. As if sensing what affects her problem might have on the employment of his people, he said: 'I will speak to the men about the extra hours. I think I can get them to agree.' He paused, embarrassed, and added softly: 'Without the time-and-a-half.'

She stared down at him. So he knows, she thought. Suddenly she reached out and touched his shoulder gratefully. Then, tightening her lips purposefully, she sat stiffly erect and snapped the reins. Bessie began to move and Carlos slid out of sight.

During the ride back to town, her mind was occupied by what the day still held in store. Hours of gruelling work and, if she could manage the time – and she couldn't afford not to – going to Coyote and trying to sort things out. Sometimes it seemed to her that no matter how hard she worked, obstacles always popped up in front of her. So far, she'd managed to work her way around them. *So far . . .*

Beyond these thoughts she could hear the steady clip-clop of Bessie's hooves on the dirt road. Then abruptly the smell of burning brush assaulted her senses. Someone was clearing fields. Her lips tightened, and she held her breath. But after a while that one overpowering odour engulfed her completely. Ever since she had been a little girl, fires – even the smell of smoke – had filled her with nightmares and dread. No matter how she tried to close her mind to it, the hideous memory was always there in the background somewhere.

The smell of burning.

The crackle and roar of flames.

The hideous shrieks of agony and the desperate cries for help . . .

There was no escaping it. Years passed and many things changed, but never that.

For with the smell of fire came the memory of death. The unshakable memory that had stayed with her ever since she had been six years old.

BOOK ONE

1895

Elizabeth-Anne

HIDALGO COUNTY, TEXAS

1

It was a sunny Thursday when a strange caravan stopped at the roadside along the parched, sloping banks of the Rio Grande near Quebeck, Texas.

The caravan was Szabo's Travelling Circus and Freak Show, and like a pioneer wagon train trying to protect itself from attacks by hostile Indians, the members of the circus drew the wagons round in a protective circle. The horses were then unhitched, led down to the water, and were allowed to graze on the dusty brush and dry tufts of grass. Since the horses were paramount to the survival of the circus, their needs always came first.

The circus people were one huge family. They drew the wagons protectively around their little compound and stuck close together because they felt more secure that way. For the most part, they were considered freaks. They had all, at some time or other, lived singly in towns or in the country, where they had been outcasts — easy marks for jeers, pranks, and ridicule. But together, they shared this common bond, their food, and their earnings. To be sure, it was a rather unnerving form of making a living, but all of them felt that it was better to be around others of their kind, and be gawked at by audiences, than to live by themselves and be at the whim and mercy of intolerants and cold-blooded pranksters. They had all suffered terrible indignities on their own, but within the bosom of the circus they felt normal, enveloped in a caring, gentle, and loving family. There was safety in numbers. As well as employment.

And so it was that Hazy and Goliath, the dwarfs; Hester, the bearded lady; Marikka, the fat lady; and Paulette and Pauline, the Siamese twins, rarely left the sides of their fierce protectors, some of whom looked quite ordinary, but whose talents assuredly weren't — Szabo, the ringmaster and circus owner, who advertised himself as 'The Strongest Man Alive'; Hendricks, 'The Human Dragon', a Dutchman who 'swallowed' kerosene and then spat it into a torch, causing frightful flames to appear to spew forth from his lips; Stavros, 'The Elastic Man', a Greek contortionist who, thanks to his unique joints, could entangle his arms and legs into unbelievable knots; Boris, 'The Human Fly', who could effortlessly walk tightropes, shin up smooth poles, and swing from trapezes; and the Tak Brothers, four young Chinese who were acrobats.

On this particular day, the circus had not stopped to give a show or to rest: it was midmorning and it should have been on the road, headed for the nearest town. But Marikka, the fat lady, had gone into labour to give birth to the child she and Szabo had conceived, and so the travelling circus had, by necessity, stopped travelling. Everyone awaited the birth with anticipation. For the circus family, it was truly an event.

Szabo, the father-to-be, was in his late forties. Essentially a kind, gentle man, he nevertheless worked at creating a forbidding, piratical appearance. He was medium of height but extremely broad and heavy, and had a domed, glossy shaved head. He wore a thick handlebar moustache and an enormous gold loop in his right ear. His body was spectacularly packed with hard muscle. Besides running the circus and being its ringmaster, he also challenged local townsfolk to fights, and invariably, his challenges were accepted. Everyone liked to watch a good fight, and every town had its resident renowned ruffian. More often than not, the bets taken at the fights brought in more money than the rest of the circus box office.

'Szabo,' his common-law wife, Marikka, had begged him in their native Hungarian, 'the fights, they got to stop. You are not so young anymore. You cannot take the punches like you used to. You will get hurt, you should stop.'

'You think I cannot fight? I never lose yet!' he boasted, puffing out his chest. Then he shrugged his massive shoulders and added softly, 'How we bring in enough money if I cannot fight? The show don't pay to keep the circus going. Then what would the others do? What about Goliath and Hazy, and Hester, and Paulette and Pauline?'

And that had settled the matter.

Marikka, the mother-to-be, was an enormous, grotesque woman who weighed over three hundred pounds, a fact that made her pregnancy all but indistinguishable. She was very shy and it tore her apart inside to be put on display in front of gawking audiences and be ridiculed and laughed at. But she forced herself to grin happily throughout her performances: she loved Szabo with all her heart and knew that she had to help in any way she could. It was an unwritten agreement that everyone who was part of the circus had to do his share, and although Szabo owned the circus and she had shared his bed for the past five years, she didn't want to be treated any better than the others.

Now that she was in labour, Hazy, the wizened dwarf, with her tiny hands, acted as the midwife. Outside the wagon, Szabo and the others gathered in silence and waited impatiently for news.

Daylight turned to dusk, darkness fell, and midnight approached. One by one, the circus people had drifted back to their own wagons until only Szabo and Goliath remained outside. 'What can be taking so long?' Szabo kept repeating over and over.

Inside the red-and-gold lead wagon, the black, pot-bellied iron stove glowed orange, and the air was humid and stuffy. Pots of water bubbled and hissed furiously as they boiled over. Hanging kerosene lamps cast gigantic, grotesque shadows across the walls and cove ceiling. From behind the blue floor-length curtain that divided the long, narrow wagon in two came the feverish moans, gasps, and heavy panting of a woman in labour.

Despite Hazy's chasing him out each time he poked his head in past the curtain, Szabo couldn't stay away. The bone-chilling screams of his wife tore him apart inside. Now, pulling the curtain aside for the hun-dredth time in so many minutes, the sight of her pro-fusely sweating, screwed-up face and her massive breasts and rolls of flesh rising and falling like bellows was more than he could bear.

'Out!' Hazy practically flew at him, her wrinkled, child-like dwarf's hands blurring through the air. She shoved him backwards with all her might: even under the best of circumstances, childbirth does not lend dig-nity to the female anatomy, and she did not wish for Szabo to see his wife thus.

'Out!' Hazy ordered again, and her expression was so fierce that Szabo reluctantly obeyed.

This time, Hazy shot the bolt across the door behind him.

'And stay out!' the dwarf called out the window when Szabo climbed up the wagon wheel to peer inside. Then she slammed the little window shut and drew the check-ered curtains tightly across it.

The hours crawled past with interminable slowness: midnight . . . one o'clock . . . two. The later it got, the more Szabo thought he would go crazy. He and loyal Goliath, Hazy's tiny husband, had been pacing circles together around the wagon all afternoon already, and

36

still Marikka was in labour. Above them, the tall thin chimney rising up from the wagon roof emitted showers of sparks, and all around, the windows of the other wagons glowed yellow; no one was sleeping. Everyone was awaiting news of the birth.

'Something is wrong,' Szabo muttered. 'It takes too long. Listen.' He paused and cocked his head. 'Listen to the horses. Even they can sense it. I never seen them this restless.'

Goliath scoffed. 'It's only the screams, Szabo,' he soothed. 'It's only that which frightens them.'

'They can smell death,' Szabo said stubbornly. Clumsily, he rolled a cigarette, lit it with shaking fingers, and puffed on it nervously, the smoke becoming pale plumes carried backwards along the wind. He rubbed his thick bare arms with his hands. Despite it being mid-August, the summer night was chilly.

He and Goliath froze in mid-pace as Marikka howled, her eerie, blood-curdling cry causing faces to pop out of every window of the wagons all around.

'It's all right, Szabo,' Goliath assured him in a bare whisper. 'If it weren't, Hazy would have called us.'

As if on cue, the door to the lead wagon suddenly exploded outwards and in the rectangle of blazing light the tiny, bow-legged figure of Hazy motioned urgently for Szabo to come. Grinding the cigarette out under his heel, he leapt up on to the wagon's little back porch. 'What is it?' he demanded.

But Hazy only looked up at him with frightened, moist eyes before slowly turning away.

Alarmed, Szabo pushed Hazy aside and rushed into the wagon. Yanking the blue divider curtain aside, he sank to his knees beside the sturdy bunk on which his enormous wife lay, pale and damp and quiet. Her eyes were closed and her breathing sounded weak and shallow. He noticed that one of her arms was coiled around a small, blanketed bundle.

With a surge of paternal warmth, Szabo gently pushed the blanket aside. The child Marikka was holding was tiny and red, with strands of dark wet hair. The breath caught in Szabo's throat and his naturally fierce features became docile and awed. Smiling, he touched the child gently with his fingertips.

His smile froze and he found himself falling through a nightmare.

The baby felt ice cold. It was dead.

Stunned, he slowly turned around. Hazy had come up quietly behind him and was standing there, silent tears pouring down her wizened cheeks. She wiped her eyes with a knuckle. 'I . . . I'm so sorry, Szabo,' the dwarf sobbed. 'I did the best I could do. Really, I did. But the little boy . . . he was stillborn.'

Szabo's lips tightened grimly. 'And Marikka?' he demanded softly, staring at Hazy. 'My wife? She will be all right?'

Hazy averted her gaze. 'I . . . I don't know,' she whispered.

Szabo jumped to his feet and bounded over to the door in three swift strides. 'Goliath!' he bellowed from the porch.

Hazy's tiny husband pushed his way through the circus people who once again crowded around outside. 'Yes, Boss?' he called up.

'Hitch up two horses,' Szabo ordered. 'The fastest we got. Then come with me. We must drive Marikka to a doctor.'

'Just give me two minutes, Boss,' Goliath said, and sped off.

'Szabo?' Marikka's low, slurred voice drifted out to him. 'Szabo!'

He hurried back to her bedside. 'Sssssh,' he said gently. 'You must not tire yourself, Marikka, my darling.'

She looked up at him, her eyes searching his. 'You

38

are angry with me, Szabo?' Her voice was weak and husky, barely more than a whisper.

'How can I be angry with you?' He took her hand and raised it to his lips. 'I love you, Marikka.'

Shadows deepened around her puffy red eyes. 'The baby . . . he is dead.' A keening moan gurgled in her throat. 'Our baby is dead, Szabo. Dead.'

'Quiet,' he said gently. 'Everything, it will be all right.'

'No.' She took his arm and gripped it with astonishing strength. 'I have failed you.'

'We will have other children.'

'No, Szabo. My . . . my insides. Something is not right there. I can feel it.' Her hand gripped his arm even more desperately. 'I am frightened, Szabo.'

'Hush. I take you to see a doctor.'

'It is too . . . late,' she said wearily. Then her grip weakened and her hand loosened from his arm.

'The horses are hitched, Boss!' Goliath called from outside.

'I must go now,' Szabo said.

But Marikka did not hear him. She had already drifted off into feverish unconsciousness.

It was only when he got back to his feet that Szabo noticed the blood staining the sheet. He lifted it up and stared. More blood was slowly welling from Marikka's vagina.

'I want you to stay here at Marikka's side,' he told Hazy. 'We take her to see a doctor.' And with that, Szabo went back outside and climbed up to the driver's seat atop the wagon. He held out his hand. Goliath tossed a whip up to him and, showing remarkable agility and strength for someone so tiny, fearlessly leapt bareback on to one of the horses, his sturdy little hands clutching its mane. No sooner was he mounted than Szabo snapped the reins and cracked the whip.

With a mighty jerk, the horses heaved the creaking wagon out of the circular formation and into the road.

39

More cracks of the whip rent the night, and with a burst of speed the horses were off at a gallop.

They raced along the rutted country road at breakneck speed, the top-heavy wagon swaying precariously and bouncing as it crashed in and out of deep potholes. It was not a vehicle designed for speed, but Szabo kept whipping the horses until he felt he was racing the devil. Had he had even a little moonlight to guide him, he would have slowed down. The road was more treacherous than he dared imagine.

But Szabo was driven by desperation, and he guided the horses by feeling and instinct alone. Squinting against the wind, his eyes smarting and watering, he cracked his whip mercilessly while peering fiercely ahead into the darkness from under brushy, furrowed brows. Nothing mattered – not the horses' safety, not Goliath's, least of all his own – nothing but Marikka.

The wagon ate up one mile after another, and Szabo cursed the vast distances between towns in this gigantic sprawling state. From where the circus had pulled up at the roadside, the last town lay some twenty miles distant; he prayed that in this other direction he would reach one sooner.

Too late he heard Goliath's scream of warning. Too late he heard the approaching thunder of hoofbeats. Far, far too late he saw the oncoming obstruction looming larger and larger out of the darkness in front of his eyes. The breath froze in his throat. Out of the blackness of the night, another team of horses and a wagon were headed towards his, and in that split second before impact, he could hear the shouts and screams from the people in the other wagon.

Time froze. The horses and wagons converged almost in slow motion. And then time sped up again, and the horses collided head-on and went crashing down to the ground in a whinnying, snorting tangle. Szabo grabbed hold of his seat just in time and hung on

40

for dear life. He saw Goliath leaping through the air and sensed rather than saw the other wagon hanging suspended in midair before flipping cartwheels. Two short screams of terror receded into the distance as its occupants were tossed out under the impact.

Then everything was silent save the horses struggling noisily to their feet. The spatter of their fear-induced urination and the stench of their faeces were loud and strong.

Miraculously, through sheer weight, perhaps, the circus wagon had somehow remained upright.

'Goliath?' Szabo called out hesitantly in sudden dread. Then he roared: '*Goliath!*'

'I'm down here, Boss,' the dwarf called uncertainly from the darkness to Szabo's left. 'I jumped just in time.'

'Thank God.' Szabo let out a deep breath of relief, and from one of the windows heard Hazy shrilly demanding explanations. A moment later Goliath climbed up from the bottom of the dark embankment and limped over to the wagon.

Szabo jumped to the ground and held his little friend by the shoulders. 'You are hurt?' he asked worriedly.

'No, Boss.' Goliath tried to laugh lightly. 'I just got all jiggled up inside, that's all.' Then his voice turned serious. 'But the other people . . . I better go get a lantern, Boss.'

'Hurry.'

'Yes, Boss.' Goliath scrambled to the back of the wagon, climbed painfully up on to the little porch, and returned with a lit kerosene lamp, which he held high.

Szabo looked at him. 'Did Marikka awaken?'

Goliath shook his head. 'No, Boss. But Hazy's on a tirade.' He laughed softly. 'So what else is new?'

'Let's start.' Szabo turned to Hazy, who was hanging out a window. 'You stay here with Marikka,' he commanded.

Together, the two men, one huge and massive, the

other tiny and bow-legged, slid down the stony embankment and systematically searched for the people in the wagon.

They found the man and the woman thirty feet away. The impact had tossed them face-down atop jagged rocks in a dry creekbed, where they lay like limp, unmoving rag dolls, arms and legs splayed.

For an instant, Szabo had to turn his face away. There was so much blood . . . such an awful lot of blood. He felt the bile rise in his throat, and fought it back down. He took a deep, steadying breath and forced himself to kneel down over them to check for their pulses. Finally he slowly got back to his feet and shook his head. 'There is nothing we can do for them,' he told Goliath quietly. 'They are both dead.'

Suddenly Goliath grabbed Szabo by the leg. 'Listen, Boss!' the dwarf hissed.

They both cocked their heads. At first, they could hear nothing but the frightened movements of the nearby horses.

And then the cry came again. It drifted like a high-pitched, eerie song along the currents of the wind.

'It's coming from over there!' Goliath shouted, pointing. Still holding the lantern high, he led the way through the scratchy, thorny brush.

They found a newborn baby, swaddled in thick blankets, nested in the branches of a stunted tree.

With an expression of wonder, they both slowly drew close to it.

'It is a miracle!' Goliath whispered.

Carefully Szabo lifted the baby from the branches. It stopped crying the moment he held it. 'See?' he said. 'It likes me.'

While Goliath held up the light, Szabo examined the baby closely. It was truly a miracle, he thought. The baby had not suffered so much as a scratch. The branches had cushioned its fall after it had been thrown.

42

'It's a girl,' Szabo said. 'A beautiful, blue-eyed baby girl!'

'Do you think she belongs to the people we found back there?' Goliath asked.

'I do not know. But it looks newborn to me.' Suddenly something occurred to Szabo. 'We will go back there. I want to see something. Here. You hold the baby. Give me the lantern.'

They made the transfer and backtracked to the creekbed where the two bodies lay sprawled across the rocks. Almost tenderly, Szabo lifted the woman up and turned her around, laying her face-up across the rocks. Then he lifted up her skirts and held the lantern close. He nodded to himself. She had been haemorrhaging badly from her womb, and he could see afterbirth sticking to her thighs.

'What do you see, Boss?' Goliath asked nervously.

'Look. See how she recently gave birth? They must have been on their way to a doctor, like us!' Szabo exclaimed. He let her skirt drop and stood there thoughtfully, rubbing his chin.

The baby started crying again.

'She needs milk,' Goliath said.

'Marikka has milk,' Szabo said softly.

In unison, they turned to each other and stared.

The dwarf drew a deep breath. 'Are you thinking what I am thinking, Boss?'

Szabo did not reply.

The dwarf's voice was hushed. 'Kidnapping?'

Szabo was silent a moment longer. 'I prefer to think of it as . . . substitution.' His midnight-blue eyes were like wet stones. 'The child needs a mother, and Marikka needs a child. What is more natural?'

Suddenly Goliath felt the chill of mortal fear. Never before in his life had he seen such determination in anyone's eyes as he saw now in Szabo's. 'And Marikka? What will we tell her?'

43

'We tell her nothing. Let her think this child is hers.'

The dwarf did not speak.

'Marikka was feverish,' Szabo continued. 'She will think her baby's death was but a bad dream.'

'And this accident? Don't we report it?'

Szabo shook his head. 'Tomorrow, someone will ride by and find these people. They will also find a dead child. Now to the wagon. Tell Hazy to bring me my own child.'

'Szabo . . .'

'Do as I tell you!' Szabo roared, and took the crying baby girl from Goliath's arms.

The dwarf ran off. When he came back with Hazy and the dead child, Szabo wordlessly wrapped his own dead son in the baby girl's blanket, and then he wrapped the baby girl in his dead child's. Tenderly, he stooped over and put his son down beside the dead woman. When he straightened, he looked around at the terrible tableau. 'It is done,' he said with finality.

The two dwarfs stared at him expressionlessly.

Szabo handed the crying baby girl to Hazy. 'Take my daughter back to her mother,' he ordered.

Hazy stared at him. Then she exchanged glances with Goliath, and a silent communication seemed to pass between the little people. They nodded at each other almost imperceptibly. 'Now can we take Marikka to a doctor?' Hazy asked softly.

'No. We return to the camp.' Szabo's voice had gained confidence. 'This child will do more for Marikka than all the doctors in the world.'

2

The drive back to the campsite was a slow and careful one, its tedium dictated by the precious treasure they were now transporting – a treasure far more valuable than gold or silver. Szabo didn't need to be told that finding the infant had been one chance in untold millions, and he wasn't about to jeopardize its safety by having another accident. So the two dwarfs sat atop the driver's seat, the reins in patient Goliath's hands, while Szabo was inside the slowly moving wagon with Marikka.

For a long while he had just been sitting there beside his huge wife, shushing the tiny child he cradled gently in his massive, powerful arms. But as time went by, his lullabies and hushes could no longer keep the newborn silent. Her hunger demanded milk, and she sensed the source of it nearby. She started crying fitfully.

'Quiet, my little princess,' Szabo sang softly, and rocked her back and forth in his arms.

But the baby cried even louder.

'All right, all right, little princess,' Szabo soothed. 'You are hungry. Then you will eat. Never let it be said that Papa Szabo starves his little princess, eh?' Carefully, he pulled the sheet down off Marikka's huge, pendulous breasts and placed the child beside one teat.

Instinctively, the baby's mouth searched for the nipple, clamped its lips purposefully around it, and began to suckle contentedly.

Szabo watched the timeless portrait of motherhood with a sense of warmth and awe. It filled him with an overpowering love which was entirely new to him. Already it seemed impossible, even to him, who knew better, that the child could be anyone's but his and Marikka's. As he looked on, he could almost see the ticklish, sensual sensation of feeding lips reaching down through the layers of Marikka's feverish unconsciousness. Then her eyelids fluttered and slowly opened. Tears welled in her bright blue eyes as she caught sight of the baby. 'I thought I was dreaming,' she said softly.

Szabo smiled indulgently. 'Then it is good you woke, eh?'

Marikka reached tentatively to touch the child, her face registering surprise and relief that this was no illusion, no fever-induced hallucination. 'Why, he . . . he's really alive!' she marvelled softly in Hungarian, and turned wonderingly to Szabo. 'Our little baby is alive, Szabo! *Alive!*'

'Yes, Marikka,' he said, 'our child is alive. But you are mistaken. Is not a boy. Is a girl. A beautiful, plump baby girl.'

'That's funny.' Her big moon-face creased into furrows. 'I would have sworn a boy, and born dead.' She looked at Szabo curiously.

'It was the fever, Marikka,' he said softly. 'Our baby is fine. You were confused, that is all.'

Marikka stared at him for a moment, then she nodded. 'She's so beautiful, Szabo. Like little princess.'

'That is because she looks like you,' he said staunchly.

She smiled. 'No, no. She looks like you. She has your eyes!'

He laughed. 'Now you must get well quickly,' he said.

'Yes,' she nodded, her eyes glowing. And in that moment, he knew that he had been right. The baby would do far more good for her than all the doctors in the world.

'Oh, Szabo,' Marikka sobbed and reached for his hand. 'I am so happy. So wonderfully, wonderfully happy.'

'So am I, Marikka, so am I.' By the time they pulled back into the campsite, the baby had finished nursing and Szabo was standing on the railed porch of the wagon, infant in one arm, the other extended exultantly in the air. All the circus people spilled out of their wagons and converged, eager for news of Marikka and the child. 'Is a girl!' Szabo roared proudly, and everyone broke into cheers and excited chatter.

Then, one by one, they filed in to 'ooh' and 'aaah' over the beautiful baby and to congratulate Marikka. Age had its privileges, and since she was the oldest member of the circus, Olga, the fortuneteller, was the first to go inside. A toothless, slack-jawed crone, she looked as tiny and frail as a starved bird, but the rest of the circus people had long since learned that she was the toughest of them all: there was iron in her fragile, twisted bones. Maybe she hobbled along painfully when she walked. Maybe her hands were so crippled with arthritis that her fingers were contorted claws and she shuffled her tarot cards with difficulty. But she compressed her gums determinedly and shooed away anybody who tried to help her. 'You think because I am an old woman that I cannot take care of myself?' she'd snap – then cackle and spray spittle as the good Samaritan fled.

Her predictions had never been known to be proved wrong, but still it was only the townsfolk who had their fortunes read and believed what she told them. The circus was one big flashy show – a sleight of hand here, a bundle of tricks there. Everyone had his own routine and act down pat, so none of the performers took her seriously. With a little make-up and a lot of concentration and practice, the impossible became possible – on the surface – but reading the future from palms, crystal balls, tarot cards, and tea leaves? Everyone in the circus scoffed at that. No one could read the future, was the unanimous consensus. Not even old Olga.

But old Olga knew better. Let the fools laugh, she told herself. What did they know, anyway? Even after Alexi had lost his balance and fallen to his death from the tightrope, no one had credited her with that prediction, had they? But, yes, she had foreseen it.

'We in the circus know that any of us can have accident,' Szabo had gently scolded her afterwards in his broken English. 'Is bad luck to suggest. Then we

47

become nervous and cannot concentrate. That is ho~
accident happen. You tell audience their fortune, okay:
Do not tell *ours*.'

No, they didn't really believe, not even after Alexi's
fatal fall. They hadn't *wanted* to believe. But they *were*
superstitious – which was why, for a long time following
Alexi's death, everyone in the circus steered clear of
old Olga's fortunetelling. Ha! Let them all scoff, Olga
thought contemptuously. Let them be like ostriches and
bury their heads in the sand. But I? I *know*.

When she came into the wagon to offer congratulations to Szabo and Marikka, she did nothing of the
sort. Instead, she immediately seized the baby's tiny
clenched hand in her claws and forced it open, finger
by finger.

The baby protested, but old Olga ignored the indignant cries. She leaned forward into the tiny palm, studied it closely, and slowly nodded to herself. She turned
to Szabo, her black eyes flashing. 'This child, she will live
a long, prosperous life!' she cackled with satisfaction,
spittle spraying from between her withered lips.

'And me?' Marikka asked in good humour, holding
out her plump red hand. 'I will live a long, prosperous
life, too?'

Olga took Marikka's hand, looked at it for a single
split second, then let it drop as if it were a poisonous
snake. 'Is not good to know everything!' she whispered
hoarsely.

Szabo, who suffered Olga in good humour, began to
laugh. 'Tell us, Olga, what you see?'

'I don't see nothing!' Olga snapped. And she
clamped her gums shut and stumbled blindly out.

When she got to her own wagon, Olga closed the
curtains tightly, took her crystal ball out of its padded
velvet case, and laid her fingertips on the cool, smooth
surface. But as hard as she tried to conjure up the

future, she saw nothing but dark shadows and white wisps of swirling mists.

Before the sun rose, the circus left camp – and Szabo and Marikka's baby was named Elizabeth-Anne – Elizabeth for Marikka's great-aunt, and Anne for Anna, Szabo's mother. Though she was illegitimate, since Szabo and Marikka had never bothered with the formality of marriage, Elizabeth-Anne's father gave her his last name: Gross. Szabo, a Hungarian immigrant, had actually been born Szabo Godebska, but at Ellis Island, through which he had entered America, Godebska had been both unpronounceable and unwritable. The immigrations officer, a semi-literate German and an immigrant himself, had taken one look at Szabo's broad shoulders and massive tree-trunk arms, and that had done it: he was renamed Gross, German for large.

For Szabo and Marikka and their circus family, Elizabeth-Anne was an enigma over whom everyone puzzled. Most babies at birth are red and ugly and angry looking, but not Elizabeth-Anne Gross. She was pink and adorable, a cherub with a disposition to match. And the older she got, the more her beauty surfaced. It seemed unbelievable that she was born of such an enormous, freakish mother and such a massive, muscular father. The circus family unanimously agreed that she was special, and they all called her 'Princess'. Since she was so young and beautiful, with luxuriant curls the colour of wheat, and huge, inquisitive, aquamarine eyes, everyone did his best to shelter her from the curious townsfolk they came across. They were afraid that a child of such exquisite beauty would stand out among the rest of them, and be stared at and ridiculed as they were. This fear was not at all unfounded, for in a circus of freaks, Elizabeth-Anne's beauty was, perhaps, the most freakish thing of all.

But Elizabeth-Anne never thought of herself or the

49

others as freaks. Throughout the most formative years of her life they were her only family and friends. They were generous and loving, and she loved them right back. To her, it was the outside world that was peopled with freaks. She adored her circus family, and she was never aware of the gaudy seediness of the tattered tent or the tiredness of the third-rate acts. From her earliest memory, it was a paradise. The brightly painted wooden wagons, with curtained windows and tiny porches mounted on heavy axles; the old calliope puffing raucous music; the horses fitted with brightly dyed plumes just before the circus paraded through a town; the tinny blare of trumpets and the deep, resonant bass beat of the drums; the costumes, rent and mended but extravagantly sumptuous to her eyes; and the excited eyes of the local townsfolk who seldom ventured from their sleepy little townships and were so starved for entertainment that the arrival of the circus signalled a momentous occasion – for Elizabeth-Anne it was, quite simply, pure magic.

And the travelling! It was indeed a nomad's life, but she knew nothing else and loved nothing else. The smells of horse sweat and manure, of greasepaint and mothballs, of sawdust and choking road dust – those were things both familiar and comforting to her.

But the circus life was drudgery. The pomp and excitement of the parades and shows belied the days consumed by wearisome, monotonous travel; the rehearsal of new tricks until they seemed effortless; the ceaseless sewing and mending of costumes which suffered immense wear and tear; the repairing of the rickety wagons; the care of the horses, the big tent, and collapsible bleachers – it was anything but the glamorous life the outsiders perceived it to be. It was harsh, back-breaking, grim manual labour, but it was done with no shirking of duties. Chores were, indeed, gladly done – with a sense of camaraderie and good humour. With whistling and singing.

No one could imagine another, better life.

There was little time to devote to a child, but Elizabeth-Anne never wanted for anything, and if she did, she was never aware of it. When Szabo and Marikka were too busy to spend time with her, then the circus family cheerfully passed her back and forth between them like a favourite niece, enveloping her in their warm, protective fold. She was kissed and hugged, played with and given treats on the sly, and entertained with new tricks and stunts during practice. Those occasions when everyone *was* too busy to spend time with her, she would rummage through the costume wagon, dress herself up in absurdly huge outfits, and play 'pretend'.

But one thing never changed. The beautiful child was always sternly instructed to stay out of sight in her parents' wagon while the parades and shows were in progress. She was allowed to peer out from behind the filmy, grey curtains of the lead wagon, but that was the limit. From outside she was but a ghostly shadow, a silhouette which never materialized before the eyes of the curious public.

Each new day – monotonous as it might seem to the others – swept Elizabeth-Anne up in its whirlwind of excitement, and she seized upon it as an adventure. Each sunrise brought with it new wonders, new delights. The world was hers to discover, and so, still, was the circus. With her boundless energy, she never tired of anything. There were a thousand things to do, a million things to see and smell and touch. But it rankled her that she was only a child. She dreamed of growing up overnight, so that she could be a real participant in the circus world. She wanted to be able to help set up the big tent and water the horses and do a hundred menial chores which to her weren't menial at all. They were necessary, and that made them seem important and grown-up.

'Not yet,' Szabo would tell her patiently. 'Still you must grow a little more, my Princess.'

And first thing every morning, she'd grab his trouser leg, give it a desperate tug, and ask hopefully: 'Did I grow enough during the night, Papa? *Now* can I help?'

And he would laugh and scoop her high into the air and twirl her around until she was breathless and dizzy. 'Not yet, my Princess,' he would say softly, giving her an affectionate squeeze. 'But soon. You will see. Time flies.'

When she was five years old, he stroked her wheat-gold curls and said: 'Take advantage of your youth, my little Princess. A time will come when you will wish to be young again and not have to work. Be happy you don't need to do nothing yet.'

But she frowned thoughtfully and then shook her head. 'Noooo,' she said slowly. 'I don't think I'd like that, Papa. I'll never want to do nothing. I'll always want to work.'

When Elizabeth-Anne turned six, two things of great importance occurred. First, Marikka and Szabo were married by a justice of the peace in Mansfield, Ohio. And Elizabeth-Anne was finally allowed to pitch in and help around the circus, which made her feel very grown-up. Her chores consisted of cleaning wagons, washing dishes, and mending costumes. Everyone smiled at her encouragingly, patted her on the head, and told her how indispensible she was and what a fine job she was doing. The words of praise were music to her ears. But she never realized that in actuality she was a hindrance to the smooth efficiency with which the circus was run. Her childish stitches had to be torn out of costumes and redone once she went to sleep, the dishes she washed had to be rewashed behind her back, and the mess she made cleaning the wagons invariably had to be straightened. No one ever let on what a nuisance she was. She took her chores so deadly serious that no one could find it within his heart to wound her pride. Besides, she was such a joy, and everyone's favourite, that no one really minded the extra work she caused.

Elizabeth-Anne was momentarily satisfied. At long last, she was a somebody . . . a somebody who worked and paid her own way. Even at her tender age, she grasped, instinctively, what was never said but understood. That everyone had to pull his share. But despite everything, she soon felt left out again. She liked her chores well enough, and took pride in doing them, but what she really ached to do was perform in the ring and join in the parades. She needed to be part of the glitter and the noise and the hubbub of the performances. Her yearning to be more a part of it all consumed her.

Early one morning, Hazy and Goliath were perfecting a new clown routine in the meadow where the circus had camped for the night. Both were in white-faced make-up and sported bulbous red noses, but there their similarities ended. Hazy's lips were smeared in a malicious, exaggerated grin of red; Goliath wore an equally exaggerated but pathetic red frown and black greasepaint tears.

Elizabeth-Anne sat down in the moist, dewy grass to watch. She drew her knees up to her chin and wrapped her arms around her legs.

Goliath began the routine by waddling up to Hazy and tweaking her bulbous nose. Simultaneously, the hooter Hazy held let out a loud honk. Startled, Goliath looked around and scratched his head. Then he carefully tweaked Hazy's nose again.

Honk.

Elizabeth-Anne hunched her shoulders and giggled.

Goliath tweaked Hazy's nose a third time. There was a long, drawn-out honk as the nose came off in his hand. He peered at it closely, squeezing it again and again.

Honk. Honk-honk. Honk.

Elizabeth-Anne clapped her hands in delight. She was enthralled.

Suddenly aware of the loss of her nose, Hazy felt her face and let out a shriek. Then she turned around and, with the enormous, two-foot-long shoes she wore, tried to kick Goliath in the buttocks. She missed twice, but on the third try she kicked him neatly. There was a honk as he went sprawling. Then he let out a howl, jumped to his feet and, clutching his buttocks with both hands, took off running. Hazy took off after him, kicking away wildly. Each time her foot made contact, there was another honk.

Elizabeth-Anne covered her mouth with her hands and laughed so gleefully that tears ran down her cheeks. Realizing what joy the performance brought her, she decided then and there what she wanted to become. A clown. It wasn't just something she wanted to do. It was something she felt she *had* to do. She could not have explained it if she had tried, but she knew, intuitively, knew deep down inside with a sudden burst of surety, that greasepaint flowed in her veins. Then and there, she made up her mind to speak to Szabo, who had always made it all too clear that she would not be allowed to perform.

Later that same day, when the circus was moving along again, Elizabeth-Anne was perched in her usual place between Szabo and Marikka high on the driver's bench of the lead wagon. The wagon rattled and swayed perilously from side to side as the horses picked their way carefully along the rutted dirt road.

Elizabeth-Anne didn't notice the jolts and jars of the ride, nor the asphyxiating clouds of dust raised by the horses' hooves. For the past few hours she had been sitting silently, deep in intent contemplation. She had been rehearsing a method of approaching Szabo with her request to be a clown. She realized that her father, and

54

everyone else for that matter, had a soft spot for her. She could get almost anything she asked for — anything except permission to mingle with the spectators, watch the shows, and sit proudly costumed atop the wagon during the parades. Now she would have to ask for something he would be even more dead set against. Well . . .

She took a deep breath and glanced timidly sideways at her father. He was so massively big and brawny, so frightening looking, yet so gentle and overprotective. Yes, she decided, she could get anything she wanted from anybody in the circus. Especially him. But on this one issue . . . She sighed miserably, trying to summon up all her courage. Now that the time to bring up the subject was at hand, she felt more unsure of herself than ever. Over the past hours, her initial certainty had evaporated like the morning dew in the sun. Finally, she forced herself to open her mouth. 'Papa?' she squeaked in a tiny voice.

'What is it, Princess?' Szabo asked gently. He took his eyes off the road and turned to look down at her.

Elizabeth-Anne's eyes fell to her lap and she fidgeted with her hands. She swallowed nervously and looked back up at him. 'Papa,' she croaked so weakly that she had to clear her throat to get the frog out of it. 'Papa, I'm six years old? Right?'

'Yessss . . .'

'And growing bigger?'

'So?'

'You said that means I'll soon be grown-up.'

He narrowed his eyes suspiciously. 'Well?'

'I was thinking . . .' She could feel a red warmth creeping from her neck up to her face. 'Can't I? . . . don't you think? . . . I could . . .?' Her eyes didn't waver from his, but the words she had worked out so carefully in her mind suddenly failed her, with only disjointed fragments of phrases spilling out, all punctuated with lilting question marks.

Over Elizabeth-Anne's head, Szabo exchange glances with his wife. A silent signal seemed to pass between them.

With one finger, Marikka stroked a stray lock of hair out of her daughter's face. 'What is it, angel?' she asked gently.

Elizabeth-Anne bit down hard on her lower lip.

'Come, come child,' Marikka scolded softly. 'Do not be afraid.'

Elizabeth-Anne turned and looked into her mother's gentle, red moon-face with its slack, purple-veined cheeks and countless folds of corpulent flesh cascading into her collar. 'I need . . .' Elizabeth-Anne paused for an interminably long moment, her face reddening even more, her heart pounding violently against her ribs. Then suddenly the words burst out of her, like a flood, 'I need to become a clown!'

There! It was out! She glanced timidly at her father, but his forbidding expression caused her to slump and grow tiny.

Szabo's calculatedly brutal features had spread into a fierce scowl, but his voice was soft. 'No, Princess,' he said emphatically. 'When we get to towns, you stay in the wagon as always.'

Elizabeth-Anne felt her hopes deflate even further. She turned away, defeated. 'Yes, Papa,' she said with quiet resignation.

Szabo shook his head sadly, her disappointment tearing at his heart. Didn't she realize how hard it was for him to deny her anything? How could he explain to her that she was too beautiful, too special for her own good? That this was a circus of freaks? That she would be the target of ridicule, of stares? *That if people caught sight of her, the circus might even be accused of kidnapping this beautiful child from somewhere?*

He passed the reins to his left hand, and with his right, reached over and placed his cocked forefinger

56

under Elizabeth-Anne's chin. He turned her head around to face him, and his voice was gentle and warm. 'I tell you what,' he said slowly. 'For starters, from this day on you do the oiling. All right?'

Elizabeth-Anne nodded. Before each show, Marikka smoothed oil on Szabo's torso so that he would appear to be even more muscular and well defined than he was. Now Elizabeth-Anne would be allowed to aid in this chore. She was glad to be of help, but still, she couldn't help feeling vast disappointment. The oiling, she realized instantly, was nothing more than a way to pacify her so that she wouldn't feel totally let down.

Szabo frowned. He could see that she still wasn't happy. 'Well . . . maybe soon you can be a clown,' he said grudgingly against his better judgment. 'We will see, okay?'

A hopeful smile wobbled tentatively at the corners of Elizabeth-Anne's lips.

Szabo grinned suddenly, his gold tooth flashing in the sunlight. 'And when the time comes to be a clown, I teach you myself, eh? Me – I can be a clown too, right?'

Elizabeth-Anne's smile broadened now.

'Yes, *I* teach you!' he roared, and then he threw back his shaved, gleaming domed head and laughed. It was an infectuous laugh, loud and resonant and clear. A happy laugh straight from the heart. It was enough to make Elizabeth-Anne, and everyone else within earshot, join in.

But Szabo was never to teach her to be a clown, nor was he ever to laugh again. For up ahead, across the parched fields, was a town. A wooden plank with the name of the town painted on it poked up out of the weeds at the roadside.

'*Quebeck, Texas, Pop. 431*,' the tilted letters read proudly.

It was the first time in six years that the circus had passed through this particular town.

57

It would also be the last.

Neither Szabo nor any other member of the circus could know it, but they were about to give the last performance of their lives.

3

The circus wagons pulled off the road to pitch tent in the fields just south of Quebeck. The locals called them Geron's Fields, after the farmer who owned them. The ground was dry and pebble-strewn, but Szabo knew from long experience that the location was perfect. The fields were close to town and, most important, were beside a pond that was clean and clear, from which the circus could draw its water supply.

Even before the lead wagon creaked to a stop, Szabo had one foot over the side of the driver's bench. He put all his weight on one hand, twisted himself up off the seat, and jumped nimbly to the ground, landing gracefully on both feet. Then he reached up, grabbed Elizabeth-Anne around the legs, and lifted her down. She followed him around to the other side of the wagon and watched in silence as he planted his feet squarely apart, took a deep breath, held it in, and then let it out slowly as he gently grabbed his 300-pound wife and lifted her down.

Szabo squinted up at the sky and frowned. There were perhaps seven hours of precious daylight left. Time was of the essence; as a rule, it took between ten and twelve hours to set up the circus, and it was imperative to keep Elizabeth-Anne from getting in the way. The rest of the day had to be devoted exclusively to setting up the tent, bleachers, and sideshow since tomorrow would bring its own frenzied activity: getting made up and costumed, holding the parade, the fight, and the show itself. Then before nightfall, the tent and bleachers would come down, everything would be packed up, and by dawn the circus would move on again. At least that was the way he had planned it. It was a routine perfected over many years.

He gave Elizabeth-Anne a swift hug. 'I tell you what, Princess. Why don't you go play?'

Elizabeth-Anne pulled away from him, visible disappointment clouding her usually angelic face. 'Don't you want me to help?'

'Sure I do. But for weeks you have been working hard. You deserve a day off.'

'All right.'

Szabo could see the muscles tighten in her face. He sensed that her mind was consumed with hurt. He glanced around slowly, then took her aside and lowered his voice to a confidential tone. 'See all those sunflowers?' He kneeled and pointed at the fields all around them, where tall sunflowers with blooms the size of black-eyed susans grew profusely.

Elizabeth-Anne's eyes followed his finger. Then she nodded slowly and looked into his face. 'Yes, Papa?'

'Remember how once you made those garlands of daisies?'

Elizabeth-Anne smiled. 'Yes.'

'Go pick as many sunflowers as you can and make garlands out of them. Then we decorate all the wagons with them. What you say?'

'There are a lot of sunflowers,' she mused thoughtfully. Then her voice brightened. 'Should I really pick them all?'

'As many as you can.' He rose to his feet, clapped her warmly on the shoulder, and strode off briskly, shouting instructions to the wagon drivers.

Elizabeth-Anne watched the wagons draw up, one behind the other, in the usual circle. Then she took a deep breath, blew the golden hair that hung down over

59

her face aside, and began to push her way through the weeds. She plucked one sunflower after another, laying them neatly in the crook of her arm. Bees buzzed about, and she saw a dragonfly swoop and then heard its drone as it flew off towards the pond. Butterflies flitted all around. The air was warm and fresh.

After a while she had gathered an armful of flowers. She sat down at the edge of the road, oblivious to the shouts and yells as the tent was pitched, and skilfully wove the flowers into a wreath. Then solemnly, she placed it atop her head, a radiant, gold-and-brown crown. She got back up, proceeded to pick more armfuls of sunflowers, and deposited them in a huge, ever-growing pile by the roadside.

The next day dawned bright and sunny. Summer held sway and not a cloud was to be seen in the powder blue sky. Overnight, Geron's Fields had metamorphosed into a sprawling fairground.

Word of the circus had spread like wildfire throughout the county, and people from miles around converged on the fields on horseback, in buggies and wagons, or on foot. Since most of the county's population was scattered among far-flung farms, and most of the people did not see each other for weeks at a time, except at church services, the circus was deemed as good an excuse as any at which to socialize, catch up on gossip, and have fun. There was a cacophonous party atmosphere in the air, a wild hearty, electrified holiday spirit.

Women dressed in their Sunday finery chattered amongst themselves as they hiked up their flowered gingham dresses so that the hems wouldn't get dirty as they carefully picked their way around the grounds.

Men congregated amongst themselves, smoking pipes and cigars, sneaking drinks of liquor, comparing crop harvests, and talking man talk.

Screaming flocks of children, many of whom hadn't seen each other since last Sunday's church service, or longer, raced about holding aloft the colourful, whirling paper pinwheels they'd just purchased for a penny.

Money jingled and changed hands rapidly. There were a staggering array of impulse purchases, shows, and games it could be spent on. In Quebeck, Texas, there was little else that could entice people to part with their hard-earned coins, and they parted with them willingly.

People paid a nickel apiece to be allowed within the circular wagon compound to inspect Hazy and Goliath's wagon. No matter where the circus pitched tent, that particular wagon always proved to be the show-stopper.

It was a small, narrow wagon; not counting the wheels it stood a mere five feet high and was fifteen feet long. What made it so novel were the picture windows on all four sides, and the roof, a mullioned, greenhouse-like expanse of clear glass so that a child, stepping up on a platform, could gaze unimpeded down inside in wonderment. And there wasn't a child alive who didn't yearn for that wagon to be his own. It was like a playhouse on wheels, and everything was miniaturized for the dwarfs.   Unlike all the other wagons, the interior of this one was palatial. The little carved head- and footboards of the beds gleamed darkly, the petite couches boasted carved, gilded frames, and the chairs were upholstered in red velvet. Even the carpets, with their cabbage-rose design, and the incredibly detailed, tiny porcelain dishes laid out on the little waxed dining table, were perfectly scaled. Every last item in the wagon, save for the huge windows, was identical to its normal-sized counterpart, except that all of it was child size.

Not only was the wagon on view, but its occupants as well.

Hazy, her wizened dwarf's face seemingly unaware of the voyeurs pressing their noses flat against her windows like giants peering into a fish bowl, was seated in one of the miniature chairs knitting a tiny sweater with a pair of short, thin needles. Goliath was in an armchair, legs on a footstool, miniature book in hand.

There were no end of other delights to entice money from the circus goers. Games requiring either skill or coordination or just plain luck could be played at the numerous booths and stalls. Prizes were pressed glass vases from St Louis, treasured paper flowers, and cute stuffed dolls and animals.

There were feasts for the palate as well. Vendors hawked spicy hot dogs liberally smeared with mustard and ketchup, popcorn served in brown paper cones, candyfloss, and foil-covered chocolates. From every corner of the circus grounds came good-natured shrieks and shouts, laughter, cries, announcements over the megaphone, the scuffle of an occasional drunken fight – all of it drowned out by the raucously insistent, vibrant cheer bursting forth from the steam-powered calliope.

Even though the doors and windows were closed, the circus noises penetrated the dim, airless confines of the lead wagon. Elizabeth-Anne knelt on a chair by the window, looking out at the activity through the chink in the curtains. The excitement was infectious, and she felt a desperate longing to be out there amid it all.

She sighed painfully to herself. Maybe it was best if she tried to ignore everything – if she just pretended nothing was happening. Maybe that way she wouldn't feel she was missing out on all the fun.

She was about to turn her back on the window when she noticed Goliath, a fat cigar in one hand and a huge megaphone in the other, pushing his way through the throngs. She knew from experience what that meant. The prizefight was about to be announced.

She wondered who her father would have to fight today.

She stayed glued to the window.

Elizabeth-Anne was in the smaller front 'room' of the curtained-off wagon; Szabo and Marikka in the larger room in the rear.

Marikka stood watching her husband in impassive silence. Szabo was dancing from foot to foot, his fists clenched as he shadowboxed an imaginary opponent. Marikka knew what he was doing. Limbering up. Getting himself primed.

Preparing for the fight.

With an air of resignation, Marikka Gross picked up the embroidered, red satin cape which lay neatly folded on the bed. She waited for her husband to be still. Then slowly, she draped the cape around his broad shoulders.

Elizabeth-Anne watched Goliath approach the platform which had been set up in front of the lead wagon. He walked with the arced, bowlegged stride of dwarfs, yet there was a peculiar dignity and assurance about the way he held himself. He stuck the cigar in his mouth, stood on tiptoe, and pushed the megaphone up on the platform. Then he stepped on a crate, crawled up on to the platform on all fours, and picked up the megaphone as he got to his feet. He was standing right in front of the lead wagon, his back to Elizabeth-Anne.

She smiled as he produced a handkerchief from the pocket of his brown plaid suit, and proceeded to slap the dust off his knees with exaggerated care. Then he pocketed the handkerchief, took the cigar out of his mouth and raised the megaphone to his lips. 'Attention! Ladies and gentlemans! Attention!'

His twangy voice boomed over the crowd with surprising force. People looked up, stopped what they were doing, and began to drift over to the platform.

Curious children elbowed their way to the front of the crowd to get a better view of him, or else were hoisted on to the shoulders of adults.

Goliath puffed contentedly on the cigar, his face enveloped in a cloud of blue smoke. When everyone had gathered around him, he stretched his short arms out in front of him and gestured the crowd to silence. As if on cue, even the maddeningly cheerful blare of the calliope faded and slowed and finally died away. The sudden, total silence that hung over the circus seemed unearthly.

Goliath narrowed his eyes as he gazed over his captive audience. 'Ladies and gentlemans!' he announced again into the megaphone. 'Welcome to dee greatest show on earth —'

'I *seen* the Greatest Show on Earth, squirt!' a heckler hollered from the back. 'P. T. Barnum was in Brownsville coupla' weeks back!'

'Yeah!' another drunken voice chimed in, and there were some loud whistles and catcalls. Everyone turned to see who the hecklers were.

Goliath was undaunted. He puffed jauntily on his cigar and assumed a severe look. Quickly he appraised the crowd. The two hecklers were in the back, along with another couple of young men egging them on. No matter where the circus went, there were always a few loudmouths and drunks in the audience. But on the whole, most of the people here were decent, well-behaved family folk out to have a little fun. It wouldn't do to have the day spoiled for them.

He scratched his nose, a signal for Hazy to come out and do the routine they'd perfected long ago. It never failed to win the audience over and, if it did not always silence the hecklers, it would at least drown them out.

'Mebee Szabo's Travelling Circus ain't the world's beegest show,' Goliath hollered loyally, 'but it sure dee greatest!'

There was a smattering of applause. Then a ripple of giggles flowed through the audience. Hazy, dragging an enormous club, was sneaking up behind Goliath on tiptoe, like a cat stalking its prey. She climbed stealthily up on the table, signalled the audience to silence by holding a finger to her lips, and promptly swung the club downwards at Goliath's head. The club missed its mark and everyone roared with laughter because Goliath hadn't noticed what had happened.

Goliath pretended to be puzzled by the laughs. He scratched his head quizzically and shrugged. 'Szabo's circus has dee world's greatest acts –'

Hazy's club descended once more, again missing Goliath's head.

Forgotten now were the hecklers. Everyone was caught up in the routine. How could a club that big miss anybody? The laughter got even louder as Hazy scrutinized her club closely, seemingly trying to figure out what was wrong with it. She handled it like a baseball bat, giving it a few practice swings.

'Ladies and gentlemans!' Goliath announced. 'I would like to introduce to you dee world's strongest man!'

'Is he a shrimp like you?' the heckler called out again.

Goliath ignored him and tapped the ash off the end of his cigar. 'Before this afternoon's show, dee great Szabo challenges any man here to a fight. *Any* man!' Goliath locked eyes with the heckler: 'Even *you!*'

Goliath's lips curled into a lopsided grin. The heckler was suddenly silent. That was always the way it went. Hecklers were seldom fighters. As soon as the challenge was raised, they tended to disappear.

Goliath poked a thumb at his own chest. 'I take the bets!' He paused dramatically, and from somewhere came the roll of a snare drum. 'Ladies and gentlemans! Hailing from dee dark forests of Hungary, here is dee strongest man alive! Dee one! Dee only! *Szaboooooo!*'

And then Hazy dropped her useless club, produced a firecracker, and quickly lit it. She dropped it at Goliath's feet and dived off the table. The sudden explosion sent Goliath somersaulting down to the ground. He shrieked, jumped to his feet, and took off running in apparent terror. The audience broke into laughter and applause, the familiar calliope tune started anew, and Szabo, resplendent in his much-mended cape of old satin, strode out and hopped with ease onto the table. His shaved domed head gleamed and his earring flashed as he raised his muscular arms high in the air.

Inside the lead wagon, Marikka came up beside Elizabeth-Anne. She ducked low, parted the curtains a bit more, and peered out the window.

Elizabeth-Anne turned to look up at her mother. Marikka looked so sad, she thought. So frightened and miserable. She was always like that before one of Szabo's fights.

The misery and fear were insidiously contagious. Elizabeth-Anne found them seeping into her own body. 'Mama?' she said in a tiny voice.

Marikka did not take her eyes off the scene outside. 'What is it, child?' she asked absently.

'Is Papa going to get hurt?'

Marikka let the curtain fall back in place. The wagon dimmed and she turned slowly to face her daughter. She sensed Elizabeth-Anne's fears and pulled the child into the protection of her huge, soft bosom. 'Your Papa, he will be fine,' she said in a soft voice.

'I don't like it when Papa has to fight,' Elizabeth-Anne said.

'Neither do I,' Marikka said gently.

'Does Papa like it?'

'No, child. Your Papa, he hates to fight.'

Elizabeth-Anne's face creased into a frown. 'Then why does he do it?'

With one hand, Marikka stroked her daughter's soft, golden curls. How could she explain to a child that the money from the fights was what really kept the circus going? That without the fights, no one in the circus would have a job? That despite all the shows and all the hard work, the circus would slide into bankruptcy?

'Your Papa, he is a good man,' Marikka said in a quiet, dignified voice. 'That is why he fights.'

'Are all people who fight good?'

'No, child. Most people who fight are not.'

From outside, a sudden roar filled the air. Marikka quickly parted the curtains.

'Papa can beat anybody, can't he?' Elizabeth-Anne asked suddenly. 'He's the strongest man in the world?'

'Yes, child,' her mother repeated. 'Your Papa, he's the strongest man in the world.'

But a sudden fear seized Marikka's heart as the man challenging Szabo came forward. He was big and beefy and ruddy faced. He stood at least six foot five, and he was huge all over, built like a lumberjack. His arms were the size of hams; his enormous hands looked as if they could crush bone. And he was at least ten years younger than her Szabo.

Marikka closed her eyes. Her enormous bosom heaved painfully. 'Szabo,' she said silently to herself, 'this time, I fear you will get hurt.'

4

Old Olga sat alone in her dark wagon. The curtains were tightly drawn and the oil lamp on the table in front of her flickered, sending enormous shadows jumping up the walls and across the coved ceiling. For the time being, no one was waiting to have his fortune read. Whenever the fights were announced, or Goliath and

Hazy monkeyed around, she got a bit of respite, for which she was grateful.

She cocked her head at the applause outside but remained seated. She never stepped outside her wagon if she could avoid it. She was too old to be curious about anything any longer. Too old and too ill. She found it increasingly difficult to move. For years, her body had been letting her down, refusing to obey her commands as if it had a will of its own. But today, her inflamed arthritic joints ached and creaked worse than ever, relentlessly compelling her to thoughts of her own mortality.

She clutched her flowered, fringed shawl tightly around her and bent over the small round table. The stained tablecloth was printed in a swirling pattern of arabesques. On it were the tools of her trade: a carefully lettered star chart, the heavy, clear crystal ball on its base of carved rosewood, her ancient worn deck of hand-painted tarot cards, and a glass of tea.

Olga regarded the accoutrements and for the briefest moment her bituminous eyes dilated. It had been many years since she had read her own fortune.

She narrowed her eyes and sighed to herself. She knew it was not good to know one's fortune. She wondered what compelled her to want to know it today.

She clutched a glass of murky tea with both hands, lifted it awkwardly to her dry, cracked lips, and drank it down. She shivered. It wasn't sugared and tasted bitter. Some loose leaves stuck to her tongue. She turned her head sideways and spat them out. 'Now let's see what fate's in store for old Olga,' she muttered aloud.

She turned the glass upside down, unceremoniously dumping the wet tea leaves directly on the tablecloth. A widening dark stain slowly spread outward from the leaves as the cotton absorbed the drippings.

She ignored the stain. What mattered were the leaves and what they foretold. She scattered them around at random with her fingertips. Then she leaned forward and studied them closely.

Suddenly she sucked in her breath.

It could not be! There had to be some mistake!

She could almost hear her blood as it rushed wildly through her veins. In desperation, she scattered the leaves again, pulled the oil lamp closer, and reread the leaves.

Her heart thumped madly against her ribcage as the dark fear spread its clammy mantle around her. She gripped the edge of the table with her gnarled hands.

She had made no mistake. And she knew the tea leaves never lied.

Forgotten now were her aching joints, her inflexible fingers. For the first time in years, her grip was dexterous.

She snatched up her star chart. The thin yellowed paper crackled in her hand. She willed herself to stop shaking long enough to consult the stars' positions.

She let the paper drop.

She had gone over the chart earlier that very morning. So why hadn't she noticed it then? All the portents were there. A potent evil ruled the skies on this day. Ah, but the cards! Perhaps they would say differently? They were, after all, her strongest medium. More reliable than anything else.

She quickly snatched at the stack of tarot cards, shuffled and reshuffled and finally cut the deck. Expertly, she flipped card after card face-up on the table. Then she reshuffled and laid them out again. The order of the cards was different – but the message was the same. One card held sway over all the others. The evilly grinning grim reaper shouldering his scythe.

Death lurked in the air. *But how would he come?*

She felt frozen fingers crawling all over her skin. Down her legs. Up her arms and round her neck. Despite the sudden chill, she let her fringed shawl slip unnoticed from her shoulders. She reached out and pulled her crystal ball closer. For a moment she stared down at it, wondering if she had the courage to continue.

She sighed painfully. She knew she *must*. She had to know how Death would come for her.

She laid her trembling fingertips on the cold, smoothly polished globe.

The instant her fingers met crystal, there came a flash of searing white light. She snatched her hands back and stared at the ball. It had never done that before.

She fortified herself by taking a deep breath. Ever so slowly, she reached out again. This time there was no flash, but the crystal glowed whitely. Swirling light, like hurricane clouds seen from far above, spiralled inside the smooth round sphere. When the clouds dissipated, she saw clearly what the future held in store for her.

She gasped. The face captured inside was contorted by the shape of the sphere and resembled a head-on portrait taken with a fish-eye lens. And what a hideous, spine-chilling portrait it was! The grim reaper! He who would take her away. His ugly yellow teeth were bared in a ludicrous grin and his huge, eyeless sockets trailed wisps of smoke. She forced herself to look deep into those mad eyes which were not eyes, and then she saw the source of the smoke. A fire was burning inside the skull. As she watched, it grew bigger, more powerful. Flames crackled and sparks shot out of the eye sockets. Simultaneously, a gust of wind rushed through Geron's Fields and slammed her wagon door shut. Startled, her fingers lost contact.

Suddenly, she knew.

Fire.

Death would come by fire.

The moment her hands had left the crystal, the evil face had disappeared. Just like that. The crystal ball was once again nothing but a benign sphere of glass. Hesitantly, she touched it again. Nothing.

On a sudden impulse she extinguished the oil lamp. Then she sat back in the near-total darkness. Somehow, extinguishing the flame made her feel a bit better. Not much, to be sure . . . but a little. She knew, of course, that she could not change her fate; no one could. No matter what efforts one made to try to stave it off, fate would come for you. Find you, wherever you were, whatever you did. There was no use hiding from it. Extinguishing the lamp would make no difference.

Still, there was no reason to tempt fate, was there?

She was sitting shock still, breathing heavily, when she heard the footsteps on the wagon steps outside. When the knocks came on the door, she looked up suddenly, her eyes wide, her lips slack, exposing her rotting gums. Someone wanted to come in — and she had a good idea who it was.

The evilly grinning spectre come to carry her away.

'Who is it?' she cried out, her voice quivering with fear. Not that she was scared to die. Far from it. Death would be a welcome relief after all those painful years since her teeth had rotted and fallen out, since her arthritis had crippled her more and more. She had been looking forward to dying. She was old and feeble and bone weary. She had lived far too long, she thought. But what frightened her, what put terror in her brittle old bones, was knowing the way death would come. She had always imagined dying peacefully in her sleep. And of all the ways to die, she relished being roasted alive least of all. She regretted now that she had felt the compulsion to read her own fortune. That had been the worst mistake of her life. She realized that now.

But it was too late.

The door creaked as it was slowly pushed open. Bright light from outside spilled in, silhouetting the caller. For a moment, Olga was blinded. She drew a deep breath, then seemed to crumble as she let out a hiss of relief. 'Hazy!'

Moving with the same peculiar gait as Goliath, Hazy waddled over to Olga. 'Is something wrong?' she asked worriedly.

Olga quickly shook her head. 'No no, you just frightened me.' She managed a sickly smile. 'What do you want?'

'You sure you're okay?'

'Yes, yes,' Olga said impatiently. 'What is it?'

'The fight's about to start. Soon the women and children will flock to have their fortunes read. Can you tell me mine first?'

Olga shrank back, a terrible fear knotting her stomach. 'No!' she spat out so vehemently that her spittle sprayed Hazy.

Hazy frowned, wiped the spittle off her face with her forearm, and regarded Olga queerly. Nevertheless, she held out a tiny hand, palm up. 'A quick palm reading, then?'

Olga stared at Hazy. Then her eyes dropped. Reluctantly, she took the proffered hand and looked down at it, holding it sideways so that it caught the light flooding in from the door.

And experienced one of the worst shocks of her life.

The wagon suddenly began to reel around old Olga. Hazy's lifeline had never been extraordinarily long, but it hadn't been very short, either. But now . . . now the lifeline was *gone*. How was that possible? *How could a deep crease in someone's flesh simply disappear?* Olga gripped the tiny hand with such fierceness that Hazy let out a howl.

'Ow!' Hazy snatched her hand back. 'You're hurting me!' she accused.

Startled, Olga snatched her own hand away. Her eyes gleamed darkly, but her face had gone white. She felt a peculiar sickness in the pit of her stomach – an awful churning sensation. She had to fight to keep the bile down.

Slowly, Olga's gaze dropped to her own right hand. The fingers were clenched into an unyielding claw. Hesitantly, she forced the hand open by pulling the fingers back with her left hand.

What she saw made her close her eyes. *Her own lifeline, too, had disappeared.*

She pushed her chair back and rose unsteadily to her feet. Thunderbolts of pain shot through her joints with the movement, but she compressed her gums and stifled her cries. There was no time to concentrate on the pain. Another, far more pressing matter took priority. Hazy's lifeline had disappeared, and so had her own.

Maybe others' had, too.

She *had* to find out.

5

As she hobbled by the big tent Olga could hear the raucous commotion coming from inside. That meant the prizefight was already in progress. She knew from experience that the spectators were all men: it was unseemly for women and children to watch fights and place bets. That was a man's sport. Meanwhile, the women and children would be occupying themselves in a more genteel manner – gossiping, playing games at the booths, watching the puppet show. Olga relentlessly pushed her way through the flocks of women and children, occassionally grabbing a hand and staring at it before the stranger snatched it back indignantly. But she neither explained nor apologized for her mysterious behaviour. She *had* to grab palms at random. She was driven to *know*.

73

She was satisfied. Every spectator still had his or her lifeline.

Then she ran across Hester, the bearded lady. Her lifeline was gone. The Tak Brothers' were, too. Hendricks, the fire-swallower, was walking with a flaming torch in one hand, blowing flames from his mouth to the delight of a crowd of children. Olga steered clear of him. She need not be reminded of fire.

Finally, Olga reached the lead wagon. She was tired and breathing heavily, but she ignored Marikka's surprised greeting and seized her plump red hand immediately.

No lifeline.

"Olga! What is it?' Marikka demanded.

Olga was balefully silent. She took Elizabeth-Anne's hand and studied it closely. She felt an immeasurable wave of relief settling over her. The child at least would be spared.

'Olga . . .' It was Marikka again.

'It is nothing!' Olga snapped, and took a seat.

'What about the fortunetelling concession? The women and children —'

Olga cut her off. 'I must speak to Szabo,' she said gravely.

Marikka shook her head. 'But the fight, it's started already! It will be a while!'

But Olga wouldn't budge. She folded her gnarled hands in her lap and stared resolutely ahead. 'Then I wait,' she said succinctly.

Szabo felt himself bouncing off the ropes. His opponent was waiting for him and punched him with a left. Instinctively, he dropped his hands to protect himself, but he was too slow. His body jerked and his kidneys exploded with a searing pain.

He looked stupidly at his opponent, only dimly aware of the men who sat excitedly around the ring. They all

74

sat hunched forward, eyes gleaming, feet stomping a noisy rhythm. He could hear their shouts, but he paid no attention to them.

'Give it to 'im, Barney!' the men crowed.

'I got ten dollars ridin' on you, Barney!' someone called out hoarsely.

'Think of Marikka!' Szabo chanted over and over to himself under his breath. 'Think of the money the circus needs! Think of my Princess!'

The mantra seemed to give him strength. He hopped forward and thrust a right to the big man's jaw.

Even before the blow hit, Szabo realized his mistake. So did his opponent. The big man's eyes looked confident as he effortlessly warded off the fist with one arm and simultaneously jabbed Szabo's unprotected chin.

A ringing filled Szabo's ears. He could feel himself swaying. He planted his feet apart to get a firmer footing and shook his head, trying to clear it of cobwebs. Never in his memory had he faced such a tough opponent. The man was huge. Powerful as an ox. And he moved elusively with the speed of lightning.

The big man's eyes gleamed as he circled confidently around Szabo, clenched fists raised in front of his face. Szabo turned warily, keeping his eyes on the constantly moving body. The man glistened with sweat and he knew that he did, too. He could feel it running down his forehead and into his eyes. The salt burned and made his eyes water, and in his right eye he could already feel the beginnings of a swelling coming on.

He blinked as the big man lunged forwards with a jab to his left. Szabo danced backwards to avoid the blow, but his body failed to respond in time. Even before he felt the pain, he knew what was happening. So did the spectators: their roars of excited approval were turning into shouts of contempt.

Szabo rallied all his remaining strength. He knew that he was steadily wearing down, that the big man was too powerful for him. Too powerful and too fast. All it would take was another couple of well-placed blows, and then it would be over.

'*Think of Marikka! Think of the circus! Think of Marikka! Think of —*' He tried to focus his thoughts on the litany, but now the shouts of the crowd were disorientating him, drowning out his ability to concentrate.

'That's it, Barney, thatta boy!'

'C'mon, Barney! Finish him off!'

A rage of humiliation flooded through Szabo and his heart hammered wildly against his ribs. He knew that he had to turn the tables on his opponent, yet he found it impossible to make his body respond. *What was happening?* he wondered. He had never lost a fight before. Nor had he ever felt so hurt or so humiliated in his entire life.

More pain exploded, white hot and exquisite. Szabo frowned at his opponent.

The big man feinted with his left. Szabo's eyes followed the blur; he saw the opening and made his move. A split second later, a right snapped into his face.

He blinked and shook his head again. Then he saw another blur. The fist was coming at him as if in slow motion.

He raised his own fists to parry it, but his arms felt as if they were made of lead, as if they were no longer a part of his body. The fist crunched into his jaw.

He jerked back as a blinding white light dazzled his eyes; then brilliant shards of colour exploded in a kaleidoscope of pain. His eyes rolled upwards, the whites fluttering. He could feel a soothing, peaceful, floating sensation. It felt somehow delicious, and he gave himself up to it.

Everything receded into darkness.

He reeled, swayed dizzily, and fell heavily forwards.

He had passed out.

Marikka could tell something was wrong the moment the fight ended. She knew from experience that the locals always bet on their resident bully, never on a transient fighter like her husband. It didn't matter who looked the strongest, or which opponent was the most experienced. It was simply a matter of local pride. Then, when Szabo invariably won, the spectators would file out of the tent with an air of quiet resignation or forced good humour.

Not once had she known the men to pour out of the tent ecstatically, as they did today, five of them hoisting the winner aloft. Nor had she ever seen them licking their thumbs, counting thick sheaves of money as they walked.

She stared out the window, unwilling to trust her eyes.

'He met his match today,' a voice cackled behind her.

'Be quiet!' she blurted irritably. She whirled in disgust at Olga, turning her wrath on the old gypsy as if she were to blame for Szabo's losing the fight.

Olga's cracked parchment face was a mask of imperturbability, but the ancient eyes were pained.

'I'm sorry,' Marikka sighed softly. She lowered her eyes guiltily, and turned slowly back around and let the curtain drop. She gripped the windowsill, bowed her head, and closed her eyes. So what she had most feared had finally come to be. She had known it would, sooner or later.

Was Szabo hurt? She quivered in fear and was now surprised to discover that she was afraid to know the answer. Before, during, and after each fight, she mouthed silent prayers for him. Her greatest nightmare was that he would be badly wounded. Much as she tried to stifle such ugly thoughts, they wormed their way into her mind, uninvited and unwelcome. She envisioned him bloody, broken-boned, or even worse, dead.

She took a deep breath. Well, she would know soon enough which it was to be today.

Suddenly she spun into action. She couldn't bear to wait another instant to find out! She rushed to the door and wrenched it open just as the Tak Brothers carried her husband out of the tent. Marikka's hand flew to her breasts and she made a keening noise. She stumbled down the wagon steps and hurried as fast as her bulk would allow. 'Szabo!' she screamed. '*Szabo!*'

When she reached him, she quickly fell into step beside the strange entourage.

'I am okay,' Szabo mumbled angrily from between swollen lips. His head lolled from side to side and he swallowed with difficulty. 'Put me down.'

The silent Tak Brothers glanced questioningly at Marikka.

She nodded and watched as they gently stood her husband up. He put one arm around Marikka's shoulders and held onto her for support as they limped together up the steps and into the wagon.

'Lie down,' Marikka commanded. She sat him gently down on Elizabeth-Anne's bed, lowered his head back on the pillow, and lifted his feet up. Elizabeth-Anne and Olga drew close around him.

Marikka knew where her priorities lay. 'Not now!' she snapped sharply at Olga. Then she turned to Elizabeth-Anne. The girl's aquamarine eyes held a peculiar look. 'Alcohol,' Marikka commanded succinctly.

Elizabeth-Anne stood frozen to the spot, her hands clenched at her sides. She was disappointed and frightened. Papa wasn't supposed to get hurt. He was the strongest man in the world.

'Well! What are you waiting for?' Marikka shouted. 'Get the alcohol!'

Elizabeth-Anne hurried to fetch it. When she brought it back, Marikka already had a rag ready. She

78

doused it with the alcohol and dabbed it gently on her husband's cuts and bruises.

Szabo hissed as the alcohol burned his wounds. He scowled at Marikka.

'Keep still,' she urged gruffly.

'We lost a lot of money,' Szabo whispered hoarsely. 'Hurry. We have a show to put on.' He started to sit up, but she pushed him back down and shook her head.

'No,' she said firmly, 'today's show we cancel. Today you got to rest. Tomorrow we move on.'

Szabo stared up at her for a moment. Then he sighed wearily. 'The show, we got to give'

'But —'

'We got to.' Szabo shut his eyes. 'Today we lost too much.'

'Was there that much betting?' In her shock, Marikka accidentally rubbed a cut too roughly. The moment he sucked in his breath, she instantly snatched the rag away. She touched his cheek contritely with her finger-tips. 'Did I hurt you?'

He smiled ruefully. 'Get ready for the show. Me, I will be up on my feet in a minute.'

'How can you —'

'Get ready,' he repeated firmly. He sat forward, sought her hand, and squeezed it. 'Nothing is so bad a little greasepaint will not cover it.'

She hesitated, but he shook his head. Sighing with resignation, she pushed the cork back into the alcohol bottle. Then she got to her feet and moved to the back of the wagon.

He slumped down and closed his eyes as he heard her moving around. After a while he became aware of someone staring at him. He turned his head sideways. Elizabeth-Anne stood silently in a dark corner, her eyes dulled with disappointment.

'What is the matter, Princess?' he asked. 'Why the face?'

79

A strangled sound came from deep within Elizabeth-Anne's throat. 'You lost the fight, Papa?' she asked in a small voice.

He managed a weak smile. 'Sometimes you win, sometimes you lose.' He stifled a grunt as he struggled to sit up. He patted the mattress with his hand. 'Come over here, Princess.'

Reluctantly Elizabeth-Anne moved to the bed. Once she was seated, he put an arm around her and gave her a squeeze. Usually it would make her squeal with delight, but today she stiffened and looked away.

'Princess,' Szabo said softly.

Elizabeth-Anne turned to face him.

'You are upset?'

She nodded gravely.

'You want to talk about this?'

She stared into his eyes. 'You lied to me, Papa,' she said quietly. 'You told me you were the strongest man in the world.'

He shook his head from side to side. 'All papas want their little princesses to believe that,' he said sadly. 'Me? I am no different from any other man.'

She knitted her brows. 'But don't you see, Papa? I *believed* you.'

'And now you do not?'

She bit down on her lower lip and sat in stony silence.

A feeling of shame came over Szabo. He had never realized just how sensitive and perceptive the child really was – how she believed his every word. He knew suddenly that she would never take anything at face value again. Not without questioning it first. He knew that now at a mere six years, his princess had become a sceptic.

'Sometime when you are older,' he said slowly, 'maybe then you will understand.'

She looked at him without speaking and nodded.

A feeling of overwhelming sadness ran through him. He wished that the show did not have to go on . . . that he could take the time to sit down with her and try to explain. It was important that she understood.

But without the proceeds of the show, the circus would be in severe jeopardy.

'Now I must get ready,' he said sadly. He reached behind him for the bottle of oil which was kept on the shelf. He held it out to her. 'You still want to help?'

She nodded gravely, and he poured some oil into her outstretched palm. Carefully she smoothed it over his arms and chest until he gleamed. Several times he nearly had to cry out in pain, but he didn't let on that he hurt. Somehow that, too, seemed important.

Finally, when she was finished, she spoke up. 'Are you still going to pick up four people at once like you always do, Papa?' she asked.

For a moment Szabo did not speak. 'It is important to you, Princess?' he asked finally.

She nodded.

'Then four people I will still pick up at the same time,' he assured her. 'Maybe I am not really the strongest man in the world. Say I am *one* of the strongest, eh?' He smiled and kissed her smooth forehead. Then he got wearily to his feet. 'Now I must go to the tent and help put on the show.'

After Szabo and Marikka left the wagon, she was alone. Olga had slipped quietly out, unnoticed. For a long time Elizabeth-Anne thought about what her father had told her – that perhaps she would understand when she was older. That maybe he *wasn't* the strongest man alive, but *one* of the strongest. Somehow she felt a little better now. But still, he *had* lied to her, and if you couldn't believe your own father, who could you believe?

But forever after, sceptic though she had become, what she was to remember and berate herself for was her own despicable behaviour. She had been too

81

involved with her own disappointment to show any concern for him.

She had never even asked him if he was hurt.

While the show was in progress, she decided to see for herself whether he could still pick up four people simultaneously. She knew that if anyone caught her sneaking out of the wagon, she would be in severe trouble. But she decided to take the chance. She *had* to see if her father had told her the truth this time.

Her heart thumped with fear and excitement as she left the wagon and walked over to the big tent. Slipping unnoticed into it was a lot easier than she had anticipated.

For a while, the show was magical and mystical, funny and exciting, and she could understand the gaiety of the people who flocked to see it.

Then suddenly it turned into a nightmare.

Hendricks was performing his fire-eating act, when he accidentally swallowed some of the kerosene and gagged. He dropped his flaming torch in the sawdust, clawed at his throat, and spewed the kerosene out from between his lips.

It was the worst fire that Quebeck, Texas, or Elizabeth-Anne were ever to see. Before her horrified eyes, she watched the conflagration begin.

At first a tiny flame licked lazily across the sawdust; a moment later there was a sea of flames. When Hendricks had spat out the kerosene, a roaring plume of fire and smoke shot skyward and set off the roof of the tent. From all around, she could hear the cries of fear and panic, pain and anguish. She watched in shock as the oil she had rubbed onto her father's body turned him into a roaring human torch. She started to run towards him, but was shoved to safety by the fleeing, screaming mob.

For interminably long minutes, she stood outside in the field and watched the fierce fire burn itself out.

When it began to die down, she headed back to the smouldering rubble that was left of the tent to search for her mother and father. They lay dead, pinned down by a still-burning pole. She grabbed hold of it with her bare hands to pull it off them, in her shock unaware of the flames licking her hands, burning her palms and fingers. Then she smelled the nauseous odour of frying, sizzling flesh, her own and her family's, and she dropped the pole and threw up.

The townsfolk had succeeded in stampeding to safety and miraculously only three of them suffered burns, two of them minor. Mrs Pitcock, the mayor's wife, suffered the most. She was burned on the forehead and cheeks, but that eventually healed, blemishing her face slightly. Not one townsperson died.

But the holocaust took its toll on the circus family – all but Hazy and Hester, the bearded lady, died before they could be taken to the nearest hospital. Hester died in agony that same night.

Elizabeth-Anne would never forget that terrible sight and the horrible stench of burning flesh for as long as she lived. She would be unable to bear to look at her hands, even long after their wrinkled, parchment-like skin had healed, for they were a constant reminder of tragedy and loss and death.

Elizabeth-Anne would never discover the terrible irony which fate had so cruelly meted out.

She had been orphaned twice in the space of six years – both times in the very same town.

And so it was that things ended where they had begun.

6

It had been a flash fire, ravenous, indiscriminate, and all-consuming. It had fed itself on the circus and was over within minutes. But the remains smouldered for days. There was little entertainment in Hidalgo County, and the news spread like wild-fire. Even those who had not come to see the circus travelled from miles around to gawk with morbid fascination at the destruction first-hand.

Elender Hannah Clowney was not one to thrive on sensationalism and misery. Neither was she a gossip. She was far too busy to squander her time uselessly by prying into other people's affairs – she had enough headaches and problems of her own, mainly her rooming house on Main Street, where she lived on the ground floor with Jenny, her niece, and rented out the upstairs rooms by the week, as well as the Good Eats Café across the street.

Twenty-six years earlier, Elender Hannah Clowney had been born in Boston. That legendary streak of New England frugality, coupled with an implacable calm and a no-nonsense approach to life, was ingrained in her bones. She rented out rooms by the week instead of the month because of a simple matter of arithmetic: she figured that there were fifty-two weeks in a year. Divided by four, that came to thirteen months. Renting out rooms by the calendar month, on the other hand, would have netted her only twelve months. It just made plain old Bostonian common sense to squeeze an extra month out of every year – and the money with it.

If she'd known about the fire, she'd have been the last person to hop into her buggy, drive out to Geron's Fields, and survey the damage. As it was, she didn't hear about it because, for the past two days, she'd been in Brownsville.

She'd taken Jenny, who had just turned nine, along with her. Since Quebeck was not even a pinpoint on a map, she decided it wouldn't hurt the girl to be exposed to something bigger, more cosmopolitan. Coming from Boston, Elender Hannah Clowney knew the world offered much more and was certainly faster-moving than sleepy little Quebeck, where time stood still. She considered ignorance dangerous and exposure all-important. And yet . . . yet *she* had moved to Quebeck a little more than eight years ago. By choice. It had seemed the perfect place to settle down and carve out a new life for herself. When she'd arrived, no one had known her, and she had since become a model citizen, admired and respected.

She'd paid for her past mistakes. Her slate had been cleansed.

She had to admit that her new life in Quebeck hadn't turned out half bad. No, not bad at all, everything considered, which was why she had gone to Brownsville. Her rooming house was paid for, the Good Eats Café was making money, and she'd managed to save five hundred dollars – two hundred of which was going for new paint, fabric, and furniture. The rooms she was renting out could do with refurbishing, and she could finally afford it. The remainder of the money would go towards buying the house the café occupied. It was much smaller but had a big porch encircling it and was structurally sound; she'd be able to own it instead of renting, and equity was something which just made good old common sense.

She'd enjoyed Brownsville – the dressing up, the shopping, the bargaining, and the two nights spent at a real hotel. She'd almost forgotten how much fun a big town could be. Of course, it wasn't as exciting as Boston or New York or Philadelphia, but still, it would have been a perfect trip had it not been for Jenny. The trouble had started as soon as they'd left Quebeck. Driving past Geron's Fields, they came across Szabo's Travelling Circus and Freak Show. The big blue tent was just being pitched, and suddenly Jenny no longer wanted to go to Brownsville. She wanted to stay and see the circus instead.

She had bounced up and down on the buggy seat. 'Look, Auntie!' she squealed. 'A freak show's come to town!'

Elender frowned disapprovingly at the brightly painted wagons.

'Can't we stay here, Auntie?' Jenny begged. '*Please*? I want to see the freaks!'

'We will *not* put off this trip,' Elender said concisely. She narrowed her eyes. 'You have looked forward to it for two weeks and so have I. And I still am.' And with that, she tightened her lips and determinedly snapped the reins to make the horse trot even faster.

But it did not move fast enough: Jenny caught sight of two dwarfs, obviously arguing. Elender, who did not like to come face to face with human misery, quickly averted her eyes. And in doing so saw the child.

She was at the roadside, pushing through the weeds, plucking sunflowers. As Elender watched, the little girl brought the bouquet up to her nose and sniffed it. Then she wrinkled her nose and looked up.

What a beautiful child she was! So tiny and delicate, so perfectly . . . *angelic*. For an instant their eyes met, and the girl smiled disarmingly. There was a happiness in that smile such as Elender had never seen.

The magical moment was broken by Jenny. 'She's one of the freaks, isn't she?'

Elender did not reply. She could only wonder how Jenny had turned out the way she had. *She is so unlike me*, Elender thought. *How had that happened? I've tried to*

*do everything for her. Give her everything. Is that the problem?
Or is it because the child has no father?*

Everyone in Quebeck knew that Elender Hannah
Clowney was a spinster and that Jenny was her
orphaned niece – because that was what she had told
them when they had first arrived. It was the first and
last lie she had ever told.

Spinster. Well, it wasn't far from the truth. After all,
she didn't have a husband. But Jenny wasn't her niece.

She was her daughter.

Elender had never planned to have a child, certainly
not one out of wedlock. She'd just turned sixteen when
it had happened. When Arthur Jason Cromwell's
parents had sailed for Europe. She had been one of Mrs
Cromwell's chambermaids, and the night of the sailing,
she and Arthur had been alone in the big brick house
on Beacon Hill. He'd given the rest of the servants a
free night out. And told her to stay. She'd never forget
that night for as long as she lived.

She was in the kitchen when he rang for her. She
looked up at the bell register, surprised that the ringing
did not come from the public rooms or his own. It came
from his father's bedroom, which was just next door to
the missus'.

She went upstairs and knocked on the door.

'Come in!'

Slowly she opened the door. The room was dark and
warm, and he was sprawled in a tufted armchair in the
corner, his feet up on a hassock. There was half a bottle
of brandy on the marble-topped table beside him.

'You rang, sir?' she asked respectfully.

He nodded. 'Turn down the bed.'

Automatically she walked over to the bedside cabinet.
If he wanted to sleep in his father's bed, that was his
business. She shivered at the impropriety of the idea,
but did as she was told. When she finished, she looked
over at him. 'Will there be anything else, sir?'

87

He smiled slowly, his eyes travelling over her body. She was tall for her age, slim but full-breasted. Much more so than most girls her age.

She could feel her face reddening under his obvious scrutiny.

'Get undressed,' he said softly.

She stared at him, suddenly feeling helpless and frightened.

'I told you to undress!'

And slowly, she fumbled with the buttons on the back of her dress. She knew what he wanted to do was wrong, but with the Cromwells gone, he was master of the house. She dare not disobey him. He could dismiss her at his whim, and without references, all jobs would be closed to her.

She was, after all, the orphan of poor Irish immigrants, had no family, and had blessedly been taken in by the rich and all-powerful Cromwells. A bad word from any of them, and her life might as well be over.

Her fear only seemed to excite him all the more. Swinging his legs off the hassock, he got up from the chair and crossed over to her. Placing his hands on her shoulders, he pushed her roughly to her knees and tore at her petticoat. When she was naked, he pulled her back up and took hold of her arm. He led her to the bed.

The sheets were cool and clean and crisp, but she felt hot and dirty and used. She had never been to bed with a man, and the agony was supreme. Arthur smelled of brandy and sweat, and when he tore savagely into her, the pain was so great she nearly fainted. It was the worst experience of her life, but mercifully quick.

As soon as he fell asleep, she gathered up her torn clothes and stumbled out of the room. She felt humiliated and empty. Mortally wounded. Tears streamed down her face. Her thighs were wet with blood.

At least it's over, she told herself. *Now I can die in peace*.

But it wasn't over, nor did she die. He took her to bed every night, and soon the other servants suspected what was going on. As a whole, they were ruthlessly respectable, and blamed Elender. She became a pariah.

Six weeks later, it was all over. This time it was she who came to see him. Her face was pale. 'I'm pregnant,' she told him quietly.

He stared at her and then ordered her to undress. The next day, he gave her five hundred dollars and one instruction: 'Go down to New York and get rid of the baby.'

So she went to New York, but she didn't get rid of the baby. She worked one job after another until she 'showed', and was frugal with her money. When the baby was born, she named her Jennifer Sue and headed west, perfecting her cover story on the way: that she'd had a widowed sister-in-law who'd died and left her some money and custody of her child.

When she came to Quebeck, Elender knew it was the perfect place to start a new life. The town was small and no one knew her. Her story was plausible and accepted. Not even Jenny ever learned the truth.

In over eight years, Elender and Jenny had never left sleepy little Quebeck. Except for the trip to Brownsville.

Now Elender couldn't help wishing she hadn't taken Jenny, who had been sour and had pouted during the entire drive. Only when they'd checked into the hotel had Jenny finally forgotten the circus. Elender Hannah Clowney may have been frugal, but for the one time in years they would stay overnight in a real city, she had decided to splurge and stay in a first-rate hotel.

The Hotel Garber was a huge, square, red brick structure of four storeys, with ornamental black iron fretwork and tiers of balconies, and boasted its own livery stable. She and Jenny were helped down from their buggy and escorted inside to the front desk by a uniformed porter who carried their luggage.

Elender's breath caught in her throat as she gazed around the huge, luxurious lobby. This . . . this palatial hotel . . . this was what she dreamed of owning, not the modest rooming house in Quebeck, but she was practical enough not to confuse simple dreams with hardcore reality. Still, it did no harm to dream a little, and so her envious eyes took in the plush red carpeting, the shiny, red damask walls punctuated with graceful white plaster columns with gilded capitals, the electric globes on brass sconces, the sweeping brass-railed staircase, the palms in Chinese export pots, and she wondered how it felt to own all this. All the while, her New England mind attempted to grapple with all that luxury and translate it into a mind-boggling sum of dollars and cents.

They were shown up to their second floor room by yet another porter. As soon as the door opened, Jenny headed straight for one of the twin beds and hopped on it to test its springs. Elender looked around and smiled, savouring the luxury of the quilted, pale blue satin bedspread and the matching swag drapes hanging elegantly on either side of the arched French doors.

The porter cleared his throat. She turned and found him waiting expectantly. She dug into her purse for a coin, handed it to him, and smiled. He frowned into his hand and Elender's smile faded. She snapped her purse shut with a decisive click. Generosity had its bounds. Money did not grow on trees, at least not for Elender Hannah Clowney. The amount she had already spent on the room alone seemed outrageous. 'A fool is easily parted from his money,' Mrs Cromwell used to warn, and she cautioned herself about being more thrifty; it seemed remarkable how, in a city, money had a habit of changing hands with alarming regularity. There were altogether too many temptations.

When the porter left, snapping the door behind him with no less decisiveness than Elender had closed her purse, she noticed a framed sign affixed to the back of the door. She leaned forward and read the thick block letters. GUESTS WISHING TO TAKE A BATH KINDLY RING THE BELLPULL BESIDE THE BED AND INFORM THE CHAMBERMAID A HALF HOUR BEFORE THE DESIRED TIME.

Yes, Elender thought, a bath would be nice. It had been a long ride, and she felt tired and gritty. She could use some freshening up.

She started to reach for the tasselled bell rope. Suddenly she frowned, her hand hesitantly poised in mid-air.

Ring the chambermaid for a bath. She wondered why she felt so peculiar about such a simple action. Was it because *she* had been a chambermaid once? Or was it, quite simply, that she still felt the class distinction she had known on Beacon Hill, and was still herself a chambermaid at heart?

She lowered her hand slowly and decided to wait until later. In the meantime, she tried to shove the unpleasant memories out of her mind by investigating the room.

She pushed her hand down into the plump mattress and slid back the covers to feel the blinding white, stiffly starched sheets. Ever neat, she found herself remaking the bed, as well as smoothing the covers of the one on which Jenny had sat. She could not help wondering whether this instinctive reaction was yet another throwback to her tenure as a servant.

She peeked into the closets, felt the wallpaper with her fingertips, and judged the quality of the towels which were folded in precise squares beside the ceramic bowl and pitcher on the washstand. To her surprise, she discovered the room was no more comfortable than those she rented her roomers back in Quebeck. Less so, despite the impact of luxury, because upon close examination she discovered the lack of little things. The personal, thoughtful touches the hotel did not provide

– an extra blanket, toiletries a hurried traveller might have forgotten, a dressing gown, a reading lamp that could be moved just where you wanted it.

Her inspection over, Elender went through the open French doors that led out to the balcony. She drew a sharp breath. Jenny was leaning over the railing, precariously perched on her toes. 'Jenny!' she scolded sharply. 'Get away from there at once!'

'Yes, Auntie,' Jenny said with glum resignation.

'Come and wash up. We'll have a late lunch downstairs in the dinning room.' She watched Jenny skip inside, glad to see her more cheerful.

The dining room was quiet and empty; the lunch crowd had long since finished and left. The waiter was a wizened, white-jacketed, white-haired negro. He let them have their choice of a table. Elender chose a large round one beside a window looking out onto the street. This way they could watch people pass, seeing what the latest fashions were.

'We still have the special from lunch, ma'am,' the soft-spoken waiter said solicitously. 'Rabbit stew with dumplin's.'

Jenny licked her lips.

'We'll order in just a moment,' Elender told the waiter, who withdrew quietly and busied himself snapping fresh tablecloths out over the tables and laying silverware and glasses for the evening meal.

Elender picked up her menu, glanced at it, and stiffened. The prices were exorbitant, and her immediate inclination was to get up and leave. Even if price were no object, she would have difficulty swallowing such expensive food. Surely there were modest places where they could find something to eat for much less. But Jenny had never been to a city or a nice restaurant, she reminded herself. The child would be sorely disappointed.

Elender glanced across the table at Jenny, who was hidden behind a menu. 'Don't read with your eyes so close to the page, dear,' Elender said automatically. 'You'll ruin your eyesight that way.' She closed her own menu and laid it down. 'We'll have a slice of apple walnut cake and a nice cup of tea,' she decided quickly, folding her hands on the edge of the tablecloth.

'Aw, Aun-*tie*!' Jenny wailed.

'I needn't remind you that we're not rich, Jennifer Sue Clowney,' Elender said. 'Besides, cake and tea will hold us over quite nicely until supper.' She did not add that supper would be inexpensive: while shopping, she would pick up some bread and cheese which they would take back to the hotel and eat in their room.

After finishing their tea and cakes, which were small in portion, but delicious and beautifully served on gold-rimmed china, they explored the shopping streets. The hum of activity around them was contagious, and Jenny quickly forgot about the lunch she could not have. She was mesmerized. Life was faster-paced here in Brownsville than it was out in the country. The salt air from the Gulf was invigorating. Shop windows were chock full of enticing merchandise of all kinds.

'Look, Auntie!' Jenny squealed, suddenly tugging at Elender's hand and pulling her towards a shop. She stood enraptured in front of the window and sighed deeply. 'Isn't that a *beautiful* doll?'

Elender nodded. Seated in the window was the most exquisite doll she had ever seen. It had long, lustrous golden hair, a porcelain face with a sultry expression, and languorous, dark blue eyes. It was dressed in a pink crinoline gown with flounces.

'Oh, Auntie, I'd love to have that doll! Please, Auntie?' Jenny shook Elender's hand. 'Oh, please say yes!'

'I'm sure it's expensive,' Elender said carefully.

'Oh, I know.' Jenny was silent for a moment. Then she looked up hopefully. 'But for Christmas?'

'We'll see, Jenny.'

Jenny's face fell, and as they continued walking, she lagged further and further behind.

On the next street corner, Jenny came to a stop and stood, mesmerized, in front of another shop. When Elender realized Jenny wasn't beside her, she stopped walking, turned around, and slowly backtracked.

Jenny pointed excitedly at a boudoir set of gleaming gold-tone metal. There was an ornate oval hand mirror, an embossed, white-bristled brush, and a matching ivory comb.

'Oh, Auntie! *That's* what I want for Christmas!'

Elender smiled tolerantly. 'But I thought you wanted the doll.'

'Oh, no,' Jenny said loftily, shaking her curls. 'Dolls are for children.'

Elender hid her smile. 'I see,' she said.

'Auntie, do you think . . .' Jenny bit down on her lip.

'Perhaps you will get it for Christmas,' Elender said vaguely. 'If you're good, that is. But not now.'

Jenny was glum the rest of the day.

The following morning, Elender left Jenny at the hotel while she went looking for new furniture and curtains for the rooming house. Prices being what they were, she decided against buying anything. Besides, she rationalized, the rooms she rented out were comfortable and homely just as they were. Much more so, in fact, than the hotel.

They stayed one more night at the Hotel Garber. In the morning, they climbed up on the buggy and drove back to Quebeck. Jenny was gloomy, pouting from not getting the boudoir set. *Christmas*! she thought. *Christmas is ages away! I'll never get it*!

But unknown to her, Elender had bought the set and had it secreted in her luggage.

As they neared Quebeck, they passed Geron's Fields

again. Where the circus had been was a charred, skeletal ruin. Even the wagons had burned.

Elender stared at the destruction with horror. And then she saw the child again. The one who had been picking sunflowers. She was ragged and filthy, and her angelic face was stony. She walked aimlessly about, as if in a stupour.

Jenny saw her, too. 'Look, Auntie!' she piped up. 'There's one of the freaks!'

Elender stopped the horse and turned to Jenny. Her hand blurred and there was a sharp crack. Jenny cried out. 'You *hit* me!' she accused.

'And I'll hit you every time you call another human being a freak,' Elender said with quiet rage.

Jenny stared at her with vitriolic hatred, but Elender didn't notice. She hopped down from the buggy and waded through the tall weeds out into the field.

The girl's eyes were dulled with shock.

Elender stooped down, put her arms around her, and picked her up. 'Come, child,' she said gently. 'Everything's going to be all right.'

7

The shock Elizabeth-Anne had suffered was so great that she lost her power of speech.

'What's your name?' the nice woman kept asking her over and over, but much as she wanted to reply, she couldn't. Her mind simply would not allow her to form the words.

After Elender took Elizabeth-Anne home and bandaged her hands, she asked around in town and learned that there was another survivor of the circus fire: a dwarf was being treated by Dr Purris. But when Elender mentioned Elizabeth-Anne, everyone expressed astonishment. No one had known that a beautiful little girl had been part of the circus, and that she had also survived the inferno. In all the commotion, the child had been completely passed over.

'*Nobody* noticed a stranger?' Elender asked in disbelief. 'I find that extremely hard to believe.'

Mr Preston, the owner of Preston's Drygoods Store, shrugged his narrow shoulders. 'Everyone was panicking,' he muttered, 'tryin' to round up their own families.'

'Does she have any other relatives?' Elender asked. 'Please, it's very important.'

But Elender didn't hear his answer. She was already outside, climbing up into her buggy. She snapped the reins decisively and headed straight for the doctors where she spoke to Hazy, the dwarf, who was suffering from severely infected burns.

'It's gotta be Elizabeth-Anne,' the dwarf mumbled painfully. 'She's Szabo Gross' daughter. He owned . . . the circus. Her mother . . . her mother . . . was the fat lady. Now . . . now poor Elizabeth-Anne got no mother . . . no father.'

'Does she have any other kin?' Elender asked. 'Please, try to remember. It's very important.'

Hazy sighed deeply. Besides Szabo and Goliath, only she had been privy to the truth. Until now the circumstances of Elizabeth-Anne's birth had been a carefully guarded secret shared by three . . . and two of them were dead. Soon now, she herself would die. Should she blurt out the truth . . . that Elizabeth-Anne had been the child of local farmers who had died in an accident six years before?

'Please,' Elender urged.

Hazy stared at the kind woman and then made up her mind. God only knew what kind of relatives Elizabeth-Anne's real parents had had. Better she should mention

96

Szabo's half-sister, who lived back East. 'There is no one,' Hazy murmured. 'Just a half-sister . . . Elspeth . . . somewhere . . . somewhere . . . in Pennsylvania.'

'Where in Pennsylvania?' Elender pressed. 'Please, it's very important. Try to remember.'

The dwarf screwed up her blistered face, whether in concentration or pain, Elender couldn't tell. 'I . . . I don't know. A little town. Starts . . . starts with a "Y".'

'Yes?' Elender said eagerly. 'A "Y"?'

'A little town. York. Yes. York . . . York, Pennsylvania.'

Elender thanked Hazy and left. She returned to visit her two days later, but she had died from her infected burns.

Now all that was left of the circus was Elizabeth-Anne. The letters Elender sent to York, Pennsylvania went unanswered.

'I'm Auntie,' Elender would tell Elizabeth-Anne gently. 'Until we can get in touch with your next of kin, you'll be living with Jenny and me. She'll be your sister. Don't be frightened, Elizabeth-Anne. Your mother and father are in heaven, and we both love you. Don't we, Jenny?' Elender glanced at Jenny, who made a production of nodding her head.

Elizabeth-Anne could only stare blankly at both of them, but Elender was patient and kind. Unfortunately, Jenny wasn't. The cruel streak she had inherited from Arthur Jason Cromwell was surfacing more and more all the time. She despised Elizabeth-Anne. For weeks, the slap she had received from Elender still burned hotly on her cheek, but she especially hated Elizabeth-Anne because she usurped *her* place at home and received most of the attention. Jennifer Sue Clowney could not and would not tolerate the situation. She must have *all* of Auntie's affection for herself, and she made a silent vow to destroy Elizabeth-Anne. But Jenny was guileful, careful never to go too far while Elender was watching or within earshot. She perfected her technique of torturing Elizabeth-Anne in little ways. And Elizabeth-Anne, unable to speak, had no way to fight back. She had to take her lumps in numb silence. She would look Jenny in the eye and pretend nothing had happened. She hoped that if she didn't respond, maybe after a while Jenny would get bored and leave her alone.

Since Elizabeth-Anne hated anything that reminded her of the circus, it was only natural that she despised her hands. The shrivelled, dry skin was an ever-present reminder of the horrors she had witnessed. She got into the habit of hiding them behind her back, or keeping them out of sight at her sides, but as much as she tried, she still caught sight of them too often. She had to wash and eat, and she could do neither without using her hands.

One day, out in the backyard alone, she forced herself to take a good look at them.

They're just ordinary hands, she told herself. *There is nothing wrong with them. Nothing at all.*

But the vision of the fire leapt up in front of her, and only when she hid her hands did it disappear.

Elizabeth-Anne did not know it, but as she tried to come to terms with her hands, Elender had been watching from the window. That night, Elender stayed up until early morning sewing Elizabeth-Anne three pairs of white gloves.

'Here,' she told Elizabeth-Anne when she went in to wake her in the morning. 'Now your hands won't distress you so much anymore.'

At lunchtime, Elizabeth-Anne stared at her plate hesitantly. Then she looked over at Elender and held up her gloved hands.

'Yes,' Elender told her gently, 'you may wear them while you eat.'

When it was time to wash before bedtime, Elizabeth-Anne stared at her washbowl. She looked questioningly at Elender and held up her hands.

Elender hugged her and handed her another pair of gloves. 'You may wear them while you wash, too. Only, don't forget to change to dry ones afterwards.'

Elizabeth-Anne looked at her gratefully.

At bedtime, Elender sat at Elizabeth-Anne's bedside and said her evening prayers for her. Once again, without saying a word, Elizabeth-Anne questioned her about the gloves.

'You may wear them anytime you please,' Elender told her, 'anytime at all. Even while you sleep.' Then she kissed Elizabeth-Anne good-night.

It's strange, how well we can communicate, Elender thought. *Even without Elizabeth-Anne's saying a word, she always manages to get her point across.*

I love Auntie, Elizabeth-Anne thought, *but I don't like Jenny at all. Maybe if I don't show any fear of her, she'll leave me alone for good. Things aren't too bad. Everyone else treats me nicely.*

But she was wrong. The ladies were on their way.

Jenny saw them first. She was sitting on the porch swing with Laurenda Pitcock who was a year younger than she, when the contingent of women marched briskly down Main Street, their long dark skirts flapping around their ankles. The Sunday afternoon was warm, pale yellow with sun, but cool and shady on the porch. From the open kitchen window behind them wafted the sweet, mouth-watering fragrance of baking blueberry pie.

Laurenda's alert nostrils picked up the scent first. Jenny heard her deep, appreciative sniffs and promptly jabbed her elbow sideways into her ribs. Laurenda turned to her angrily, and Jenny put a finger to her lips. 'Ssssh!' she whispered.

Laurenda sighed heavily and leaned forward with weary resignation, her chin resting on the palms of her upturned hands, her elbows digging into her thighs. She was bored, but neither she nor Jenny dared speak. It was a strictly enforced rule that each Sunday, during the two hours that Auntie's roomers and Elizabeth-Anne took their afternoon naps, Jenny and her friends were not to make a sound. They didn't even dare swing back and forth, for fear the rusty chains supporting the porch swing might creak and awaken someone. Playing was strictly forbidden while the roomers slept, as was laughing and speaking. Sometimes Jenny and Laurenda would whisper to one another, but before they did so they would first glance suspiciously back over their shoulders to make certain that Auntie wasn't at the window, watching.

After a while, Laurenda began to swing her legs impatiently up and down, watching the tips of her Sunday boots appear from under the swing, then disappear again. She twisted around. One of the swing's slats began to creak and Jenny jabbed her with an elbow once again.

'Ow!' Laurenda mouthed soundlessly, promptly poking Jenny right back.

'Now what did you go and do that for?' Jenny hissed.

Laurenda glanced over her shoulder at the kitchen window. The gingham curtains were still open to the breeze, but she couldn't see anybody. She turned back to Jenny. 'If we wake somebody up, your aunt'll be real mad,' she whispered ominously.

'I wish we *would* wake everybody up. I'm sick and tired of just sitting here.'

'So am I.' Laurenda kicked her legs morosely. 'I wish I'da stayed home.'

Jenny sat up straight, craned her neck, and nudged Laurenda again. The ladies, with Mrs Pitcock in the lead, were approaching the house. Their steps were purposeful, and Jenny could see that their faces were set in grim, uncompromising lines. 'Your mama's coming,' she said in a low voice. Looks like she's on the warpath.'

Laurenda made a face. 'Now I know I'm in *big* trouble,' she whispered morosely.

Jenny watched the women come to a stop. They waited for Mrs Pitcock to open Auntie's picket gate, then they marched towards the porch like a flock of birds, their starched skirts ruffling indignantly in the breeze. Jenny turned back to Laurenda. 'Why you in trouble?'

Laurenda shrugged miserably. 'I wasn't supposed to come over here and play with you,' she said.

'What did you do this time to deserve that punishment?'

Laurenda looked hurt. 'Nothin'.' She lowered her voice and glanced at her mother out of the corners of her eyes. 'Mama just said I gotta stay away from here while the freak's stayin' with you.'

Jenny felt a cold chill settling over her. She had known from the start that Elizabeth-Anne was trouble, that she was *poison*. Now it looked like she would lose all her friends because of her, too. 'Then why'd you come?' Jenny whispered.

Laurenda screwed up her face. 'I didn't have nothin' better to do. Mama doesn't let us work on Sundays. Says it's the Lord's Day. I get bored sittin' around the house.'

Jenny felt relieved. At least Laurenda didn't hold Elizabeth-Anne against her. 'Are you going to get whupped?' She looked at Laurenda with keen interest.

'Naw,' her friend said in a grown-up voice. 'I don't ever get whupped.' She fell quiet and waved to the

101

women as they stepped up on the porch. Mrs Pitcock's face was frozen.

'What are you doing here, Laurenda Pitcock?' she demanded.

'I was just passing by and —'

'You go on home right this very minute, Laurenda Pitcock!' Mrs Pitcock hissed at her daughter. 'Your pappy's going to wallop you good for disobeyin' me!'

Laurenda paled and jumped off the swing. In her hurry, she lost her footing and went sprawling. There was a thud as she hit the porch and let out a grunt. Quickly, Jenny helped her scramble back up on her feet. 'You hurt?' she asked with concern.

Laurenda didn't bother to reply. She leapt off the porch and dashed across the lawn.

Jenny turned around and stared up at Mrs Pitcock. The left side of the woman's face was brown and crinkly, where she had been burned during the circus fire. The other side was still perfect, and she had positioned herself to show her good side.

Virginia Evins Pitcock, strong as the proverbial rock, stood tall and straight as a board, one gaunt hand clutching the shawl she wore draped over her shoulders. The other women clustered around her. She was clearly their spokeswoman.

Mrs Pitcock's bituminous eye flashed as she took a deep breath. She looked as if she could barely control herself . . . as if a thousand buried burdens were ready to burst to the surface. 'Is your aunt at home?' she asked in a voice quivering with anger.

'Hello, Mrs Pitcock,' Jenny said politely. 'Yes, she is.'

'Then could you be so *good* as to tell her that we'd like to speak to her?' Mrs Pitcock asked sarcastically. 'We'll wait here.' She folded her hands in front of her.

Jenny hesitated for the barest fraction of a second. She knew that Auntie did not like disturbances while her roomers were napping. Yet what choice did she have? Mrs Pitcock had been forbidding and intimidating at the best of times, but ever since she'd been burned in the circus fire, two months earlier, she had become positively condemnatory.

Jenny preferred invoking Auntie's anger to Mrs Pitcock's any day. She dashed inside the house to find her.

In the bedroom dimmed by the drawn curtains, Elender was gratified to hear the gentle snores. She looked down. Elizabeth-Anne's white-gloved thumb was in her mouth, and her long golden lashes were pressed down against her freckled cheeks. She was fast asleep.

Slowly Elender shook her head, a sad smile on her lips. Ah, the sleep of the innocent, Elender thought to herself. How lucky the poor thing is to be able to retreat into its protective, healing mantle. Yet how tragic to be orphaned at so tender an age, and by so horrible a calamity. The worst was surely yet to come — it wasn't easy to adjust to a new life.

Elender, if anyone, could easily sympathize with that.

While she watched, Elizabeth-Anne rolled onto her side, tucked her knees up to her stomach, and continued to snore. Elender had come to wake the child, but now she decided against it. Better to leave her sleeping, she thought. Let her at least have her dreams.

She had so little else.

Elender leaned over the bed, brushed her lips ever so lightly against Elizabeth-Anne's cheek, and pulled the cover up over her. Then, straightening and tiptoeing from the room, and keeping the door open a crack so that she could hear the child if she cried out in her sleep, she collided with Jenny.

Elender could see the grim expression on Jenny's face. For an instant, she felt guilty for having kissed Elizabeth-Anne. What if Jenny had seen? She knew that Jenny was, by nature, extremely jealous. Jenny never wanted to share anything with anybody, least of all attention and affection.

Jenny cleared her throat. 'Mrs Pitcock and a lot of other ladies are here, Auntie,' she blurted. 'They want to talk to you!'

Elizabeth-Anne didn't know for how long she had been asleep. When she awoke, she opened her eyes and frowned up at the ceiling. Then she turned her head to one side. It was starting to get dark out, and the curtains were drawn. But the stream of pale yellow light coming in from the cracked door gave the room a comforting glow. Somewhere in the house she could hear sharp voices raised in anger.

She sat up in bed, wiped the sleep from her eyes, and fidgeted with the gloves. She despised wearing them. They were hot and made her hands sweat. But she hated seeing her disfigured hands much more.

She looked around the room, trying to orientate herself. She wasn't in her own small bunk in the circus wagon, nor in the storeroom which Auntie had made into a bedroom for her. She was in Auntie's bedroom, in Auntie's own bed, but Auntie wasn't here.

Her ears picked up another muffled wave of conversation coming from the parlour. She turned towards the door and frowned in concentration. A woman whose heated, strident voice she did not recognize was doing most of the talking, but she couldn't make out what she was saying.

Drawn by curiosity, Elizabeth-Anne tossed aside the covers and slid off the bed. The floor felt cool against her bare feet. Soundlessly, she padded over to the door, pulled it open a trifle further, and slipped out into the hall.

As she neared the parlour, Mrs Pitcock's voice gained loudness and clarity.

'I tell you, she's not normal!' Mrs Pitcock was hissing

104

vehemently. 'She was with that motley group of frea[k]
wasn't she? Well, this is a respectable town, and if w[e]
have anything to say about it we aim to keep it tha[t]
way! We do not intend for our children to associate with
her kind!'

Elizabeth-Anne heard the other ladies making indistinguishable clucks of agreement as Mrs Pitcock continued her tirade. She peered into the parlour from
behind the door. On a side table, Auntie's kerosene
lamp, the one with the hand-painted roses on the frosty
yellow glass shade, gave off a wavering light, casting the
women's shadows high onto the walls. Mrs Pitcock and
another lady were sitting side-by-side on Auntie's red
Victorian love seat; they were facing Elizabeth-Anne,
but were too agitated to notice her. Elender and the
other women sat on the matching side chairs, Elender's
body and face in rigid, shadowy profile. Elizabeth-Anne
felt an overwhelming urge to run in and throw her arms
around her, but she hesitated and stepped back silently.
Some instinct told her that she would be intruding, so
she positioned herself behind the open parlour door.
This way she could squint into the parlour through the
crack between the door and its frame.

While Mrs Pitcock was speaking, Elender had been
studying her thin, folded hands. Now she raised her
head in dignity and rose to her feet, her long black
skirt swirling about her legs. 'But she's only a *child*!' she
gasped in a low voice, her hands clenched angrily at her
sides. 'An innocent! How can you all be so cruel? Just
this morning, you were sitting in the church, not two
pews away from us!' Elender looked accusingly around
the room. 'If my memory serves me correctly, you were
all there. And each of you listened intently to the Reverend's sermon on Christian charity!'

Several of the ladies averted their eyes. It was clear
that they didn't like the direction this conversation was
taking.

Mrs Pitcock sat forward and looked up at Elender, careful to show the good side of her face. 'Why do you think Moses led the Israelites to the Promised Land? So they would be in a land of their own, among their own kind, that's why!' She nodded her head in triumphant righteousness. 'It's not natural for normal people like us to mix with abnormal freaks.'

'She's as normal as you and I.' Primly Elender sat back down on the edge of her chair and folded her hands in her lap. 'It's not the child's fault that her parents were circus people,' she said quietly. 'Why should she be made to suffer the sins of her elders? If sinners they were.'

Mrs Pitcock jumped to her feet. 'I suppose it's not that circus' fault that we suffered the worst scare of our lives? And I suppose it wasn't that circus' fault that I ended up looking like this?' Her voice had risen to a shrill screech and she leaned down in front of Elender to display the burned side of her face.

'No one likes you any the less for it, Mrs Pitcock,' Elender said gently, taking the woman's hands.

Mrs Pitcock snatched her hands away. 'All I can say,' she replied ominously, 'is that I'll not allow my Laurenda to associate with anybody in *this* house! Not while you harbour that freak. If you've got to keep that creature, I warn you, we'll drive her out of this town, and you along with her! You and your Boston airs! We'll have a town meeting! My husband is mayor! These ladies all support me a hundred percent!'

'Mrs Pitcock, *please*.' Elender fought to keep herself under control. 'The child's suffered just as much as you. And she's lost both of her parents, and all of her friends on top of that. Can't you show just a tiny bit of compassion? Can't any of you?' Elender glanced pleadingly around the room, but the women refused to meet her gaze.

Quietly, Elizabeth-Anne slipped into the parlour. It

106

was a moment before the adults noticed her. Elender spied her first and quickly rushed towards her. Elizabeth-Anne looked up at her with wide, hurt eyes.

Elender gently placed her hands on Elizabeth-Anne's shoulders. 'Nod hello to the ladies, dear,' she said gently.

Elizabeth-Anne nodded shyly.

'She cannot speak,' Elender explained with tears in her eyes. 'That's how much the fire has affected her.' She reached for Elizabeth-Anne's hands and held them out for inspection. 'She wears these gloves because she cannot bear to look at her hands. Like you, Mrs Pitcock, she was badly burned.' She paused to catch her breath. 'Does any one of you have the heart to be so cruel to someone who has suffered so. Who *still* suffers?'

The ladies looked silently at one another and a signal seemed to pass amongst them. Without speaking, they got to their feet and filed out, leaving Mrs Pitcock behind.

Elender looked at the woman and smiled tentatively, but Mrs Pitcock sniffed and marched out with self-righteous indignation.

Elender drew Elizabeth-Anne close and held her tightly. 'If your kin from York, Pennsylvania, don't show up, I want you to stay here with us, Elizabeth-Anne,' she said softly. 'This will then be your real home. Would you like that?'

In reply, the child flung her arms around her neck and kissed her gratefully.

8

'Just sit here while I finish up,' Elender said pleasantly.

Obediently Elizabeth-Anne took a seat on top of the stairs while behind her, Elender breezed into Mr

Saunder's room and collected the sheets, blankets, and pillows which had been airing out in the open window all day. Elizabeth-Anne twisted around and watched her.

With an economical flick of her wrists, Elender briskly snapped the bottom sheet and let it billow out over the bed. Before it even settled down like a slow, soft cloud, she quickly went from corner to corner, tucking the sheet under the horsehair mattress, her nimble fingers stretching it taut as she made expert, neat hospital corners. The fresh autumn air wafted in through the open window, and it smelled good.

Elender stood the pillows up against the shining brass headboard and plumped them with her hands. Downstairs, a door banged shut and cowbells jangled. It was the outside door.

Elender quickly took one last look around the room. Convinced that it was indeed spotless and all was in order, she briskly crossed the oval rag rug and came out onto the landing.

She smiled at Elizabeth-Anne and then grasped hold of the banister and leaned over it. 'Jenny? Is that you?'

Two floors below, Jenny took a few steps backwards and came into view. She leaned her head way back and looked up. 'Yes, Auntie, it's me,' she called up sweetly. 'I'm sorry I'm late, but Miss Welcker wanted to go over some arithmetic problems with me. It's been hard and I'm dead tired, but it was worth it.' She covered her mouth and pretended to yawn. 'Can I do anything to help?'

'Nooo . . .' Elender said slowly. 'I'm almost done.' She waved a thin hand fluidly through the air. She had picked up that elegant mannerism from Mrs Cromwell, and believed it gave her an air of 'quality'. 'There's some milk and biscuits in the pantry. Then why don't you go and play while it's still light? You can do your homework later.'

Jenny beamed.

'Oh, and make sure Elizabeth-Anne gets some milk and biscuits, too.'

Jenny's beam froze and her voice was filled with patent resignation. 'Yes, Auntie.' And she called out: 'Come on down, 'Lisbeth-Anne.'

Elizabeth-Anne gazed silently at Elender, her aquamarine eyes pale and expressionless.

'Go on,' Elender prodded gently.

Elizabeth-Anne got up and, carefully holding onto the banister, started slowly down the stairs. At the second floor landing, she hesitated and looked back up. Elender smiled and clapped her hands. 'Go on, now.'

Elizabeth-Anne obeyed. She could understand what people said and what they told her to do, but she still had not regained her power of speech. All Elender's efforts at trying to get her to talk had been in vain.

In the pantry, Jenny quickly stuffed her pockets full of biscuits. They looked big and crunchy and smelled delicious.

She nibbled on one and peered out into the kitchen. Elizabeth-Anne was just coming in. Quickly Jenny swallowed the biscuit, then lifted the white ceramic milk pitcher and plate of biscuits, and tiptoed with them out into the kitchen.

Jenny had grown nearly half an inch over the past few months, and her heart-shaped face was covered with freckles. Her eyes were a fathomless robin's egg blue and her dark brown hair was neatly parted in the middle and plaited in two thick, long braids. At the moment, her lips were decidedly turned down at the corners.

As Elizabeth-Anne carefully pulled one of the chairs out from under the kitchen table, Jenny deliberately sneaked behind her so that she couldn't help but back into her. 'Watch it!' Jenny cried when she knew it was too late. Elizabeth-Anne spun around and looked at the plate and pitcher in horror. For a fraction of a second, they seemed suspended in mid-air. Then, as if in slow motion, they crashed to the floor. The pitcher shattered into a thousand ceramic shards as milk flew everywhere and biscuits rolled across the floor in all directions.

'Now look what you made me do!' Jenny yelled.

Elizabeth-Anne could only stare at the mess in open-mouthed horror.

Elender's footsteps came in a quick cadence down the stairs. She stopped in the doorway, her hands on her narrow hips as she surveyed the damage. 'All right,' she said quietly. 'What happened?'

Jenny spun around and pointed an accusing finger at Elizabeth-Anne. 'She did it! It's all her fault! She came barging right into me!'

Elender stepped forward. 'You'd both better clean up this mess immediately,' she said calmly.

'But it wasn't *my* fault, Auntie!' Jenny wailed shrilly. 'Why should *I* have to do it?'

'I'm sure that if Elizabeth-Anne was to blame, she didn't mean to do it,' Auntie said judiciously. 'But you'll both clean it up. *Before* you go out and play. There've been altogether too many accidents around here lately.'

Jenny glared malevolently at Elizabeth-Anne.

'I'll be back in five minutes,' Auntie warned. 'By that time I expect this kitchen to be spotless. And for the remainder of the day, neither of you shall have any biscuits. It that clear?'

Jenny lowered her eyes demurely. 'Yes, Auntie,' she murmured in a contrite voice. 'I'm sorry.'

Elender swept out, and as soon as she was gone, Jenny raised her head. A wicked kind of triumph glinted in her eyes.

Elizabeth-Anne stared at Jenny blankly. But when Jenny reached into her pocket for a biscuit and began nibbling deliberately on it, the blank expression disappeared. Silent tears of rage welled up in her eyes. She longed to speak up – to cry out – against the injustice. She even opened her mouth. But not a sound would come out.

And that only made her cry all the more, as she cleaned up the mess Jenny had made while Jenny watched her, relishing each bite of the biscuit she took.

9

One morning, after several days spent wrestling with herself about what was best for Elizabeth-Anne, Elender dressed her in freshly laundered clothes and, holding her hand, escorted her to the local schoolhouse, a one-room, red-painted building situated at the edge of Quebeck. Jenny and all her friends attended the school, and Elender figured that although Elizabeth-Anne couldn't speak, that she was of school age. It bothered her that the child had no friends. Perhaps at school she would make some.

There were six grades in the Quebeck schoolhouse. The teacher, a thin, stern-faced spinster by the name of Miss Welcker, had previously taught in New Orleans. Tuition cost ten dollars per year for each student.

'That'll be eight dollars for Elizabeth-Anne, since school has already been in session for two months,' Miss Welcker told Elender.

Elender thought it a highly worthwhile investment.

It turned out to be a waste of money.

Elizabeth-Anne neither learned anything, nor did she make any friends. The fact that she could not speak was bad enough, but the fact that she had been part of the travelling circus was worse. All the other children regarded her as a freak. She was an outcast. A pariah.

It began that first day, during recess.

'Maybe she's a dwarf and won't grow any more?' one

of the girls whispered loud enough so that Elizabeth-Anne could hear.

'Or maybe she'll grow hair all over her body?' one of the boys suggested. 'Then she can go off and join a sideshow!'

And everyone hooted with cruel laughter.

Day after day, the ruthless taunts continued. Elizabeth-Anne learned to ignore them as best she could, usually by pretending not to hear them. Even Jenny, who had always enjoyed being one of the most popular girls, found her popularity waning dangerously. Because Elizabeth-Anne lived with her, she was sometimes included in the verbal assaults. She complained bitterly to Elender about it.

'Auntie, you've *got* to take 'Lisbeth-Anne out of school!' she begged.

'But why, for heaven's sake?'

'Everybody's making fun of her!'

'Perhaps they'll soon stop.'

'But they're making fun of me, too!' Jenny wailed.

Elender Hannah Clowney had no pity for strong youngsters who couldn't stand up for themselves. 'You're old enough to ignore that kind of rubbish,' she told Jenny severely. 'Anyway, you're fortunate because you can take care of yourself. But Elizabeth-Anne's a special child. You've got to stick up for her, be her big sister.'

But Jenny soon discovered how to regain her lost popularity. By being the ringleader and thereby avoiding association with Elizabeth-Anne. She became even more cruel and heartless towards her than all the others combined. In fact, it was she who began to mastermind the assaults.

In class, Elizabeth-Anne felt reasonably safe. Miss Welcker ruled her students with an iron hand, and Elizabeth-Anne's desk was in the front row. But she dreaded going to school, dreaded walking there and home, and dreaded recesses most of all. That was when the others really got their chance to torment her.

This gnawing fear of recesses refused to leave her, and she always tried to stay as close to Miss Welcker as possible.

Elizabeth-Anne's fears were not without foundation. Because it was not long before she was physically abused.

The same routine greeted Elizabeth-Anne and Jenny each school morning. Elender woke them up at five-thirty sharp, poured pots of boiling water into two enamel wash bowls, and sent the girls outside to fetch their own buckets of cold water from the pump. After they had washed up and got dressed, they all headed across the street to the Good Eats Café, where Elender cooked and served the girls breakfast while she rushed around, getting things ready for the Café's first customers of the day. Then, when Elizabeth-Anne and Jenny finished eating, they each split up and did their hour of morning chores. Finally Elender would hand them their lunches – usually two slices of home-baked bread spread liberally with congealed, salted bacon fat, and an apple or a pear, all neatly wrapped in newspaper and tied with a string. Then she would inspect each girl to make sure she was neat, admonish her to be good and study hard and kiss them both good-bye. She would watch proudly from the porch as they walked off together down Main Street to school.

They look just like sisters, Elender would think warmly, grateful that they were finally getting along better with each other.

Little did she know how wrong she was.

Jenny glanced over her shoulder. Auntie's house was out of sight. 'Go on by yourself, freak,' she said caustically.

113

Elizabeth-Anne stared at her and then went on to school alone.

Jenny watched her for a moment before turning down a side street and slowly walking past the Pitcock house. At the end of the street, she turned around and passed the house again.

A few minutes later, Laurenda Pitcock caught up with her. 'What do you think you're doin'?' she hissed breathlessly. 'You were supposed to wait by the bandstand for me! We had a deal.'

Jenny tossed her pigtails defiantly. 'I can walk where I like,' she said with laughter in her voice.

'If my Mama saw you and thought you were waitin' for me, I'd be in big trouble.'

'And get whupped again?' Jenny said slyly.

Laurenda scowled. 'I told you before, I don't get whupped.'

'That's not what I heard. 'Sides, for a few days after your Mama and all the ladies came to visit Auntie, you had trouble sittin'!'

'That's a lie!'

'Is it?' Jenny narrowed her eyes. 'Just ask anybody.'

'I fell,' Laurenda said with dignity.

Jenny hooted with laughter. Angrily, Laurenda grabbed her arm. Jenny stopped laughing and looked at her challengingly. After a moment, Laurenda let go of her. She kicked a pebble and watched it skip down the road. 'Sometimes I think you don't like me,' she mumbled.

Jenny shrugged. 'I don't care what you think.' She offered Laurenda her lunch pack. 'Want my apple?'

Laurenda shook her head, and for a while they walked on in silence. Then, as they neared the school, Jenny turned to her, a smile on her face. 'I have an idea,' she said slowly. 'But I need your help. And everybody elses' too.'

114

'Is it about the freak?' Laurenda looked at her with quickening interest.

Jenny nodded. 'It'll keep her from coming to school.'

Laurenda stopped walking and stared at her. 'You're sure?'

'I'm sure. Can I count you in on it?'

Laurenda squirmed uncomfortably. 'Will I get into trouble?'

'I don't think so,' Jenny said slowly. Then she brightened. 'And if you do, your Mama won't care, will she, as long as it keeps the freak out of school?'

Laurenda grinned and Jenny put an arm around her shoulder, confidentially drawing her head close to hers. They walked slowly towards the schoolhouse. 'I've got it all figured out,' Jenny said in a low voice. 'We'll do it tomorrow at recess. That'll give us enough time to get everybody ready. I'll distract Miss Welcker, so you don't have to worry about her. Now, here's what you and everybody else needs to do . . .'

Midmorning. The following day.

Miss Welcker frowned at the class, her hard dark eyes and thin lipless mouth set into disapproving lines. What she saw brought on a feeling of uneasiness. The roomful of children facing her, sitting ramrod straight and still, with hands folded in total obedience, was too good to be true.

Melissa Welcker was a middle-aged woman with a complexion like glazed ceramic and unmanageable greying hair escaping a tight bun. She had been teaching for over twenty-two years, and relied greatly on instinct. She prided herself on being able to sense it when some elusive mischief or other was brewing, and she could sense it now. The children had been too well-behaved this morning, and their faces, though carefully set like masks, could not hide the eager anticipation in

115

their eyes. Something was definitely up. If only she knew what.

Slowly, she reached for the brass bell she kept on her desk and picked it up by its wooden handle. She held it thoughtfully for a moment, then gave it a single shake.

The moment the clang reverberated through the room, the children rushed to the door, their feet stampeding the scrubbed floor like a herd of cattle. By prearrangement, everyone would play pin-the-tail-on-the-donkey. On her way out, Laurenda Pitcock reached for the 'tail', which was kept on a shelf. It consisted of several lengths of rawhide tied together with a thick pin stuck through the knot at the top end. The 'donkey' was cut from a large board and was nailed to the fence in the schoolyard. For as long as anybody in Quebeck could remember, that donkey had been there, the wood gradually weathering into a dull pewter patina until it looked the colour of a real donkey. Parents remembered playing with it, and over the years, only the tail had had to be regularly replaced.

Melissa Welcker gathered up several books, scraped back her chair, and started to rise from her desk when she noticed a lone pupil standing in front of her. She looked up in surprise. 'Yes, Jennifer? Aren't you going outside to play?'

'I've got some division problems I don't understand,' Jenny said timidly. 'I wondered . . .'

Miss Welcker folded her hands on the desktop and frowned at Jenny. 'But you're doing just fine, Jennifer! You got an "A" on your last test.'

Jenny smiled tightly. 'I know, but I would like to do even better. I'm still a little confused, especially with the fractions . . .' She bit down on her lower lip and stole a glance behind her at the open door.

Melissa Welcker sighed. 'Very well, Jennifer,' she said. 'Shut the door and we'll see what we can do.'

Jenny could barely keep the triumph off her face.

Now all she had to do was come up with enough questions to keep Miss Welcker occupied for the next half hour. That way, recess wouldn't be supervised.

The others were counting on her.

Outside in the playground, Elizabeth-Anne was happily unaware of what the others had in store for her. As usual, she kept to herself and walked around the yard slowly with her head tucked down. The day was cool and crisp and invigorating, and there was a decided nip in the air that told her winter was not far off. She could almost smell it in the wind that blew down from the north. Despite the sweater she wore, she rubbed her forearms briskly with her hands.

She was oblivious to everything going on around her. Of course, she had seen Laurenda Pitcock reaching for the donkey's tail before leaving the schoolhouse, so she was vaguely aware that they were going to play pin-the-tail-on-the-donkey. But she couldn't care less. Unless she was being taunted, she was always excluded from their games, and that was fine with her. If they didn't want her, well, then she didn't want them, either. She preferred to wander around in solitude, her chin tucked down against her chest, her thoughts on things far away. She felt protected by this invisible wall she erected between herself and the others.

She was so involved in her own introspection that she never noticed everyone drifting quietly towards her from all sides. Once she did become aware of it, it was too late. She was entirely surrounded.

Her heart skipped a beat and she looked about in confusion. She took a step forwards to walk away, but Laurenda Pitcock blocked her. She turned in another direction, but Nadine Derrick stood in her way. She felt a chill racing up her spine. She hadn't realized that she had strayed so far from the schoolhouse. Suddenly she wished she had stayed near the porch.

Laurenda Pitcock put her face so close to Elizabeth-Anne's that she could smell Laurenda's warm breath. 'You scared?' the bigger girl growled.

Elizabeth-Anne's eyes filled with tears, but she shook her head defiantly.

With two fingers, Laurenda held up the black handkerchief that was used as a blindfold while playing pin-the-tail-on-the-donkey. Having always been excluded from the games, Elizabeth-Anne now stared at the handkerchief with special terror. She took a step backwards and bumped into somebody.

'Aw, come on, 'Lisbeth-Anne,' Laurenda urged. 'Don't be such a sissy. We only want you to play with us. Right, everybody?' She looked around.

There were soft laughs and grunts of agreement.

'See?' Laurenda said.

Elizabeth-Anne stared at her, lips trembling. She didn't like Laurenda Pitcock. She was mean and frightened her. And, Laurenda was very chummy with Jenny. Besides, Elizabeth-Anne knew quite well that Mrs Pitcock had headed the delegation of women who had visited Auntie.

Her eyes now darted towards the schoolhouse. She prayed that Miss Welcker was around so she could make a quick getaway. But the teacher was nowhere in sight. *Where was she?*

Against her better judgment, Elizabeth-Anne found herself letting Laurenda blindfold her. She could feel her knees buckling as the black handkerchief was tied firmly around her head. Now she could neither talk nor see, but she bravely tried to keep from showing her terror. She would play the game fearlessly, she decided. Perhaps then they would get bored and leave her alone.

She held the 'tail' straight out in front of her, trying to remember in which direction the fence with the donkey was.

She took a deep breath, dreading what was coming.

118

She had no idea what the children were up to. All she knew was that it couldn't be nice.

She knew she was in trouble the moment she felt a dozen rough hands grabbing her and spinning her savagely around. And then around again. And then around again . . .

Even with the blindfold on, she seemed to be able to see the world reeling dizzily around her. Again and again she was spun around, the hands slapping at her, grabbing her, spinning her ever more fiercely like a dervish gone out of control until she felt herself tripping and starting to collapse.

At a signal from Laurenda, the children stepped back simultaneously and Elizabeth-Anne fell heavily to her knees. She made a strange hiss as the wind whooshed out of her, and her scraped knees burned terribly. Tears stung in her eyes, and she reached up to undo the handkerchief.

A rain of slaps forced her hands away. She let out a silent cry as her arms were grabbed and her gloves were pulled off. She could hear the awe and laughter as her hands were examined.

Why are they doing this to me? she wanted to scream, feeling as humiliated as if she had been stripped naked. *I only want to be left alone! I never hurt anybody!*

She started to crawl along the ground to get away.

'Get up, freak!' someone hissed. She thought it was Laurenda Pitcock, but she couldn't be certain.

Slowly, she staggered to her feet. Then she felt it. A bite on her hand. More bites. No! Not bites . . . *Burns.* They were throwing matches at her hands! Holding them to her flesh!

Terror overcame her and she tried to break away and run, but someone tripped her and she fell on her face. She raised her head and tried to cry out. Tried, in vain, to call for help.

But not a sound would come out of her throat.

Melissa Welcker checked the watch she wore pinned to her dress, stepped out onto the side porch, and rang her bell. Recess was over.

The children ran to the door, lined up quietly, and filed inside. Jenny got up from the front row and passed the teacher on her way back to her usual seat. 'Thank you for helping me, Miss Welcker,' she said politely. 'I understand everything much better now.'

'Fractions are difficult,' the teacher nodded, 'but not impossible. Anytime you need help, don't hesitate to ask.'

'I won't, Miss Welcker,' Jenny promised.

The children found their seats and sat quietly, waiting for class to resume. Jenny pointedly avoided looking at anyone.

At first, Melissa Welcker wondered why this ominous, pregnant silence hung heavy in the air. Usually the children were agitated and noisy after recess, and she had to silence them. But not today.

Frowning, she eyeballed the classroom, trying to figure out why they were behaving so peculiarly out of character. Then it struck her.

'Where is Elizabeth-Anne?' she asked quietly.

Everyone stared at her. The silence was deadly.

'Well?'

Still no one spoke up, but furtive eyes darted around.

Miss Welcker picked up her yardstick and brought it crashing down on the top of her desk with a sharp ca-RACK!

Everyone jumped.

She pointed the yardstick threateningly at the class. 'I do not want to hear as much as a peep out of any of you!' she snapped grimly. 'Is that understood?'

No one dared speak.

'I said – is . . . that . . . under . . . stood?'

The chorus came: 'Yes, Miss Welcker.'

'Then don't forget it,' Miss Welcker warned, and

marched briskly from the room. When she got outside, she looked around, then walked quickly to the back of the building. She saw Elizabeth-Anne lying on the ground near the donkey. Hurrying towards her, she cringed at the sight that greeted her. The girl's knees were scraped and bleeding, the blindfold was still tied around her eyes, and vomit stained her mouth and the front of her dress. She could hear her sobbing quietly.

'There, there. It's all right, Elizabeth-Anne. Everything's all right.' Gently, Miss Welcker bent down, untied the blindfold, and helped her to her feet. Together, they slowly headed back to the schoolhouse. Once there, the teacher stood in the doorway and cleared her throat.

The class turned and stared at her.

'Some of you may think this is very funny,' Miss Welcker said with quiet anger, 'but I do not. I am going to leave now. You will all remain here until I return. During that time, I will let you discuss this incident among yourselves and you can decide whether it was worth it: starting today, and continuing every day for the next four weeks, none of you will have recess privileges. Furthermore, you shall *all* have to clean the schoolroom and the yard every day after school for one hour. Do I make myself clear?'

A pin could have been heard dropping.

Miss Welcker took a deep breath to calm herself. When she spoke again, her voice cut the air like a knife. 'Jennifer!'

Jenny jerked guiltily, her face ashen.

Miss Welcker's voice softened. 'Come with me. We'll take Elizabeth-Anne home.'

Jenny fought to keep the relief off her face. Careful not to meet any of her friends' accusing eyes, she hurried to the back of the classroom, eager to escape. She was only too well aware that the incident had been her brainstorm. Now, with everyone being punished, it was quite likely that they would turn on her.

On the way to the rooming house, Jenny looked Miss Welcker in the eye and asked innocently, 'What happened, Miss Welcker?'

Melissa Welcker looked at her. 'The others played a despicable, cruel trick on Elizabeth-Anne.'

'Did they hurt her?'

'Harm,' Miss Welcker said, 'can be achieved any number of ways. I'm afraid I'm going to have to tell your aunt that I think it's best that Elizabeth-Anne doesn't attend school just yet.' Miss Welcker paused. 'I'm glad that you weren't in on it, Jennifer.'

Jenny made an effort to keep from smiling. 'Still, I feel so guilty,' she said softly. 'I'll have to be punished too.'

Miss Welcker looked at her strangely. 'And why is that?'

Jenny lowered her eyes. 'I should have looked out for 'Lisbeth-Anne, you see, but I was only concerned with my arithmetic problems.'

Miss Welcker favoured Jenny with one of her rare smiles. 'You're a fine young lady, Jennifer Sue Clowney. I'm very proud of you. Your aunt should be, too.'

This time Jenny beamed. 'Thank you, Miss Welcker.'

Elizabeth-Anne tore her hand out of Miss Welcker's and ran on ahead of them.

For all her good intentions, Melissa Welcker had no idea why.

10

It was the sixteenth of December.

Amanda Fritts sat primly erect beside her husband as the train sped into the night through the dark, snow-covered hills of western Pennsylvania. Silently, she watched the showers of glowing red sparks shooting past her pale reflection in the window. From under the carriage came the steady, monotonous clickety-clack, clickety-clack of the iron wheels on the spliced rails, and the coach rattled and swayed back and forth.

After a while she tired of staring at her reflection. She relaxed in her seat, tucking her fleshy chin forwards into her neck as she untied the string of her cloth purse. She tugged it open and took the letter out again and unfolded it. The paper was thin, creased from folding and unfolding and reading and rereading, but the penmanship was neat and concise, almost brisk in its efficiency. It was distinguished by its lack of flourishes. Clearly, the writer was not one given to wasting time unnecessarily.

She reread the letter for what must surely have been the hundredth time:

> *Quebeck, Texas*
>
> *Thursday, September 12, 1901*
> *Dear Miss Elspeth Gross,*
> *If perhaps this letter should reach you, Mr Szabo Gross, the circus proprietor, and his wife died in a tragic accident. They are survived by their 6-year-old daughter, Elizabeth-Anne, who is in my care. I heard you are her next of kin. Could you, agreeable to convenience, of course, send for her or come to Quebeck as she has no other kin I know of? Or, if that should prove impossible and she has closer kin, please contact them or myself.*
> *Respectfully,*
> *Miss Elender Hannah Clowney*

'You rereadin' that letter agin?' her husband, Bazzel, asked.

Amanda nodded soberly and folded it. Carefully, she slid it back into the envelope, then slipped that in her purse. She tugged on the string. 'Bazzel . . .' she said slowly.

'What's the matter?' His voice was dry and clipped.

She stared down at the purse on her lap. Then she turned to him. He looked stern and thin and forbidding, like the farmer in Grant Wood's 'American Gothic'. Corded neck, protruding Adam's apple, round, rimmed glasses. 'Maybe . . . maybe it ain't such a good idea?' she suggested meekly.

His pale eyes narrowed. 'We're goin' through with it and that's the end of it. We come this far. This ain't no time to chicken out.'

She could feel a familiar ache knotting up her insides. Every time she got nervous, her stomach would act up. She bit down on her fleshy lip and closed her eyes. She had grown weary of the constant shams. Of bilking people out of their life's savings and then skipping out of town at night. Of constantly staying one jump ahead of their victims and the law. It wouldn't have been so bad if things had turned out the way they'd intended – pulling a fast one just once or twice, and getting enough out of it to be able to buy a farm and settle down. Unfortunately, the victims usually weren't much better off than Bazzel and herself. More often than not, they were even worse off.

Amanda Fritts was afraid that any day now the trail of fraud they had left behind would finally catch up with them.

It was high time to stop, she thought. She was tired of running, always running. And she was frightened, too. But worse, she was starting to have severe pangs of sincere guilt.

Especially this time.

This time, their victim would be an orphaned child.

She didn't know how Bazzel had managed to get hold of Elender Hannah Clowney's letter to Elspeth Gross, but somehow, it had landed in his hands. When he had brought it to her, his eyes had glinted greedily.

Amanda knew that look only too well. Quickly she came up beside him and glanced at the letter, but it was impossible to read it, he was waving it around so excitedly.

'A circus!' he whispered, and smiled coldly at her. 'How many times did I tell you that sooner or later we'd make a killing?'

'What you talking about?' she'd asked in a puzzled voice.

'Here. See for yerself. Whoever this here Elizabeth-Anne is, she owns a circus now!'

Amanda snatched the letter out of his hand, quickly scanned it, then handed it back to him. Her initial excitement faded. 'That's not what it says,' she corrected him in a dull voice. 'It only says that there's a child. That her pappy was the proprietor of the circus.'

'That means there's a circus!' he growled. 'And she's the heiress. You got any idea what P. T. Barnum brings in in a week? Tell you what. We're goin' to git one last bundle of money out of that Browder woman you been cottonin' up to. Then it's off to Texas!'

'No, Bazzel! Mrs Browder's such a nice woman! We *can't*!'

His eyes narrowed. 'You ain't never said that before.'

She wrung her hands in anguish. 'I didn't *know* her before. Now I like her. And . . . and she likes me.'

'And once she finds out about the worthless silver stock we sold her? How's she going to like you then?'

Amanda was silent.

'We'll sell her another five hundred shares,' Bazzel said with finality. 'That'll give us the money to git to Texas. Plus it'll leave some left over.'

Amanda's stomach churned. They were counterfeit shares; the mining company didn't exist. The mine did, although it had long since been shut down. There wasn't an ounce of silver in it. Bazzel had simply had the stockholders' certificates printed and over the past year had sold a few shares here and a few shares there. But never five hundred at a time. A block that large brought too much attention to the defunct mine. It was begging for an investigation.

An investigation. Just the thought was enough to make Amanda Fritts shudder.

In the beginning, she hadn't minded. Somehow, it had been different back then. It had seemed more harmless, like a game, almost. But back then, she hadn't been as afraid of Bazzel as she'd learned to be over the years.

She sneaked a glance over at her husband and shuddered. Bazzel looked so gaunt and righteous and tight-lipped – which was why, she supposed, she, like so many other people since then, had let themselves be taken in by him. He just didn't look like a con artist. He never dressed in fancy city togs. Never talked smoothly. In fact, he looked more like a hellfire-and-brimstone preacher with his protruding Adam's apple and stretched fleshless face; he looked, she thought, as honest and homespun as they came, as trustworthy as the flag or mum's apple pie. And since he *looked* so fiercely honest, people they met invariably thought he must surely *be* fiercely honest, too. They trusted him immediately, just as she once had.

When they realized their mistake, it was always too late.

It just went to prove how looks could deceive.

Amanda Fritts was a fleshy, red-faced, and withdrawn woman. She looked simple and prim and proper. Her dark eyes moved nervously.

There was something no-nonsense about her. Skin scrubbed shiny, features pointed and on the coarse side, everything clad in a home-spun disguise. Starched white bonnet. Pilgrim-grey dress. But her hands were too simple and soft for the sincere, hard-working look she strove for.

126

She saw her husband look towards her and swiftly averted her gaze. He had that ability to make her feel he could read her mind.

She hoped he couldn't. The last thing she wanted or needed was to invite his ire. She had been pummelled black and blue once too often.

Amanda wondered where her life had gone wrong. Ever since she had met Bazzel, eight long years ago, they had been on the road pulling off scams and then making tracks.

They had left York, Pennsylvania, as they had left everywhere else: in a hurry. That had posed no problem. They had been prepared to flee at a moment's notice. Their suitcases had been half packed, a lesson they had learned in Baltimore when they'd had to leave all their belongings behind. Now, they never bought anything they couldn't carry.

And in York, it had been a close call, too.

Just thinking about it was enough to make her insides turn cold.

Oh God, she thought, I never thought it would turn out like this. People hurt. A child taken advantage of. To have to pretend to be Elspeth Gross, whoever she is, just to become an orphan's guardian and steal a circus out from under her.

How in the world had things come to turn out this way?

11

She thought she would go mad from the crazily sped-up music of the puffing calliope.

As she fought her way up from the depths of the nightmare, the dream still stayed with her. Always it was that same ghastly nightmare. The one she couldn't shake. The one about the fire . . .

Once again she was on the trapeze and her father was chasing her through the burnt-out circus. He, too, was on a trapeze, and his skin was charred and blistered, and parts of his flesh were burned away, showing blackened bone underneath. The charred tent poles plunged down to dark infinity, to burning hell itself. Occasionally, one-dimensional cut-outs of Hazy, Goliath, or the other performers glided silently by below her, under their own mysterious power. Overhead, from horizon to horizon, the sky was oppressively low and red. Ablaze.

It was a hellish landscape untouched by humans as she knew them.

From the charred tent poles hung the rickety trapezes, all that stood between her and the fires of hell. It was a delicate balance. Each time she or Szabo swung from one trapeze to the next, the poles quivered and creaked under the strain like fragile, spun glass . . . always threatening to break.

For what seemed an eternity, she had been swinging from one trapeze to the next. She was terrified that her weary, blistered hands would miss one of the bars. That she would lose her balance and fall into that bottomless inferno. Or worse, that Szabo would catch up with her.

'Your oil, it burned me, and now I will burn you, my Princess!' he cackled over and over, his hideous voice echoing back and forth.

After a while she could no longer hear him, and she thought she was safe. She sat on a trapeze and rested. Then she turned around and looked behind her, and a scream died in her throat.

Szabo was gaining on her. His legs were spread apart, each burned foot balanced on a different trapeze, and the flaming torches he held in his hands sent flickers of orange across his blistered skin. His familiar face was contorted into an unfamiliar evil, and bits of his nose and cheeks crumbled away, showing the charred skull beneath. Then his lips curved into a horrible satanic grin. And his eyes . . . his eyes bulged and leered, blood-red and vicious, and pierced right through her.

As she watched, he swung closer and closer towards her, the crackling torches sending showers of sparks into the hot wind.

Then he was nearly upon her.

Maliciously he thrust the torches towards her. She knew she had to swing over to the next trapeze to avoid being burned, but her fingers were frozen to the smouldering ropes. She could only watch in horrid fascination as he and the torches came closer and receded. Came closer and receded. Already she could feel the intense heat of the flames.

'You will join me!' he cackled. 'You will join me, my Princess! Your oil, it burned me, and now I will burn you!'

She tried to scream, but no sound would come from her throat. And then, with a terrible searing pain, the torches flared against her body . . .

And her eyes snapped open as she awakened, trembling violently, uncontrollably.

She drew a deep breath and glanced around, trying to orientate herself. After a moment, she could feel herself begin to calm down. She was no longer in the nightmare world. She was at Auntie's – and everything was all right.

The house was dark and unearthly quiet, and right away she knew she was the first one awake. All she could hear was the sharply whistling wind outside and the creaking of the house as it shifted on its foundations. She didn't like to be the first one awake, because she didn't like the stealthy sounds of the night. She wanted to wake up to comforting sounds – to muffled brisk footsteps moving about upstairs, to the muted chatter of voices, the scraping of chairs. But at this early hour, she only had smells to keep her company – smells of aged wood and musty walls and clean laundry . . . the exotically fragrant odour of herbs. It was a disconcerting, overpowering, medicinal odour that wafted down in stifling waves from the tangles of dried herbs hanging upside down from all over the ceiling.

She shifted and sat up slowly in bed, looking around timidly, her eyes wide as saucers. It was not completely dark and she could make out the shapes around her: from between the curtains, a chink of silvery moonlight fought its way into the room. Winter moonlight it was, cold and icy, and somehow that was comforting. Warm sunlight, yellow and red sunrises, flaming sunsets – those were things that frightened her, reminded her all too clearly of the . . .

She forced herself to swallow and tried to shove the awful memory aside. But her throat felt dry and clogged, and it was difficult to make the memory go away. It was always there, if not lurking in the front of her mind, then worming restlessly somewhere in the back, constantly trying to wiggle its way into her consciousness. Anything could trigger it and push it forwards. Anything at all.

She leaned sideways and reached for the thick, green glass tumbler of water Auntie had left on the bedside cabinet. Holding it carefully between both hands, she took a sip. The glass felt smooth, and the water was cold and refreshing. She licked her lips and set the tumbler down. The patchwork quilt had fallen to around her waist, and the chill air bit through her flannel nightgown.

She shivered and quickly lay back down, pulling the quilt up around her neck. For a while she stared up at the dark ceiling.

She wished she could go back to sleep. This large, rough-hewn room made her feel tiny, lonely, and frightened, but it had been the only unused room in the house. Auntie had wanted to put her in with Jenny, but since Jenny had kicked up a fuss, Auntie had put her in here. 'Besides, every young lady needs a room of her own,' Auntie had told her kindly, trying to make her feel better.

Elizabeth-Anne glanced around the room. It was

actually a storeroom, where Auntie kept all her herbs, staples, unused furniture, and anything else that was not used regularly or which she wanted to keep out of sight, and there was something disconcerting about it. The big, heavy pieces of stored furniture loomed threateningly, like mute giants, and in the midst of it all was Elizabeth-Anne's bed, a huge, towering, spiral-posted bed with a lumpy horsehair mattress. When the house had first been built, the plasterwork had been stencilled with primitive green leaves and yellow thistles, but they had long since faded away, leaving a murky, trailing pattern that Elizabeth-Anne's imagination took for other, more monstrous things: thorns and nettles and monsters and snakes.

She had tried, desperately, to communicate to Auntie how much the storeroom frightened her, but the words had never come. She had opened her mouth and struggled to form them, feeling the effort in her throat.

The only sound that had emerged had been a garbled, hideous, high-pitched squabble.

She had seen Auntie's stricken expression, and Jenny's horrified look the first time she had made that sound, so she had stopped trying to talk altogether.

But Auntie hadn't given up that easily. Every day, for half an hour, Elender Hannah Clowney sat her down in the parlour and tried to teach her to speak.

'A,' Auntie said slowly, drawing the sound out so that it lingered musically in the air. 'Aaaaa . . . Now try to repeat it, Elizabeth-Anne. Just watch my lips. Aaaaa . . .'

Elizabeth-Anne sat in the chair and stared at her.

'A,' Auntie said again. She pointed at her own lips and then moved her hand gracefully, as if she were conducting an orchestra. 'Aaaaa . . . Aaaaa . . .'

Elizabeth-Anne dutifully formed the vowel with her lips, but not a sound could be heard.

Auntie drew her chair closer to Elizabeth-Anne's. She took the girl's hands and looked into her face. 'Let's try it again, dear,' she said gently. 'Aaaaa . . .'

Elizabeth-Anne eyed her sadly. She had never felt so miserable. She wished Auntie would give up on her.

Elizabeth-Anne knew she would never be able to speak again, no matter how much coaching she got. It wasn't that she didn't want to speak. She just *couldn't*.

'Aaaaa . . .' Auntie gave Elizabeth-Anne's hands a little squeeze. 'Please, dear. Just give it a try?'

Elizabeth-Anne nodded solemnly. She had loved Auntie since that first day, and she wanted to please her in any way she could. She'd do anything for her. *Anything*. But couldn't Auntie understand that the one thing she just *couldn't* do was speak? That she would never talk again? That as hard as she tried, it just wouldn't happen?

'Aaaaa . . .' Auntie prodded again, and Elizabeth-Anne closed her eyes, and furrowed her brow in concentration. She took a deep breath. Then, summoning up all her strength, she opened her mouth and once again formed the sound with her lips. She fought to force it out from deep inside her, and she could feel the back of her throat hurting from the strain, but still there was only silence.

She fought to bring out a sound. Any sound.

'Eh-eh-eh-eh-eh-eh-eh-eh.'

All she could produce was that inhuman clucking noise. Defeated, she slumped in the chair and opened her eyes. She stared at Auntie helplessly.

I've failed, she thought miserably. *I've let Auntie down again.*

But Elender smiled reassuringly, quickly got up, and bent down to hug her. 'That was very good, Elizabeth-Anne!' she said. 'I'm very proud of you. We'll continue again tomorrow.'

And Elizabeth-Anne thought, *Oh, what's the use?*

12

It was the twenty-third of December and rain was lashing down in thick sheets. In the warm parlour, Elender hummed 'Silent Night' to herself as she stood atop the stepladder and carefully draped the last glittering garland around the top branches of the Christmas tree. Then, clapping her hands together in a gesture of finality, she stepped down, moved the ladder away, and stood back. She surveyed the trimmed tree with pleasure.

The pine was perfectly cone-shaped and stood nearly six feet tall. It was crowned by the angel she had made years earlier out of gold paper and white lace, and the crocheted ornaments and the silver glass balls she cherished sparkled and looked lovely. The angel's hair was feathery white, stretched from branch to branch like snow drifts. All that was missing were the candles.

In the past eight years, Elender's Christmas festivities had become a tradition. All her roomers were single or widowed, and she made an effort to ensure that they enjoyed a nice holiday. On Christmas Eve, she would light a yule log in the fireplace and hang mistletoe above the door, just as the servants in the Cromwell house on Beacon Hill used to do. Then, when she rang the dinner bell, all the roomers would come downstairs and gather in the cosy parlour to share a smörgåsbord of roast beef, smoked ham, fried chicken, and plum pudding. There were freshly baked Christmas biscuits and glasses of punch for everyone. Afterward, the roomers would gather around the tree while she lit the candles, and she would sit down at the upright spinet and everyone would join in singing the carols.

But this year, there would be no yule log in the fireplace and no candles on the tree. Elender didn't need to be told that they would terrify Elizabeth-Anne. Since the circus fire, the child had become alarmed of flames of any sort. She would steer clear of the kitchen when the stove was lit, and refuse to stay in any room while a candle was burning.

Elender glanced at the pendulum clock ticking away on the mantel. It was nearly eleven o'clock, long past her usual bedtime. Tomorrow would bring a long, gruelling day. She would have to get up by five. There were the gifts to be wrapped, the smörgåsbord to be prepared, the house to be cleaned, and any multitude of last-minute things she had overlooked to be taken care of.

She crossed to the window, parted the curtains, and looked out. She sighed. The night was unusually dark because of the rain, and a chill draft blew in from around the windowframe. She had never quite got used to Chrismases here in southwest Texas. They could be rainy and cold or dry and cold. But never cold enough for a white Christmas. Just cold enough to settle in your bones.

Elender let the curtains fall back in place and walked around the parlour. She checked to make sure the embers in the fireplace had died. Then she lifted the frosted hurricane shades from the lamps and blew out the flames. She'd bought the frosted shades especially for Elizabeth-Anne. The girl didn't seem half as frightened of them as the clear ones. Of course, they didn't give off as much light, but at least the flames weren't visible.

She left the last lamp lit and carried it to her room. On the way, she looked in on the girls. Jenny was curled up on her side under a mountain of quilts, breathing peacefully. Silently Elender kissed her on the cheek and then closed the door. Then she went to the storeroom and looked in on Elizabeth-Anne.

The child was having another bad dream.

She sighed to herself as she approached the bed and held the lamp high. She could see Elizabeth-Anne squirming. Her forehead was creased in agitation and she was flushed and sweaty. She could hear her making frightened clucking noises – those same clucking noises that were the only sounds she could produce.

Quickly Elender set the lamp on the bedside cabinet, leaned over the bed, and reached out and shook Elizabeth-Anne gently. 'Elizabeth-Anne,' she called out. 'Elizabeth-Anne!'

The girl awakened with a start, her eyes wild with fear. Immediately, she sat up and threw her arms around Elender's neck.

Elender sat down on the edge of the mattress and held her tightly, patting her reassuringly on the back. 'There. There,' she whispered soothingly. 'You've just had a bad dream. Everything's going to be all right. Auntie chased the bad dream away.' Gently she uncurled the girl's arms and made her lie back down.

Elizabeth-Anne's aquamarine eyes were wide. Don't leave me, they seemed to plead. Please stay here.

Elender read the expression and stroked Elizabeth-Anne's cheek reassuringly, but she was worried. Elizabeth-Anne's nightmares had been recurring ever since the day she had found her wandering in Geron's Fields. But lately, they seemed to have increased in frequency. Perhaps . . . She frowned thoughtfully to herself. Perhaps a tiny dose of laudanum would help her sleep more peacefully. Would keep the nightmares at bay. It was, after all, a harmless mixture of alcohol and opium.

'I'll be back in a moment,' Elender said decisively. 'I'm going to get you something to chase away your dreams.'

Elizabeth-Anne sat up again and clung tenaciously to her, afraid to be left alone with her nightmare.

'I'll only be a moment,' Elender assured her gently.

Elizabeth-Anne looked at her doubtfully, but obediently lay back down.

Elender left and soon returned with the bottle of laudanum she kept on a shelf in the kitchen and poured a mere drop in a teaspoon.

Elizabeth-Anne licked the spoon dry and grimaced, but for the rest of the night she slept peacefully. The next day, for the first time, she awakened without a haunted, restless look.

The next night, without the laudanum, the nightmares returned. Elender gave her another tiny dose of laudanum, and Elizabeth-Anne slept soundly.

From that day on, before bedtime, Elender would give her a drop or two.

She did not know that it was the beginning of Elizabeth-Anne's opium addiction.

13

Amanda stood uncomfortably beside Bazzel Fritts in front of the big clapboard house. The ground floor windows were all lit, and from inside came the tinkling of a piano and voices raised in a carol. They were mostly men's voices, deep and off-key, but a woman's strong voice overpowered them and kept the tune going:

> 'Deck the halls with boughs of holly,
> Fa la la la la, la la la la,
> 'Tis the season to be jolly,
> Fa la la la la, la la la la . . .'

Amanda glanced sideways at Bazzel. 'I still don't like this,' she murmured. Her lips were numb from the cold and her nose was running. She wiped it on the sleeve of her coat. 'It ain't right, Bazzel. 'Specially not at Christmastime.'

Bazzel stared at the house through the sheets of rain. For the first time, he, too, felt misgivings. They had begun at the railroad station. Night had fallen by the time they had got off the train, and all the while they'd ridden here in the horse-drawn buggy they'd hired, he'd been on the lookout for signs of the circus. In the night, he hadn't been able to see a thing, and there wasn't even any moonlight due to the rain. He'd thought it best not to ask the old man who drove the buggy anything about the circus. These small towns were all alike. As soon as one person as much as sneezed, the next day everybody within miles knew about it.

Amanda sensed his misgivings. She took his arm to turn him around and leave – not that they had anyplace else to go.

He looked at her coldly, his pale eyes glittering like steel behind his wet, round, wire-rimmed glasses. 'You're Elspeth,' he said quietly, 'and don't fergit it. That's all that matters. Answer to that name only. Case anybody asks, when you married me you became a Fritts. Elspeth Fritts.' He shivered suddenly. 'It's cold out here. Let's git inside.'

Amanda sighed deeply as he picked up his suitcases, and she reluctantly picked hers up, too. She followed behind him climbing the three steps up to the porch. The familiar strains of the music inside stopped, but a moment later *Hark the Herald Angels Sing* began.

Bazzel knocked loudly on the door.

> *'Hark the herald angels sing,*
> *Glory to the newborn king,*
> *Peace on earth . . .'*

In the parlour, Elizabeth-Anne slid quietly over to the far side of the settee and kept one sharp eye peeled on Jenny's feet, since Jenny had been giving her painful little kicks on the ankle with the tips of her boots. With her other eye, she watched the gentlemen standing

137

around the spinet, which had been moved from its usual spot in front of the windows. Elizabeth-Anne knew that Auntie had moved it there especially for her — so that it hid the fireplace completely. The gesture made her feel safe. Now, if only Jenny would leave her alone, life would be almost perfect.

Elizabeth-Anne felt prettier than she ever had. Auntie had bought two identical dresses — one for Jenny and one for her. They were white, with eyelets down the front, and were the prettiest dresses she had ever seen. And, because it was Christmas Eve, Auntie had parted their hair in the middle and tied it at the sides with red and green silk ribbons.

Abruptly Auntie stopped playing, her fingers poised in midair. She cocked her head to one side and frowned as, one by one, the men stopped singing. She craned her neck up over the top of the piano. 'Was that the door?'

Jenny jumped to her feet. 'I think so,' she said. 'I'll go see who it is!' She skipped out of the parlour and into the hall.

Elender scraped the piano bench back, got to her feet, and looked at her gentlemen roomers clustered around the piano — she knew that they were tired of singing and were anxious for refreshments. 'That's enough carolling for now, I should think,' she said, smiling warmly. 'Why don't we have some punch and some food?'

The men murmured grateful agreement and moved over to the table which Elender had festively draped with a white tablecloth she'd embroidered with green holly leaves and clusters of red berries. The big cut-glass punch bowl was the centrepiece, and around it, mouthwatering platters of artfully arranged delicacies were heavily laden.

As she did each Christmas, Elender took her place behind the table and ladled out cups of punch and handed them around. Then she circulated among her uests. A good hostess, she knew, made everyone feel welcome and important.

'Auntie?'

Elender stopped in midstep and frowned. Jenny was standing in the doorway with two well-bundled strangers. She had never seen the plump, red-faced woman or the tall, cadaverous man before. In the hallway behind them, she could see four suitcases.

Quickly she crossed the room, folding her hands in front of her. 'Yes?' she inquired pleasantly.

Bazzel Fritts' eyes swept around the warm, cheerful parlour. In one long glance he took in the tall Christmas tree, the wreaths hanging in the windows, the little pine twigs sprouting from behind picture frames and mirrors, the lavish platters of food. He exchanged glances with Amanda and then stepped forwards and cleared his throat.

'I'm Bazzel Fritts, ma'am,' he said in a dry, unemotional voice, 'and this here is the missus, Mrs Fritts.' He took Amanda by the arm and pulled her forward.

Amanda smiled shyly at Elender and lowered her eyes.

'Up till nine months ago, Mrs Fritts here was Miss Gross.' Bazzel paused and added pointedly: 'Miss Elspeth Gross?'

'We jest got married lately,' Amanda said nervously. 'We moved an' we jest got yer letter. We come as soon as we could cause a' l'il Elizabeth-Anne.'

Bazzel turned to Jenny and smiled thinly. 'You're a mighty pretty young thing, Elizabeth-Anne.'

Jenny raised her pointed chin indignantly. 'I'm Jenny,' she said loftily. *That's* 'Lisbeth-Anne.' She pointed disdainfully at the settee and sniffed. 'She can't talk. We think it's because she was scared speechless when the circus burned down.'

Bazzel's smile faded and his eyes narrowed. He didn't

139

even catch Amanda's 'I-told-you-so' look. 'The cr̅
cus . . . burned?' he asked in a faltering voice, all hi̅
hopes and dreams of easy money crumbling down
around him.

Jenny nodded vigorously. 'It was the biggest fire ever
seen in these parts – '

'Jenny!' Elender hissed.

Jenny froze in midsentence. Nothing she might have
let slip out in front of Auntie could bring about worse
repercussions; in the excitement of the Frittses' arrival,
she had totally forgotten Auntie's stern warnings about
what would happen if she ever as much as hinted about
the fire while Elizabeth-Anne was within earshot.

Jenny's heart sank abysmally. For once, she hadn't
even been trying to torment Elizabeth-Anne. *Oh, dam-
nation!* she thought. It had simply slipped out! And
now . . . She could feel the tears stinging at the corners
of her eyes. Now she would be well and truly punished.

She raised her eyes fearfully to meet Auntie's gaze,
half expecting her wrath at this very moment. Instead,
she saw a peculiar mixture of compassion and hopeless-
ness in Elender Clowney's eyes.

Jenny immediately felt better. She sniffed and wiped
the tears away with her knuckles. She sensed that her
fear of punishment was without foundation, and that
Auntie mistook her tears of self-pity for sorrow towards
Elizabeth-Anne. Then she noticed her aunt's odd
expression, and wondered what could have caused it.
Elizabeth-Anne's relations finally having arrived? Jenny
could not conceive that that could be the reason. For
her own part, she was more than delighted that they
had finally come to rid her of that freak once and for
all. Now it wouldn't be long before everything would be
back to normal, and she would again be the sole object
of attention in this house.

And Jenny had to struggle to keep from smiling.

Elender nervously fingered the locket watch which

hung from the thin gold chain around her neck, but otherwise she maintained her composure, and pasted a weak, quivering smile on her lips. 'You must be cold and hungry,' she told the Frittses in the warmest voice she could muster. 'Why don't you give me your coats, and then we'll see about getting you some refreshments.' She turned to Jenny and fluttered her hands to shoo her towards the kitchen. 'Jenny, be a dear and fetch some hot tea for Mr and Mrs Fritts, would you?'

'Yes, Auntie,' Jenny said with patent resignation.

Amanda Fritts slowly unbuttoned her coat. She looked surprised as Bazzel helped her slip out of it. He had seldom ever done that before.

Bazzel handed Amanda's coat to Elender, took off his own, and handed it over, too. Then they made a beeline for the piano and stood behind it, their backs to the room as they leaned down, gratefully holding their icy hands out in front of the warming fire.

'The kid's a mute!' Bazzel hissed so vehemently that Amanda could feel his spittle on the side of her face.

'Sssssh!' Amanda glanced quickly over her shoulder and wiped her cheek with her sleeve. 'Somebody might hear you!'

Out in the hallway, Elender hung their coats in the closet under the stairs. As she closed the closet door, she felt a light tug on her skirt. She turned around and looked down. Elizabeth-Anne stood there, her eyes wide with fear.

Elender pulled her close and held her tightly. This unexpected visit by Elspeth Gross . . . Elspeth Fritts, she corrected herself . . . was a totally surprising turn of events. Over the months, she had become extremely attached to Elizabeth-Anne, and had begun to think of her as her own. She loved her (dared she even think it?) more than she loved Jenny. Elizabeth-Anne had a

141

fragility, a sweet vulnerability that Jenny had never possessed.

People were wrong, she thought. Ties of flesh and
blood weren't necessarily the strongest. Emotional
bonds were far stronger. And Elizabeth-Anne knew it,
too. She could see that in her eyes. There was something
about this child which filled her heart with all the warm
hopes and dreams that she had once reserved exclusively for Jenny, and she had been secretly relieved when
there'd been no reply to her letters. But now, here were
the Frittses . . . in the flesh. Waiting in the parlour to
take her beloved Elizabeth-Anne away.

Elender felt as if a vice-like grip had been applied
around her heart.

For the first time that her roomers could remember,
Elender's Christmas Eve party ended early. After they
had reluctantly gone to their rooms, Elender, Jenny,
and Elizabeth-Anne cleaned up. Finally, Elender
moved two settees together, brought extra linen, pillows, and quilts down from the upstairs linen closet, and
made the Frittses a makeshift bed.

They can stay as long as they like, she thought. *That way
Elizabeth-Anne will be here a little longer.*

When the parlour door closed and they were finally
alone, Amanda sank wearily into a chair. The drum-
ming of the rain was enough to make her go mad. She
rubbed her fingers over her face. She felt tense and
drained from the last hour of deception, constantly
thinking carefully before she spoke so that she wouldn't
make any blunders. Even so, she had almost slipped
once. 'Elspeth?' Bazzel had said, and she had not
responded. He'd had to repeat it, much louder and
sharper, before she finally remembered: she was no
longer Amanda. She was Elspeth.

142

'Mrs Fritts is hard of hearin' sometimes,' Bazzel had lowered smoothly, 'she's been havin' ear troubles.'

Now Bazzel waited by the door until Elender's footsteps receded. A moment later, he opened it a crack and peered out. The hall was dark, empty and quiet. Satisfied that no one could eavesdrop, he quietly closed the door and went over to Amanda. 'Been a long day. Let's git to bed.'

She lowered her hands and looked up at him, her face pinched and tired. 'I could use some sleep.' She folded her hands in her lap. 'My nerves are frazzled.'

'Pull yourself together, woman.'

'Bazzel,' she said softly, 'there ain't no circus. Nothin' but the kid.'

'Don't you think I know that?' he hissed nastily.

She hesitated a moment. 'What we do now?'

He shrugged. 'Move on, I suppose. There ain't nothin' to keep us here no more. I reckon we'll do what we been doin' all along. Sell minin' shares.' Then suddenly an idea hit upon him. They would take the kid with them. Having her around would give them a greater aura of respectability and would make it even easier to con folks. 'We'll take that kid,' he said flatly. 'We oughtta be able to sell twice as many shares with her hangin' to yer skirt. Maybe . . .' His teeth showed yellow as he smiled. 'Yep. Maybe we kin even unload some of them shares on Miz Clowney before we leave here.'

Amanda bit down on her lip. 'Bazzel,' she said softly. 'There ain't no more shares.'

It was a moment before her words registered. 'Sure there are.' He turned and pointed to their luggage. 'They're in the bottom o' that suitcase.'

'No they ain't,' she said meekly.

He crossed the room quickly, pulled the suitcase out, and got to his knees. Snapping the catch open, he rummaged through it. She watched quietly as he flung

143

clothing out on the floor. Then he froze. The bundl
of silver mine shares were not there.

He got to his feet and turned around slowly.

Amanda could feel the familiar pain in her stomach start up again. She knew him well enough to see that he was in a rage – whenever he got that icy, implacably calm look in his eyes, there was no telling what he might do. 'Where they at?' he demanded tonelessly, stepping towards her.

'B-Bazzel,' she stammered. 'I-I thought – '

'What did you do with them, woman?' he demanded with an icy edge to his voice.

Her face went white. 'I-I burned them.'

'You *what*?'

She averted her eyes. 'I burned them just before we left York,' she whispered. 'You've got to believe me, Bazzel. I didn't want to do it. I-I just couldn't be part of it no more.' She closed her eyes. 'Not cheatin' old women out of their life's savings.'

He stared down at her, his fists clenched at his sides. At that moment he wanted nothing more than to lash out at her and beat her senseless.

She glanced up at him, her eyes filled with fear. 'Please, Bazzel,' she begged timidly. 'Don't beat me? We'd have to explain – '

'*We'd* have to explain?' He shook his head. 'No, woman. *You'd* have to do the explainin'. Jest like you got a lot of explainin' to do to me.'

She stared at him miserably.

He was silent for a moment before he spoke again. 'Soon as we're gone from here, you're gonna git yer punishment,' he threatened slowly. 'Don't think yer gonna git out of it.'

She felt a cold chill settle over her. Bazzel was not one to make idle threats. He never forgot a slight or a double cross. She shuddered to think what the punishment might be. 'Bazzel . . .' she said in a tiny voice.

144

'Git to bed,' he said coldly. 'One more word outta you and you'll git punished right now.'

She crawled meekly under the covers and pulled the quilt up around her, wondering how he was going to get back at her and how she might avoid it.

Perhaps she should just pack up and leave him? Be rid of him for good? No, she'd considered doing that before, but she'd always come to the same conclusion. There was no way she could make it on her own. She was too dependent on him. Strange as it seemed, she and Bazzel were a family of sorts.

She could hear Bazzel's loud, sharp snores. He always snored loudly since he'd developed adenoid trouble.

She glanced around the dark room, smelling the redolent fragrance of pine emanating from the Christmas tree. A strange ache of loneliness and despair stole over her. In the rush to leave York and come here, she'd almost forgotten.

It was Christmas.

She could feel tears stinging in her eyes.

It was hours before she finally cried herself into a fitful sleep.

14

While she had been pregnant with Jenny, Elender had promised herself that, no matter what, she would create a warm, loving home steeped in honest values and traditions for the child she was bringing into the world. Subsequently, she had selected what she considered to be the best of all possible worlds – what she'd known from her own poor but happy childhood, and the good things (yes, there had been good things, too) which she'd observed as a servant in the Cromwell mansion on Beacon Hill. As a result, she mixed these select experi-

ences judiciously so that, together, they created a g..
ciousness, a warmth, and a sense of ethics rarely see..
outside the best homes. She had kept her vow, providing Jenny with everything that an 'aunt' possibly could.

And now, with Elizabeth-Anne, her generosity and love knew no bounds. Since this was Elizabeth-Anne's first – and last – Christmas here, she intended to make it truly, truly special.

Christmas Day began early for Elender. She got up long before anyone else stirred, quietly preparing for the festivities ahead. There was breakfast to be cooked and served across the street at the Good Eats Café, as it was every morning, but the late lunch in the rooming house was a feast that needed more than half a day to prepare. There would be the cream of vegetable soup she'd learned to make from the Cromwells' cook, the big goose which had been brought, slaughtered and already plucked, by the farmers who supplied all her meats and poultry, the sweet cherry syrup which would accompany it, the mashed potatoes and candied yams, the vegetables, glazed in caramel, the apple and pumpkin pies topped with dollops of thick, rich clotted cream . . . everything had to be cooked to perfection, and that took time.

She started the day by carrying the gifts, tagged and gaily wrapped, downstairs from their hiding place in the attic. Traditionally, she would arrange them under the tree, but because the Frittses were rooming in the parlour, she stacked them on the hallway table instead. She had to make two trips – not only were there gifts for Jenny and Elizabeth-Anne, but a thoughtful little something for each of her roomers, be it tins of home-baked cakes and biscuits, a shawl or sweater she had knitted, a pair of gloves or woollen socks she knew they needed.

In the midst of arranging the packages, she paused and eyed herself thoughtfully in the mirror above the

146

...ble. She had always prided herself on her fairness, kindness, and sense of decorum, was and had always been acutely attuned to other people's sensitivities, and now she realized that the arrival of the Frittses put her in an embarrassing position. There were gifts for everyone but them. Of course, how was she to know they'd arrive? And on Christmas Eve yet? Still, she would have to come up with a little something for them. Christmas was, above all, a time for sharing what one had with those who were not fortunate enough to be in their own homes . . . a time for celebration and joy.

But it was not a time of joy for her.

The Frittses had come to take Elizabeth-Anne away.

It would be a miserable Christmas.

When Elizabeth-Anne entered the kitchen she was wearing thick woollen stockings, a flannel skirt, and heavy knit sweater. She could already hear everyone moving about in the house, but only Elender and Jenny were in the little-used kitchen; with special exceptions, cooking was usually done at the café across the street.

Elizabeth-Anne glanced into the big adjoining dining room. It was still empty, but places had already been set on the gleaming, waxed table in anticipation of breakfast. She noticed that two extra place settings had been squeezed in for the Frittses.

The big kitchen was snuggly warm and smelled delicious. A half hour earlier, Auntie had put the big Christmas goose, stuffed with a mouthwatering mixture of breadcrumbs, finely chopped goose offal and drippings, herbs, and diced Granny Smith apples, into the wood stove, where it roasted slowly.

When she heard Elizabeth-Anne's footsteps, Elender looked up from the pastry she was rolling and smiled. Quickly she wiped her hands on her apron, rushed across the room, and scooped her high into the air.

'Good morning, Elizabeth-Anne!' Elender kissed her warmly. 'Merry Christmas!'

In reply, Elizabeth-Anne coiled her arms around her neck and returned her kiss.

Elender set Elizabeth-Anne down, placed her hands on her shoulders, and propelled her towards the kitchen table. 'As soon as you finish your breakfasts, you and Jenny can open your presents,' she said.

Elizabeth-Anne nodded, and Elender busied herself at the stove. There was a sizzling sound as pancake batter hit the hot, greased skillet.

With all the heat from the cooking, Elizabeth-Anne didn't need her sweater. She pulled it off and draped it over the back of her chair. Then she scraped the chair out from under the table and sat down. A moment later, Elender placed a mug of steaming hot milk and slid a plate with a big, golden pancake in a puddle of rich syrup down in front of Elizabeth-Anne. Then she went back to her pastry.

Jenny, who'd already finished eating, shot Elizabeth-Anne a piercing look from across the table. 'Hurry up and finish eating, 'Lisbeth-Anne,' she hissed impatiently.

'Leave her be,' Elender called from over her shoulder. 'Eating fast makes for bad digestion. The presents are not going to run away.' Then she turned around slowly, placed her hands on her hips, and looked questioningly at Jenny. 'Well? I didn't hear you wishing Elizabeth-Anne a Merry Christmas.'

'I didn't hear her wishing me one, either,' Jenny retorted tartly.

'Jenny . . .' Elender's voice held a warning note.

'Merry Christmas, 'Lisbeth-Anne,' Jenny sang in a loud, sweet voice.

Elizabeth-Anne looked at her and smiled hesitantly.

'Even if I don't see why I should wish you anything,' Jenny added under her breath.

'What's that?' Elender asked sharply.

'I was just telling 'Lisbeth-Anne that I wondered what our presents are, Auntie,' Jenny replied innocently.

Elender fixed her with a long look before she turned around again.

Elizabeth-Anne picked up her teaspoon and carefully skimmed the thick, wrinkled layer of cream from the top of her milk. She blew on it so it would cool and then ate it with relish. She licked the white moustache off her upper lip with her tongue. She loved the sweet richness of the cream; it was her favourite part of breakfast. She took two cubes of sugar from the china bowl and plopped them into her milk. With the spoon, she tapped the cubes gently to break them up and stirred.

Jenny glanced at Elender. She was busy pinching the pastry around a shallow round pastry tin, her back turned. Taking advantage of the situation, Jenny gave Elizabeth-Anne a swift sharp kick under the table. 'Hurry up!' she mouthed silently.

When Elizabeth-Anne ignored her, Jenny's patience snapped. She reached out, grabbed the pancake off Elizabeth-Anne's plate with her fingers and began gobbling it down, all the while glancing at Elender from the corners of her eyes.

Elender's back was still turned.

The pancake finished, Jenny slid Elizabeth-Anne's mug over to her side of the table and exchanged it with her own empty mug. She blew on the hot, sweet milk and sipped it, blew on it some more, and took big gulps. Elizabeth-Anne could only stare curiously, astonished at her speed.

A moment later, Jenny scraped back her chair and jumped to her feet. ' 'Lisbeth-Anne's finished, Auntieeeeee . . .' Her words trailed off into silence. Elender had turned around, arms akimbo, and was glaring at her through narrowed eyes.

Jenny suddenly turned pale.

'I saw what you did, Jennifer Sue Clowney.' Elender's voice was unnaturally harsh as she wagged an admonishing finger at her. 'I'm ashamed of you!'

Jenny burst into tears and ran from the kitchen. A moment later, the slam of her door reverberated from down the hall.

Elender shut her eyes and took a deep, painful breath. She felt a tightening in her stomach. She wished now that she'd pretended that she hadn't noticed what Jenny had done. Of all the days of the year, Christmas was one she didn't want spoiled in any way. Not for the roomers, not for Jenny, and not for herself. And this year, especially not for Elizabeth-Anne since she wouldn't be here for very much longer. But, Jenny had been getting away with far too much lately, constantly testing her authority. If she didn't put her foot down now, she would only get more and more selfish and spoiled.

When she opened her eyes, she saw that Elizabeth-Anne had twisted around in her chair and was gazing at her with wide and sympathetic eyes.

Elender smiled sadly at her, slid a saucepan from the burner over to the cold side of the stove and then marched, with grim, terse footsteps, down the hall to Jenny's room. Elizabeth-Anne slipped off her chair and followed quietly.

Jenny was lying face-down on her bed, sobbing into her pillows. Elender motioned for Elizabeth-Anne to go back to the kitchen; then she shut the door softly and approached the bed. 'Jennifer.'

Jenny sniffed noisily, lifted her head, and turned around, a bitter, challenging look on her wet, red face.

'You deserve to be severely punished,' Elender said in a quivering voice. 'Ever since Elizabeth-Anne came here you've treated her miserably. Don't think that I haven't noticed. But this time you've gone too far.' She shook her head in exasperation. 'Don't you have any

.eart?' she whispered. 'Don't you know what she's been through?'

'*She's* been through!' Jenny wailed uncharitably, hopping up into a sitting position. 'She's taken *over*, Auntie! Everything's 'Lisbeth-Anne this, 'Lisbeth-Anne that! You don't even love *me* anymore!' Jenny's tears poured down her cheeks.

'You know that's not true, Jenny,' Elender said quietly. But she bit down on her lip, knowing that Jenny's accusation was close – too close – to the truth. She loved Jenny. Always would, no matter what she did. Jenny was, after all, her only daughter, even if she could never admit it publicly, let alone share it with her privately. It was just that, compared with Jenny, Elizabeth-Anne was so . . . *angelic*. So sweet and obedient and good-hearted. After witnessing the devastating fire and the nightmarish deaths of her family and friends, and suffering her subsequent loss of speech . . . well, how could one's heart *not* go out to her?

'Get up, Jenny,' Elender said wearily, 'and dry your tears. You're not going to be punished because it's Christmas. But let me warn you . . .' Her voice was stern and icy. 'One more incident . . .'

Jenny got up slowly, but her words came swiftly. 'I'll be good, Auntie,' she promised. 'I'm sorry, really I am! It's just that I didn't think you loved – '

Elender swiftly embraced her. 'I'll always love you, Jenny,' she said softly, pressing the child's head towards her bosom. 'I'll always love you. More than anyone else in the world. You've got to believe that.'

But in her heart, Elender knew she was telling a lie. Perhaps she could fool Jenny, but she wasn't fooling herself. She would always love her daughter, yes, but she could not love her more than Elizabeth-Anne. Jenny would simply not permit such unquestioning, pure, blind love. She was, at heart, cold, conceited,

selfish, and spiteful. She always had to have her ow
way, even if it meant hurting others.

And whose fault was that?

Mine, Elender thought to herself, suddenly feeling a
hot rush of guilt. *Mine, and mine alone. Jenny inherited
those traits from Arthur Jason Cromwell. She is his daughter,
as well as mine. If I'd been strong enough, brave enough, to
flee the Cromwell mansion when he . . .*

She frowned to herself and cast those thoughts away.
She hadn't been strong or brave enough: it was water
under the bridge.

Her lips quivered into a smile. 'Come on, Jenny. Let's
go open the presents and forget all this, all right?' She
placed a finger under Jenny's chin and lifted it.

Jenny nodded and smiled slowly. 'Yes, Auntie,' she
said softly.

Elender put her arm around Jenny's shoulder, and
together they left the room.

That wasn't so hard, Jenny thought. *All I had to do was
appeal to her emotions. I can always play on Auntie's soft spot.*

Elender lowered two large, brightly wrapped packages
each into Jenny's and Elizabeth-Anne's outstretched
arms. She smiled as the girls struggled under the weight
of them. 'You may open them in the kitchen,' she said,
turning as she heard footsteps behind her. The Frittses
were coming down the hall. 'Merry Christmas,' Elender
greeted them warmly.

'Mornin',' Bazzel said crisply.

Amanda smiled bleakly and pushed a limp lock of
stray hair out of her eyes. 'Good mornin', Miz Clowney.'
She looked shyly down at her feet. 'Merry Christmas.'

'And a very Merry Christmas to you, Mrs Fritts.'

Amanda Fritts looked even more unhappy than she
had the night before. Elender noticed that she kept
pulling nervously at the frayed white cuffs of her blouse
with her fingers, and she wondered whether this ner-

vous reaction had something to do with Bazzel Fritts. Had they had words between them? Or could Elspeth be frightened of him? After all, there was something remote and formidable . . . almost forbidding . . . about him. Not only that, but somehow the Frittses just didn't give the impression of being a warm, loving couple. There was an odd coldness there, a chilly distance between them which she couldn't figure out. And . . . although she couldn't quite put her finger on the precise reason why such a strange idea should suddenly pop into her head, Elender was unable to prevent the perceptive thought from forming: call it intuition or suspicion, for some reason, she just *knew* in her heart of hearts that Elizabeth-Anne would be far better off with her than with the Frittses. But what could she do? Elspeth and Bazzel Fritts were the child's flesh and blood, while she herself was merely a stranger who had befriended her.

What rights did strangers, however loving and well-meaning, have to an orphaned child?

Bazzel cleared his throat, his Adam's apple bobbing up and down. 'We was wonderin' if we might talk to you in private fer a few minutes, Miz Clowney.'

Elender glanced into the dining room. The roomers were already gathering for Christmas breakfast. 'We can talk in the kitchen as soon as I serve the food,' she said. 'Girls!'

Jenny and Elizabeth-Anne turned around slowly, their faces barely visible above the tops of the packages.

'Why don't you go into the parlour?' Elender glanced at Mr Fritts and lowered her voice. 'Did you build a fire in there?'

'Seein' how cold it was, and since there was wood stacked right next to the fireplace – '

'Did you move the piano?'

He looked at her queerly but slowly shook his head.

'Good. The only reason I asked you that is because

153

Elizabeth-Anne is terrified of fires, the poor thing. After that terrible circus fire she witnessed, I shouldn't wonder.'

Elender moved aside and smiled automatically as she let the girls pass. Then she steered the Frittses into the kitchen. 'Have a seat, won't you? I'll serve you your breakfasts in here instead of the dining room. That way we can talk in privacy while you eat. I'll be right back.'

Elender smoothed the front of her apron and busied herself. The Frittses sat watching quietly as her footsteps beat a brisk circular cadence from the kitchen to the living room and back again. Between her trips, she set steaming mugs, filled half with sweetened coffee, half with hot milk, down in front of the Frittses. She added plates of eggs, sausages, and homemade cranberry muffins, finally closed the dining room door, and poured herself a mug of well-deserved coffee. Then she brought it over to the table, sat down, scooted her chair forwards, and folded her hands on the tabletop. 'There. Now what was it you wished to talk to me about, Mr Fritts?'

But Bazzel held up his hand to silence her, closed his eyes, and bowed his head over his plate. Amanda clasped her hands in her lap and did likewise, murmuring in unison with him: 'Oh Lord, bless this bounty which we are about to receive, amen.'

The moment Bazzel's eyes clicked open, he reached for the gravy boat which was filled with syrup. He poured some liberally over his fried eggs and grey pork sausages. Then he punctured the egg yolks with his fork, speared a whole sausage, and dipped it into the liquid yolk. He bit off a piece and talked while chewing, his long, uneven teeth moving steadily up and down. 'Miz Fritts and I had a long talk.' He gestured towards Amanda with his fork and swallowed, his Adam's apple bobbing again. ' 'Bout 'Lisabeth-Anne . . .'

Elender looked at him. 'She's such a sweet child,' she

154

said. 'And so pretty with that gold hair and those pale blue eyes. I can guarantee you'll have no problems with her.'

'We never expected any, ma'am,' Bazzel said. 'She's right pretty, jest like her mama.' He glanced at Amanda. 'Ain't that right, Elspeth?'

Amanda bowed her head and murmured: 'Yes, jest like her mama, God rest her soul.'

'Amen,' Bazzel added.

Elender frowned. On her deathbed, Hazy had told her that Elizabeth-Anne's mother had been the fat lady of the circus. That certainly didn't suggest that she would have been a pretty woman. *Were the Frittses talking about the same woman?* But then, people did gain weight. Perhaps Elizabeth-Anne's mother had been pretty at one time.

' 'Course, we love little 'Lisbeth-Anne, seein' how she's a relative and all,' Bazzel said. 'I'm sure she'll grow up to be a fine lady, jest like her mama.' He reached for a muffin, tore it in half, mopped the syrup up off the plate with it, and chewed on it reflectively. 'I'm 'fraid livin' with me and Elspeth, though, that could be mighty rough on her.'

Elender cocked her head to one side and looked at him questioningly. 'I beg your pardon?'

Amanda looked up. 'You see, Miz Clowney, we don't have no home,' she explained quietly. 'And children, they need a home. Like we told you yesterday, we been on the move. That's why it took us so long to git here.' She spoke with deceptive conviction and chose her words carefully, praying that what she was about to say would appease Bazzel's anger with her for destroying the silver mine shares. She took a deep breath and continued in a trembling voice: 'Mr Fritts and me, we're God-fearin' people. That's why we travel the country spreadin' the word of Jesus wherever folks'll listen. And that takes money, Miz Clowney, and lots of it.' She

155

exchanged glances with Bazzel, whose flinty eyes urged her on. 'When we got yer letter, me and Bazzel, we took it as a sign from the Lord. We decided that if you was willin', Miz Clowney, we . . . we might be willin' to sell you little 'Lisbeth-Anne, seein' as how you git on so well and all. You know, jest for enough money so's we could keep spreadin' the Lord's word.'

Elender sat in stunned silence, unable to believe her ears. *Sell* Elizabeth-Anne? Is that what she had heard? Did these . . . these . . . *cretins* offer to sell her the beautiful child? Elender Hannah Clowney had never been so outraged in her entire life.

But before she could recover from her shock and muster up the words she wanted to say to these monsters, Bazzel Fritts broke the silence: ' 'Course, if you ain't willin' to give us a good price fer 'Lisbeth-Anne, Miz Clowney, ma'am, then we can sell her in Dallas or somewheres. I figger she'd bring in a nice tidy little sum, seein' as how she's so pretty 'n all – '

But his salespitch was interrupted by a shrill, unearthly scream that tore through the house.

15

At first, Jenny and Elizabeth-Anne had been too pre-occupied with their own presents to take notice of each other's. They ignored the conversations and the clinking of cutlery and china drifting in through the open door from the dining room.

Jenny had set her two packages down on the parlour table, and then picked them up, one by one, and shook them. She quickly proceeded to tear the wrapping off the smaller, heavier one.

Elizabeth-Anne put her presents on the settee, and knelt there, fumbling clumsily with the pretty ribbon on the larger of her packages. The ribbon was difficult to remove because of her gloves. They wouldn't let her get a firm grip.

'Ooooooh!' As she tore apart the paper, a black, velvet-covered box came into view and Jenny let out such a loud squeal of delight that Elizabeth-Anne stopped what she was doing and craned her neck to look over at Jenny.

Jenny undid the brass catch, lifted the lid, and proudly held up the box, tilting it to show Elizabeth-Anne what lay inside. Cool, polished, gold-tone metal and silvery mirror flashed luxuriantly against plush red velvet.

'It's the boudoir set I wanted!' Jenny breathed with smug satisfaction. She lifted out the hand mirror with its oval, bevelled glass and held it up, preening visibly at her reflection. Then she snatched up the matching brush with its pristine white bristles and started brushing her hair with the exaggerated movements of a lady in her boudoir. After a moment, she glanced over at Elizabeth-Anne, who finally had her ribbon and paper undone. She was about to lift the lid off her carton.

Jenny frowned, wondering what in the world could be so huge as to require a carton of such copious size. Probably a winter coat, she thought. Well, that was all right with her. From past experience, she knew that Auntie always gave a plaything or something unnecessary as one gift, and something sensible, but dull and unwelcome – like underwear – as another.

Triumphant with her aquisition of the boudoir set, as well as Auntie's ready forgiveness for her stealing Elizabeth-Anne's breakfast, Jenny was capable of being particularly expansive. 'I'm sure it's something real nice,' she said over her shoulder without bothering to see what lay beneath Elizabeth-Anne's mountainous nest of white tissue paper. She busied herself tearing open her second package instead. She grimaced and pushed it aside. Just as she'd expected. *Underwear.*

Carefully, Elizabeth-Anne parted the white tissue. She let out a deep breath. Inside her cushioned box sat a flaxen-haired doll . . . the most beautiful doll imaginable.

Her eyes shone as she took hold of the doll and, ever so gently, lifted her out. The matt-finished porcelain face looked so real it could have belonged to a living lady, and the sky-blue, wide-set eyes were framed by thick, fine lashes. Never in her life had she seen such a beautiful doll, or such a beautiful, frilly, lace-trimmed gown. Not even the most extravagant circus costume would have compared with it.

Jenny turned around and let out a cry of indignant envy. 'That's *mine*!' she hissed with blazing eyes. 'That's the doll I saw in Brownsville!'

But Elizabeth-Anne was too busy to hear her. She sat down, set the doll on her lap, and began stroking its real, soft blonde hair in wonderment. She didn't see Jenny lunging for it until it was too late.

Jenny snatched the doll off her lap. Elizabeth-Anne tried to grab it back, but Jenny was too quick. 'It's *mine*!' she hissed from between her teeth.

Elizabeth-Anne shook her head and jumped off the settee. She pounced at Jenny, but Jenny hopped back behind a table.

A soft, strangled noise came from the depths of Elizabeth-Anne's throat. Tears streamed down her cheeks as she held out her gloved hands beseechingly.

Jenny made a face, turned her back on her, and held the doll against her chest. 'You're mine!' she hissed over and over to the doll. 'You're *mine*. Auntie made a mistake. You're the doll I saw in Brownsville!' She felt Elizabeth-Anne's angry hands clutching at her dress and quickly tore herself out of her grasp. She tossed her head. 'Go away, you freak!' she hissed over her shoulder. 'Nobody wants you here! Leave me alone!'

In desperation, Elizabeth-Anne tried once again to grab the doll away, but Jenny held it high and smiling with hideous triumph, skipped around to the back of the piano. She was certain that Elizabeth-Anne would stay away, for hidden behind the piano was the fireplace with its crackling, leaping yellow flames.

Elizabeth-Anne never went near a fire.

But Jenny hadn't counted on three things – Elizabeth-Anne's outrage, tenacity, and what the doll symbolized to her. It was more than just a toy; for Elizabeth-Anne it was a gift from Auntie, whom she loved more and more with every passing day. Auntie had given it to *her*, not to Jenny – and now Jenny was using it to torture her once again.

Suddenly, all the months of suffering at Jenny's hands came to a head.

Enough was enough. Elizabeth-Anne was not about to sit back and take any more of the cruelties Jenny dished out without putting up a fight.

Despite the hot fire leaping in the fireplace, Elizabeth-Anne darted behind the piano and flew at Jenny, managing to wrest the doll from her clutches. Jenny was surprised at the younger girl's fierce determination. For a moment, they fought a bitter tug of war, then Jenny tightened her hands around the doll, and Elizabeth-Anne could feel it slipping from her grasp. Her grip was hindered by the gloves – they wouldn't let her gain purchase.

Jenny drew back, and as she did, Elizabeth-Anne tried to give the doll one last, fierce tug.

What happened next astonished – and shocked – them both. The doll flew out of their hands and tumbled into the fireplace. Greedy flames hissed and crackled as they engulfed it.

Jenny stared in horrified fascination as the frilly lace dress caught fire.

For Elizabeth-Anne, the world seemed to stop. As the flames leapt up around the doll, her hands flew up to cover her face. Unlike Jenny, she was not seeing the doll burn – *she* was seeing the flaming bodies of Szabo and Marikka.

A high-pitched, hideously blood-curling scream burst forth from her lips, echoed out into the hallway, and from there into the dining room, where it abruptly stilled the clinking of cutlery on china; it rolled into the kitchen, down into the cellar, and up the stairs; it escaped, muffled, through the closed windows and froze a hopping rabbit outside, its ears drawn back in fear at the unearthly noise. Then a crash reverberated from the kitchen, and Elender came tearing into the parlour, the Frittses at her heels. She looked around wildly and spied the two girls behind the piano. She moved behind it and glanced into the fireplace. Her hand flew to her breast and her heart skipped a beat at the terrible vision.

'Oooooh, Auntie, Auntie, Auntie! *They're burning, Auntie! Ooooh, Auntie!*'

Elender stared at the flames as if mesmerized. Then she glanced at Jenny.

'Ooooooh, Auntie. The fire – the hot fire. The horrible hot, hot fire!'

Elender frowned at Jenny; Jenny's lips weren't moving at all. Then, slowly, she turned to Elizabeth-Anne. The girl had fallen to her knees, her hands clutching her belly as her body rocked from side to side, her lips moving in anguish.

'Ooooooo, Auntie! Auntie! *Help them, AUNTIE!*'

Elender fell to her knees and held Elizabeth-Anne tightly. The girl was speaking! Actually speaking! She had found her voice! It didn't matter how or why. Nothing mattered anymore but that she could speak!

160

It was a miracle!

And as she held the girl, swaying back and forth with her, Elender began to shout with joy as the tears streamed forth from her own eyes.

From that moment on, Elizabeth-Anne was her own child, her own child more than Jenny or anyone else ever could be.

BOOK TWO

1890

Zaccheus

DENT COUNTY, MISSOURI

1

Three memorable events in United States history occurred in 1890: the Battle of Wounded Knee, in South Dakota, the publication of *How The Other Half Lives* by Jacob Riis, and the first-ever execution of a criminal through electrocution. Not so memorable was the birth of Zaccheus Howe on a struggling farm near Muddy Lake, ninety miles southwest of St Louis, Missouri.

It was an early September morning when Sue Ellen Howe, who had never heard of Jacob Riis, Wounded Knee, or electrocution, leaned on her scythe and looked out across the field. It was a breezy day, and the alfalfa undulated like the waves of the ocean. In the distance, she could see her husband, Nathaniel, and her daughter, Letitia, expertly scything the west field with economical, fluid arcs, their blades reflecting the sunlight with flashes of silver. The air was redolent with the smell of fresh-mown hay.

Sue Ellen was heavy, swollen with child. For the past nine months, this had not deterred her from her dawn-to-dusk chores. But suddenly she knew she had to stop. She wiped the sweat off her brow with the back of a hand and called out to her eleven-year-old daughter: 'Letitia!'

Letitia stopped scything and hurried over. She was a sturdy, flaxen-haired girl with strong teeth, muscular arms, and a long face full of freckles. She looked at her mother questioningly. 'Mama?'

'My time's come,' Sue Ellen said concisely. 'Let's git to the house. I need yer help.'

Nathaniel did not turn around as the two women strode purposefully towards the small farmhouse. The alfalfa had to be cut; without it, the horse and the cows would starve during winter. And before it could be stored in the barn, it had to be completely dried. If it was stored damp, then the dampness could cause a chemical reaction, generating incredible heat from within, and the hay would erupt in flames and cause an inferno. Not that Nathaniel Howe knew anything about chemistry. But he was a farmer, as his father and grandfather before him, and there were certain things farmers knew that had been handed down through the generations. It did not matter *why* something happened; what mattered was that it *did*.

Nathaniel squinted up at the sky. It was clear and powder blue; the birds danced weightlessly in the air and the sun was strong. Hopefully the weather would hold for a week or two. After the alfalfa was brought in, then the rain would be welcome. Meanwhile, he hawked and spat and continued scything while his wife, assisted by his young daughter, gave birth to a healthy boy. By sunset, Sue Ellen had nursed the child and cooked a hot supper in the big black iron pot in the hearth. Nathaniel glanced impassively at the boy, named him Zaccheus, then ate his meal and went straight to bed. The next day, Sue Ellen hopscotched between the house and the field, breast-feeding her baby while continuing to scythe.

Sue Ellen Howe was twenty-five years old that autumn. She had married Nathaniel when she was fourteen, a lovely, pale-complexioned girl who promised to grow into a real beauty. It never happened. She looked forty, her face browned and burned by the sun, her back stooped by the heavy farmwork, her hands callused and rough. If she was no longer lovely and her pale complexion was forever gone, a certain pioneer hardiness and inner strength replaced them. She could neither read nor write, but she knew how to plant and harvest crops, mend and sew, salt pork, raise chickens, and can vegetables. Her eyes were hard and unyielding, her lips dry and cracked and purposefully sealed. She accepted her life unquestioningly and was never heard to utter a complaint. She did not love Nathaniel, but it never occurred to her that she should. She was content with him. He worked hard, never hit her, took her to bed with a kind of animal purposefulness, drank little and spoke even less.

Nathaniel was only ten years her senior but looked like her father. He was a taciturn man, not given to displays of affection. His family had once owned a large, flourishing farm and several slaves, but the War between the States had ravaged the farm, decimated the family, and freed the slaves. Nathaniel and the twenty-odd acres of soil from which he, his wife, and his daughter eked out a meagre living were all that remained of any glory the Howe family had ever aspired to. Now the arrival of Zaccheus meant an extra mouth to feed, but Nathaniel consoled himself with the fact that, before the boy turned eight, he would be able to put in a full day's work.

Zaccheus was six when he first learned how poor he was. The spectre of hunger always hovered nearby, as there was never enough food to go around, and he learned to accept the gnawing emptiness in his stomach. Accept it, but not like it. Once when things got really bad and the crops failed to yield even what it took for survival, his father loaded his shotgun with buckshot and headed across the fields to shoot blackbirds. They were tough and stringy and virtually meatless, but somehow, sucking on the crunchy, brittle bones seemed to make the hunger go away for a while.

He was seven when he received his first present. His parents had taken him to the county fair, and he'd found a big Negro selling baby chickens for a dime each. Zaccheus gazed into the cardboard boxes and immediately fell in love with a fuzzy yellow chick. It seemed to single him out, staring up at him, begging him to take it home.

He pointed at it. 'His name's Zack, too,' he told his father.

'It ain't a he, Zack. It's a hen, so it's a her,' his father said tersely.

'Can I buy her, Pa? Fer my very own?'

His father thought about it. 'We'll see,' he said vaguely, wondering what on earth a child would want with a chicken. They were filthy and served no purpose as a pet.

'Please, Pa?' Zaccheus begged desperately, awarding his father with a toothy grin.

Sue Ellen smiled at her husband. 'C'mon, N'thaniel. Havin' one chick o' his own ain't gonna hurt none. 'Sides, it's only a dime.'

Nathaniel frowned. 'Reckon it won't,' he said at last. He dug into his pocket and produced a much-coveted dime. He held it up. 'All right, son, go buy yer chick. It's yers. But you gotta feed it and take care of it.'

'Sure, Pa! Thanks!' Zaccheus raced up to the Negro and puffed out his chest proudly. His heart hammered inside his ribcage. 'I want to buy a chick!' he squeaked.

The Negro, a length of straw stuck between his pearly white teeth, scowled down at the boy. 'Run along, young'un, them chicks cost a dime.' He turned away, trying to catch sight of a real customer.

Zaccheus yanked on the Negro's blue overalls. 'They're a dime, ain't they?'

The man didn't bother to look down at him. 'Go on, young'un. Skedaddle.'

'But I got a dime!' Zaccheus wailed fiercely, holding up the bright coin.

The Negro turned slowly to look at him, and grinned. 'So you do, sir. You is a mighty rich young man, if I says so myself, being able to afford to buy your own fine chick, yessir.'

Zaccheus beamed up at him, because now the big Negro really believed he could afford a chicken of his very own.

The dime changed hands quickly, and Zaccheus reached into the box and lifted out his chick. It chirped protestingly, but when he held it close, it quieted down. It felt soft and warm and cuddly, and he didn't even mind the sharp, needle-like pecks of its beak.

'Sue,' he said softly, pressing his chick against his cheek. 'That's yer name, l'il chick. Sue.'

Nathaniel found a cardboard box and punched some holes in it. He handed it to Zaccheus. 'Put the chick in here so you won't lose it, son.'

Zaccheus shook his head. 'I wanna hold her,' he said. 'Ain't no way she's gonna git away from me.'

Nathaniel shrugged and tossed the box away.

It was dusk by the time the Howes headed home. In the back of the mule-drawn wagon, Zaccheus held the chick tightly. He cooed softly and petted it, then yawned noisily. A beatific smile was on his face as his lashes slowly fell down against his cheeks.

Sleep came easily, despite the shaking and rattling of the wagon, and his fingers slowly went slack.

The chick squirmed and slid out of his loosening grip, hopped lightly across his chest, and explored the wagon. It hopped on to the tailboard and perched there, looking back at the receding moonlit road.

A deep rut came up and the wagon wheels crashed down into it. The sudden jolt didn't awaken Zaccheus, but the chick lost its footing and was thrown off the wagon and into the night.

Half an hour later, Nathaniel unhitched the mule and led it into the barn while Sue Ellen climbed up into the back of the wagon. She shook Zaccheus gently. 'C'mon, son,' she said softly. 'We're home.'

Zaccheus sat up blearily, rubbing his eyes. Then he looked around groggily and drew a deep breath. 'Sue!' he cried, realizing he wasn't holding his chick any longer. He scampered desperately around the back of the wagon, looked under a pile of blankets and moved some crates, but Sue was nowhere to be seen. Shattered, he retreated into a corner, pulled up his legs and wrapped his arms around them, his chin resting on his knees. 'Sue's gone!'

'C'mon in the house, Zack,' Sue Ellen said calmly. 'We'll find yer chick in the mornin'.'

He shook his head defiantly and stared up at her. 'No. I gotta find her now. She's my pet, Ma. She's probably cold 'n scared 'n hungry.'

Sue Ellen grasped his wrists firmly and pulled him towards her. 'It's way past yer bedtime, young man. I said we'll look fer it tomorrow.' There was no mistaking the authority in her voice.

'But she might be gone by then!' he cried.

'Don't cry, son,' Sue Ellen said firmly. 'You know yer Pappy don't like a boy who cries.'

Zaccheus shook his head adamantly. 'I ain't cryin'!' he said forcefully as a single huge tear, highlighted by the moonlight, glistened and slid slowly down one cheek.

'Ain't no use to look fer it till daylight anyways,' Sue Ellen said. 'You 'n me, we'll set out after breakfast.'

He looked at her hopefully. 'Promise, Ma?'

'I promise, son.'

The next day, despite Nathaniel's grumbling, Sue Ellen and Zaccheus drove back the way they had come the night before until they reached the field where the county fair had been held. Then they turned around and drove slowly home, all the while on the lookout for the chick. They never came across it.

That night, after they returned, Sue Ellen whispered something to Nathaniel. For a moment he stared at his wife. Finally he nodded and cleared his throat. 'All right,' he said, raising his voice so that Zaccheus would be sure to hear. 'Since you 'n him couldn't find it, I'll see what I can do. If'n anybody can find that chick, it'll be me.'

The following morning, Nathaniel set out to find the chick. Zaccheus waited at home with bated breath. His father was gone all day, but in the evening, when he returned, sure enough, he had a yellow chick in a perforated box.

'You found her!' Zaccheus whooped delightedly. 'You found Sue, Pa! Jest like you said you would!'

Nathaniel exchanged glances with his wife. Then Sue Ellen smiled tenderly and squeezed her husband's hand affectionately.

In later years, Zaccheus would wonder whether Nathaniel had really found Sue, or if he had set out to buy another chick. It was a mystery he would never solve.

Hunger won out.

For a week, Zaccheus followed his chick around and played with it between chores. Eights days later, when the family didn't have much to eat, he approached his mother. 'Cain't we eat Sue?' he asked.

Sue Ellen eyed him sadly. 'No, son,' she said slowly, 'she ain't near big enough yet.'

Whenever he was hungry, he would continually appeal to his mother: 'I'm hungry, Ma. Cain't we eat Sue?' And his mother's reply was always the same.

As month after month went by, Zaccheus began to eye his pet hungrily. Sue was getting bigger and plumper all the time. He could just imagine how juicy she would be cooked. Every time he looked at her, he couldn't help smacking his lips.

Finally Sue had grown enough and Sue Ellen nodded her head. 'We'll have yer hen for supper tonight, Zack,' she announced. And that afternoon, she went after the nearly grown hen and wrung its neck. Like all the chickens killed on the Howe farm, this one, too, managed to flip-flop its way under the thorny rose hedge to die. Zaccheus crawled in after it and pulled it out. He brought it to Nathaniel and watched his father behead it. He felt swollen with pride. Because of him and his pet hen, the family would eat well.

When Sue Ellen brought the succulent roast chicken to the table, Zaccheus smacked his lips without compunction.

Pet or no, it never occurred to him that the hen was anything other than to eat.

Like many fathers, Nathaniel planned for Zaccheus to someday take over the farm. But Zaccheus was not destined for the life of a farmer. He was a dreamer, and possessed a quick, lively intelligence and a natural inquisitiveness. He was a very handsome boy, tall, fair-haired, and blue-eyed. Despite the starchy foods which were the Howes' dietary staple, he was as lean as his mother and father. The farmwork was exhausting and burned off every ounce of excess fat.

When Zaccheus turned nine, his life took on an unexpected turn.

Reverend Flatts of the Muddy Lake Methodist Church paid the Howes a visit.

Visitors to the Howe farm were rare. When Zaccheus cried out that a horse and buggy were headed their way, the entire family put down their work and gathered on the roadside, watching the approaching visitor with curiosity. As the buggy drew closer and Nathaniel recognized the Reverend, he scowled. He harboured an inbred suspicion of politicians, churches, and anyone who did not work the soil with his hands. So it was with less than a modicum of friendliness that he watched the short, rubicund man with the huge paunch struggle down from the buggy.

The Reverend mopped his forehead with a handkerchief. 'Morning, Mr Howe,' he wheezed formally.

Nathaniel squinted at him, then turned sideways and let fly a squirt of tobacco juice. He turned back to the Reverend. 'Rev'end,' he nodded.

'Fine looking boy you got there.' Reverend Flatts nodded at Zaccheus.

Nathaniel did not speak.

'He seems to be a bright boy. It's time he went to school.'

Nathaniel put his hands over his son's shoulders and drew him close. 'That why you drove out here? To take my boy away from me?'

'Not to take him away,' Reverend Flatts assured Nathaniel smoothly. 'The boy needs to learn to read and write.' The Reverend suddenly took on a more country air. 'Time's a changin'.'

'We're farmers,' Nathaniel insisted. 'We don't need no book learnin'. Besides, I need 'im on the farm.'

'He'll do you a lot more good knowin' how to read and write, Nathan. 'Member last week I saw you at the Muddy Lake General Store?'

Nathaniel looked at him suspiciously. 'What about it?'

'You was cheated, that's what. Cause you couldn't do no 'rithmetic.'

'Cheated!' Nathaniel roared, his eyes flashing. 'You mean I was gypped?'

The Reverend hadn't counted on the fury of Nathaniel's anger. He took a step backwards, swallowed, and managed to nod. 'You bought dry goods, if I remember rightly,' he said, suddenly unsure of himself and sweating even more profusely. 'Beans an' flour an' tobacco.

173

The tobacco should have cost you nineteen and a quarter pennies. Course there's no such thing as quarter-pennies. But you paid twenty-one cents instead of twenty. Same with the beans and the flour. And since you couldn't pay in cash, you're bein' charged interest by the week. One percent a month. Even there you're overpayin', since you can't figure it out right yourself.'

Nathaniel shoved Zaccheus away, lunged at the Reverend, grabbed him by the lapels, and half-lifted the fat little man off his feet. The Reverend did a little dance on tiptoe as Nathaniel shook him fiercely. 'You dirty, double-crossin' swine,' he snarled. 'Posin' as a man o' God! I got a good mind to put you outta yer misery! Why didn't you tell me I was bein' cheated at the store?'

'Because telling you then wouldn't have done you any good in the long run!' the Reverend sputtered, reverting to the King's English in his fear. His already florid face was getting redder by the second. 'Not without learning to read, write, and do arithmetic. If Zack learns, he can help. Then you'll never be cheated.'

Nathaniel let the Reverend go.

The fat man gulped air and brushed his crumpled lapels with his fingertips. 'If he learns to read, he'll have a chance at a future. Nowadays, everybody's got to read and write to get ahead.'

Nathaniel glowered. 'Zack'll be a farmer jest like me. There ain't no shame in that. We're honest, hard-working folk.'

For the first time since she had married Nathaniel, Sue Ellen stepped forwards and spoke up. 'Maybe the Reverend's right, Nathaniel. Maybe Zack should go to school,' she said quietly.

Both men stared at her. Nathaniel turned to the Reverend. 'It costs money, don't it?' he snapped.

The Reverend nodded. 'Fifteen dollars a year.'

Nathaniel shrugged. 'Well, I ain't got it.'

'I do,' Sue Ellen said softly.

Nathaniel stared at her open-mouthed.

'I got that gold locket my Mama left me. It's worth at least fifteen dollars.'

Nathaniel shook his head. The locket was the only thing Sue Ellen's mother had left her, and he knew how much she treasured it.

'I'll sell it,' she offered quietly, avoiding her husband's eyes. ' 'Sides, I never get a chance to wear it, noways. 'Course, we'll have to switch the chores around, but they'll git done. Zack cain get up at three, do half the chores, go to school, and finish the rest when he gits home.' She nodded. 'Zack'll go to school.'

Her voice was so level and firm that Nathaniel was speechless.

It was the first and last time that Sue Ellen ever spoke up and came to a decision without conferring with her husband.

2

Zaccheus dedicated himself to learning. Instinctively, he knew that the only way to escape the poverty in which he was entrenched was through education. He saw how those townsfolk who could read and write lived, and he attributed their higher standard of living to education. For the first time, he became ashamed of the mean way he and his family lived. He knew how poor they were, but worse, now he saw that they hadn't tried to better themselves, but were content as they were. That realization triggered a hunger for learning he had not known could exist.

Within six months, he could read better than others who had gone to school for three years. Diligently, he practised his penmanship over and over, always striving for neatness and legibility, and he constantly tried to decipher that which still held mysteries for him. He spent hours lying awake at night with a candle, memorizing words and definitions in the Webster's Miz Arabella, Reverend Flatts' stern wife, had lent him. She was his teacher, and in the second year, knowing that the Howes couldn't spend any more money on Zaccheus' education, she took him on in exchange for chores.

Nathaniel grumbled, but somehow Zaccheus, working with an almost superhuman energy, managed to do his farm chores, as well. By mid-term of that year, he was able to read, memorize, and explain entire passages of the Bible. He had a gift for the English language – and a gift for getting what he wanted. The vocabulary he had learned gave him a smooth, glib tongue. He contrived to become friends with the widow who lived next to the Flattses because she had an enormous library; she lent Zaccheus her books.

He devoured every volume she owned. Whereupon Miz Arabella's primer initially opened the magic door to knowledge, and the Bible explained many things and recounted marvelous stories and heroic deeds, it was the Widow McCain's books which brought an ache and excitement into his life – and the realization that his own life was dull. In the books, he read of faraway places which seemed far more real and exciting than the parochial world of Muddy Lake – magical places such as China, Japan, Greece, and Russia.

The more this new world opened up to him, the more Zaccheus hungered to become a part of it. He grew to despise Muddy Lake. He yearned to visit the lands of pale, delicate women with almond eyes and tiny lips; he hankered to roam through the Winter Palace of the czars; he longed to stumble through the ruins of ancient civilizations. His entire being was consumed with wanderlust and an insatiable thirst for knowledge. But he carefully kept these feelings to himself, fearing that if his father discovered how his imagination swirled, he would put a stop to his schooling. And slowly – inevitably – Zaccheus felt a distance growing between his family and himself. It was a gulf that was widening by the day. He knew why it was happening: because he couldn't share things with them. He couldn't share his thoughts and ambitions and dreams. They would never understand.

It was nearly five years before he finally confided in anyone.

It was a breezy Sunday afternoon when his sister, Letitia, her husband, Theoderick, and their shrieking children came for a visit. Theoderick was a farmer several miles away, and Sue Ellen had been very proud of Letitia's marriage to him. He owned tobacco fields, and that made him a man to be reckoned with, even though he had little money. Nathaniel, on the other hand, had taken the marriage with no show of emotion and had withdrawn into himself more than he ever had before. He had not only lost his daughter, but with her had gone a fourth of his workforce. He was afraid the time would come when Zaccheus, too, would finally sever ties and be gone for good.

But these disturbing thoughts Nathaniel kept to himself. Besides, he knew from the look in Sue Ellen's eyes that she knew, too. In a strange way, she seemed to be closer to Zaccheus than he.

They ate lunch on the porch, on a trestle table made of rough-hewn planks long weathered silver. In honour of the occasion, Sue Ellen had gone all out. There was fried chicken, mashed potatoes with gravy, cornbread, and for dessert she'd made her speciality, a tangy rhubarb pie.

There was little conversation during the meal; everyone was too busy eating, the children included. In the Howe household, this meal amounted to a feast, and it was eaten with intense concentration, as if it were some sort of solemn religious ceremony.

The food disappeared quickly, and every last drop of chicken drippings was mopped up from the cracked plates with pieces of cornbread. No one knew when another feast such as this might be forthcoming, so they all ate what they could. Miz Arabella had taught Zaccheus to eat quietly and mind his manners, and throughout the meal, the noisy slurps of his family shamed him.

While Sue Ellen cleared the plates away, Nathaniel and Theoderick stayed on the porch, chewing tobacco, smoking pipes, and drinking cider. The children chased each other off into the woods, playing games they'd made up.

Zaccheus, having seen little of Letitia since her marriage, walked with her to the far end of the fields, where a creek divided the Howe farm from the Swaggertys' in a natural, meandering boundary. For a long while they were both silent.

As they walked, Letitia glanced worriedly at her younger brother from time to time. She could sense that something weighed heavily on his mind, but she was a Howe, and Howes never pried into each other's business.

She waited until he was ready to speak.

Zaccheus picked a dry stalk of weed and nervously snapped it into little bits and pieces. He threw them, one by one, into the creek and watched them being carried downstream by the current. Finally, he could no longer bear to keep his yearnings to himself.

'Letitia?'

His sister raised her freckled face, her strong chin jutting upward. His eyes darted to the distant house in which he had been born. A lazy wisp of smoke trailed skyward from the crooked chimney. All around him, the crickets chirped noisily from the depths of grass, and a steady trill came from within some clumps of bushes. A frog croaked. 'I can't bear it here any longer, Letitia!' he blurted in a rush.

Letitia frowned as he spoke. Ever since he had started school, his language had changed, and she had trouble following what he said. Gone forever were the 'ain'ts', 'cain'ts', 'jests', and 'fers' which had always inhabited his vocabulary.

'An' what's wrong with this place?' she asked indignantly.

His eyes glowed with the intensity of smouldering embers. 'There's a whole world out there, Letitia!' he cried, no longer trying to contain his excitement. 'It's so big and sprawling and beautiful! Did you know there are such things as snow-covered mountains that belch smoke and fire?'

'Oooooh!' she squealed, clapping a hand over her mouth. Her eyes looked like horror-stricken saucers. 'Lawdy, but I wouldn't wanna see that. It would scare me to death!' Then she lowered her hand and smiled. ' 'Course, your jest tryin' to pull my leg.'

'No,' he said quietly, 'it's true.'

'How'd you know?' she accused. She leaned forward. 'You been there?'

'In a way.' He looked defiant.

'When?'

'I . . . I read about it.'

'Oh.'

The way she said it took the wind out of his sails. He cursed himself for revealing his innermost secrets to her. She couldn't read, couldn't possibly begin to imagine the power and magic of words. And therefore, she couldn't begin to believe what was written in books.

He had been a fool to confide in her.

She looked at him sharply. 'You ain't thinkin' of leavin' here and runnin' after some squirrely fairy-tale mountains, are you?'

He bit down on his lip and nodded. Then he clutched her hands so tightly that she let out a squeal of pain. 'I've got to get away,' he said, 'but you've got to promise me you won't tell Ma and Pa.'

'It's the Rev'end.' She tossed her flaxen head. 'He's been puttin' funny ideas in yer head. Yep, funny ideas. 'Fore long, people here'll say *you're* funny, too, if you don't keep things like that to yourself.'

He shook his head. 'No, it's not the Reverend. It's the books. They talk to me, Letitia! Really, they do!'

She looked at him as if he was crazy.

'When you're reading,' he said patiently, 'it's just like there's a storyteller right beside you, telling you all about the marvels he's seen.'

Letitia still looked unconvinced. 'Where you wanna go?' she asked with incisive practicality.

He shrugged and rocked frontwards and backwards on the balls and heels of his bare feet. He looked down and studied his toes thoughtfully. 'I don't really know,' he said reflectively. 'Everywhere, I guess.' He raised his head and squinted in the sun. 'I think I'd just like to travel for a while. See everything I can.'

'Don't that take a lotta money?'

He nodded. 'But I'm not going to leave just yet.'

She frowned. 'How's come?'

'Oh, I still got a lot to learn,' he said vaguely, avoiding her eyes by looking out across the fields.

What he couldn't tell her was that he was at odds with himself. On the one hand, he yearned to take off immediately, walk to St Louis or else head north, south, or west – the direction itself didn't matter, only that he begin his journey. On the other hand, Miz Arabella's beautiful niece, Miz Phoebe, had just come from Natchez to stay with the Flattses. Phoebe Flatts was sixteen, two years older than he, and she mesmerized him. Her face was as cool and white as porcelain, her long, white-blond hair gleamed like satin, and her eyes were dark

180

and liquid. Whenever she passed by him, she would lower those eyes and smile demurely with her tiny, heart-shaped lips, and his pulse would race and a blush would rise up from his neck. He'd never known that a woman could have that kind of effect on him, and now that she'd come into his orbit – however peripherally – he couldn't bear to tear himself away from her. Not even for his travels.

But what he had found even more disturbing was that he had difficulty putting his feelings for Miz Phoebe into words or even thought – nothing he could think or say could ever do her justice. Finally, in desperation, he had gone to the Widow McCain and borrowed her slim volume of verse again. The first time through he'd been unimpressed, but now he understood why poetry existed – to describe the indescribable. And from that moment on, each time he thought of Miz Phoebe, one of Shakespeare's sonnets sprang to his mind:

Shall I compare thee to a summer's day?
Thou art more lovely and more temperate;
Rough winds do shake the darling buds of May,
And summer's lease hath all too short a date.

Those words, and those alone, he thought, did Miz Phoebe Flatts justice.

Now, standing with Letitia at the bank of the creek, a romantic vision flashed in front of Zaccheus' eyes. Up until now, Miz Phoebe had been a dreamlike apparition that had filled him with yearning. He knew how he felt towards her, and how to put it into words. But he suddenly realized that that was not enough.

He would marry her.

3

He swung his legs out of his bunk; the wooden planks on the floor creaked and groaned under his weight. He shivered from the cold air that blasted in through the leaks in the caulking. It was still hours before dawn.

He reached behind him and rubbed the small of his back with his fingertips. His muscles were stiff and knotted from sleeping in a half-curled position. The slats of his bunk, which was hammered in a kind of framework against the east wall of the cabin, were already too short to accomodate his body full-length.

He stopped moving about and listened carefully. From behind the curtain which divided the cabin in two, Nathaniel's snores and Sue Ellen's even breathing continued without interruption.

He nodded to himself, tiptoeing cautiously around the dark cabin with the familiarity which comes from living in the same place for many years. He knew each loose floorboard, the location of each piece of hand-hewn furniture. And he knew only too well how sounds travel. Last night, after they'd all eaten and gone to bed, his father and mother had made love. Their grunts and groans, and the creaks of their iron bed, had been barely muffled by the wall of curtain.

Not that Zaccheus was mystified by the noises. Raised on a farm, he had learned about copulation at an early age. It was just that recently he had become aware of needs of his own; therefore, there was something perverse to him about the proximity of the act, especially since it was his mother and father.

By touch and feel, he gathered up his clothes, pulled them on quickly, slipped into his worn boots, and laced them high. He reached for the loaf of bread Sue Ellen kept on a shelf above the stove and tore off a large hunk.

He chewed the tasty, floury crust on his way outside, moving carefully across the loose floorboards lest they creak too loudly and awaken someone.

When he closed the door of the cabin quietly behind him, he took several long, deep lungfuls of fresh air. He glanced around. The purple night was velvety, high-lighted by pale white moonlight on the endless fields.

At the well, he drew a bucket of water, dipped the tin ladle into it, and drank thirstily. The water was cold and delicious.

He splashed the rest of the bucket's contents on his face. It had an instant wakening effect.

From the lean-to shed at the side of the cabin, he took out the gardening tools. Then, whistling softly to himself, he set out in the pale moonlight to work on Sue Ellen's vegetable garden. Mondays through Saturdays were spent out in the fields; Sunday mornings were reserved for toiling in the kitchen garden, repairing tools, and doing the wash; Sunday afternoons offered the family their much-deserved, bone-weary rest. Today was a Sunday.

He swung his hoe swiftly into the moist ground, throwing clumps of earth up all around him. He was driven with a kind of superhuman purpose and energy. He had to get the garden hoed and raked by nine o'clock. That way, he would have enough time to wash up, get dressed, and head to town for the eleven o'clock church service at the Muddy Lake Methodist Church.

He had never set foot in a church before, even though Reverend Flatts and his wife had tried their best to per-suade him. But today . . . yes, today he would go! Not because he was filled with religious fervour – but because Miz Phoebe would be there.

The gardening chores took longer than he'd planned, and he finished half an hour later than expected. His body glistened with sweat. He had long since taken off his jacket and shirt. His back, chest, and face were burned red, and his wiry muscles stood out clearly.

He picked up his shirt and jacket where he'd left them, tucked them in his belt, gathered up the tools, and hurried back to the cabin.

Sue Ellen was crossing the yard, a flat basket of folded laundry wedged between her hips and her hand. She paused and watched her son curiously as he cleaned the tools. She had never seen him work so feverishly before. Only after he finished, and had put them away, did she speak. 'You was up early, son.'

He turned to face her. 'I know, Ma. I wanted to finish off so I could go into town.'

'Inta town? You're in town most ever' day. Why you goin' today, too?' She followed him to the well and watched as he drew a bucket of water and reached for the bar of lye soap.

'I'm going to church,' he announced quietly.

'*Church*! Since when's a Howe set foot in a church?' Zaccheus heard Nathaniel sneer.

He spun around. He hadn't heard his father approach. 'Morning, Pa. I got up early so I could get the gardening finished before I left.'

Nathaniel squinted closely at him. 'First it's school, now it's church. Where you gonna go next?'

'Going to church won't do me no harm,' Zaccheus said softly.

'Since when did you git religion?'

'It isn't because of religion,' Zaccheus said defiantly. His blue eyes were challenging.

'What then?'

Sue Ellen's eyes were wise and knowing. She reached out and touched her husband gently on the arm. 'Leave 'im ʋe, N'thaniel,' she said quietly.

ʋthaniel shrugged and spat into the weeds.

ʋe Ellen nodded to Zaccheus. 'I'll git you a clean shirt out.'

Zaccheus hurried and washed.

The service was half over by the time he got to the church. The double doors were open, and the sounds of a hymn spilled out into the quiet, dusty street:

> *'Onward Christian soldiers,*
> *marching as to war.*
> *With the cross of Jesus*
> *going on before . . .'*

He hesitated and glanced up at the white clapboard building. It was little more than a small rectangular house with a porch facing the street and a small steeple housing a bell. Yet, despite its spartan simplicity, it seemed somehow imposing and ecclesiastical.

And intimidating.

Suddenly he felt unsure of himself. He had never been in a church, let alone one in which a service was taking place. Maybe he was making a fool of himself? Maybe his motive for coming was so transparent that everyone would know the reason? Maybe . . .

He swallowed nervously and turned away. Then he stopped and chastized himself. *What a fool you are. Why would anyone think you came to church just to see someone you lust after?* He glanced over at the Flattses' house, right next door.

Hadn't Reverend Flatts and Miz Arabella constantly invited him to attend services?

He frowned to himself. Yes, they had. Then, before he could change his mind again, he summoned up all his courage, turned to face the church again, and willed himself to climb the wooden steps to the porch.

He tightened his lips and looked past the open doors, into the sanctuary. It was dim, and speckled with a kaleidoscope of colours from the single stained glass window above the altar. The congregation was standing, hymn books in hand, their voices raised in chorus. From the balcony just inside came the deep, majestic cords of the organ. That would be Mrs Flatts, he thought.

Zaccheus removed his hat and took a deep breath. Then he slipped quietly inside. He stayed at the back. He knew he didn't belong; yet for some strange reason, he couldn't leave. He felt compelled to stay and accomplish what he had set out to do.

When the hymn ended and everyone sat down again, he remained standing, hat in hand. Trying his best to look unobtrusive, he stepped sideways into a corner so he wouldn't be silhouetted against the brightness of the open doors. But when Reverend Flatts stepped up into the pulpit and surveyed his congregation kindly, he noticed Zaccheus and held out his plump red hands in greeting and smiled. With his fingertips, he motioned for the young man to step forward. 'We have a visitor today,' the Reverend announced in a friendly voice. 'Welcome, Zaccheus Howe. Come forward, into a pew.'

Heads turned. Zaccheus saw people eyeing him curiously, but without malice.

Self-consciously, he slipped into the last row of pews. A dour-faced woman smiled tightly at him and moved over to make room for him. Smiling his thanks, he sat down and craned his neck, trying to catch sight of Phoebe Flatts, but in front of him was a sea of bare heads and dark bonnets. And all the bonnets looked distressingly alike from behind.

Reverend Flatts launched into a long sermon about honouring thy father and thy mother. Zaccheus squirmed in his seat. He was bored and impatient – bored by the interminable slowness of the service, and impatient to catch sight of Miz Phoebe.

Finally, the sermon was over and everyone rose to his feet again. Zaccheus followed suit. The woman beside him pointed down at her hymn book, the organ started up again, and everyone began to sing:

> *'On a hill far away*
> *stood an old rugged cross,*
> *an emblem of suffering and shame . . .'*

He stood on tiptoe and craned his neck restlessly. The woman beside him gave him a sharp poke in the ribs. He glanced sideways at her. She was eyeing him sternly.

He bowed his head solemnly and pretended to catch up with the hymn. When it ended, the organ music changed to a quicker-paced, higher-pitched spiritual march. He instantly sensed that the service was over.

People began to step out from the pews and shuffle towards the doors. Zaccheus made room for the woman to squeeze past him, but he remained in his pew, waiting for Miz Phoebe to come past him. Suddenly he was afraid that he might already have missed her, or that perhaps she hadn't come to church, that she could have taken ill, or be off visiting someone . . .

No, there she was, standing in the front pew, her body in profile, the hymn book clasped in front of her! His heart surged. She was waiting patiently for the people in the back to file out.

The moment she walked past him, she glanced sideways at him, and her heart-shaped lips parted, showing tiny, even white teeth. Then she flushed and lowered her dark, liquid eyes.

Zaccheus' breath caught in his throat. Phoebe Flatts was so stunning that even the severity of her black bonnet could not detract from her beauty. Strange, how he'd never really noticed the little things about her – her delicate tininess, for one, and the narrowness of her miniscule, cinched hourglass waist, for another.

He slipped into step behind her, breathing appreciatively. She smelled faintly of violets.

Outside the church everyone milled about, greeting Reverend Flatts and socializing with each other. Zaccheus was dying to stay, but he wasn't a Methodist. He felt a gulf between himself and these people. They had their denomination in common. They knew each other. They had better clothes than he.

Oh, but how he wished he could wait around just to be near his beloved Phoebe a little longer, but he felt too out of place.

He slipped away quietly, but for the next several weeks, he regularly attended church services. A few weeks later, he was invited to share Sunday afternoon lunch with the Flattses. Soon it became a standing invitation.

Attending services had paid off. Sundays with the Flattses became a weekly tradition.

Zaccheus was Arabella Flatts' pride and joy, sure proof that her teaching was paying off handsomely. No matter his social station, Zaccheus did far better than the brightest wealthier students because he applied himself so diligently. And Reverend Flatts liked him because he was hard-working and attended church services regularly, something none of the Howes had ever done.

The Sundays Zaccheus spent at the church services and at the Flattses' afterwards were boring and dull, but to him the hours fled by all too quickly. They were the only times he could be near his precious Phoebe. He suffered the interminably long sermons gladly, and no longer sat in the back pew. Reverend Flatts had invited him to sit in the front row beside his niece.

Each Sunday, Zaccheus' pulse raced as he snuck little sideways glances at her. He never heard the sermons, only Phoebe's sweet breaths and her crystal clear voice as she sang the hymns. His greatest excitement was when she shared her hymn book with him, so that he could hold one side of the heavy book while she held the other, their fingers occasionally brushing against each other as they turned the pages. When that happened, he felt a crackling rush of electricity surge through him.

His greatest disappointment was when Reverend Flatts gave him his own hymn book as a gift, and he could no longer share Phoebe's.

4

Arabella Flatts pressed her fingers down on the organ keys and let the last rich chord of the hymn linger forcefully. Then she lifted her hands, twisted soundlessly sideways on the bench, and gazed down from the church balcony. Her sharp topaz eyes surveyed the sea of heads. From up here, she could almost imagine the view the Lord had if He deigned to look down from Heaven to focus His all-seeing eyes upon this inconsequential congregation. Of course, she knew He had better things to do than watch the people of Muddy Lake, but still, it was nice to imagine how He would see them if He did.

Arabella Flatts was a thickset homely woman in her fifties. Long ago, she had dedicated her life to God, first, and her husband, second. Unlike most of Muddy Lake's congregation, the majority of which worked the land, her face and hands were pale and scrubbed scrupulously clean. The rest of her body, which nobody ever saw – not even her husband, since she slept in a full-length, long-sleeved nightgown, and the few times they made love was in total darkness and silence – was even paler. She favoured ankle-length skirts and dresses, and blouses with long sleeves and high, tight collars so that her neck was perpetually and ruthlessly squeezed red.

She held herself with the stately poise required of a minister's wife, and her kindness and shrewd mind, coupled with the Reverend's ecclesiastic enthusiasm, had made the Flattses very popular among the congregation.

She smiled dreamily as her husband entered the raised white pulpit. Raptly, she listened as he delivered another of his sermons. Even after all these years, his sermons never failed to enthral her. On the street, or at home, he looked like such an inconsequential, almost comical fat little man, huffing, puffing, and wheezing because of his weight. But once in the church, his whole demeanour seemed to change. He seemed to somehow . . . yes . . . *grow* in stature. She, who lived with him daily, who shared his table and his bed, never failed to be aware of how he changed during the services . . . how he was bathed by the magnificence of the Lord.

Arabella Flatts was very proud of her husband, the Reverend. The Lord had seen fit to bless him by calling him to serve, and she felt sure that He was as proud of him as she herself was.

She nodded her head as her husband raised his voice, emphasizing a point. Below her, the congregation of Muddy Lake, listening raptly to his every word, drew back and flinched. Reverend Flatts' words and voice had that kind of effect on them. Everyone liked to boast that he was the best minister they had ever seen or heard.

Arabella let her eyes roam.

Suddenly she frowned.

She could see Phoebe in the front row, sitting up straight beside Zaccheus, her bonneted head tilted back. As Arabella watched, Zaccheus slowly turned his head sideways. Not all the way, and probably nobody noticed it since he had to look sideways and up to face the pulpit. But from the organ balcony, Arabella could see that he wasn't facing up. He was studying Phoebe.

190

Arabella looked thoughtful, her spiritual concentration momentarily broken.

So that's it, she thought. *He's in love with her. That's why he's coming to church.* She frowned to herself. *Does that make it an ulterior motive? Or . . . could the Lord be moving in one of His mysterious ways? Was that why He had seen fit to visit tragedy upon Phoebe's parents? So that Phoebe would come here and gain another member for the congregation?*

Arabella couldn't be sure.

She continued to stare. For almost a full minute, Zaccheus had his head turned. Then Phoebe turned to glance at him, but Arabella couldn't see her expression: her niece's face was hidden by the sides of her flaring black bonnet.

Arabella smiled faintly to herself. Then she turned quickly around again. The sermon was over.

She poised her fingers above the keyboard and brought them crashing down in a hymn.

That night, in the cool darkness of the second-floor bedroom, Arabella turned her head sideways on the pillow. For a long moment, she stared at her husband. He was a large, shadowy mound of blanket. 'Reverend,' she said hesitantly.

He stirred and she could feel him turning to face her. 'Yes, Arabella?'

'The Lord . . .' She bit down on her lip. '. . . sometimes He moves in mysterious ways, doesn't He?'

'Yesss . . .' Elias Flatts' voice sounded puzzled. 'Is something bothering you?'

'N-noooo,' she said slowly. 'It's just that sometimes I wonder why He makes the things happen that He does.'

'What kind of things?'

'Oh,' she said vaguely, 'just things.'

Reverend Flatts reached over and patted his wife's hand. 'Ours is not to question why,' he quoted softly.

She nodded her head in the dark. 'No, it isn't,' she

191

replied. She felt suddenly better for not telling him about Zaccheus' eyes for Phoebe. The Reverend would find out soon enough for himself.

And besides, it was the Lord's doing.

She smiled faintly up at the dark ceiling. Even long after her husband's wheezy breathing grew deep and regular, she lay awake, remembering how, long ago, she had met him. How young she had been then – barely two years older than Phoebe was now. And her husband had been a young seminary student, slim and handsome and filled with shining fervour.

He was no longer slim and handsome, of course, but his religious fervour burned deeper than ever. Some things, at least, did not change.

And with those comforting memories, she fell soundly asleep.

The Methodist services themselves may not have particularly appealed to Zaccheus, but the readings from the Bible did, since it was filled with parables, heroic deeds, and age-old history. It was sweet poetry to his ears, something he could both appreciate and respect. But what he liked most of all about the services – besides the opportunity to be with Phoebe – were the hymns. They were writings of another kind. Poetry set to music.

Without telling anyone, he composed the words to a hymn of his own, *The Mighty Golden Gates of Heaven*. He did it while toiling in the fields or walking to and from town, keeping a scrap of paper and a stub of pencil handy in his back pocket. This way, whenever he had an inspiration, he could quickly jot it down.

Slowly, the hymn began to take shape:

> *The Mighty Golden Gates of Heaven,*
> *Behind which our Lord is throned,*
> *Where angels glide in paradise,*

Is our true heav'nly home.

The Mighty Golden Gates of Heaven,
Inside which we serve our Lord,
Saint Peter, guardian of the gates,
Give us our Christian sword.

The Mighty Golden Gates of Heaven,
In the bright blue sky above,
A place where Christian brothers
Find undivided love.

The Mighty Golden Gates of Heaven,
Dazzling, brilliant and pure,
A mecca for the Lord's servants,
A place where we'll endure.

The Mighty Golden Gates of Heaven,
Our one true spiritual choice,
Where God in all His glory reigns,
A place where we'll rejoice.

The Mighty Golden Gates of Heaven,
Our own true spiritual home,
The only place for brothers
That we can call our own.

Finally the hymn was completed. Zaccheus showed it to Arabella Flatts.

She was amazed. She studied first the lyrics and then the handsome, remarkable lad who had written them. '*You* wrote this?' she asked incredulously, tapping the sheet of paper with an index finger.

Zaccheus nodded timidly, his long gangly body ill at ease.

The Reverend was right, Arabella thought, the Lord truly worked in mysterious ways. There was no longer any doubt in her mind but that the Lord had sent

Phoebe here in order to attract Zaccheus to the congregation.

Each afternoon of the next week, Arabella sat down behind the church organ and set the words to music. Then she had the *Muddy Lake Gazette* print up sheets of the hymn. The Easter Sunday when it was first sung, there were tears in the Reverend's, Arabella's, and Zaccheus' eyes.

Zaccheus' tears were misconstrued for revelation, piety, and pride. The truth was, he was immensely sad. This was the first time anything he had created had moved himself and others, and rather than feeling thrilled, he was plunged into a deep depression: the first time his hymn was sung was the most important day of his life, but his family wasn't there to share in his pride. On that Easter Sunday, like every other Sunday of his life, Nathaniel refused to go to church. There was work to be done. Without Letitia's help, and with Zaccheus around less and less, the time wasn't there to squander. Letitia and Theoderick weren't church-goers either, so they stayed away. And Sue Ellen, who had planned on going for the first time in her life, awoke that morning with a burning fever. The flu she had caught would last a week.

From that Easter Sunday on, *The Mighty Golden Gates of Heaven* was sung during at least two services a month. The Reverend and Arabella sent copies of the hymn to neighbouring towns, and it soon became the most popular hymn in the county. In one fell stroke it elevated Zaccheus above everyone in Muddy Lake. He had found his forte. Poetry.

Arabella Flatts was humble enough not to verbalize the credit that was due her for recognizing Zaccheus' potential and nurturing his genius, but every time she

194

looked upon him, her eyes glowed with deep pride. Even Phoebe seemed to glance at him more often.

The Methodist community welcomed him with open arms.

5

Arabella Flatts dabbed her lips delicately with her napkin and pushed her carved, lyre-backed chair back from the oval mahogany dining room table. Phoebe took her cue and rose to her feet. Reverend Flatts, Zaccheus, and Reverend Tilton, who was visiting from Salem and had delivered this Sunday's sermon, also touched their lips with their napkins.

'A feast,' Reverend Tilton, whose wife had died the previous year, proclaimed in his rumbling voice. He placed his rumpled napkin down beside his plate and rose to his feet. He was a tall man, and towered high above Arabella Flatts. 'You are a hugely accomplished cook, Mrs Flatts. I envy the Reverend.'

Arabella flushed with pleasure. 'You must visit us more often, Reverend,' she said demurely.

'That I shall, that I shall.'

Reverend Flatts came around from the head of the table and stretched out his arm in order to clap a hand on Reverend Tilton's shoulder. 'Let us retire to the study,' he suggested, stifling a burp. He turned and nodded. 'Come along, Zaccheus. There's something we'd like to discuss with you.'

Zaccheus looked puzzled. He had never before been invited into the sanctum of the Reverend's study, to which the men who dined at the Flattses' traditionally retired after eating. He glanced first at Reverend Flatts, then at Reverend Tilton, and finally at Mrs Flatts.

She smiled encouragingly, her topaz eyes sparkling,

and watched as the men, followed by Zaccheus, went out to the hall and into the Reverend's study, which was right next door. When the study door snapped shut, she and Phoebe began clearing the table.

Arabella smiled with satisfaction as she gathered up the white bone-china dinner plates she'd inherited from her grandmother on her father's side. Every last morsel of food was gone, eaten with relish and lavish compliments. The compliments were neither wasted nor undeserved. The beef liver, served cold in a mustard sauce, had been piquant and savoury; the mushroom ragout, spooned atop the fried grits, had had just the right consistency and delicacy; the coarse yellow cornbread, spread with homemade honeybutter, had never tasted better; and the strawberry and rhubarb pie, which she'd baked fresh early that very morning, had all been eaten up, down to the very last crumb. There were no leftovers. Normally she despised vanity, but even so, she had to admit that the lunch she had prepared had turned out exceptionally.

Arabella always made certain that her Sunday lunches were feasts commemorating the Lord's day. On Sundays, she summoned up all her culinary skills and happily improvised on her favourite recipes which she had collected over the years. During the week, meals in the Flattses' home were far simpler, though the portions, due to the Reverend's usually limitless appetite, were not.

'Reverend Tilton delivered an inspiring sermon, don't you think?' Arabella said pleasantly as she made a stack of the plates.

Phoebe looked at her and nodded.

'Well, soon as the dishes are done, we'll go sit out on the porch. You know the saying, "Men work from sun to sun, but women's work is never done". Well, on Sundays I don't prescribe to that. We may have to cook, but we'll sit and rest, just like the good Lord intended.'

Phoebe nodded, her face impassive. She didn't like doing dishes, nor did she like just sitting around. In Natchez, she'd always had plenty of friends around; here, young and old alike always seemed to be working. And the little rest there was, was usually taken up sitting around.

Phoebe Flatts was bored to tears.

From behind the closed door of the study, the two women could hear the men talking. Phoebe ignored the voices, but Arabella nodded to herself. She knew what it was the men were discussing. Last month, she herself had broached the subject with her husband, and he had gone to see Reverend Tilton about it.

Which was why Reverend Tilton was here.

'It's time you gave your future some thought,' said Reverend Flatts. He was pacing the book-lined study where twin oval portraits of Reverend Flatts' grandparents gazed down in oil-painted solemnity; his grandmother, tight-lipped and severe, wearing a starched white cap gathered in scalloped edges; his grandfather, grim and resplendent in a frockcoat. 'Do you have any idea what you would like to do with yourself?'

'Sir?' said Zaccheus, who was seated on the edge of a settee upholstered with worn fabric. Reverend Tilton was seated opposite him, tea cup in hand.

Reverend Flatts tucked his thick red fingertips into his waistcoat pocket. He took a deep breath, tucked his chin down into his voluminous neck and looked thoughtful, his grey brush eyebrows knitted, his lower lip jutting out. Then he looked up again and met Zaccheus' gaze. 'You're fourteen years old.'

Zaccheus nodded his head, frowning in puzzlement. 'Yes, sir?'

'I don't need to tell you how bright you are.' Reverend Flatts met the youth's gaze with his small porcine eyes. 'We're all very proud of you.'

Zaccheus looked away in embarrassment, a lump blocking his throat. He had learned some manners and gained some education, but he had yet to acquire the polish it took to accept a compliment gracefully.

'It's never too soon to start planning for your future,' the Reverend continued. 'Within two years, you'll have to decide what you want to do with your life.'

'My Pa wants me to work the farm,' Zaccheus said quietly.

'I can understand that,' Reverend Flatts said, 'but do you think you're cut out for a life of farming?'

'What else can I do?' Zaccheus blurted out helplessly.

The Reverend smiled and glanced at Reverend Tilton. A silent signal seemed to pass between the two men. Reverend Tilton set his cup down, got to his feet, and cleared his throat. 'Have you considered a career in the ministry?' he asked softly.

'The . . . ministry?' Zaccheus' voice was a squeak.

'The ministry,' Reverend Tilton nodded. He gestured to Reverend Flatts. 'We are both in agreement that the Lord has blessed you extraordinarily. For a young man your age, you're filled with talent. We think you should put it to good use to do the Lord's work.'

'But I don't know if – '

'You have a calling?' Reverend Tilton asked gently.

Zaccheus nodded. He was unable to speak. Everything was moving too quickly for him.

'Many who are called to do the Lord's work do not even realize it in the beginning,' Reverend Tilton said flatly. Then he smiled benevolently down at Zaccheus. 'But the Lord knows, Zaccheus. He has singled you out to do His work.'

'Doing the Lord's work is doing fine work,' Reverend Flatts added emphatically. 'It's a highly respected career. A man can go far in the ministry.'

Zaccheus turned to Reverend Flatts.

'In the ministry,' Reverend Flatts continued, 'we do

198

not only hold church services. We're . . . doctors of the soul. We take care of people's spiritual needs. We help heal their pain.'

'But . . . *me*?' Zaccheus' voice was thick with emotion and confusion. 'I don't know anything about it.'

'On the contrary,' Reverend Tilton said smoothly. 'Your hymn proves how sensitive you are. You have a mighty talent for translating the untranslatable and putting it into words for all to understand.'

Reverend Flatts cleared his throat. 'You don't have to make up your mind just yet,' he said, 'but if you're interested, you should let us know soon. These things take time. You must be interviewed and approved, take tests, go to college – '

'*College!*'

'Yes, college.' Reverend Flatts frowned solemnly. 'All ministers are thus trained. And once you're trained and ordained, you will get a congregation of your very own. Even the chance to do missionary work overseas.'

'Overseas!' Zaccheus sat up straight. He didn't dare believe what he had heard. It was as if some distant siren were whispering sweet dreams into his ringing ears.

'Of course, should you decide to pursue such a career, we would have to find a suitable wife for you. One who willl attend to your needs and the needs of your congregation, just as Mrs Flatts attends to things here. There are many fine young devoted women. Women like our Phoebe, for instance.'

Zaccheus turned red.

Reverend Flatts coughed delicately, glanced away, and flushed slightly. Arabella Flatts might not have been aware of it, but he had not been totally blind to Zaccheus' attentions to Phoebe, either. And hadn't he, on the deathbed of his niece's parents, vowed to care for Phoebe? To help find her a suitable husband? No simple task.

Of course, there was still time. But slowly, things

199

would have to be arranged, little wheels set into motion. The first of these was to make certain that something would become of Zaccheus.

'You think about it,' Reverend Flatts said quickly. 'There's no need to decide just yet. For the time being, we'll keep it between us three, eh?'

Zaccheus tried to swallow the lump which was blocking his throat. The book-lined study seemed suddenly to reel dizzily around him.

He couldn't believe it. It was too good to be true.

An education.

A career, even if not one of his choosing.

The possibility to travel around the world, to the far-distant places of which he had dreamed so long.

And, possibly, Phoebe for a wife.

Everything, on a platter.

For a moment, a feeling of choked love rose up within him. He, who had never felt anything for religion, now felt something overwhelming stirring deep within him. Was this an accident? Was this fate? Or . . . was it truly the Lord's doing? Perhaps . . . just perhaps, it was.

Before Reverend Flatts showed Zaccheus out, he took him aside. 'Just remember,' he told him in that special tone of voice which implied both confidentiality and the caring, good advice of an elder, 'no good decision was ever reached in a rush. Take your time coming to a decision about this. Think it over well and consider all the consequences. Now go home and try to get a good night's sleep.'

6

It was an autumn day much like the one on which, fifteen years previously, Zaccheus had been born. Nathaniel leaned wearily on his scythe and squinted up at the sky. A few yards away, Sue Ellen sensed that he was taking a rest. She shouldered her scythe and came over to her husband. For a moment, they stood side by side, their clothes whipped by the wind which was starting up, both of them looking up at the approaching, roiling grey clouds like two hardy, tough-skinned pioneers.

'It's gonna rain,' Sue Ellen said with surety. 'Last night, my leg was actin' up agin.'

Nathaniel turned his head sideways and spat. 'If it does, we'll lose this here crop,' he mumbled. He wiped his sweaty brow with his forearm and tightened his lips savagely across his yellow teeth.

Sue Ellen turned to look up at him. 'It's gonna work out,' she said quietly. 'We'll git the crop in.'

'Don't know how.' He let out a deep breath and turned to her. 'Not with Zack spendin' all his time at the Rev'end's.'

'He's learnin' things, N'thaniel. He wants to be a somebody.'

Nathaniel scowled. 'Whatdya mean, "be a somebody"? We're all somebody. Ploughin' and growin's respectable work. What good does it do a man when he's a somebody but he ain't got no respect?'

Sue Ellen looked at her husband steadily. 'Our son is respected,' she said quietly. 'Time's a' changin', N'thaniel.'

'Not fer the better, that's fer sure. Well, I better git goin' before the rain starts. Don't do me no good to jest stand here.' He started to turn away.

'Wait.' Sue Ellen placed a hand on his arm. 'Here comes Zack now.' She brushed the greying, stray strands of hair out of her eyes and squinted across the fields. In the distance, she could see Zaccheus hurrying towards the alfalfa field, scythe over his shoulder. He walked with a natural surety and grace which she realized was lacking in the rest of them, which none of the Howes besides him ever had. She watched as he came to a stop at the edge of the field, leaned his scythe against the fence rail, vaulted nimbly over it, and unbuttoned his shirt. Then he stuck it in his back pocket and picked up the scythe. For a moment, he looked across the field and waved.

Sue Ellen lifted her hand slowly and held it, raised in the air, for a long moment. Then, ever so slowly, she put her hand down and watched as her son expertly swung the tool.

It's amazing how quickly time flies, she thought to herself. It seemed only yesterday that Zaccheus was born. It had been the same way with Letitia. They grew up right before your very eyes.

'Ain't he a tall drink of water?' Sue Ellen wondered proudly out loud.

Nathaniel grunted.

Sue Ellen turned to her husband. 'Zack's a fine young man,' she said. 'He ain't like you or me, N'thaniel. He's been blessed.' She nodded her head positively. 'We should be proud o' him.'

Nathaniel turned slowly towards her. 'You proud o' him, Sue Ellen?' he asked softly.

'I am.' She nodded sagely. 'He's the first o' us to git a chance to be somebody, N'thaniel, n' he's doin' it. That's good for a mother's heart. It ain't all been wasted, know what I mean?' She eyed her husband closely. 'Ain't it good for a father's heart, too?'

He looked at her sadly.

'Zack is like one o' the wild animals. He's free, N'thaniel. He looks at things different from you 'n me. He sees how purdy the world is. Why, only yesterday, you know what he said?' She smiled bleakly. 'He said, "You're purdy, Ma".' She shook her head. 'Imagine me – purdy!'

Suddenly Nathaniel felt a powerful surge coursing through him. He touched his wife's cheek with his rough, soily hand. 'Your life ain't been good with me, Sue Ellen,' he said quietly. 'You was the purdiest woman in these here parts. You coulda had any man you wanted. Any kind o' life for yourself.' He paused. 'You made a bad choice marryin' me.'

Her eyes glistened with tears and she breathed deeply the moist freshness of the field and the salty, masculine sweat of her husband. 'No, N'thaniel,' she said softly. 'You's what I wanted. You's what I got. I'm satisfied. Really I am.' Then quietly, almost under her breath, she whispered: 'I love you.'

Nathaniel swallowed and looked away so that his wife wouldn't see the tears that threatened to spill from his eyes. Then he took her in his arms without any fierce animal longing.

For the first time in his life, he felt the urge to kiss her gently.

7

It was the following day that Reverend Flatts rode out to the Howe farm to see Nathaniel.

Nathaniel had a pretty good inclination just why the Reverend had come. He signalled for the short, fat visitor to follow and led him from the bright sunshine into the dark dankness of the cabin. The single big room, divided in two by the ragged curtain, smelled stale and rancid.

The Reverend fought to refrain from twitching his nose in disgust. It was a peculiarly repugnant odour, one which he had smelled too often hereabouts – the offensive, intermingling stench of old grease and poverty – only here, inside the Howe cabin, it seemed somehow more pronounced. More repellent. The Howes were among the poorest farmers in the county.

Nathaniel reached up into a cupboard, lifted down a stone jug of moonshine and banged it down on the rough-hewn kitchen table. He pulled out the cork, which plopped noisily, and poured two Mason jars full to the rim before sitting down. The Reverend sat down, too. From outside, at the other side of the lean-to shed, came the steady cracking sound of Zaccheus splitting firewood.

Nathaniel took a hearty swig before noticing that the Reverend wasn't touching his drink. He gestured with his thumb at the Reverend's jar. 'Cain't trust a man none who don't drink,' he said tersely.

The Reverend felt Nathaniel's dark eyes boring into his. Slowly, he picked up the greasy jar which no amount of Sue Ellen's rinsing in cold, soapless water could adequately clean, and, squashing a grimace, sipped delicately. He suppressed a shudder. The corn liquor was strong and burned raw all the way from his throat down to his stomach. He never touched spirits, but he didn't dare turn down Nathaniel's hospitality: the farmer would be offended. More importantly, he needed Nathaniel to be in as good a mood as possible; otherwise, the mission on which he had come would surely fail.

'Lord forgive me,' Reverend Flatts prayed soundlessly each time he took a tiny sip.

Both men sat there quietly for a long time, Nathaniel draining one jar after another, the Reverend making ginger attempts at sipping his. Nathaniel scowled when he noticed that the level of moonshine in the Reverend's jar was barely dropping. 'You ain't drinkin',' he accused softly. 'Come on, Rev'end, drink up like a man. It ain't gonna kill you.'

Reverend Flatts closed his eyes and drained his jar. He started coughing uncontrollably and his eyes bulged like a carp's.

Nathaniel leaned sideways and slapped Reverend Flatts heartily on the back, which only made the fat little

204

man's eyes bulge even further. Nathaniel filled both jars again. He raised his. 'Bottoms up.'

The Reverend watched, fascinated, as Nathaniel drained his fourth jar in one long gulp. Then he realized, with a shock, that Nathaniel was waiting for him to follow suit. 'Lord forgive me,' he prayed silently and drained his jar. He sputtered painfully, his stomach began to churn, and it took all his strength to fight to keep the bile down. Nathaniel filled the jars again.

The Reverend was feeling peculiarly light-headed, a feeling he had never been subjected to before, and sweat suddenly began to pour from his body. His limbs felt weightless and the room began to reel all around him. Amazingly, though, the more Nathaniel Howe drank, the more sober *he* seemed to become.

Finally, Nathaniel leaned back in his chair, his eyelids drooping as if to sleep. But it was a deceptively sleepy look: he was very much alert. 'So you come to take my boy away from me,' he drawled slowly at last.

The Reverend didn't speak immediately. He had been trained to handle almost any situation gracefully, but here at the Howes' he was a fish out of water. He had never been inside the cabin before, and he found everything about it stifling. The claustrophobic stuffiness. The leaky caulking between the uninsulated boards. The creaky, hand-hewn furniture, as uncomfortable to sit on as it was ugly. Sue Ellen's heartbreaking attempts at making the place homely: the patchwork quilts; the tattered curtains over the cracked windows, which he recognized had been made from clothes donated by the church; the bottles, filled with multicoloured liquids on the windowsills, so that they caught the sunlight and made a strange, stained-glass effect; the meagre wildflower-and-weed arrangement on the table. Everything spoke of a desperate attempt at making the unlivable livable. It depressed him, revolted him, made him feel more ill at ease than he had ever been in his life and, strangely enough, at the same time gave him strength for what he had come to do. Making a better life for at least one member of this abjectly poor family – eliminating the spectre of poverty for Zaccheus – that was, at least, a beginning for the Howes. That was, the Reverend believed, the Lord's will.

Nathaniel suddenly scraped back his chair and jumped to his feet. He crossed the creaky floorboards and flung open the front door. 'Sue Ellen!' he called out gruffly.

It wasn't long before his wife appeared, her lined face weary, her eyes dull as she nervously wiped her red, raw hands on her dirty apron.

'The Rev'end's hungry!'

Sue Ellen nodded and managed a timid smile as she squeezed past her husband into the cabin.

'Really, you don't need to go through any trouble for me, ma'am,' the Reverend protested unsteadily. The very thought of food only seemed to make him that much queasier. He watched Sue Ellen reaching for a grease-coated iron skillet, and winced.

'You visit us, you eat with us,' Nathaniel growled, stubbornly. 'My boy, he's eaten enough meals at your house. Now you'll eat here.'

Reverend Flatts nodded unhappily and tried to form a smile. He was white-faced and ill, but it was important that he shared the offered hospitality, no matter how much it revolted him. 'I'm . . . much obliged,' he said softly.

'Zack!' Nathaniel roared out the door.

The chopping and splintering noises stopped instantly. A moment later, Zaccheus appeared at the door. He looked nervous, at once ashamed but willing. 'Pa?'

'Kill us the fattest chicken we got. You know the one.'

Zaccheus nodded. 'Yes, Pa,' he said hesitantly.

'And git a move on, boy!'

'Yes, Pa.' Zaccheus nodded, his eyes meeting t̶
Reverend's. He was ashamed of the poverty and the dir
which his mother, much as she tried, just couldn't begin
to cope with. What made it all so much worse was that
he had dined so often at the Flattses', and was only too
aware of the trouble Arabella went through when she
prepared a meal. Everything in the Flattses' house was
succulent and beautifully served. All things aside, the
fact that his own family's meals were rather unappetiz-
ing and, out of necessity, hastily thrown together, was
not lost on him. But there just wasn't the time to devote
hours in the kitchen. Nor was there any gleaming china
which had been passed down through the generations;
everything was cracked and chipped and coated with a
perpetual layer of grease.

'Go on, Zaccheus,' Reverend Flatts said kindly. He
quickly cupped his hand and raised it to his lips as he
stifled a burp. 'Do as your father says. Isn't that what
the Bible teaches us? To honour thy father and thy
mother?'

'Yes, sir.' Zaccheus spun around and left immediately.

The immediacy of his departure was not lost on
Nathaniel. His shoulders slumped and he seemed suddenly to age as he stared after his son with a terrible
sense of misgiving and loss. He realized at once that
what he had so often feared had come true. Zaccheus
respected the Reverend far more than he would ever
respect his own father. Worse, Nathaniel knew that
there was nothing he could ever do about it. He couldn't
read. He couldn't write. Abstract thought was lost on
him. The things which were important to Zaccheus
were the things with which not he, but the Reverend,
was endowed.

He had lost his only son.

With a loud clatter, Sue Ellen slid the iron skillet onto
the stove and then went outside carrying a wooden

...ket. At the well, she filled it with water and brought inside. She poured a huge pot full and carefully stoked the big iron stove with wood. Then she twisted a piece of newspaper into a kind of stick, scratched a match against the wall, and lit the paper. With it, she poked inside the stove until the wood began to burn. Then she grabbed a basket and headed outside again. For a moment, she stopped in the front yard and regarded her son. Zaccheus was holding a bowl of chicken feed in one hand and was spraying it all around him with the other. 'Here, chick-chick-chick-chick-chick,' he cooed softly.

Smiling and shaking her head, Sue Ellen quickly strode towards the other side of the cabin, where the kitchen garden was located.

Zaccheus watched the chickens come running towards him. They were certainly quick. Although it was not yet feeding time, the prospect of food lured them towards him. But the fat brown hen? Where was she? He glanced towards the coop and then let out a painful sigh.

There she was. The fattest, best-fed one of them all. Not only the fattest, but the best egg layer of the whole bunch. He knew that his father meant him to kill that very hen, and he was very much aware of the sacrifice that entailed. That one hen was the family's prime chicken. When times were tough – and they were always tough for the Howes – but *particularly* tough, it was that hen which laid the large, protein-rich eggs which staved off hunger. The rest of the hens just didn't like to lay much. They were runts in comparison.

Now was the moment, Zaccheus knew. He lunged suddenly forwards, his arms outstretched in front of him.

The hen darted sideways, racing panic-stricken across the yard, her wings flapping for greater speed as

208

she squabbled hysterically. She turned the corner of the cabin and headed past Sue Ellen's kitchen garden.

Zaccheus ran after her, only dimly aware of his mother as she stopped what she was doing and looked up at him. She was picking vegetables for lunch, baby peas which she had planned to harvest much later on, when they would be mature and go further, but which would be a mouthwatering delicacy right now.

Zaccheus lunged at the chicken and caught hold of her. With a flurry of her wings, she flew out of his grasp. He lost his footing, tripped, and went crashing down on his belly, sliding a little way before he managed to pick himself up again. Without losing any more time, he dashed after her.

Finally he caught up with her. He curled one fist tightly around her thick, feathery neck and craned his head sideways in order to avoid her flailing legs and the beating of her powerful wings. His face was grim and determined. Feathers flew all about him.

He held her at arm's length, then lifted her high, and started swinging her around way above his head. He heard the loud pop as her neck broke, and he let her go.

The hen dropped heavily to the ground and began a spastic dance, her body rolling and jerking. For a moment, he was reminded of that other chicken, so long, long ago . . . the one he'd named Sue. The one which had been his pet. Like that one, this one, too, ended up under the thorny rose hedge. It lay there in agony, gave a series of short jerks, then finally one long, drawn-out contortion, and it was over.

He got down on all fours, crawled as far under the hedge as he could get, and reached in with one arm to retrieve her, his arm and face getting scratched from the thorns. On the way back to the house, he held the chicken in one hand by its feet and picked the thorns out of his arm with the other. He stopped by the shed nd tossed the hen onto the tree stump which served as the chopping block and picked up the heavy axe. He raised it high over his head and then brought it crashing down. In one deft blow the hen was beheaded. As the head fell he jumped dextrously backwards to avoid the blood which shot out in a geyser.

Sue Ellen skirted the scene of the slaughter, went into the cabin with her vegetables, and then came back out, gripping the two rags which she'd wrapped around the scalding handles of the big pot of boiling water. She set it down on the ground and Zaccheus picked up the chicken and threw her in. The rest was Sue Ellen's job. The boiling water would loosen the feathers so that she could pluck them easily; then she would chop the chicken into parts, dip them in flour and eggs and fry them.

Zaccheus made himself scarce. He knew that the Reverend and his father wanted to discuss his future in private. Still, he couldn't help wondering how he was faring.

'Oh, God,' he prayed silently, 'make my father see the light.'

It was only after he had uttered these soundless words that he realized what he had done.

For the first time in his life, he had said a prayer.

Reverend Flatts belched noisily, no longer bothering to stifle the noises or cup his hand over his mouth. He grabbed hold of the edge of the table and hung on. It was funny what drink could do to you, he was thinking. The cabin walls were positively *reeling* madly around him, like some carnival ride gone berserk. He felt hot and sticky, too. The glowing stove let off too much heat and the chicken, frying in the pan of splattering grease, made him ever more nauseous.

Nathaniel placed his bony elbows on the table and leaned suspiciously across it. He looked deep into the

Reverend's eyes. 'Zaccheus is the only boy we got. need 'im here. Tell me why I ought to let him go o and leave his family 'n his farm?'

Reverend Flatts pushed his empty Mason jar towards Nathaniel and smiled meekly. Nathaniel grabbed the jug and expertly filled the jar to the brim. The Reverend took a long pull at his replenished liquor and burped contentedly. He sat back and folded his plump red hands over his ample belly. Funny, too, that the concoction no longer burned down his throat. 'It's for hish shake. Heesh a shmart kid. Heesh got a lot to offer people,' he said laboriously, vaguely aware that his words were slurred. He frowned deeply, concentrating on the pronunciation of every word, but it didn't help. 'He'll get a lot in return. Heesh shpecial.'

Nathaniel smiled thinly. 'What do I git outta it?' he asked quietly.

'You?' The Reverend frowned. 'N-nothing.'

Nathaniel nodded slowly. At least the Reverend wasn't going to try and bullshit him with that 'you're-going-to-be-blessed' routine. 'An' Zaccheus? What's my boy git?'

'An edu-ca-shun. Hard work.' The Reverend swallowed, blanching suddenly as he fought down the most massive wave of nausea yet. After a moment, it seemed to recede. He let out a sigh of relief. 'Zaccheus won't have to worry about where heesh nesh meal ish coming from,' he said.

Nathaniel nodded again. For a moment he looked defeated. Then he raised his head with pride. 'Tell me one thing, Rev'end. Will my boy make a good preacher?'

Reverend Flatts drained his jar and set it down with a bang. He scraped it forwards, towards Nathaniel. 'More.'

'You're sure?' Nathaniel asked with a wry grin.

'I'm shore.' Reverend Flatts nodded emphatically. He watched his jar closely as Nathaniel filled it. Then he

211

ed it towards him, spilling half of it on the table. 'I
n't ansher whether Zaccheush'll make a good
reacher, Mr Howe. Thash up . . .' Reverend Flatts
ourped noisily again. ". . . up to Zaccheush.'

'All right,' Nathaniel said. 'You got him, Rev'end. You
and your Lord. My son's yours.'

The words barely registered. Reverend Flatts jumped
to his feet, knocking his chair over backwards in the
process, and lunged desperately to the door. As he
stumbled outside, he grabbed hold of the porch post
with both hands and took a series of deep breaths. But
it was too late. He threw up all over himself. Then his
eyes rolled backwards in their sockets, the pupils seem-
ing to disappear under his eyelids until only the whites
showed. He fell heavily, unaware that Nathaniel had
come up behind him.

Nathaniel caught the Reverend and lowered him
gently to the porch boards. He shook his head and
chuckled to himself. Reverend Flatts had done passed
out.

The Reverend never did get to eat the chicken, but six
months later, Zaccheus was on a train headed for
Centre Hall College in Tigerville, Virginia.

8

'Zaccheus Howe?'

Zaccheus spun around and found himself face to face
with a breathless, pock-marked freshman. 'Yes?'

'Reverend Astin wants to see you,' the freshman whispered in a hushed, reverential voice.

'Thank you,' Zaccheus said, but his thanks were
obviously lost; the freshman's fleet feet were already

carrying him off on another important errand across the campus.

Zaccheus frowned as he hurried towards the imposing administration building. He wondered what could have occasioned the president of the college wanting to see him. In the two years since he had arrived at the Centre Hall College in Tigerville, he had only caught occasional glimpses of the imposing, leonine Reverend Astin. True, he heard the prominent minister's sermons in the campus chapel every other Sunday (on alternating Sundays the much-revered Reverend travelled to Abingdon or Richmond, where he delivered sermons in large churches to which hundreds flocked just to hear him, making him one of the country's most famous orators; and he had twice watched the senior class graduation ceremonies on the Great Lawn, listening to Reverend Astin's inspiring words of wisdom and admonishment before sending a flock of newly ordained ministers out into a sinful world. But in two years, Zaccheus had yet to meet the man personally.

Nervously Zaccheus licked the palm of his hand and patted the back of his head to ensure that his stray cowlick was smoothed down. Then he stopped, laid down his books and straightened his tie. He, Zaccheus Howe, was finally going to meet Reverend Astin, one of Methodism's – indeed, America's – foremost ministers. And once again, he wondered what could have prompted such an important summons.

He made a shortcut across the rolling campus lawns to the administration building, a splendid, ivy-clad, mock-Tudor castle whose steeply sloping, blue slate roofs bristled with chimneys and dormers. As usual, Zaccheus couldn't help but admire the splendid surroundings. It was a far, far cry from the world of Muddy Lake, Missouri.

The campus was set in an undulating park of manicured lawns shaded by venerable oak trees and a smattering of delicate magnolias, dogwoods, and azaleas, which were now in full bloom. The sloping land gave the campus much of its character and beauty, since no matter where you stood, some of the buildings always seemed half-hidden behind hills, as if they were huge stone ships viewed from in front of rolling green swells.

With one exception, the six Tudor-style buildings which comprised the campus were solid and clad in ivy, with arched Gothic windows and thick leaded glass. The exception stood in the exact centre of the college, surrounded by the other buildings. It was the chapel, and it crouched there amidst the Kelly-green lawn, its proportions classic and graceful, its red brick walls rising majestically to scrape the fleeting clouds of the heavens.

Zaccheus skirted a gardener cutting grass with a sickle. For an instant, he stopped to watch the gleaming blade slicing through the green. It had been a little more than two years since he himself had wielded such a tool, and it served as a potent reminder. He couldn't help but marvel, momentarily, at how events had taken a turn. Inhaling the sweet perfume of the grass, he smiled and wondered if that fresh, earthy smell would ever fail to move him. Probably not, he thought. It was ingrained in his bones.

He had loitered far too long. Now he hurried up the sweeping stone steps and took another deep breath outside the big double doors of the administration building – this breath was for courage – and shifted the books he carried under his arm. He pulled one of the doors open. It was heavy and creaked noisily.

Inside the hall, it was dark and chilly. If the chapel was the spiritual symbol of the college which endowed it with purpose and importance, then it was the administration building which was the pragmatic nucleus of the campus.

As such, it had a utilitarian air about it, but the church's influence was still apparent, Zaccheus noticed

214

as he crossed the dim hallway to a refectory table, a simple cross resting in its centre. Behind the table, to either side of the cross, sat two young sophomores, their faces pink and scrubbed and wholesome.

Zaccheus stepped forwards and cleared his throat. 'I'm here to see Reverend Astin,' he said nervously.

The nearest student looked up at him. 'And you are . . .'

'Zaccheus Howe.'

The young man consulted a ledger; then he glanced at his partner. 'Please hold the fort, Brother Charles.'

'Certainly, Brother Arthur,' the other student replied, 'and may the Lord be with you.'

'And with you, Brother Charles.' Brother Arthur got to his feet and came around from behind the table. 'Follow me, please, Brother Zaccheus,' he said pleasantly. 'You may leave your books here.'

Zaccheus put them down on the table and turned towards a staircase curving up to the second floor. Automatically, he began to cross towards it.

'Brother Zaccheus.'

He stopped and turned around. The sophomore was heading in the opposite direction, towards another staircase.

'It's this way.'

Zaccheus followed him down a long corridor. Tall doors lined both walls. Then the corridor narrowed. At the end of it, his guide opened a small door. Zaccheus could see a flight of narrow stone steps spiralling down to what was surely the cellar. He looked questioningly at Brother Arthur.

'Reverend Astin is a great believer in humility,' Brother Arthur explained virtuously. 'He lives what he preaches. His quarters are a small cell in the cellar.'

'Oh.'

Brother Arthur ducked through the doorway and

Zaccheus did likewise, and they descended the narrow spiral stairs, their heels echoing on the stone.

The cellar was dark and dank and moist with mildew. It was lit at intervals by low wattage, bare electric light bulbs. At the end of the long maze of corridors, the guide stopped and knocked at a door.

'Yes?' The voice which filtered through was a deep baritone, rich and resonant.

Brother Arthur pulled open the door. 'Brother Zaccheus is here to see you, Reverend Astin.'

'Good. Send him in.'

Brother Arthur stepped aside to let Zaccheus by. Zaccheus glanced at him and then slipped past him into the room. He heard the door close softly behind him. Slowly, he turned around.

The room was indeed a cell, much plainer even than the students' dormitories. Stone-walled and stone-floored, it was no larger than eight by twelve feet. Placed diagonally across one end was a small desk; along one wall was a neatly made narrow cot with a well-worn Bible resting on the pillow. Except for a small painting of Jesus in three-quarter profile, there was no other decoration. No carpet. No curtains at the single tiny window near the ceiling which let a dim shaft of light into the Spartan quarters.

Reverend Astin was seated behind the desk, a sheet of paper and an envelope in front of him. He looked up.

The Reverend Thomas Astin looked twice as imposing in that small, simple room as he did in the pulpit of the chapel. But no matter how squalid or splendid the surroundings, he dominated everything around him. He was without doubt the most handsome man Zaccheus had ever seen.

He was tall and erect and slender, and held himself with inborn dignity. But it was his face, framed by that leonine head of hair, which arrested. His eyes were of the purest heavenly blue, yet they were not a cold blue, but were warm and sincere. His aquiline nose and clean-shaven face with its strong, square-boned jaw gave him a look of power.

Yet warmth and goodwill flowed from this man and seemed to reach Zaccheus in waves, enveloping him, casting their spell, putting him instantly at ease.

The feeling intensified when Reverend Astin rose to his feet and held out his hand to shake Zaccheus'. His grip was firm but friendly and sincere, the gesture, elegant and at once eloquent.

'Brother Zaccheus. Please sit down.' Reverend Astin motioned fluidly to the bed. Once Zaccheus was seated there, the Reverend slowly sat back down behind his desk. For a long moment they looked at each other, one digesting the other. 'So we finally meet, Brother Zaccheus,' Reverend Astin said at last. 'Your teachers speak highly of you. In the two years since you have come here, you have consistently been at the head of your classes. It seems a pity that we cannot meet under anything but the most happy circumstances.'

Zaccheus frowned. He did not know what the Reverend meant by that, or how to respond, so he remained prudently silent.

Reverend Astin folded his hands elegantly and seemed to study his cuticles. 'I have received a sad Western Union telegram,' he said slowly. He looked suddenly weary and soulful; his rich voice dropped an octave, and his eyes moistened. Even his shoulders seemed to slump. Then he looked up again and met Zaccheus' gaze. 'I never enjoy being the bearer of sad tidings, even though that, too, is part of my job.'

Zaccheus stiffened. 'Has something happened?' he whispered. A terrible sense of foreboding overcame him. 'At home?'

Reverend Astin nodded. 'It's your mother.'

Zaccheus felt a chill. 'Is she . . .' He couldn't get himself to say the word.

Reverend Astin shook his head. 'No, she's alive,' he said soothingly. 'But she is apparently very ill.'

Zaccheus slumped back, his emotions mixed. On the one hand, he was flooded with relief; on the other, he felt frightened and helpless. When he spoke, his voice trembled. 'How . . . bad is it?'

'Not good, it seems, otherwise Reverend . . .' Reverend Astin quickly consulted the telegram before him. '. . . Reverend Flatts . . . would not have requested your return home. It is his opinion that you should leave immediately.'

Zaccheus swallowed. His throat felt parched. 'But I –'

'Your examinations can be delayed.' Reverend Astin cupped his hand and coughed delicately. 'I realize you're not well-to-do, so I've already made arrangements for your travel. Here are railroad tickets.' He pushed an envelope across the desk. 'Also, you will find five dollars inside. For incidentals.'

Zaccheus felt something which he had never quite felt before – a strange, peaceful glow of love seemed to settle over him. A lump came up in his throat.

'We will all be saying prayers for your mother,' Reverend Astin promised gently. 'Now go and pack, Brother Zaccheus, and honour thy mother.' He scraped back his chair and rose, signalling that their meeting was over.

Zaccheus took his cue. Unsteadily he got to his feet and reached for the Reverend's proffered hand. He held it tightly. 'Thank you, Reverend Astin,' he said gratefully. 'You're . . . very kind. I-I don't know how I can ever repay you.'

Reverend Astin patted Zaccheus' hand and smiled. 'Mothers are very precious, Brother Zaccheus. You just take care of her.'

'I will,' Zaccheus promised him fervently.

218

'You will find a carriage waiting in front of the dormitory.' Reverend Astin released Zaccheus' hand and consulted his pocket watch. 'If you hurry, you can still catch the train. You'll have to change in St Louis.'

The tears pushed their way out of the corners of Zaccheus' eyes.

'Whatever happens,' Reverend Astin said slowly, 'is the will of God. Rest assured that He will be there with you. He will look after you and your mother. We are all His children.'

Zaccheus stared at him.

'God go with you,' Reverend Astin said.

And Zaccheus was gone.

9

In St Louis, he had time to kill between trains. The station was near the centre of town and, although he was ravenous with hunger, he decided it was a good opportunity to explore the city. Better that than eat. Food cost money, but sightseeing was cheap. He felt the five, crisp one-dollar bills in his pocket. For him, five dollars represented a fortune, but still, it was all the money he owned. Was that what his life was worth? he wondered. Five dollars?

He ignored the rumblings in his stomach and lugged his battered cardboard suitcase outside. He looked up and frowned. The sky was a uniform battleship grey and it was drizzling steadily. With a sigh, he set down his suitcase and turned up his collar. A little rain was not enough to deter him. Not after all those years on the farm. Whistling softly to himself, he picked up the suitcase and began to walk.

He didn't get far.

Without warning the drizzle gave way to thick, heavy

raindrops. Lightning flashed yellow in the sky, followed by reverberating peals of thunder. A moment later, a solid silver sheet of water came pouring down. He took refuge in the doorway of a shop.

Set into each side of the recessed doorway was a small glass window lit from somewhere above. He stared, mesmerized, first at one narrow window, then the other. On his left, behind the thick glass, was an elongated, deep-blue velvet neck draped with a strand of gleaming pink pearls. On his right, an identical velvet neck displayed a fine gold chain from which hung a filigreed charm. The centre of the charm was a dried purple pansy with a lemon-yellow centre pressed between two rounds of glass.

His eyes misted over as he remembered the locket his mother had given Reverend Flatts so long ago in exchange for a year's schooling. He knew how much she'd prized that locket, that it had been a treasured keepsake and the only pretty thing she had ever owned. Even though she had never worn it, his mother had sometimes taken the locket out, carefully unwrapping it from its nest of faded pink tissue simply to admire it. A slight smile would play on her usually tight lips, and her eyes would suddenly seem far away, as it transported her somewhere into the past.

Of course, the pressed pansy would hold no memories for her, but he could imagine how she would treasure it. Especially if . . . He took a deep breath. He'd never given his mother a beautiful gift. Ever.

And in his pocket he had five dollars.

On an impulse, he picked up his suitcase and turned to face the door behind him. It was made of gleaming brass, its glass rectangle screened with a pink, gathered curtain. Gold script letters, outlined in black, read BENSEY'S JEWELLERS.

The expensive sheen of brass and the elegant script letters intimidated him, and a keen instinct told him that he was out of his element. He had never before set foot in a shop that sold anything but the barest necessities. But before he could change his mind, he grasped the doorknob and turned it swiftly.

The door opened smoothly, soundlessly. Somewhere in the back of the shop, soft chimes announced his arrival. A current of air coming in from outside stirred something else: he heard a soft, musical tinkling above him.

He leaned his head back. Directly above him, suspended from the high, ornamental plaster ceiling was an enormous, cut-glass chandelier, its prisms spraying myriads of rainbows in all directions. For a moment, he stared open-mouthed at it. Never in his life had he seen anything quite so beautiful.

He closed the door softly behind him. Then slowly, he set down his suitcase, his eyes wide and curious. The carpet underfoot was plush maroon, a soft, muffling sea of velvet. From somewhere wafted the elusively sweet, feminine fragrance of lilies-of-the-valley. He sniffed appreciatively and tried to locate its source, his eyes flicking around the shop.

He drew another deep breath as the luxurious surroundings sank in, boggling his mind. The entire shop was sheathed in pale-green watered silk, and lining all four walls were mahogany-framed, clear-glass counters filled with the deep, rich glow of tier after tier of sparkling, dazzling jewels. He had no idea of their value, but even to his untrained eye it was surely a king's ransom in gold and silver and gems.

His eyes roved on and his initial awe gave way to a heavy, sinking feeling. There was no one in the shop.

Sighing softly to himself, he bent down to retrieve his suitcase and leave.

'May I be of help?' The musical, cultured voice seemed to float from nowhere.

Startled, he spun around. As he watched, two long,

221

spiderlike hands parted a pale-green curtain behind one of the counters.

The woman was tall and patrician. Her gleaming, jet-black hair was pulled back into a tapering braid which was tightly coiled into a nautilus-shaped bun. She was dressed entirely in black, but the gold-and-ivory cameo brooch at her throat softened her otherwise funereal appearance and gave her an elegance he had never known anyone to possess. He felt her sharp grey eyes regarding him shrewdly.

Zaccheus gestured nervously towards the display window at one side of the door. 'That charm?' He cleared his throat. 'The one in the little window? How much does it cost?'

The woman cocked her thin eyebrows. Her appraisal of him took no longer than a split second. Bensey's Jewellers was St Louis' purveyor to the carriage trade; the young man standing before her had obviously stumbled in here by mistake. That happened on occasion, and over the years she had perfected her routine of tactfully showing those who did not belong here to the door. She did it so proficiently that those who were shown out never really knew quite what had happened. She was prepared to dispense with Zaccheus in just this manner when something about him — something so vulnerable, so painfully awkward, but deadly earnest — changed her mind. Just this once, she decided, she would be genuinely helpful. She smiled thinly, clasping her elongated hands in front of her. 'The pressed pansy charm?'

Zaccheus nodded wordlessly.

The woman took a key ring out of her pocket, strode over to the built-in display case, and unlocked it. She reached inside and lifted out the gold chain and held it looped between two extended fingers, the pansy charm dangling at the end. 'It's beautiful, isn't it?' She lowered her voice confidentially. 'It's imported. Eighteen gold and Venetian glass.'

Zaccheus looked at her. 'Is that good?'

'Good?' The woman laughed softly. 'Heavens! Eig een carat is as pure as you can wear. Anything purer too malleable. It would bend or break.'

'How much is it?' Zaccheus managed to whisper. He reached out, gingerly touching the fragile charm with the tips of his fingers. The glass felt glossy and cool.

'Ten dollars.'

'Oh.' Zaccheus' face fell and he let go of the charm. 'It's . . . I'm sorry . . . it's too much.' He turned away.

The woman nodded. 'If you are interested, we also carry them in sterling silver. For four dollars.'

Zaccheus perked up. 'Could I see one?'

'Of course.' The woman replaced the chain on the velvet neck, closed the display case, and locked it. Then she selected another key from her ring. 'I'll be just a moment.' She went back behind a counter, parted the curtains, and disappeared again. Through a crack between the curtains, he could see her bending down in front of a big iron safe.

Zaccheus leaned over the counter to wait. Placing his elbows on it, he stared down. Displayed beneath the thick glass top were gold rings with tiny rubies, sapphires, and diamonds. He peered closer, trying to make out the miniscule price tags tied to them. The cheapest ring he saw was forty dollars.

He let out a soft, impressed whistle. And then he saw something that really made him blink. One ring, a diamond surrounded by ruby baguettes, had a label that read . . . could it be? Two thousand dollars? Was it possible? He had no idea that jewellery could be that expensive.

'Here we are.' The woman was back with a tiny, purple velvet box. She set it down in front of Zaccheus and lifted the lid.

charm was identical to the one in the window.
only difference was the chain and filigree casing.
y were sterling silver, not gold.

Zaccheus dug into his pocket and came up with four
amp one-dollar bills. He parted with them easily. So
ne wouldn't eat until the next day. So what. Hunger was
nothing new to him. And besides, the pansy charm was
far more important than a few meals.

Reverend Flatts frowned at his pocket watch and then
clicked the brass cover shut. He stared down the length
of the platform. 'The train's late,' he said.

Phoebe did not answer. She remained seated on the
bench, her expression taut and pained. She hadn't
wanted to come along to meet Zaccheus' train, but when
the telegram from the college came with the time of his
scheduled arrival, her uncle had insisted she be there.
'It's a bad time for Zaccheus, his mother having taken
so ill. He'll need to be among friends, Phoebe. Besides,
it's quite a long drive from the station out to the Howe
farm. I'm sure he'll be grateful for the company.'

It had been impossible to argue.

Phoebe clutched her shawl tighter around her shoulders and hunched forwards, her chin resting on her
clenched fist. The sun had already gone down, and a
sliver of moon floated like a white gondola in the twi-
light sky. It was turning decidedly chilly. Besides her
and her uncle, only three other people were waiting on
the train. She glanced towards them. A young man was
standing with his arm coiled around his wife, who was
holding their baby.

Phoebe flinched and quickly turned away. Her head
had been pounding all day, but now, seeing the baby,
she felt an acid pain gnawing into the pit of her stomach.
She took a series of deep breaths, but the pain in her
stomach refused to go away and her head continued to

224

throb, had hardly ceased to for more than tw
now.

She squeezed her eyes shut. *Why did I let it happe*
hissed soundlessly to herself.

She had asked herself that same tormenting quest
over and over despite the fact that she knew the answ
perfectly well — *Because Chester Savage is so irresistibly hand
some, so irresistibly rich, and so very, very virile. Because he is
everything and anything a woman could possibly want, all
rolled up into one stunning package*.

She had discovered, in fact, that there was only one
thing lacking in Chester Savage. Decency.

Phoebe sighed to herself.

It had begun so innocently on a fine, autumn afternoon. The trees had been a romantic cornucopia of
golds and rusts, and the breezes had been caressing with
summer's afterglow. Birds had swooped and chirped,
bees had hovered over late blooms, and butterflies had
fluttered quietly across the fields. Strange, how time
seemed to have come to a stop that afternoon.

How she could still conjure it up without consciously
meaning to! How the sweetest song of a bird or the buzz
of a bee could transport her straight back to that fateful
afternoon when it had begun. That afternoon which
had seemed so very perfect.

That afternoon which had been the beginning of the
end.

It had been the perfect day for a picnic. She had
packed a lunch, placed it in the straw basket between the
handlebars of her bicycle, and then was off, pedalling
through Muddy Lake and down the dusty country road,
a cool breeze against her face. She had not even planned
to ride far, and had no destination. But the afternoon
had been so enticing, so superbly entrancing, that she
had ridden nearly six miles before she pulled over to
the side of the road and pushed the bicycle to the stream
which flowed smoothly along the edge of the wheat

...e sat down to rest and eat lunch, and had then
...off.

...had felt something tickling her nose. She
...hed it and continued sleeping, but the fly, attracted
...he remains of the picnic, buzzed angrily around her.
...he opened one eye and waved it lazily away. Then she
sat up straight. She didn't know how long she had been
asleep, but the sun was already beginning to weaken.
Soon it would set. She rubbed the sleep out of her eyes
and slowly turned her head around. She had a distinct,
queer prickling feeling – the feeling that she was being
watched.

There was a copse of old trees on the other side of
the road, no more than ten yards behind her. And he
was standing there, one hand holding the rein of a
beautiful grey gelding, the other on his hip, one shiny
boot resting on a felled tree. She had never seen him
before, but his ruggedly handsome face, thick black
hair, and trim physique – not to mention the boldness
of his stare – both appealed to her and repelled her in
a way no man ever had before. She glared at him, but
he remained standing there, a cocky smile on his lips.

Quickly, she gathered up her things and hopped
indignantly to her feet. By the time she stuffed the picnic leftovers into the handlebar basket and pushed the
bicycle to the road, he and the horse had moved.

They stood squarely in the middle of the single-lane
road, blocking her way.

'Do you mind?' she asked icily.

He grinned, his teeth white and strong, his eyes filled
with masculine sureness. 'A lady would say "please",' he
reminded her in a soft, cultured voice.

Her face reddened. 'And a gentleman would take it
for granted that a lady doesn't need to be taught her
manners.' She tossed her head. 'Now will you *please* let
me pass?'

He remained frozen, his horse shifting its weight

impatiently from one leg to another. 'Ah, so you're strong spirited as well as no lady.'

'How long have you been spying on me?'

He chuckled. 'Oh, about an hour, give or take a few minutes.'

'Get out of my way!' she said angrily. She made a pretence of pushing the bicycle into him, but the ploy did not work. He neither batted an eyelash nor moved an inch.

'You've been trespassing,' he said quietly.

She glared at him, her eyes glowering. 'If I'm trespassing, then so are you.'

His eyes flashed with amusement and he waved a languid hand all around. 'That stream. Those fields. In case you didn't know it, the properties on both sides of the road are part of the Savage holdings.'

'And so is the flour mill.' With her chin she gestured to the complex of buildings far across the fields; then she eyed him closely. 'So what? Who are you to complain?' It was her turn to be amused.

'I'm Chester Savage,' he grinned.

She stood there, frozen with embarrassment, unable to speak. It was a moment before she finally found her voice. 'Well, I'm sorry to have trespassed,' she said with testy defiance. 'Now are you satisfied?' She leered at him and put her right foot on the pedal of her bicycle.

He led his gelding aside to let her pass, but in her nervousness she got off to too slow a start. The bicycle, with her on it, toppled over with a clatter.

She let out a cry. 'Now look what you made me do!' she wailed accusingly, more hurt by her loss of poise than any real physical damage suffered.

'Here, let me help you.' He let go of the horse and bent down, lifting the bicycle off her. He held out a hand to help her up.

For a moment she stared up at him. Almost reluctantly, she extended her arm.

With one swift movement he pulled her to her feet and she stumbled awkwardly against him. Despite herself, her heart thumped wildly.

'Are you hurt?' He seemed genuinely concerned.

She pushed herself away from him and bent over to brush off her skirt with the back of one hand, strangely disturbed that he was still holding on to her arm. She was at once aware of dark, smouldering eyes burning with intensity. She felt curiously weak, and the beating of her heart seemed to grow louder and louder, until it reached a thundering crescendo.

That was how it started. The initial meeting. The mutual attraction. The passion. The fire. The love on her side and the love-making on his.

The deceit.

Phoebe Flatts had always harboured a weak spot in her heart for the Brontë sisters and Jane Austin. The lonely moors, the empty countryside, the wind whistling through the tors or whipping through tall meadow grass while an attractive, tall, dark, brooding man hiding some terrible secret swept an innocent but strong-willed heroine off her feet . . . that was what she spent her idle hours reading and rereading and dreaming about. In the stories, the hero was always rich and strong and powerful, and romance was fraught with danger, but in the end, true love would triumph. And the heroine, no matter how spirited, was ripe for the picking.

As was she.

The Savages were one of the richest, most powerful and influential families around, and Chester Savage was an only son. Heir to thousands of acres of prime farmland, a flour mill, and grain storage facilities, he was a dream come true. Everything about him fit Phoebe's romantic notions to a tee.

They met again and again. She lied to the Flattses, cunningly contriving one excuse after another for her absences while she wove a web of charm to trap Chester Savage.

Only, she never realized that *he* was the spider and *she* was the fly. It never occurred to her that she could be caught up in the wrong plot. That the Brontë romance she imagined their affair to be could turn into one of those cheap, sordid little novels neither ladies nor true gentlemen would be caught dead reading.

They rendezvoused at discreet places where no one would see them. In a clearing in the woods while the weather held. In a deserted shed after the first frost set in.

At first, she tried to resist temptation, but her resistance was weak, and her romantic naïveté held sway. She had visions of Chester Savage pulling up in front of the Flatts home, hat in hand. Wooing her. Begging Reverend Flatts for her hand in marriage.

That was the way it was supposed to happen.

Instead, the secret rendezvous continued. She cajoled Reverend Flatts into buying her a mare, and horseback riding proved the perfect cover. She could come and go as she liked, no questions asked.

The trysts, for the time being, at least, were enough. Phoebe would have done anything to feel Chester Savage's powerful arms around her, his moist kisses on her lips.

One thing led to another.

It was not long before the kisses progressed to more serious matters. His lips sought not her lips, but her breasts. Then his hands sought her smooth, round buttocks and the mound between her thighs. Ultimately, of course, he had mounted her, entered her, and ridden her to peaks of ecstasy she had never quite imagined could exist.

She had been afraid, but it had felt so good. Lovemaking became a drug like no other. She felt compelled to be used by Chester Savage, to feel him inside her, to

mp her naked legs around his naked buttocks. She
arched her soul and kept telling herself that something which felt so good . . . which was so beautiful . . .
simply couldn't be wrong. She decided that Aunt Arabella had once lied to her: sleeping with a man did not
hurt at all. On the contrary. What it did do was fill her
with the most exquisite ecstasy she had ever known to
exist, and she lived and breathed solely for those heady
moments. She thrived on the passion. Her face glowed
radiantly at all times; she had come alive as she had
never come alive before.

Arabella noticed the change in her and told Reverend
Flatts: 'I'm so glad Phoebe has finally got over her
parents' death, the poor thing. I was worried about her,
she was so listless. The fresh air is doing her a world of
good. I'm so glad you bought her that horse.'

Phoebe, overhearing her aunt, had smiled to herself.
If Aunt Arabella only knew! she thought. But *she* knew
better than to tell her. Still, she wished she had a friend
to confide in, to share her exhilarating, secret life with.
But there was no one. She had made no friends. Since
coming here, she had remained aloof from everyone
except Chester Savage.

Their trysts continued like clockwork. And then, suddenly, Chester missed one of their prearranged meetings. For three panic-stricken days Phoebe returned to
their place of rendezvous. For two days he did not show
up. She waited outside the shed for hours, pacing hysterically, her ears searching the wind for the sound of
his horse, her mind racing over the terrible things which
might have happened to him. She imagined accidents.
Illnesses. Even death.

On the third day, he was there, waiting for her.

She was so flooded with relief that she ran into his
arms and burst into tears. And he held her close, pep-
pering her with kisses, whispering the sweet words she
needed so desperately to hear. She summoned up her

courage to speak of marriage, but his hungry lips wei
always on hers; then they coupled again and again
There was simply no time for talk. Not after so many
days apart.

Somehow, the love-making seemed enough. He was
back. She had him wrapped around her in more ways
than one. He *needed* her. Obviously, no one else could
satisfy him. He was hers.

Or so she thought.

Over the next few months he missed a few more of
their meetings, but his explanations were always smooth
and soothing and sounded sincere enough. Besides, she
wasn't about to doubt him. He was her lover and she
needed to believe that whatever he told her was the
truth. She *had* to believe that, for if she didn't . . .

. . . If she didn't, then they had no basis for an endur-
ing relationship.

And then she missed her period. At first she didn't
give it a second thought. She simply ignored it.

Then she missed another.

Finally, she had no choice but to tell him that she was
pregnant.

Without replying, he pulled her towards him and
they made love more fiercely than ever before. They
coupled like savages, his child she was carrying a bond
between them. Now she knew that she had him – that
he would finally come to the Flattses' house and beg for
her hand. He had no choice. He was a gentleman.

She floated; she soared. 'Phoebe Savage', she
repeated to herself over and over, falling in love with
the sound of it more and more. 'Phoebe Savage. Mrs
Chester Savage.' *The young, powerful, exceedingly beautiful
Mrs Chester Savage.*

She was at the top of the world.

She was not ready for the crash.

He did not see her again. *Ever.*

Desperate, she saddled her horse and rode out to the

vage estate, a sprawling complex of buildings at the edge of the flour mill. When she got to the majestic, pillared house, the butler told her that Mr Savage was out of town on business. 'Would you like to speak to the missus, ma'am?' he asked.

She had nodded, expecting his mother. But the cool, haughty young beauty was obviously not the woman who had borne him.

'I'm Phoebe Flatts,' Phoebe said softly. 'I've come to see your brother.'

The woman laughed softly. 'So you're the one!' she said with a hint of laughter in her voice as her amber eyes appraised Phoebe thoughtfully.

'Pardon me?' Phoebe asked in confusion. She expected his sister to put her arms around her, perhaps kiss her on the cheek. But no matter what the reception, she would try her best to make friends with her.

'You're here about Chester, aren't you?' the woman asked.

Phoebe smiled and nodded. 'Yes. Will he be back soon?'

'I certainly hope so,' the woman said. 'But of course, I have a vested interest in him. You see, he's not my brother. He's my husband.' Seeing Phoebe freeze, she added: 'Don't you read the papers? We were married only last week.'

Phoebe took a step backwards as icy chills rippled through her. *This can't be true!* she thought. *This can't be happening to me! This is a nightmare. I'll awaken at any moment —*

'In a way, I have a lot to thank you for,' the new Mrs Chester Savage said saccharinely. 'After all, you've been a great help to me, you know. What Chester couldn't have with me, he had with you. But take my advice.' She smiled conspiratorially and lowered her voice. 'From one woman to another, next time, *don't put out.* I mean,

men love to be with women who do, but they nev
marry them.'

And she slammed the door with such force that Pho
ebe felt the force of the wind.

'Noooo!' she wailed shrilly, her voice warbling with
pain. She took a faltering step backwards, her hands
covering her ears. '*Noooo*! It can't be true!'

Then she turned and fled the stifling estate with its
majestic house, the house she would have given her
eyeteeth to live in as her own. The house which, she had
been certain, would be hers. Which now belonged to
someone else.

Someone who had played a different game for the
very same man. Someone who had won while she had
lost.

Phoebe never remembered how she managed to get
home. The ride was a blur. Nothing registered in her
consciousness. Nothing but the terrible pain and confusion which filled her with knife-like stabs. In a split
second, her beautiful, controlled world had disinte-
grated, and she wanted to die. Yet, despite her pain, one
thought instinctively rose to the surface of her tortured
mind.

No matter what happened, no one must ever know.

She stumbled through the successive days and weeks
in a daze. Somehow, the masks she pulled down over
her face and heart must have been convincing. No one
seemed to suspect that anything was wrong. No one
seemed aware of her pain.

The days were sheer torture. Only the nights were
soothing, when her subconscious would conjure up
dreams of Chester Savage. When his warm dream
lover's arms would once again be around her, bringing
her exquisite love and pleasure. Yes, the nights were
bearable . . . but they were far too short.

Phoebe was realistic enough to know that she would
have to do something, and soon. There was the child

233

within her, growing more each day. But which way to turn? She didn't know how to have a baby, or how to get rid of it.

She had heard of miscarriages, and considered falling off her horse. But when the doctor examined her . . . no, that was no good, either. The doctor would surely discover what was wrong. Worse, she was liable to hurt herself badly — not that she cared, anymore — but the prospect of being crippled, or suffering broken bones, with the baby perhaps still safe inside her, was an idea she did not relish.

She receded into her books. Sang in the choir. Went through the ordinary motions of daily life. The glow of lust and ecstasy, which had lit her from within was gone now, replaced by a countenance of shame.

Soon, the baby would show.

She cringed, the vice around her heart tightening ever more and more. She knew what would happen when her belly swelled. She would be jeered and ridiculed, would become an outcast. She had brought shame and degradation upon a house which must remain above suspicion.

But still, her feeling that something had to work out persisted. There *had* to be a solution.

Now, sitting at the railroad station, waiting for Zaccheus, she raised her head slowly. In the distance, she could hear the long, drawn-out whistle of the approaching train.

It was the sound of salvation.

Why hadn't she thought of it before? There *was* a solution after all.

He was arriving on the train.

10

The first thought which crossed his mind was: *She's grown even more beautiful.*

The first thought which crossed her mind was: *He's not as bad as I remember. Rumpled, perhaps, by the journey, but neat and clean. Presentable. Rather attractive, in fact. No, he's not at all as bad as I thought. He's no Chester Savage, but I could do a lot worse.*

Phoebe flashed Zaccheus her most dazzling smile and forced herself to take his arm and squeeze it affectionately. Unwittingly, she had a vision of squeezing Chester's arm, but instantly blotted out that thought. She might as well face the facts. Chester Savage was gone from her life. She must forget him.

Reverend Flatts drove and they sat side by side in the back of the buggy. Phoebe unfolded the lap robe and pulled it over their knees, her clever fingers brushing his legs. The buggy rattled, swaying and bumping across the rutted road into the night, and they were repeatedly jostled against one another.

Phoebe thought: *No, he's no Chester Savage. But, if everything goes according to plan, I'm in the clear. He'll think the baby is his.*

She said softly, 'I've missed you. I waited a long time to see you.'

Zaccheus turned towards her, his eyes glowing in the light of the white country moon. 'You have?' He sounded pleased.

She did not meet his gaze. 'I have.'

He didn't speak.

'It's so quiet here,' she said with a sigh. 'Nothing exciting ever happens.' She laughed quietly. 'Of course, you know that.' She paused, hating having to show her hand by asking the question, but it was imperative that she knew just where she stood. 'Did you make any . . . friends . . . at college?'

'A few.' He swallowed nervously, feeling simultaneously thrilled, yet peculiarly discomforted, by her closeness.

A note of caution crept into her voice. 'Were they all . . . ministerial students?'

'Yes.'

No hesitancy there, she thought with satisfaction. *So far, so good.* Her voice relaxed. 'Now that you're back, I hope we can see quite a bit of each other. That is, if I'm not intruding on someone else's . . .' She shrugged delicately. 'You know. Territory.' Her eyes glowed at him in the dark.

'No, no, you're not,' he said positively. 'Do you want to see me? I mean, *really* want to?'

'Of course I do!' She smiled, lowered her voice, and hooked one arm through his. 'Remember the way you used to follow me around while you were working outside the house? Always sneaking little sideways glances at me? I'll never forget that. As soon as I'd turn a corner, sure enough, there you were – clipping or pruning right behind me! I used to feel you were my shadow.' Her laughter tinkled in the night. 'You always seemed to be lurking around me.'

'I'm sorry. Did I . . . annoy you?'

'Hmmmm. Anyway, times change, and so do emotions.' She summoned up all the warmest sincerity she could muster. 'I found I missed you. And now you're finally back!' She disengaged her arm from his, clapped her delicate hands together, and held her index fingers, as if in prayer, poised at her lips. She looked at him expectantly. 'Did you bring me a present?'

'A present?'

'You know . . .' She waved one hand deprecatingly. '. . . A little something from college.' She swallowed distastefully, despising herself for what she was about to say. She knew she had no choice but to spell out the feelings she pretended to have towards him. Had to make them crystal clear. He mustn't, under any circumstances, misunderstand her. Time was of the essence; there was none left for mistakes. "Don't young men usually bring . . . their lady friends a little something? You know. A souvenir?'

'Oh, I –' He stammered, suddenly embarrassed and felt his face heating up. 'Yes, I . . . I brought you something,' he managed.

'Oh! What?' She sat forward eagerly.

Reluctantly, he reached into his trouser pocket and touched the little velvet case with his fingers. It felt smooth and warm. For a moment, he gripped it fiercely. Inside it was the sterling chain and the Venetian pansy charm. He had bought it for his mother, not for Phoebe.

How stupid of me! he cursed himself silently. *I should have bought Phoebe something, too. Why didn't I think of it?*

But he knew the answer to that one. Even if he had, his finances wouldn't have permitted it.

He hesitated, his mind in sudden turmoil. He knew how much his mother would treasure the keepsake. Perhaps he should tell Phoebe that, in his hurried departure, he'd forgotten her present? Or had lost it? But the warm reception he'd received from her filled him with pride, massaging his male ego and cementing, once and for all, the feelings he'd always harboured for her. Somehow he had to reciprocate the warmth she was showing him. He had to please her. Prove he loved her.

Slowly, he pulled the velvet box out of his pocket. 'Here,' he said quietly, handing it over.

'Oooooh!' she squealed, seizing the case and hurriedly lifting the lid. She peered closely into the box, trying to make out the shape in the moonlight. 'A necklace!' she breathed. 'Oh, Zaccheus! You shouldn't have! I mean, I'm so glad you did, but nobody's ever given me anything like this before!' On an impulse, she leaned sideways and pecked his cheek.

Zaccheus smiled shyly and looked down into his lap. He'd always been attracted to Phoebe, but he'd never dared believe that *she* could feel the same way about him. Did she *really* like him that much?

Slowly, he lifted his hand and touched the spot on his cheek where she had kissed him. It seemed to tingle warmly.

It seemed too good to be true.

Half an hour later they pulled up to the Howe farm. The tiny cabin windows glowed with weak kerosene light.

Zaccheus hopped off the buggy, swung his suitcase to the ground, held Phoebe's proffered hand between both of his, and then waved to Reverend Flatts. He stood there, watching the buggy drive off until it was completely swallowed up in the night.

He glanced around and breathed deeply. The night wind was sweet and moist, exactly as he'd remembered it. Cicadas and crickets chirped shrilly; wind rustled in the trees. From somewhere in the distance, the breeze brought the sound of a barking dog wafting towards him.

Suddenly he felt all alone. Visitors to the farm had always been rare events, and he remembered how everyone always rushed out to meet anyone who arrived. But no one came out to meet him.

Slowly he made his way up to the cabin's rickety porch and set his suitcase down. He stood staring at the door's weathered wood before turning the knob. Then he pushed the door open and stepped into a room alive with flies. They swarmed over every surface.

The tattered curtain dividing the cabin was drawn aside, and Zaccheus could see his mother lying quietly on the bed. Her eyes were closed, and her chest rose and fell with every rasping, laboured breath she took. The noisy snores which punctuated them came from Nathaniel. Keeping vigil beside the bed, his father had fallen asleep in the rocker, his hands folded in his lap, his head tilted sideways against his shoulder.

Zaccheus slowly approached the bed and stared down at his mother, his heart tightening and contracting painfully. With a shock, he saw how much weight she'd lost. She'd always been on the gaunt side, but sturdily gaunt, and fit as a fiddle. Now, the skin of her face hung with a slack translucence, one of her arms, poking out from under the covers, seemed ghostly pale and skeletal, and her emaciated body was drenched with sweat. Even the covers were soaked through.

She seemed to sense his presence: her eyes flickered open. 'Zack,' she whispered listlessly, her lips barely moving. 'My son.' She lifted one arm slowly, holding a trembling hand towards him.

'Ma!' The word was a sob caught in his throat. Then he was kneeling beside her bed, holding her clammy hand tightly. He brought it up to his lips.

She turned her face sideways on the pillow to face him, her eyes deep and dull, yet moist with a peculiar shine. 'Let your Ma look at you!' Her lips curved into a faint smile. 'You've grown taller, son. My, but you're a fine-lookin' man, if I say so myself. Life at that college shore seems to be agreein' with you.'

'Ma? Soon's I heard how sick you were, I came hurryin'.' For some strange reason, for the first time in many years, he found himself slipping into the country dialect of his childhood. It was as if he wanted her to know he was hers, that he was no different from her, that they were equals.

'I know you hurried, son.' She sighed heavily and sat suddenly forwards, her body wracked with coughs. They came from deep within her and seemed to last forever. She turned away, felt for a rag, and spat noisily into it. Then she balled the rag up, sank back on the pillow, and smiled apologetically. 'It's the sickness,' she said weakly.

'How long you been sick, Ma?'

'Since right after you left,' she said quietly.

'And you didn't tell me? Why didn't you have Reverend Flatts write to me?'

'He wanted to, but I wouldn't let him. You're busy, son. You got your whole life ahead o' you. I didn't want to mess that up for you.'

Tears blurred his vision. 'I love you, Ma!' he said with quiet forcefulness.

'I know that, son,' she said gently. 'And I'm so glad that you're doin' well. I'm so proud of you. That's what kept me goin' all this time. Even ole Doc Fergueson sez so.' She paused. 'By all rights I shoulda been six feet under a long time ago.'

'Don't talk like that, Ma!' he whispered huskily. 'You're gonna live. I'm not gonna let you die!'

She smiled painfully. 'Sooner or later, we all gotta die, son.'

'Then I'll make sure it's later,' he vowed.

'Will you do somethin' fer me, son?'

'Sure, Ma. Anything you ask.'

'Jest hold me? Jest fer a minute?'

He nodded and drew close to kiss her.

She turned abruptly away. 'Don't kiss me!' she whispered.

He stared at her uncomprehendingly. 'Why not?'

'Doc Fergueson said so. No kissin'. An' don't touch my spit rag, neither.'

'Why? What have you got?'

'It's my lungs. I fergit the word fer it. Doc Fergueson sez it's from the cold winters and the bad heat here in this house.'

'Tuberculosis?' he asked softly.

'Yeah. That's it!' She smiled again at him, this time

radiantly. 'You shore are gittin' an education. My! Jest listen to you rattlin' off them big words!'

In his rocker, Nathaniel awoke with a start. He stared at Zaccheus, then pushed himself painfully to his feet. The illness was taking its toll on him, too. He looked thinner, older. Worn out.

Zaccheus forced himself to smile. He held up a hand in awkward greeting. 'Hi, Pa!'

'Hi, son.'

Then Nathaniel did something he had never done before in his life. He swiftly crossed to the bed, put his arms around his son, and held him tightly.

11

It was raining. One of those warm, steady country rains. Inside the cabin it sounded like a ceaseless scratching on the roof. When Zaccheus looked out the window, all he could see was steady silver rivulets of water running down from the eaves. He could hear the steady musical plops as water dripped heavily down into the buckets from leaks in the roof.

Nathaniel continued his listless vigil in the armchair. He seemed to lack interest in anything. The crops were suffering, but he didn't seem to care. The fences needed mending. He didn't care about that either. Even the tools were rusting. The only thing he did do was feed and water the animals so they wouldn't die. Nothing else seemed to matter much anymore.

Zaccheus boiled a large pot of water and kept busy for a while scrubbing the crusty dishes and pots and pans which had accumulated over the weeks. It was a thankless chore, but he was glad to be able to do something – anything – as long as he could keep occupied. This cabin was home, but he'd never realized just how

241

dark and cramped and confining it was. Occasionally, he would step out onto the porch, quickly closing the door behind him so as not to let in too much cool air, and then merely breathe deeply, inhaling the goodness of the fresh country air. Maybe it was a mistake, because every time he went back inside the cabin he was hit with the offensive, hot odour of stale air and illness.

After he finished the dishes, scrubbing the pots with steel wool until they shone with a lustre they hadn't seen since they were new, he began to tidy up the cabin.

'My!' Sue Ellen marvelled softly from the bed. 'Cain't fer the life o' me b'lieve how hard you're workin'.'

Zaccheus smiled thinly. 'I never minded work,' he said lightly, but the truth was, if he didn't keep busy he was certain he would go out of his mind. He had to keep himself occupied so he wouldn't dwell on his mother's illness. But despite all his pottering, his mind was consumed with it.

When the cabin was tidy, he stepped out onto the porch for a well-deserved break. For a while, all he did was watch the rain dribbling steadily, hypnotically, down over the edge of the porch eaves. A sudden change in wind slanted the rain sideways and a mist of cool needlepoints hit him. After the stifling heat inside the cabin, it felt good.

He sat down on the porch bench, his back to the cabin wall, savouring the freshness and cleansing effects of the rain. He stifled a yawn. Strange, how until now he hadn't realized how bone-weary he was. The last three days must be taking their toll. First there had been the long train trip during which he'd hardly managed to catch a few winks. And last night, he'd barely been able to shut his eyes. All night long, his mother had been having night sweats and coughing fits. It had been difficult to sleep through them.

Now, he found his eyelids drooping. His head slowly lolled forward into his chest, and he nodded off.

He awoke abruptly, suddenly aware that someone was standing over him. He lifted his head. "Doc!' he said with surprise.

Doc Fergueson was a short, stout man with tufts of unruly white hair and a pleasant, reddish face. 'Zaccheus,' he greeted gravely.

Zaccheus got to his feet and they shook hands. The doctor's grip was surprisingly firm and warm.

'Mind if I sit down and join you?' Doc Fergueson asked.

'No, not at all, Doc. Make yourself comfortable.'

They shared the bench, Doc Fergueson putting his black leather satchel carefully down beside him. 'You're worried, son,' he said.

Zaccheus nodded. 'Did you examine my mother yet?'

Doc Fergueson nodded. 'I arrived about half an hour ago.'

'And?'

'It doesn't look well, I'm afraid. Not well at all.'

Zaccheus felt the weight on his shoulders increasing. 'Is there anything we can do?'

'I'm afraid not,' Doc Fergueson sighed, staring out into the rain. 'All we can do is try and make it easier for her. If you had the money, I'd suggest a clinic back East in Asheville, North Carolina. Otherwise . . .' He shrugged helplessly. 'I'm afraid she'll die, and soon. In her condition, this cabin isn't a very healthy place for her. Not with all the draughts and leaks.'

'It's the only home we got,' Zaccheus said miserably.

Doc Fergueson nodded. 'I know that,' he said softly.

'Can I go in and see her?'

Doc Fergueson nodded and Zaccheus went inside.

Sue Ellen appeared to be asleep, her stringy hair fanning out over the thin pillow beneath her. Her face was pale and drawn, and there were dark shadows under her eyes.

'Ma,' Zaccheus said softly.

243

Her eyes slowly opened. They seemed less shiny, but the dark pupils contrasted sharply with the pasty complexion of her skin. She reached out to touch Zaccheus' hand. 'Mornin', son,' she said weakly.

He cupped both his hands around hers and felt a stab of pain: even her fingers felt brittle and fragile. He sat down on the edge of the bed. 'You had a bad night, Ma. How do you feel now?'

'A lil' better. I'm worse nights than days. Hope I didn't keep you from sleepin'?'

'No,' he lied, 'I could sleep through a thunderstorm.'

'Could you?'

He smiled.

She sighed and knitted her brows. 'I'm jest so bored lyin' in bed all the time! That's the worst of it. I ain't used to doin' nuthin.'

'Soon as you're well you'll be up and about.'

'No.' She shook her head. 'I ain't never gonna be up'n about agin.'

'Did Doc Fergueson tell you that?' Zaccheus asked sharply.

She shook her head. 'No, son, he didn't. But I can see it. It's in 'is eyes.'

'Maybe you're seeing things, Ma,' he said gently.

She shook her head. 'I hope I die soon, that's all. That way your pappy'll be able to git on with things.' She sighed weakly. 'I ain't nothin' but a chain round 'is neck.'

'No, you ain't.'

She pulled her hand out of his and turned her face sideways; when she spoke her voice was muffled by the pillow. 'I tried to be a good wife to yer pappy. I tried to work hard and raise his children best I could. But now it's all over.' She turned around, her eyes wide and glistening with hot tears. 'Once I'm dead, do me a favour, Zack? Take care o' yer pappy fer a lil' while? He's a lot more sensitive than he lets on, and he's been takin' all this mighty hard.'

Tears blurred Zaccheus' vision. 'I promise,' he said quietly. 'But I don't want to hear talk like that no more, Ma. You're gonna get well. I'll see to it.'

But he didn't know if she heard him. Her eyes were already closed and her breathing came softly, regularly. She had fallen asleep at last.

Doc Fergueson was still waiting for him out on the porch. 'She's weak, son,' he said.

Zaccheus closed his eyes for a moment and nodded. 'I know. She's had a bad night.' Trembling, he sat down slowly and stared at the doctor. He hesitated a moment. 'This clinic you mentioned, Doc. What can you tell me about it?'

'It's expensive, son. Too expensive for most people. Only the rich can afford to go there.

'But it *could* help my Ma?' Zaccheus persisted.

'Well, yes and no,' the doctor said carefully. 'It'll never get rid of the tuberculosis, I'm afraid, but with a lot of rest and the right care, it could arrest the disease for a while. She could even improve a little.'

'Then we've got no choice,' Zaccheus said firmly. 'We'll have to send her there. How much would it cost?'

Doc Fergueson looked at him. 'A hundred dollars a month: something like that.'

'A hundred dollars!' Zaccheus sat very still, not daring to breathe. There wasn't that much money in the world! 'And how long would she need to stay there?' he asked finally.

'Three months at the minimum, maybe four. Maybe even six or eight.'

Zaccheus' mind was reeling. Three months at the clinic would come to three hundred dollars; eight months to eight hundred. 'We just don't have that kind of money.'

Doc Fergueson's voice was soft. 'I know, son.'

'But *if* we could raise it,' Zaccheus said, 'then could you get her in?'

'Yes,' Doc Fergueson said positively. 'It's a private clinic. They'll take anybody as long as they can pay.'

Letitia, Theoderick, and their four children – Jesse, aged five, Stockley, aged four, Pearl, two-and-a-half, and Sallie Sue, barely six months – drove over to visit Sue Ellen that afternoon. Letitia hadn't known that Zaccheus was home and she gave him a warm hug. Theoderick shook his hand stiffly. The two older children let out whoops and went running off into the rain. 'Don't get too wet!' Letitia called after them, but they threw caution to the wind and didn't listen.

After the grown-ups, Pearl, and Sallie Sue visited with Sue Ellen for a while, it was clear that she was growing tired, so they all went outside. Nathaniel and Theoderick sat on the porch drinking moonshine, Pearl playing at their feet, while Letitia picked up Sallie Sue. The rain had let up, and together, she and Zaccheus walked to the banks of the creek, where he had once talked so candidly about the future with her.

The years of hard farmwork had already made their mark on Letitia. Though still sturdy and strong, she was thinner, with compressed lips and angular cheekbones. Her skin was tanned dark and crow's feet were beginning to appear at the corners of her eyes from too much time spent outdoors. She held herself rigidly erect and her steely eyes were clear and impassive, almost cool in their appraisals. She rarely cracked a smile. It was as if she had lost her sense of humour.

Zaccheus was filled with a sense of misgiving. At first he had been relatively certain that his sister would agree to at least think about what he was about to propose, but now he wasn't so sure.

He waited for the right opening to come up in their conversation.

Letitia said, 'I hear you're gittin' along well in school.'
Zaccheus nodded.

'Ever'one's real proud o' you. Don't honey!' She leaned her head sideways as Sallie Sue tried to tug on her hair.

'I hear you and Theoderick aren't hurting, either. Ma tells me you expanded the farm.'

She nodded. 'Yeah. We bought thirty more acres last year, after the Widder Dodelson died.'

This was the opening he had been waiting for.

He took a deep breath. 'Letitia?'

'Yeah?'

'We gotta do something for Ma.'

'Do somethin'?' His sister frowned. 'Like what?'

'Doc Fergueson says if we can send her to a clinic in Asheville she might get better.' He shrugged. 'Who knows? She can't get any worse, that's for sure.'

'An'?' She eyed him warily. 'What's the catch?'

He sighed painfully. 'It's expensive.'

'Uh-uh.' She shook her head vehemently. 'We ain't got no money, Zack. Not after puttin' a down payment on the new land, keepin' up the payments, gittin' new machinery, and feedin' the kids. All that eats up money. We cain't afford to lose what we got.'

He stared at her. 'But Ma's life is at stake!'

'I knows that, but what she got won't go away,' she said with her own brand of logic.

He clenched his teeth. 'The clinic can help her!' he said fervently. 'I know it will! What she needs is good medical care!'

'It ain't gonna help none.'

'Why do you say that?'

She shifted Sallie Sue to her other arm. 'Theoderick, he don't believe in doctors. 'Sides, what he sez all the time is true. When the Widder Dodelson took sick and didn't do nothin' 'bout it, she wuz fine. Soon's Doc Fergueson started meddlin' with her it wuz curtains.

Same way with Willie Brashear.' She looked at him significantly.

'Maybe. But maybe they called in Doc Fergueson too late?' Zaccheus suggested softly.

Letitia shook her head. 'Theoderick don't think so, and I don't neither. Nope, it's a waste o' good money, that's what it is. An' money's tight. They don't grow none on trees.'

Zaccheus looked at her steadily. The babbling of the creek suddenly sounded like a loud rushing in his ears. 'Does this mean,' he asked huskily, 'that you don't want to help send Ma to the clinic?'

'I wanna help Ma,' Letitia said carefully, 'but me and Theoderick, we ain't gonna help with Doc Fergueson's bills. And we ain't helpin' with no fancy clinic either.'

And that was that.

Zaccheus took a deep breath. So . . . He had no choice but to take matters into his own hands.

12

Phoebe Flatts had been waiting impatiently by the window for two and a half days now, and she still hadn't seen hide nor hair of Zaccheus. A cold panic was beginning to grip her. Perhaps he wouldn't show up at all. Maybe her charms hadn't worked. Maybe she had scared him off. Maybe . . . *Oh!* There were a hundred . . . a thousand . . . possible maybes, and if she dwelled on them too long, she knew she would go out of her mind.

Hearing the steady clip-clops of a horse and the creaking of a wagon, she parted the lace curtains and peered out for the thousandth time. Her heart soared hopefully. It was him!

She jumped to her feet, stopped in front of the mirror to pat her hair and hurried out onto the colonnaded porch. She virtually glided down the wide steps, lifting her skirt with two fingers of each hand so that the scalloped lace hem wouldn't drag on the ground.

She was in front of him almost before he hopped down from the wagon, her face flushed and glowing with relief.

He studied her intensely, if only for a split second. He hadn't seen her since two nights before last, when she and the Reverend had picked him up at the railroad station, but it had been night, and the lights had been dim, casting long, tricky shadows. Now, in full daylight, he could see that the lighting at the railroad station had, in fact, been unflattering. She was far more beautiful than he had dared remember. Just looking at her was enough to bring a lump to his throat.

She had, he thought, the most extraordinarily beautiful face he had ever seen. It was a purely classical face, but she was so petite that it was also a diminutive face, startling in its fine-boned delicacy. And it was this very delicacy which gave her such a charming appearance: her beauty didn't threaten as it would have had she been taller or larger or more imposing.

Her face was a perfect heart shape with extraordinarily high cheekbones and a refined aquiline nose which was, again since she was so petite, beautifully shaped and delicate.

Her lips were full and naturally pink. Her spun-gold, whitish satin hair gleamed richly, pulled smoothly back from her face and falling in a cluster of thick curls from the back of her head down to the nape of her neck. She was wearing her finest dress, a concoction of white lace which she had made over the winter with Arabella's help. Overall, the effect was so virginally pure that Zaccheus was at a loss for words.

Around her neck she wore the sterling chain with the pansy charm.

'Hello, Zaccheus.' Phoebe's voice was low and husky,

249

and it was at that moment that he knew he was going to marry her.

'Hello, Miz Phoebe.' He took both her hands in his and smiled down at her, for the first time aware of how short she really was.

'You mustn't call me Miss Phoebe,' she chided carelessly. 'To you, I'm plain Phoebe. You must call me that.' She gazed at him challengingly, her eyes sparkling. 'Now, greet me all over again.'

'Hello . . . Phoebe,' he said softly.

'There! Now that wasn't so difficult, was it?' She favoured him with the whitest, pearliest, most radiant smile he had ever encountered. It seemed to light up her entire face.

He found himself blushing under her gaze. Now that she had broken any existing formalities between them, there were a hundred things he wanted to say to her . . . *needed* to say to her . . . but he was unable to put any of them into words. At least not just yet. He had come here on a far more important errand. 'Is . . . the Reverend home?' he asked.

She shook her head. 'He's over at the church.'

He nodded. 'I've got to see him right away. Soon as I'm done, I'll come over and see you? Phoebe?'

She looked up into his face and smiled, her eyes steady and unwavering. 'I'll put on some hot coffee. We'll have it soon as you're back.'

He smiled. 'Thanks. I won't be long.'

The clapboard church seemed smaller than he had remembered, and the trees around it had grown fuller and greener in his absence. Both double doors in the front yawned wide.

Once inside, he stood at the back, hands on his hips, and glanced around. The interior was aglow with the familiar rainbow of colours from the stained glass window above the altar, and he could hear a steady scraping sound coming from near the front of the sanctuary. He wrinkled his nose; the odour of fresh varnish was sharp, acrid, and offensive. Reverend Flatts and a young man were bent over: the youth sanding down a pew, and Reverend Flatts brushing honey-coloured varnish onto one which had already been sanded smooth.

Reverend Flatts raised his head when he heard Zaccheus approach. Carefully he laid the brush on top of the opened can of varnish, wiped his hands on a rag, and stepped out into the aisle. 'Zaccheus!' he exclaimed pleasantly. 'My boy.' They shook hands warmly and the Reverend's florid face became concerned. 'And your mother? Is she feeling any better?'

Zaccheus shook his head. 'No, I'm afraid not.'

'I'm sorry to hear that. She's a fine woman.'

'Yes, sir, she is,' Zaccheus replied. He compressed his lips and shifted his weight nervously. For a moment he studied his feet. 'Reverend Flatts? Could we go somewhere and talk?'

Reverend Flatts glanced behind him at the youth sanding the pew. 'Oh. Of course. Right back here.' He took Zaccheus' arm and led him to the vestry. Once inside it, he closed the door. 'Have a seat, son,' he said gently. He gestured to a wooden, spindle-backed chair.

Zaccheus sat down, hands clasped in front of him. 'I know the Howe name doesn't mean much around here,' he said quietly. He looked up at the Reverend, his eyes steady, clear, and blue. 'I was wondering if you might help me. I don't know who else to turn to.'

'Yes, of course. Any way I can.' Reverend Flatts slowly took a seat opposite him and looked into his face. 'Well?'

Zaccheus cleared his throat. 'I need to get a loan at the bank.'

'And the purpose of this loan?'

'Doc Fergueson says there's a private sanitarium in Asheville, North Carolina. He thinks it'll help my Ma.'

'But it's expensive,' Reverend Flatts guessed.

'Yes, it's very expensive,' Zaccheus said bitterly.

251

Reverend Flatts nodded and glanced at his pocket watch. 'In that case,' he said, 'we'd better not waste any time. Let's go see what we can accomplish before lunchtime.'

No more than ten minutes later they stood outside the Farmer's Bank. Zaccheus halted momentarily to smooth the front of his shirt, making certain it was tucked neatly into his trousers, then lifted each foot in turn, wiping the dust off his shoes on the back of his trouser legs. He looked at Reverend Flatts.

'Are you ready?' the Reverend asked in a kindly voice.

Zaccheus took a deep breath and nodded.

Reverend Flatts clapped a hand on his back. 'Don't be nervous, son,' he advised. 'Mack Collins is a tough businessman, but a scrupulously honest one.'

Zaccheus smiled gratefully and together they climbed the two steps up to the door. 'After you,' Reverend Flatts said.

Zaccheus went inside, followed by the Reverend. He looked around curiously. In all the years he had lived in Muddy Lake, he had never once set foot inside the bank, and it held both awe and mystery for him. Awe, because this was where people put their money for safekeeping, or borrowed it for whatever purposes it was needed. Mystery, because he had always wondered what this place looked like, and because having money to take to the bank – however miniscule the amount – was something which the Howes always had a perpetual and severe shortage of.

He saw a polished mahogany counter with a single teller's cage protected by thick brass bars. Behind the bars stood a thin, myopic-looking man who wore very thick glasses and resembled nothing so much as an undertaker. Behind the man, Zaccheus noticed a big iron safe cemented into the wall, much like the one he had glimpsed in the rear room of the jewellery shop in St. Louis, only this one wasn't quite as large.

And there was a big desk off to one side, right under a small window. Like the teller's station, the window, too, was barred.

Mack Collins, the man sitting behind the desk, was the antithesis of a man bearing such a strong, tough-sounding country name. He looked much like the teller, which wasn't unusual considering they were brothers, except that Mack Collins was older and even more delicate looking, leaving one with the impression that he was part praying mantis. He was unearthly pale, with translucent skin stretched tautly over sharp, angular cheekbones. White eyebrows, stiff as wires, topped his eyes, and thinning white hair swept back from his high forehead. His insect-like appearance was emphasized by his long, bony extremities.

Reverend Flatts took Zaccheus' arm, propelled him towards the desk, and cleared his throat. 'Morning, Mack,' he said cheerfully.

The banker looked up from the paperwork he was shuffling, grumbled something under his breath, and got slowly to his feet. His eyes were a peculiar light grey and suspicious, so intense and startling they seemed to pierce straight through you. 'Reverend.' He held out a pale, palsied flipper of a hand. *'Parkinson's disease,' Reverend Flatts had told Zaccheus on the walk over. 'It makes him tremble all over. Don't take any notice of it.'*

'This is Zaccheus Howe, an associate of mine,' Reverend Flatts said quickly in his clear, resonant voice. 'You've probably heard of him. He's the bright young man who wrote the hymn for our church. He is currently studying at Centre Hall College in Tigerville, Virginia, to become a minister.'

Mack Collins slowly shifted his piercing grey gaze in Zaccheus' direction. 'Pleased,' he said concisely. He extended a trembling flipper and they shook hands.

Zaccheus had to fight to keep from recoiling; the banker's skin felt as dry and lifeless as paper.

Collins waved at the two red leather captain's chairs facing his desk. All three men took a seat and Collins came right to the point. 'Now, what can I do for you gentlemen?'

'Zaccheus is an up-and-coming young man,' Reverend Flatts sermonized carefully in his most sincere voice, 'one with a brilliant future, if I say so myself. He won a scholarship to the college, which, I assure you, is no small feat. To date he's never had the need of a bank.' He smiled pleasantly. 'But that's now suddenly changed.'

'That's mighty fine,' Mack Collins said with such a lack of conviction that Zaccheus had the sinking, and accurate, feeling that Collins' only interest lay in the contents of a well-stuffed purse.

Collins eyed Zaccheus closely. 'Now that the Reverend's given you a well-intentioned build-up, why don't you tell me in your own words what you think I can do for you, young man.'

Zaccheus took a deep breath and glanced sideways at Reverend Flatts, who smiled encouragingly. Zaccheus turned back to Mack Collins. 'I need a loan,' he said simply.

'Oh–ho.' Collins leaned forward. 'And the purpose for which you need this loan?'

Zaccheus told him and Collins listened intently, his face expressionless. 'Mr Howe. You have neither a bank account nor, as I see it, any viable income in the near, foreseeable future. Tell me. How do you intend to repay such a loan?'

'I am willing to stop my studies and work at anything until it's repaid,' Zaccheus vowed quietly. 'You can trust my word, Mr Collins.'

Collins' face creased into a frown. 'A successful banker never trusts anyone. Certainly not a young man who has not proven himself.'

254

Zaccheus stared at him. 'What does that mean?'

Collins unfolded his pale hands and ticked several points off on his long, thin fingers. 'It means, quite simply, that you have to be solvent in order to borrow money. You must be able to prove that you can repay it. Or own property. Or, you must have satisfactorily repaid loans made to you in the past, that is to say –'

'But – but I haven't had any need to borrow money before!' Zaccheus sputtered.

Collins nodded. 'Quite true. But banking is a peculiar industry, one with its own rules and regulations which have been developed through trial and error. Without a trustworthy credit history . . .' He held out his hands and shrugged helplessly.

Zaccheus frowned. 'How do I get a credit history, sir?'

'By getting a loan.'

'And if I've never had one?'

'Then it's very difficult. In that case, I would require substantial collateral.'

Zaccheus frowned thoughtfully. 'You mean – you'd lend me the money if you held something valuable of mine until it was repaid?'

'I would consider it,' Mack Collins said carefully.

Zaccheus had a sudden idea. 'What if I got my father to agree to put up our farm as collateral?'

Collins shook his head. 'I'm afraid that's no good,' he said flatly.

'Why not?' Zaccheus blurted desperately. 'The farm's worth some money!'

Collins shook his head again. 'Not as collateral.' He paused. 'I suppose you haven't heard?'

'Heard? Heard what?'

The banker's businesslike voice became gentler. 'Your father, Mr Nathaniel Howe, is mortgaged to the hilt,' he said quietly.

'I don't believe it!' A look of shock burned its way across Zaccheus' face.

'I'm sorry that you've had to hear it from me,' Collins said sincerely. 'I thought you knew. A year and a half ago, Mr Howe mortgaged the farm and he hasn't been able to keep up with the payments. Even worse, in my estimation, he hasn't been working the land to generate any income.'

Zaccheus sat there in stunned defeat. His ears were ringing from the shock. His father had mortgaged the farm? Nathaniel? The same Nathaniel who had never, as far as he knew, set *foot* in a bank? To whom nothing was as sacred as a man's outright-owned piece of land?

'He must have had to mortgage the farm because of my Ma's health,' Zaccheus said quietly. 'He's got to take care of her. There are doctor's bills.'

'And the mortgage payments?' Collins pressed. 'Why doesn't he take care of those?'

'Because,' Zaccheus said bitterly, 'he obviously doesn't have the money.'

'He's got a month,' Mack Collins said softly, 'before the bank forecloses. After that, the bank will own the farm. I'm sorry, but we have no choice.'

'A month!' The bank reeled around Zaccheus, a merry-go-round gone out of control. 'Does that mean that you're turning me down, Mr Collins?'

'Yes, it does.'

Zaccheus whirled in Reverend Flatts' direction, his blue eyes pleading. 'Please, Reverend! You've got to help!'

'Mack,' Reverend Flatts said slowly, 'what if I cosign a loan for Zaccheus?'

Collins frowned. 'Well, that depends on how much he needs.'

Reverend Flatts looked questioningly at Zaccheus. 'Well?'

Zaccheus' brain began to spin. Eight hundred dollars was what he needed, but half that amount would insure getting his mother into the clinic, at least for a while.

256

Still . . . four hundred dollars . . . Something told him to reduce even that. 'Two hundred,' he said quickly.

Collins shook his head. 'I'm afraid not. Fifty, a hundred. No more.' He glanced at Reverend Flatts. 'You're overextended, too, Reverend. I know, I know.' He held up a trembling hand and smiled grimly. 'The Lord will provide. But I'm afraid that what holds true in heaven doesn't always hold true on earth.'

'But Mack!' Reverend Flatts whispered. 'A life is at stake here! I'll personally guarantee the loan!'

Collins shook his head again. He was a member of Flatts' congregation, but he was a banker first and a churchgoer second. 'Reverend, I let the church mortgage the parsonage when the church needed a new roof –'

'Yes, yes, I know,' Reverend Flatts said testily. 'You've already told me. I've overextended my credit.'

'Not that I don't trust you,' Collins said smoothly. 'It was my trust in you that made me give you a loan in the first place.'

Reverend Flatts sighed. 'I know that, Mack.'

Zaccheus sat there numbly. He didn't know Reverend Flatts had had to borrow the money for the new church roof. Now why hadn't he thought of it before? Muddy Lake was, after all, a poor congregation.

Well, one thing was for certain. As far as a loan was concerned, there wouldn't be one. He got wearily to his feet.

As soon as they got outside, Reverend Flatts shook his head. 'I'm sorry, son. I tried. I don't know what else we can do.'

'The way I figure it,' Zaccheus said slowly, 'is this. If help isn't available here on earth, perhaps . . . just perhaps . . . it will be forthcoming from heaven.'

13

In Reverend Flatts' study, Zaccheus nibbled on the end of the pen and gazed dully at the blank sheet of paper on the desk in front of him. Composing the letter was a far more difficult task than he had imagined. Ever since he could remember, Nathaniel had instilled in him a fierce sense of pride and independence, and it had become ingrained in his bones. Asking for help was something which simply wasn't done. A Howe never went begging.

You're not begging, Zaccheus told himself fiercely. *You're asking for a loan that you'll repay.*

Phoebe came in with a steaming cup of coffee, set it down in front of him, and withdrew quietly, closing the door softly behind her.

Zaccheus hesitated, not knowing how to begin. But slowly, he began to write:

Dear Reverend Astin,

It was very kind of you to make the arrangements for me to visit my family. You cannot know how I appreciate it, and I will never forget your kindness or how much I am in your debt. My mother is far more ill than I imagined.

You told me I should stay with her as long as I deem it necessary, and I appreciate that, too. In view of all you've done for me, I am loathe to ask for more help, but in this I have no choice.

My dear mother is suffering from tuberculosis, and I don't think I need to go into the nature of that illness. However, the doctor here believes it is possible for her to improve if she is sent to a sanitorium in Asheville, North Carolina. Unfortunately, it is an expensive undertaking, one which my family and I are unable to provide. I know it is asking for a lot, but I humbly beseech you to find it in your heart to allow the college to loan us the sum of eight hundred dollars in order that my mother's health might be restored. I would, of course, glady undertake any job after college hours — or if necessary put a moratorium on my studies — to repay it speedily.

I repeat, I am loathe to beg for help, but you, Reverend Astin, are the sole person I can think of to turn to.

Thank you.

> *Very respectfully,*
> *Your brother in the Lord,*
> *Zaccheus Howe*

Zaccheus read the letter through, folded it carefully, found an envelope, and slipped it inside. He sealed the flap firmly shut.

Then he stared at it for a long time before he went off to mail it.

Nine days had passed since Zaccheus had mailed his letter. Phoebe parted the lace parlour curtains, and saw him sitting outside on the front porch steps, his back to her as he waited for Mr Peabody, the postman. He had given Reverend Astin the Flattses' return address, since mail delivery in town was more prompt than out in the rural areas.

She let the curtains drop back in place, smoothed a hand over her hair, and went outside. 'Zaccheus,' she said softly, coming up behind him.

Startled, he turned around swiftly and his eyes consumed her. She was wearing an ankle-length, peacock-blue dress with a high white lace collar which sheathed her swan-like neck in delicate arabesques all the way up to her chin. She'd strung the sterling chain with the pansy charm outside the lace; against it, the delicate filigree was set off to perfection.

'Waiting for Mr Peabody?' she asked.

He nodded wordlessly.

She tucked the dress under herself and sat down

259

beside him on the front steps, her arms hugging her knees. For a while, they sat without speaking. Then she eyed him sideways, a shrewd light gleaming iridescently in her large, black pupils. 'You're not going to become a minister once it's time for you to be ordained, are you?' she asked quietly.

He felt a peculiar sensation spread through him, as if someone had made an incision in his skin, peeled it back, and peered deep into his soul. Slowly, he turned to face her. 'What makes you say that?' he asked sharply.

'Oh . . .' She shrugged her narrow shoulders eloquently. 'I . . . I don't know.' She regarded her pale hands studiously. 'It's just a feeling I have.'

She tried to draw more out of him, but he wouldn't talk about it anymore. Still, for the moment she was satisfied.

He hadn't tried to deny it.

It was the thirteenth day since Zaccheus had mailed off his letter.

'I'm sorry, Zaccheus,' Mr Peabody, the postman, told him. 'There's nothing for you yet. Maybe it'll come tomorrow.'

'Yes, maybe tomorrow.' Zaccheus sighed painfully. Tomorrow. There was always tomorrow.

But if the money from Tigerville didn't arrive soon, his mother might not see many tomorrows.

A spectacle which Muddy Lake had never before witnessed, and which would be talked about for a long time to come, occurred seventeen days after Zaccheus mailed his letter.

Mr Peabody came *running* up the street, his black, cracked-leather shoulder bag bouncing up and down behind him as he waved an envelope in one hand. 'Zaccheus!' he was shouting hoarsely. 'Zaccheus Howe!'

On the Flattses' front porch, Zaccheus suddenly sat

up straight. Just when he had been ready to give up hearing from Reverend Astin, here was Mr Peabody doing the unthinkable: actually interrupting his regularly scheduled rounds to run – *run* – to him with a letter!

So there is *a God after all!* Zaccheus thought with crazy relief.

He jumped to his feet, let out a 'Whoop!' and charged down the street to meet the postman halfway. The excitement was infectious. People stopped whatever they were doing and came out on their porches or leaned out of windows, mouths agape. Mr Peabody had never been seen hurrying before.

The front door of the Flattses' house opened and banged shut. Phoebe, a starched white apron tied around her waist, stood on the porch, her face puzzled as she wiped her hands on a towel. Then, seeing Mr Peabody at a run, she tossed the towel aside and raced after Zaccheus.

'Thanks, Mr Peabody!' Zaccheus shouted with happiness. 'I love you! *I love you*!' He gave the stunned postman a bear hug, kissed both his cheeks noisily, and then snatched the letter out of his grasp.

Mr Peabody scratched his head and shook it. 'Shore must be one important letter,' he muttered. 'I never done got kissed by no one before!'

Important! Zaccheus laughed and jumped into the air with relief, tears of happiness flowing from his eyes. It wasn't only important – it was a matter of life and death! The money inside – a cheque or money order, surely, since the envelope was so thin – would mean his mother's salvation! Her life would be prolonged. Her suffering eased.

Phoebe finally reached Zaccheus, faint from the exertion. She watched him fumbling with the envelope, caught it for him when he dropped it, and smiled as he tore it open.

Inside the envelope were two folded sheets of vellum

261

stationary. He unfolded them and frowned. He had expected a cheque or money order, but there was neither. For a moment, he looked down at the ground, afraid he'd dropped it.

Well, perhaps it would follow under separate cover, he thought soberly. And eagerly, he began to read.

My son in Christ,

It is with a grievous heart that I received your letter stating the precariousness of your mother's health, for neither did I realize that she was so seriously ill. I suggest that you take a leave of absence from your studies in order that you can be with her in her time of need. Be assured that my prayers — and those of the entire college — are with you and your dear mother. During services last Sunday, the entire congregation offered up a prayer. I am certain that our good Lord heard them, and the rest is now in His hands.

Zaccheus stopped reading. His heart was pounding furiously and his forehead pulsed as though it would explode. It was not prayers which his mother needed so desperately, but eight hundred dollars so she could be sent to the clinic in Asheville. He skimmed the rest of the letter, his heart growing heavier with every word:

I fully understand your request for a loan of eight hundred dollars, and it is my sincerest wish that such a request were in my power to grant. Alas, we are all merely the Lord's humble servants, instruments of His will. A minister has the power to call upon God's help to heal the soul, to refresh the spirit. Unfortunately, many of the earthly needs which both the college and myself would like to help come true are outside our powers. We are not a banking institution, but a spiritual one. We do everything within our power to take care of our own — and as one of our future ministers, you are one of our own. That is why we undertook to provide you with a scholarship. You were highly recommended, and we are all proud of having you in our midst.

But even colleges need money. It is true that our kind benefactor, God rest his soul, left behind an endowment, but even we spiritual leaders are governed by the laws of the layman's earth. The money left to us — and there is never enough to do our job adequately — is stipulated by the trust to be used for education, maintaining the college, and scholarships. Not a penny may be used for any other emergency, no matter how exigent . . .

Zaccheus felt a cold seizure gripping him. The message, however convoluted, was clear: there would be no money forthcoming, at least not from Reverend Astin or his precious college. The letter, however kindly worded, was an intricate dance neatly skirting the issue, never saying 'no' outright, but making that message crystal clear nonetheless.

A low, mournful keening sound escaped Zaccheus' lips. What kind of church was it, he asked himself, that refused to help send a poor woman to a clinic so that her suffering might be alleviated? Since when were trusts and scholarships more important than human life?

He glanced scornfully at the letter. From the way it was worded, Reverend Astin — the much revered, much beloved Reverend Thomas Astin — did not sound so much a man of God as a politician.

Quickly, listlessly, Zaccheus skimmed the remainder of the letter, Phoebe, reading it over his shoulder, silently mouthing the words:

. . . As spiritual leaders, we will do everything we can, even though our hands are tied financially. But foresake not hope, my son, in Jesus Christ the Lord, the son of God, because He is all powerful. Did He not cure the leper? Did He not cast illness out of the sick? Did He not raise the dead to living? And does He not offer us all everlasting life? He is merciful,

our Lord and Saviour Jesus Christ, kind and loving, and,
let me assure you, a single prayer uttered unto Him is worth
a million pieces of silver.

> *Sincerely, I remain a simple*
> *servant of both God and man,*
> *Yours truly in Christ,*
> *Thomas V. Astin*

There was the sudden crunching of paper as Zaccheus balled the letter up. He tossed it to the side of the road. The tears which suddenly blurred his vision were tears of rage. He had seen, first-hand, the richness of Centre Hall College, the splendour of the ivy-clad buildings, the lovingly tended, manicured, rolling green acres. That campus represented all the money in the world; yet to heal the sick, there was none.

'Zaccheus.' Phoebe, genuinely worried, placed a gentle arm around his waist. 'Come on, Zaccheus. We'll talk about it at home.'

Savagely he spun in her direction, his blue eyes flashing such virulent hatred that she recoiled. 'You asked me something the other day!' he hissed. 'Do you remember?'

She only stared at him, afraid that any words would only fuel his anger.

'You wanted to know if I'll ever be ordained,' he said grimly. 'Well, I'll give you my answer now. *Never. Never for as long as I live!*'

'Zaccheus?' she whined. The sun was catching the sterling chain around her neck, and the silver flashed like a mirror.

Slowly, ever so slowly, he reached out to touch the pansy charm. Phoebe, terrified that he would take his anger out on her, held her breath, but his touch was surprisingly gentle.

Mesmerized, he felt the sterling chain with the pansy charm between his fingers. *There was a lot more than just sterling where that had come from.*

14

Celesta Bensey's chin jutted proudly forwards as she raised her head and stretched her thin, corded neck. She clasped her thin hands in front of her and surveyed the interior of her shop with a sharp, piercing gaze.

She felt extremely gratified. She could feel that everything was in order. If as much as one tiny item were out of place or missing, she would have sensed it instantly.

In the twenty odd years she had run the shop, which had been founded by her grandfather more than a hundred years earlier, Celesta had learned to rely on her acumen and instincts, and they had served her well. Her Grand Tour abroad had been cut short upon the death of her father twenty-one years ago, and she had returned to discover herself the sole heiress of a respectable business. W. Timothy Hollister, her father's lawyer, had pressured her to sell the shop. 'I'm afraid you're just not well enough acquainted with it, Celesta, and being a young woman and all . . .' he'd said with gentle sadness. 'Anyway, I think I can come up with a buyer. If you sell it, it should fetch a good price and, wisely invested, that'll give you enough to live on nicely for the rest of your life.'

'And do what?' she'd asked him in quiet outrage. 'Needlepoint? Quietly become an old maid? Men don't find me particularly appealing, except those who think I have some money. No, if I'm to be an old maid, I'd rather be one with a business that will keep me busy.'

She'd changed lawyers, found one receptive to her ambitions, and taken over the store. Since then, she had single-handedly built Bensey's into St Louis', perhaps Missouri's, smartest purveyor of luxury goods. And thanks to Guiseppe Fazio, who she'd discovered in Italy during her Grand Tour – and had subsequently sent for, along with his wife and child – the store had become the envy of everyone in the trade. For Guiseppe Fazio was an artist, and the tools of his trade – the crucibles, the mallets, the furnace, the wax, the casting platters, and the diamond cutters – all were his brushes. The delicate rings and necklaces, the sterling platters, the finely wrought flatware and bowls, the classic tea services he fashioned – no matter how grand or humble the item, he brought gold and silver and vermeil to magical, beautiful life. There wasn't a single well-to-do family within a radius of a hundred miles that didn't boast some treasure from Bensey's – a child's silver spoon, a cake service, a necklace, or a simple wedding band. In Missouri, even the most inexpensive gift item had cachet – if the box in which it came was labelled 'Bensey's'.

Yes, she had forged Bensey's Jeweller's into the most fashionable place for one-stop luxury shopping. Dowagers, socialities, newlyweds, potential brides . . . it was to her that they all flocked. Every year, indeed every *day*, brought more and more business to her door. And that, she thought, was extremely gratifying . . . not to mention exhausting.

She sighed softly to herself, a sigh half weary, half congratulatory. Today had been a good day. No, an exceptional day, even if she thought so herself. In fact, she was certain she had made more sales on this one day than on any other single day during the year, excepting the Christmas season, of course – and all because there were to be three society weddings next month. Bless the brides, she told herself. Then she smiled. Brides appealed to both her sentimentality and her sense of business.

Once again she sighed softly. Her feet hurt and her stomach was growling. There had been so much traffic in and out that she hadn't been able to take a single break, nor had she been able to close for lunch, something which hadn't happened since December. Now, she would have a huge billing to do for her regular customers in good standing; the money from her cash-paying customers was in the back room on a desk, stuffed into a cloth bag belonging to the bank. Mentally, she guessed what it contained. Probably close to five thousand dollars . . . maybe closer to six. She made it a point never to keep much cash on hand, but today had been so extremely busy, and with Guiseppe gone to Philadelphia, she just hadn't had the time to run to the bank to make the deposit. She would lock it in the safe until tomorrow morning.

She placed her clenched hands in the small of her back and stretched. She was bone-weary. It would be a relief to sit down. No, she simply *couldn't* walk to the night deposit box now.

For once, she would put something off until tomorrow. She couldn't see what harm that would do.

The room was hot and airless, but he didn't dare open the window lest a breeze part the curtains, making him visible from the street below. He wiped the sweat off his forehead with the back of one hand. The sweat he'd worked up wasn't from the heat. It was sheer nerves.

He felt physically ill. For three hours now, he had been sitting behind the curtains with the patience of the hunter, watching the comings and goings of the jewellery emporium's customers with keen interest. Every few minutes, either a well-dressed pedestrian would walk into the shop off the street, or a horse and buggy would pull up alongside the fluttering awning at the kerb. A few couples even arrived in noisy, smoke-belching horseless carriages.

He had watched the afternoon shadows lengthen steadily, a deep tide of purple creeping slowly first across the sidewalk, and then the street, until it reached the sidewalk on his side and began to climb the red brick walls of the hotel, seeping into his room. He was filled with an immense sadness, as if he knew that what he was about to do would change his life, would wreak havoc and upset the neat order of things, would forever govern his thoughts and actions, would change the very way he felt about himself. He wished there was some other way he could raise the money for his mother's stay at the clinic. But wishes were for dreamers. And he was a dreamer no more.

He parted the curtain with one finger, careful to stay hidden behind it, and glanced at the tall white church steeple in the distance. The big black Roman numerals on the round white face showed it was nearly five thirty. He glanced down at Bensey's Jewellers. The shop closed at six.

Suddenly he sprang to his feet. He could see two tiny, disembodied hands reaching down into one of the display cases next to the door. The jewellery was already being taken away to be locked up for the night.

It was time he went downstairs. He had but half an hour to finish what he had set out to do. As if to reinforce this thought, the church bell tolled once, deep and resonant.

He scraped back his chair, dumped the contents of the suitcase out on the bed, and sorted quickly through them. He grabbed the length of rope, the revolver, the rags, and the burlap hood. For a moment he looked down at the things he had sneaked out of the Howe cabin with.

He squeezed his eyes shut, his soul in turmoil. He was no thief, just as he was no beggar. But then a vision sprang up in front of his eyes. He pictured his mother, pale and weak, her body racked with painful coughs; he heard the ugly retching sounds as she spat up the thick, bloody, poisonous phlegm. He knew that he had to finish what he had started.

It was now or never.

Carefully, Celesta removed a tray of wristwatches from a display. She was grateful that Deputy Sheriff Hank Yarby had stopped by on his morning rounds to invite her out to dinner. At first, she'd made excuses, but then he'd insisted and she'd said very well, if you won't take no for an answer, we'll meet here at six. Yarby *was* sweet, really, even if he was six years younger than her. He'd been with the sheriff's office for eight years now and rumour had it he would run for sheriff once old Sheriff Caldwell retired. Yes, tonight was one night that a restaurant dinner would be more than welcome. There was no way she had the energy to go home and cook. Still, she wished her date was someone other than Yarby.

Not that she didn't like him. It was just that she didn't like him *enough*. He was strong and fearless, and handsome in a crude kind of way, but his manners left something to be desired, as did his family's background. He was rather like a diamond in the rough, she thought, but one which would never get the chance to be cut and polished.

She knew that Yarby was infatuated with her, and she knew full well, too, that his hopes were useless. She had gently rebuffed him countless times, but that had only seemed to make him that much more ardent. Still, common courtesies and a few harmless dinners didn't hurt, she told herself. Bensey's Jewellers had only been robbed twice in its hundred-year history and that had been long, long ago. Still, one never knew. Occasionally, little items would be missing, and Yarby had twice helped her retrieve them from finger-happy customers. Those embarrassing moments had been handled very discreetly by him, without her having to be involved.

It didn't hurt to have friends in the sheriff's office.

Cling-cling-cling!

Not another customer! Slowly she rubbed her eyes with her fingertips. Well, this would be the last one of the day. As she turned around gracefully, as befitted a successful lady who owned her own shop, Celesta played her little guessing game. For which of the three weddings, she mused, would this client buy —

The gasp froze somewhere in her throat and her eyes dilated dramatically. For the first time in her life, she found herself staring into the barrel of a revolver. She laughed nervously and tried to clear her throat. 'Now Yarby,' she said tremulously, 'that's not a very funny joke, you know.'

The only reply which came from behind the hideous burlap hood was heavy, rasping breaths.

Zaccheus' breath was coming hard with excitement. He couldn't seem to get enough oxygen into his lungs. He tried to swallow, but the sick icy chill of fear, combined with the sudden heady thrill of a perverse power, emotions totally alien to him, radiated from the pit of his stomach and burned down into his loins. He felt he had to urinate badly. And throw up.

He could feel the nausea rising and fought to keep it down.

With a quick backward thrust of his revolver arm, he elbowed the door behind him shut. The soft *cling-cling-cling*! seemed suddenly loud and shrill, and the woman jumped. He glanced swiftly behind him. The door was shut. They were alone.

He came slowly forwards.

The woman gazed at him in horror and shrank back, the taut cords of her neck working madly. 'What . . . do you want?'

She kept edging slowly backwards, the fingertips of one hand trying to feel the way. Nevertheless, she gasped and let out a startled yelp when her hand touched the cool smooth glass of the counter behind her. She drew up as close to it as she could, trying to flatten the lower portion of her body against it.

She squeezed her eyes shut and her lips moved hysterically as she uttered a silent prayer.

She wasn't alone in her fear. Zaccheus' heart was beating so fiercely that he felt certain it would burst. He tried to take deep, even breaths, but that only seemed to make it worse. He let the suitcase he had been carrying drop to the floor. It landed with a bang and the woman's eyes popped open as she let out a scream. When she realized the gun hadn't gone off, she looked relieved, tried to get control of herself, took a deep breath.

Zaccheus was sweating so madly that he could feel the revolver slipping in his hand. He wiped his left hand dry on his poncho, changed the revolver to that hand, wiped his right hand dry, and switched the revolver again. The woman didn't move, but her eyes followed the weapon.

He waved it threateningly. 'Where's the money?' he demanded in a trembling voice.

Celesta Bensey had one attribute which had made her admired and respected throughout the community; she was possessed of a will of iron. Now, despite the fear which clenched her in its ice-cold vice, the quick, well-oiled business gears in her mind clicked and turned and she thought of the money she would lose. Her fighting spirit was instantly roused.

'There . . . there isn't much cash around here,' she lied in a quivering whisper. 'It's . . . it's taken to the bank. Twice a day.' She swallowed, her neck cords bulging with the effort. 'That . . . that way so much doesn't lie a . . . a . . . around here.'

He brought the barrel of the revolver slowly forwards to within inches of her face, and lined her up in the sights. 'How much have you got?'

She began to scuttle sideways, like a spider. 'I'll have to go check –'

'*Don't!*' he yelled sharply, and then his voice dropped, 'move. Not until I tell you to.'

She froze in terror, one hand on her breast.

'Just tell me where you keep it.'

'In the top drawer . . . over there . . . under that display case.' She gestured sideways with her chin. His eyes followed the movement. A built-in, ceiling-high display case with glass doors, behind which several shelves of silver trays were propped, ran the length of the wall. Beneath one set of the tall doors was a vertical series of drawers built flush with the case. That was where, first thing at the end of each business day, even before she tallied the sales, she put aside the forty dollars – five singles, one five, one ten, and one twenty-dollar bill – which she traditionally kept on hand for making change in the morning.

She watched him as he backed cautiously over to the drawers, keeping the revolver pointed at her as he reached behind him and pulled the top drawer open. He stuck a hand inside, felt around, and came up with a few assorted bills. He held them up in front of his eyes, grunted something indistinguishable, reached under the poncho, and stuffed them into a pocket. Then he hopped sprightly back from the display case and landed softly in front of her.

'I don't believe this is all there is,' he said heavily. He paused, leering at her threateningly. 'You want to live?'

Her head bobbed and a cry tried to work its way up from the depths of her throat, but it became a strangled gurgle.

'If you can't come up with any more, you're dead,' he whispered hoarsely. He placed both hands on the grip of the revolver, raised it to her face, and drew even closer until the barrel pressed closely against her forehead. There was a sharp *Click!* as he cocked the firing mechanism.

Celesta squeezed her eyes shut and began to chatter

an urgent Lord's prayer. 'Ourfatherwhoartinheaven-hallowedbethy –'

'Stop *praying*!' he screamed in high-pitched hysteria. 'Stop it! Do you hear me? *Stop it*!' He struck her with the back of one hand. Her jaw snapped shut under the wallop; simultaneously, her teeth clacked painfully together and her eyes flew open. Her dark pupils danced with fright. He was mad! Stark raving mad!

'Don't pray!' he screamed. He thrust his hooded face forward so suddenly that she shrank back. 'Do you hear me! I said – don't pray!'

She trembled more than nodded.

His voice was shaky. 'I'm sorry. I . . . I didn't mean to hit you. I never hit a lady before in my life.' He paused. 'I don't want to hear you pray,' he whined softly, 'that's all. I came here to steal money.' He sniffed noisily. 'Since there isn't any more money, I'm going to take some jewels. Tell me when I have eight hundred dollars' worth.'

Careful to keep her covered with the revolver, he skirted her slowly and went behind the counter. She half turned, watching him in horror. *This can't be happening*, she told herself. *I'm dreaming a bad dream . . . a nightmare . . . that's all. I'm going to wake up at any moment and it's going to be all over . . .*

Her eyes flickered down to the mahogany-framed, clear-glass case in which some of the most expensive, most exquisite rings in the shop glittered richly. Each time his hand plucked a ring up off the maroon velvet she flinched as though mortally wounded.

Once he had a handful, he held them close to one of the eyeholes of his hood. She watched as he unclenched his hand, tilted his head, and inspected them closely, like a bird.

That hood doesn't allow him any peripheral vision! she thought. Her heart soared hopefully. *As long as he's not*

looking straight at me, I've got a chance to escape! Five quick,
normal steps, or a one-and-a-half second dash, and I'll be out
the door —

Cling-cling-cling!

They both jerked around, and then Zaccheus' world
collapsed.

'I wouldn't move if I was you,' a voice said gruffly.
' 'Round here, we don't take kindly to nice, upright
folks like Miz Bensey gettin' robbed.'

Zaccheus rolled his eyes slowly sideways. Hank Yarby
had his shotgun aimed right at his head.

It was all over. Just like that.

15

Demps Johnson, the large, powerfully built Negro,
slowly glanced up when he heard footsteps echoing
through the jail corridor. His eyes were big and soulful,
so heavily lidded that it looked as if he were perpetually
half-asleep.

He watched with deceptive casualness as Yarby
unlocked his cell door and rolled it open. The loud,
clanging roar was amplified by the stone walls and floors
and echoed back and forth, back and forth.

Yarby grinned. 'Got a buddy for you, Demps.'

Demps looked at him expressionlessly. Then the big
deputy turned to the young prisoner he'd been escort-
ing. He grabbed him unceremoniously by the scruff of
his collar and the seat of his pants and threw him into
the cell.

Zaccheus was propelled forwards so fast, and with
such force, that his legs couldn't keep up with the
powerful thrust. For a split second he seemed to be
running, then he slammed against the stone wall head
first. His forehead cracked noisily, the breath whooshed

out of him, and he saw a huge white aureole coming at him.

Then everything went dark. He didn't see the big deputy spit a wad of chewing tobacco at him. He didn't hear the reverberating clang of the cell door as Yarby slammed it shut with a bang of finality and locked it with one of the big keys on the big ring. 'What you lookin' at, boy?' The big deputy grinned at Demps, chewing the remainder of his tobacco wad with deliberateness.

Demps didn't even flinch when the wad went flying and smacked against his face. He had suffered this indignity all too often.

Yarby chuckled, shook his head, turned, and walked off, his keys jingling. Only when he was gone did Demps wipe his face with his shirt sleeve. He wasn't about to give Yarby the pleasure of seeing how being spat at burned him up.

It took about three minutes for Zaccheus to come to. He seemed surprised to find himself lying on the floor and shook his head like a wet dog shaking itself dry, trying to clear it of the cobwebs fuzzing his mind. He stopped the shaking as soon as he'd begun it. He had a splitting headache, and the slightest movement sent sharp white arrows of pain shooting off his skull.

He moaned softly, probing his forehead gingerly with the fingertips of both hands.

Demps laughed. 'You okay, boy,' he said in his deep, rich bass voice. 'You just had yourself a l'il confrontation with an inanimate object, is all. A two-foot-thick stone wall, to be precise.'

Zaccheus turned his head slowly. 'Where am I?'

'You in a free hotel, boy, courtesy of the fine city of St Louis, Missouri. Room and board provided.' His voice softened. 'You in a holdin' cell in the town jail.'

Zaccheus closed his eyes as everything which had transpired came painfully back to him. It was as if his collision with the wall had suddenly sobered his mind.

I must have been crazy, he decided. *Why else would I have done a damn fool thing like trying to rob Bensey's Jewellers?*

Because I wasn't crazy, he answered himself. *I was desperate.*

A little smile hovered on Demps' lips. 'That floor pretty hard, boy. Best set on a bunk. Ain't much softer, but it shore better'n the floor. Even got a blanket. See?' Demps lifted up a corner of threadbare grey cloth.

Zaccheus tightened his lips, rested his back against the cold corner, and remained on the floor. He drew his knees up to his chin.

'You want to talk, boy?' Demps asked softly.

Zaccheus did not speak.

Demps shrugged matter-of-factly and stretched out on the bunk, which was far too short for him, put his hands behind his head, and stared up at the ceiling. A small fly which had been crawling around the rim of the slop bucket buzzed over to him, droned little circles above his face, then gathered the nerve to land on his chin. Demps kept perfectly still, watching it with sleepy amusement as it bravely explored his face, its microscopic legs tickling faintly. Ever so slowly, he opened his mouth. The fly hopped onto his lower lip, peered into his open mouth, and rubbed its front legs together.

Suddenly Demps jerked swiftly upward and snapped his mouth shut. He put his hand up to his lips, spat the fly into it, and slammed the hand against the wall, flattening the fly into a black and red splotch. He laughed uproariously as it joined all the others thickly plastered to the wall next to his bunk. 'Learned that little trick fifteen years ago from a guy named Bad Fred,' he said. 'Teaches patience.'

Zaccheus glanced at him with revulsion and tried to recede even further into the corner.

An hour passed, then two. The slop bucket reeked. When the dinner trays were slid under the cell door, Zaccheus pushed his away.

'You should eat,' Demps advised. 'Smells like the shit in the slop bucket an' taste like it too, but you gotta keep up your strength.'

Zaccheus pushed the tray towards Demps. The big negro grinned, showing huge, pearly teeth. 'I thank you,' he said with formal dignity and bowed his head. Then greedily, he grabbed the tray and shovelled the greyish stew into his mouth with the tin spoon.

After it started to get dark, Demps stretched out again. He spoke softly, his voice sure and even. 'The bunk better, boy.'

Zaccheus was silent.

'You learn to talk,' Demps said in a sure voice. 'After a few weeks you be a regular chatterbox. After a few months you talk to the walls if you ain't got nobody to talk to. An' after 'bout a year, you even start talkin' in your sleep.' He nodded emphatically.

Zaccheus looked up defiantly, his blue eyes flashing. 'I'm not going to be here that long,' he said angrily.

'I knows that. They gonna send you to the state work farm. Next to that, this place paradise. Yes, sireee!'

'Speak for yourself!' Zaccheus snapped. 'You think you know everything, don't you?'

'Noooo . . .' Demps said slowly. 'I shore don't.'

'Well, I'm not a criminal.'

'Mebee. Mebee not. But you shore gettin' a good start in that direction.'

'I made a mistake!' Zaccheus insisted forcefully.

Demps roared with delight. 'We all did, boy!'

'I have my whole life ahead of me.' Zaccheus's voice grew hopeful. 'Maybe the judge will be lenient.'

'Lenient! Oh-ho!' Demps gave a short, rich bark of a laugh.

Zaccheus looked at him hatefully and turned away.

Demps sighed, swung his legs over the bunk, got to his feet, and stretched. He seemed to fill the small, low-ceilinged cell completely: a gleaming mahogany Atlas holding up the roof. For a moment he stood posed like that, staring down at Zaccheus. Finally, he pulled in his massive, powerful arms and squatted in front of him. 'What'd you do, boy,' he asked softly, 'to land in this here vacation spot? I hope it worth the trouble it gonna cause you.'

Zaccheus raised his head defiantly. 'My Ma's sick. She's going to die soon if she can't get into an expensive clinic, and my Pa's farm's going to be repossessed by the bank. We needed the money, so I robbed a shop.'

'Use a weapon?'

Zaccheus nodded. 'A revolver, but I don't think it was loaded. I didn't even check. It was my grandfather's.'

'Armed robbery,' Demps said. 'That's what they'll call it. First offence?'

'Do I look like a hardened criminal?'

'Heyyyy!' Demps held out both hands, pale cordovan palms extended outward as if to ward off a physical blow. 'I ain't you enemy.'

Zaccheus glared at him, but then the anger seeped out of him. He nodded contritely. 'Sorry. Yeah. First offence.'

Demps shook his head sympathetically. 'We both in the same boat, boy. Me, they gonna come down on hard. You too. Any place else you done it, maybe you get out soon. Not round here. Not with that Yarby buckin' for sheriff. Election's comin' up, see, an' the deputy, he a big man for law an' order.' His face wore a troubled expression. 'He comin' down hard on ever'body.'

Zaccheus was visibly shaken. 'What . . . what do you think will happen to me?'

'For armed robbery? In Missouri?' Demps screwed up his eyes thoughtfully. 'You probably get ten years. If you good, maybe they let you out in five.'

Zaccheus stared at him. 'I don't want to spend ten years on the state farm. Not five. Not even one. There's got to be some way —'

'Lissen, boy, an' lissen good. Nobody round here lenient to criminals.'

'But I'm not —'

'Shut up an' lissen!' Demps snarled. He thrust his glaring brown face so close to Zaccheus' that their noses touched. 'I'm a criminal. The moment you rob that shop, you a criminal. One way or other the whole world a criminal, only them people out there didn't get caught. You stand in front o' the judge an' that Yarby, he gonna crucify you, you wait an' see! He full o' tricks.'

Zaccheus hung his head low and stared down into his lap in despair.

'Lissen —' Demps glanced around cautiously and his voice dropped to a bare whisper. He hunched forward excitedly. 'What you say we get us outta here?'

Slowly Zaccheus lifted his head. 'How?'

'Ssssh!' Demps clamped a big hand over Zaccheus' mouth and looked suspiciously first over his left shoulder, then over his right. 'Not so loud, boy,' he whispered. 'Case you don't know it, jail walls got ears. You don't advertise gettin' out. But you an' me, boy, we break outta here. I was waitin' for somebody. Takes two.' He nodded sagely.

Zaccheus just sat there, staring at him. Then he laughed softly. 'Sure. We starve ourselves skinny until we can squeeze through the bars, right?'

Demps looked hurt. 'Don't be funny 'bout it. I'm serious.'

'But I don't see any way out!' Zaccheus insisted. 'That cell door's locked.' He pointed with his chin. 'Those bars are iron.'

'Shore they is, but there's ways out,' Demps whispered. His eyes still had that deceptively casual look, but when Zaccheus looked closely into them he saw that they burned with a deep, steely fire. 'There's ways out o' ever'where. We just do like the Lawd's sweet birdies in the sky.' Demps leaned sideways and looked up at the ceiling, gesturing so eloquently at imaginary birds flying above him that Zaccheus couldn't help but follow his hand and look up for the birds. 'We sprout wings and fly outta here's what we do. Relatively speakin', course.'

'And once we're out?' Zaccheus asked. 'Then what? I can't even go home. I gave the deputy my address.'

'We either split up an' you go you way an' I go mine, or you an' me, we go into business together.'

'Business!' Zaccheus scoffed. 'What business? Pulling off robberies?' When Demps didn't reply he added: 'What makes you think I want to become jail bait like you?'

Demps looked wounded. 'Me, I didn't start in crime like you,' he said, his voice icy cold. 'No, siree. But I'm a *nigger*. Some white man, he went after a white woman, an' she have to explain her condition, see? I was the scapegoat. Nearly lynched me, they did. I was in the wrong place at the wrong time. Didn't matter none that she gave birth to a lily white kid nine months later. That's life, I suppose.'

Zaccheus' face went red with shame. 'I apologize,' he said with simple sincerity. He lowered his eyes. 'I was out of line.'

Demps patted his arm. 'Thass okay, boy.' He smiled widely. 'You young. You don't know no better. But how 'bout your mammy an' pappy? They need money, right? A kid in jail can't get them none.'

Zaccheus stared silently at him.

'Just lissen to me,' Demps said excitedly. 'I knows the way to get outta here. It work before, it work again. You screams and hollers and howls and clutches you stomach. You pretends to be awful sick tonight after it good an' late an' there only one man around guardin' the place, see? Deputy or whoever come to check on you, they find you lyin' flat, clutchin' at you belly. They bends over an' I knocks him upside the head an' he see stars.'

280

'And then?'

'Then we runs like possums with they butts full o' buckshot.' Demps paused. 'What you say, boy? You in on it?'

'It won't work,' Zaccheus protested weakly.

Demps stared at him. 'It work. You do as I says, an' it work! An', once we get out, I show you how to make enough money to save you mammy an' the farm. Interested?'

Zaccheus drew a deep breath. 'Will it get me into trouble?'

'It could. But you already in trouble, so what's the difference?'

Zaccheus pondered that for a while. 'You're not suggesting we rob banks, are you?'

Demps laughed. 'Shit, no. Thass too dangerous. What I'm proposin' is just a lil' larceny by the name o' breakin' an' enterin'.'

'But why do you need me? I've got nothing to offer you. Why would you want to help my Ma and Pa? You don't know them from Adam.'

Demps grinned. 'You right; I don't. But I need *you*.'

'Why?'

' 'Cause you white.' Demps fingered Zaccheus' blond white-man's hair with quiet envy. ' 'Cause you blue-eyed. An' you got manners. An' you speak educated like.'

'So?'

'With them polite manners you got an' a new set o' clothes, you kin scout out rich folk, see? You kin wheedle 'em to become real friendly like, an' invite you into their purdy, rich, white folks' houses. That way, you scout out the territory an' see if the pickin's worth it.'

'I don't know,' Zaccheus said slowly. 'Thieving's not in me.'

'You want to send your Ma to that clinic and save your Pa's farm, don't you?'

281

'I don't want to land back in jail, that's for sure.'

'You won't. See, what you done today, you done all wrong. You don't rob stores downtown, boy. You find youself big rich houses, an' when the owners is out, then we go in. It lots safer that way, an' one o' us acts as lookout, see? An' we get jewels an' silver an' pitchers, anything we can carry away, that kind of stuff.'

'But how are we going to convert everything to cash?' Zaccheus asked. 'That had me worried about the jewellery, too. Do we sell the stuff to pawnshops?'

'Pawnshops, hell! You wants to get caught? 'Sides, even if we wasn't caught, they don't pay nothin'!'

'Well, then, what do we do?'

'I know a guy,' Demps said evasively. 'He in Charleston. He specializes in buyin' stole stuff like that. We can crate it or barrel it an' ship it by train mail. Sort o' like a regular business, if you knows what I mean. An' we never hit the same area twice. We works our way from one city to the next.'

'This guy in Charleston. What's his name?'

'Uh-uh.' Demps grinned slyly. 'That's my li'l ole secret. I tells you that now, an' you don't need me. You liable to run off on me an' do ever'thing I plan youself, and where that leave ole Demps?'

'I don't know,' Zaccheus replied worriedly. 'This isn't what I planned for my future.'

Demps laughed. 'Boy, the way things goin' now, you ain't *got* no future. You be on the workfarm for years, and when they lets you go, you be a tired ole man. I seen it. You won't know nothin' but how to steal an' kill.'

Zaccheus nodded thoughtfully. What Demps said made sense. Still, maybe if he explained to the judge why he had robbed the store, the law might be lenient. And if he said he'd been studying for the ministry, he might even have more points in his favour. Perhaps it wasn't very likely, but it *could* turn out that way, especially if he was repentent.

An escape attempt, however successful, would make the law only want him even more. But if Demps was right, and he was sent to the state farm, escape might prove impossible, or at least more difficult. There they locked big iron cuffs around one of your ankles and kept you perpetually chained to a lot of other men.

Demps seemed to read his conflicting doubts. 'Hank Yarby, he a mean sonbitch. Forget it, boy. You ain't gonna be let off easy. Yarby, he expert at trumpin' up charges. Claim you resist arrest, try to attack him, all that kinda stuff. The more he pile up on you, the longer you the property o' the State o' Missouri.'

'Is *that* what you think's going to happen?'

'How the *hell* I know, boy?' Demps whispered forcefully. 'I ain't God or no gypsy woman. I can't read no future. Yarby, he sure don't confide none in me.' He leaned so close into Zaccheus' face that Zaccheus could nearly taste his breath. 'But I tells you one thing. Ever'body knows better'n to fuck up on Yarby's turf. He want that sheriff star real bad.' Demps paused. 'But if you wants to git outta here, you needs me. An' if you wants to succeed in business and help you folks, you needs me too.'

'Why you?' Zaccheus whispered. 'Why not someone else? Why can't I do it myself?'

'You green. So far, you done it all wrong. I gots experience.'

Zaccheus could feel the conflicts thrashing about within him, bumping, grinding, slowly eroding whatever confidence he had left in either option. 'I have to think it over,' he persisted weakly.

'Don't think too long,' Demps warned. 'Come mornin', we may be separated. Won't work none if you and me locked apart in two different cells. An', closer to mornin' it gets, less time we gots to sprout our li'l wings. You know?'

Zaccheus nodded slowly. 'Okay, Demps,' he said

283

softly. 'I'm with you all the way. But I have to do something first.'

'What's that?'

'I got to see somebody back home.'

'A woman?' Demps asked suspiciously.

Zaccheus nodded.

'I don't advise it,' Demps said prophetically. 'Women's trouble.' He shook his head. 'Big trouble. You mark my words.'

Neither of them knew how true Demps' prognostication would turn out to be.

16

Zaccheus dragged the ladder around the Flattses dark house and propped it softly against Phoebe's second-floor window. As if he'd ordered it expressly for the occasion, the full white moon floated silently in the cloudless night. It was past midnight in Muddy Lake, Missouri, and the night was quiet. Even the breeze was a bare whisper in the autumn foliage on the trees.

He felt something powerful stir within him as he climbed the ladder sure-footedly, his hands flying from one rung up to the next. Demps waited in the dark cover of the bushes below.

Her window was shut. Zaccheus cursed softly to himself. Then he cupped his hands against the glass and tried to peer inside. At first, all he could make out were the dark, hulking forms of furniture, and then the breath caught in his throat. She was lying in bed, her knees tucked up near her chin in a foetal position, her body shrouded in an ethereal, almost phosphorescent nightgown.

He rapped softly on the glass with a cocked knuckle and waited anxiously for her to wake up. When she didn't, he knocked a few more times, each knock louder than the last, but the sounds did not penetrate the veils of her deep sleep.

'Come *on*, boy!' Demps hissed up at him from below. 'We ain't got all night!'

'Just give me a minute!' Zaccheus hissed back. He put a hand on the casement window and tugged at it.

It pulled open easily, with barely a squeak. Grabbing the sides of the window frame in each hand, he ducked and swung himself into Phoebe Flatts' room.

Swiftly, he crossed the creaking floor on tiptoe, all his senses assaulted in an exquisite agony such as he had never before experienced. This was the first time he had ever set foot in a bedroom which was exclusively the domain of a young lady, a room which was not shared, where the combined smells of toiling bodies, of dirt and sweat did not exist. Here the total, tangible femininity of the room's occupant was strong and potent; pervasively, puissantly sweet. He inhaled deeply of the mysteriously tempting fragrances which hovered deliciously around him, which teased his senses and roused him in pleasurable delight – the freshness of laundered linens, the honeyed sweetness of flowers, the enticingly ambrosial enchantment of perfumes and toilet waters, of soaps and powders, eucalyptus and peppermint. He took deep breaths and let the scents linger luxuriantly in his nostrils, wanting nothing more than to burrow into their source, swallowed up by the sweetness of all that nectar and myrrh.

When he reached the side of her bed, he gazed at her with silent longing. Her eyelids were quivering as she dreamt sweet lady dreams, and her soft breaths were mellifluous purrs in the night. As he watched, she stirred, her lips whispering something soft and incoherent as she changed position, one arm draping gracefully over the edge of the bed, her mouth curved in the chaste smile of the innocent. He had to suppress the sudden urge to reach out and stroke her, to pepper her face with gentle kisses, to nibble softly of her flesh and her bones and her soul. Then he became aware of something glowing richly around her neck, and his lips widened into a gentle smile. So she wore the pansy charm he had given her even while she slept!

She looked so at peace that he wished he didn't have to awaken her. He would have been content to just stand there and look down upon her for hours, but time was sweet love's enemy. He couldn't dawdle. He had to leave as swiftly and invisibly as he had come. When Hank Yarby had arrested him, he had been truthful and given his correct address; he could very well already be a fugitive even here in Muddy Lake.

He had to be careful. Anyone might turn him in. The Flattses. Even Phoebe.

He bent over her and shook her gently. 'Wake up!' he urged softly into her ear.

One moment she moaned softly, and the next she sat bolt upright, her body rigid, her mouth opening to form a scream.

He clamped a hand over her mouth and her eyes bulged in fear. Instantly, her hands flew to his and tugged at them with surprising strength.

'It's me!' he whispered. 'Zaccheus!'

She ceased struggling immediately and slowly turned to face him. Her eyes were wide and pale in the moonglow.

Cautiously, he took his hand away from her mouth.

'Zaccheus?' she said, disbelief in her voice. 'Is that really you?'

'Ssssh!' he warned.

The room came alive with the urgent sibilancy of whispers.

'Where've you been?' she demanded. 'It's been nearly a week and no one's heard a word from you!'

'I can't tell you now. I'll write you all about it in a few days.'

'You'll write me? What do you mean? Where are you off to? Why can't you just tell me everything?'

He turned away. 'I'm sorry, Phoebe. I can't ever come back.'

Her eyes went huge. 'But *why*?' She knitted her brows.

He tightened his lips. 'I just came to say good-bye,' he said quietly. 'I couldn't leave without doing that. You've been so . . . so wonderful to me, Phoebe.'

'You're not going back to college?'

He shook his head.

'Have you . . . done something?'

He nodded. 'I tried to rob a store. A jewellery store in St Louis. I had to, Phoebe! How else could I pay for Ma to go to the clinic?'

She regarded him in sad silence, and he told her the rest. When he was finished, he sighed heavily. 'At least now Ma can go to the clinic and Pa won't have to lose the farm.'

Phoebe bit down on her underlip. 'Oh, Zaccheus. Then you don't know?'

'Know what?' He frowned at her.

'You're . . . You're too late, Zaccheus,' she said softly.

He just stared at her. Cold dread, like blocks of ice, suddenly seemed to push against him from all sides. 'Too late?' He grabbed her by the arms and shook her violently. 'What . . . what do you mean, I'm too late?'

'Zaccheus! You're hurting me!'

'I'm sorry.' His hands fell from her arms.

'Your Ma passed away, Zaccheus,' she whispered thickly. 'Three nights ago.'

'What!' The strangled cry caught in his throat. 'You're joking?' he sobbed. 'Tell me you're joking?'

She took both his hands in hers and pressed them gently. 'It's true, Zaccheus.'

He shook his head. 'She . . . she died?'

287

Phoebe nodded. 'If it's any consolation, she went very quietly, in her sleep. Doc Ferguson said it was best that way. At least at the end, she didn't have to suffer too much.'

Zaccheus turned away as the tears began to slide down his cheeks.

'My uncle read the eulogy,' Phoebe continued in a low voice. 'Your Pa asked him to. He said since it happened so soon, and you're not an ordained minister yet, it was what she would have wanted. It sort of surprised us all, since none of your family ever came to church. Aunt Arabella played the hymns, and everyone sang your hymn, the one you wrote? I don't think it ever sounded prettier, there was so much feeling put into it. It was a very nice funeral. Everyone came from miles around.'

He sat in stony silence.

'Zaccheus?' She shook him gently. 'I'm so sorry. Really, I am.'

He began crying softly, and she opened her arms, held him close, and swayed him back and forth.

'I'm really so sorry,' she repeated.

'I robbed the store for her and Pa,' he said between his moans of anguish. 'Just so she could get well and Pa could keep the farm!'

'He can, Zaccheus. That's already been done. The farm's still his. We took up a special collection in church on Sunday. Everybody was generous, and Mack Collins, the banker, was the most generous of anybody. Widow McCain was sitting right beside him, and she told me he put twenty dollars into the basket. We collected more than two hundred dollars and the mortgage payments are now up to date.'

He closed his eyes. He sighed deeply, his body shaking with tremors. 'Just when Pa needed me, Phoebe, I wasn't there!' He pounded his fists on his thighs. 'And now that he needs me more than ever to help him run the farm, I'm a fugitive!'

'You tried your best, Zaccheus. That's all anybody can do. Your Pa will understand. I know he will.'

Zaccheus shook his head, sniffed noisily, and wiped his eyes with his fingertips. 'I've shamed him. I've shamed everybody. Ma's memory . . . the Reverend and Miz Arabella.' He stared at Phoebe. 'You.'

She tried to smile. 'You haven't shamed me, Zaccheus. You did what you thought was best.'

'I'll never become a minister now,' he said. 'And even if I wasn't wanted, I still couldn't. I couldn't live with myself. I took the bad road.'

'And you're going to stay on it?'

'I don't know. The way I see it, right now I don't have any choice. Not if I want to stay free. I'm a fugitive.'

Phoebe looked at him levelly. 'I don't care what road you took,' she said huskily. 'Or down what road you're headed.'

He looked at her queerly.

'Zaccheus, I don't *want* to live my life as a minister's wife. I never have. I'd hate it. Couldn't you see that?'

He couldn't help staring. 'But, I thought —'

'Sssssh,' she said soothingly. She cradled his head awhile. Then she licked her lips thoughtfully. 'Zaccheus?'

'Yes?' His voice was thick.

'What are you going to do now?'

'I . . . I guess I'll go see Pa and give him the money. Visit Ma's grave.' He sniffed again.

'That's not what I meant. I mean . . . after all that.'

'I guess I'll take off.'

'Where to?'

'Somewhere where nobody knows me, or can find me. Out of state, maybe out West.' He shook his head miserably. 'I don't know, Phoebe.'

'You shouldn't go alone, Zaccheus.'

'I'm not. I've got Demps. He and I, we broke out together. He's the only friend I've got.'

She looked at him peculiarly for a long moment. 'You're sure of that?'

He stared at her. 'What do you mean?'

'I thought I was your friend, too.'

'Yes,' he nodded. 'That's why I had to come and say good-bye.'

A sudden fear came into her eyes. 'Please don't leave me, Zaccheus. Take me with you!'

He shook his head. 'What kind of life could I offer you?'

'A better one than I have here,' she answered quickly.

'No,' he said flatly. 'I love you too much to ruin your life. Now, I'd better be going.' He bent down, kissed her chastely on the forehead, and turned reluctantly towards the window.

'Zaccheus!' she called out desperately.

He stopped and turned around slowly.

She jumped out of bed. 'I'm coming with you,' she said with finality, 'and that's that. Now be a gentleman and turn around while I get dressed.'

'But . . . you *can't* come!' he argued.

'And pray tell why not?' she asked angrily.

'I already told you. Because you'd ruin your life!'

She laughed to herself. How perfectly silly. Of course, there was no way he could know it, but she would be ruined here anyway once it became evident that she was pregnant. But if she went with him and left behind a note saying that she had eloped with him? *Yes!* That way, she would not only escape this despicable little town for which she had always held such contempt, but she would solve her pregnancy problem as well. But she wouldn't marry Zaccheus. Not now, not ever. She would remain free until the right man came along. In the meantime, she would simply let him believe what he wanted. If he mentioned marriage – and she was certain he would — she would beg him to wait a bit longer, until she was ready, and make up some excuse or other about the baby she was carrying when the time was right.

Zaccheus' flight as a fugitive was just the kind of opportunity she had been waiting for.

At that moment, a voice hissed at them from out of the darkness. 'What you waitin' for, boy?'

Startled, they both turned. Demps had climbed the ladder and was peering in through the open window. He whistled softly. 'Lawd God Almighty!' he exclaimed. 'If that ain't the purdiest sight my poor eyes ever done seen! I thinks I must a died an' gone to heaven!'

Phoebe took Zaccheus by the hand. There was a hint of laughter in her voice. 'Turn around, both of you! It won't take me but a minute to get dressed.'

17

And that was how the outlaw adventure began. They headed to Memphis, Tennessee, a 'brother' and 'sister' travelling with their faithful 'servant', Demps, and from there they went on to Little Rock and Shreveport. Everywhere, they lodged in the best hotels while gaining the confidence of wealthy people, and then they would burgle them, quickly pack the stolen goods in crates and barrels, and ship them off to the fence in Charleston, South Carolina before moving on again.

It was a neat, professional operation, one which moved with swift, clockwork precision. When the stolen goods were sold by the fence, far from where they had initially been stolen, they were virtually untraceable. And, Zaccheus, Phoebe, and Demps carefully averted suspicion from themselves. The barrels were sent off immediately, always from a railroad station far up or down the line. Most important, they never skipped town immediately after a burglary. Rather, they would stay just long enough to satisfy everyone that they were above suspicion – after all, it was common knowledge that thieves disappeared into the night.

On more than one occasion, Demps and Zaccheus were actually part of posses hunting down the 'thieves'.

Since they knew their victims, they inevitably had to sympathize with them. Zaccheus was especially compassionate, for he hated what he was doing and truly felt sorry for those he victimized. He reasoned that those from whom they stole could well afford it, but it was mere rationalization, and he knew it. The longer their spree continued, the more he came to despise himself. But a habit once begun is a difficult thing to break, especially when others are involved. Zaccheus realized that Demps' chances of survival in a conventional life were minimal, opportunities for Negroes in a white man's world being virtually nonexistent. Nor were Phoebe's chances much more promising. She was beautiful, but valuable only as an exquisite, decorative ornament. Each time Zaccheus was tempted to quit the life of crime, the obligation he felt towards Phoebe and Demps compelled him to stick with it until a better opportunity arose: after all they counted on him.

Professional as their operation was, the unlikely trio inevitably met with obstacles in their outlaw adventures. The first of these occurred near Vicksburg, Mississippi, where they were detained for four days when their hired coach lost a wheel. No one sustained any major injuries, but Phoebe was violently thrown to one side of the carriage and lost the baby she was carrying.

Demps realized at once what was happening. The soul of discretion, he picked her up and took her to the local doctor, never uttering a word to Phoebe or Zaccheus that he was aware of what had transpired. He guessed that Zaccheus was blissfully ignorant of Phoebe's pregnancy, and took no convincing to make him believe that her 'internal' injuries were caused by the accident.

Demps' discretion arose from the loyalty he felt towards Zaccheus. He did not want to hurt him, knowing that his friend worshipped the very ground Phoebe walked upon. Nor did he dare tell Zaccheus of another, more serious matter.

Whenever Zaccheus was preoccupied, Phoebe would favour Demps with sly, furtive looks of wanting, and it wasn't long before Demps became increasingly frightened of her. Phoebe's covetous, feverish desires burned more fiercely with every passing day, and he knew only too well that he was the catalyst.

She got the fever, Demps warned himself over and over. *Black fever. I got to be real careful like. Tread on eggshells. She like a bomb ready to blow. Can't Zaccheus see that?*

But it wasn't just that Zaccheus was blind. Phoebe cleverly hid any indications of the dark passions which raged within her.

Demps worked hard to create a distance between himself and Phoebe. He knew only too well the powder keg any relationship – however brief or innocent – between a black man and a white woman would ignite.

It was with this darkening cloud hovering invisibly over them that the handsome trio arrived in New Orleans.

As it turned out, it was a town none of them would ever forget. Not for as long as they lived.

18

The red velvet puff curtain dropped down over the stage. Gradually, the applause died to a smattering and then stopped completely as the electric sconces and chandeliers were turned up and the black-suited ushers flung open the doors at the back of the theatre. The audience drifted out into the hallways and down to the lobby where they milled about while discussing the first act, exchanging gossip with friends, and sipping glasses of champagne purchased from the polite black bartenders. It was intermission at the Comédie de la Quartier in New Orleans.

Phoebe sat back in the little gold-leafed chair she occupied in the front box on the right, snapped open her fan, and waved it with delicate little ladylike flicks of her wrist. After the orchestra section below her was nearly empty she rose to her feet. Beside her, Zaccheus put his hands on the arms of his chair, rose also, tugged at the hem of his dinner jacket, and followed her through the red velvet swag curtains. At the rear of the box, he held open the tufted, velvet-padded door and followed her out into the congested hall.

Phoebe smiled faintly up at him, her eyes glowing as she slipped a hand through his arm. Although she never cared what was being performed, she loved going to the theatre because it provided a wonderful excuse to dress up.

Phoebe thrived on attracting attention. She made certain that when they attended a performance, she and Zaccheus were always among the last to arrive in order to make a grand entrance; likewise, she was among the last to get up for intermission – this way, she could make a grand exit from the box and another grand entrance into the halls and lobby between acts. But she was invariably among the first to leave in the crush of departure; otherwise, her audience would be gone and could not witness her leaving in the brass-trimmed black vanadium steel Model T Ford which would take her and Zaccheus back to the hotel. 'Visibility,' Zaccheus maintained, was all-important. In the new line of 'work' he had embraced, furtiveness aroused suspicion, and suspicions had, out of necessity, to be allayed. He figured, correctly, that when you attracted attention to yourself, chances were that you were considered above suspicion.

Thus, arms hooked, Phoebe and Zaccheus gracefully paraded through the crowd of strangers and descended the wide, curving marble staircase with its intricate wrought-iron balustrade.

Zaccheus glanced sideways at Phoebe, proud as a peacock. She stood out like a diamond among glass. Even among the richest, finest women in New Orleans, she clearly held her own. To him, she was the most beautiful and desirable of them all, and his ego was satisfyingly stroked. He couldn't help comparing her with the other women.

Young or old, fat or slim, there was something stately and formidable about the well-dressed society women of New Orleans. Due to the fashion of the time, they all emulated the famous Gibson girls and seemed to share the same general physique. Without exception, when viewed sideways, their figures cut a commandingly matronly S-shaped profile. They wore gowns with long, tight puffed sleeves, belled skirts, and high collars – all balanced by piled-up hair or enormous hats.

Phoebe contrasted sharply, simply, and beautifully. She was the one woman among them who was ethereal, delicate, and bewitching. This was because, with incisive, intuitive brilliance, she used the other women as foils for her own incandescent beauty. Only six months had passed since she and Zaccheus had fled Muddy Lake so quickly and furtively under cover of night, but it seemed, somehow, as if they'd travelled not one hundred and eighty days, but many, many light-years.

Looking at Phoebe, you certainly would have thought so, Zaccheus mused with approval. She was a consummate actress, seemingly unaware that all eyes were riveted upon her. She appeared to be cloaked in years of sophistication, mystery, and . . . yes, much as he hated to admit it . . . *vanity* – she was forever stopping to admire herself in mirrors, and her spending habits knew no restraint. But he welcomed her gargantuan vanity because it worked into his scheme of things, making them both more visible.

Thereby deflecting suspicion.

Phoebe walked slowly, with that inborn, swan-like grace he'd always admired. Her long, incredibly slender neck was thin and straight, her heron's eyes seemed larger and more arresting than ever with her white satin hair pulled back and piled up on top of her head. Her wide, pale mouth with the cleft under the lower lip was curved in a smile, and her pale ivory skin and small bones gave her the fragile delicacy of a rare, exotic bird. But she had chosen not to wrap herself in too magnificent a plumage, and it was precisely that which lent her the elegance she sought. The apricot-coloured gown was Empire style, with a high bodice and a narrow, floorlength skirt which gave the illusion that she was taller than she was. Her feet were shod in low-heeled, white satin slippers, and if anyone could find fault with her, it was that her feet were too big. But that was not her fault. Zaccheus was ever cautious, and since they never knew when they might have to move on speedily, perhaps without even returning to their hotel, the slippers were a kind of insurance. They were an inch longer than her feet, and cushioned in cottonballs, two perfect diamonds, pried from their settings so they could never be traced, were stuffed inside each toe. Perhaps that was what gave her that aura of aloof confidence with which she held herself so easily.

'Champagne?' Zaccheus asked when they found an opening in the crowded lobby where they could stand without getting claustrophobia.

Phoebe nodded and he left her standing there next to a pink marble column as he threaded his way to the bar through a bejewelled group of ladies whose husbands were gathered a few feet away, lighting cigars and puffing on them importantly. The country had still not recovered from the financial panic and depression that had started two years ago, in 1907, but here on opening night at the Comédie de la Quartier you'd never have known it, Zaccheus thought.

He took his time getting the champagne. He had come to the theatre with a distinct purpose in mind – to scout out stealable wealth and get some idea of who was who and who had what. Theatres, he had discovered, were the perfect places to do this: everyone dressed up to show off their wealth.

An intent glint of calculation sparkled in his eyes as he reckoned the worth of the jewels winking at him from throats, necks, and wrists all around. He was truly astonished. Of all the places he and Phoebe had been so far, New Orleans was turning out to be one juicy plum indeed.

His eyes rested on one dowager in particular, a frowning, scrawny woman whose parched face was a cracked desert of wrinkles and whose eyes looked as though they had slowly sunken deeper and deeper into her skull. He had never seen quite so many diamonds on any one person. Bracelets, rings, earrings, necklaces, and a tiara decorated her from head to wrist.

Now *that*, he told himself, is one temptingly gratifying sight.

He made a mental note to ask around discreetly and find out who she was . . . where she lived. One theft like that and he and Phoebe could retire in luxury for the rest of their lives.

Zaccheus didn't try to fool himself. It was time to retire soon, while they were still ahead. So far they'd been lucky, but Lady Luck was a fickle mistress whose allegiances changed suddenly, indiscriminately. When you least expected it, she was liable to turn on you.

The woman he was staring at became aware of him.

She lifted the bejewelled lorgnette which hung on a chain from around her neck and stared right back at him. He forced himself to drop his eyes and look elsewhere.

'*You're a fool!*' he chided himself angrily. '*You're getting carried away. It won't do to study a future victim that obviously, especially not one who is nothing to look at except for the jewels she's dripping. Once they're missing, she's bound to remember the attention and maybe put two and two together.*'

He paid for the champagne, left a decent tip, and scooped up the glasses, one in each hand. As he made his way back to Phoebe, tongues were wagging. He overheard a quartet of women gossiping.

'Is that the new fashion nowadays?' The woman leaned sideways, all the better to study Phoebe. 'In London or Paris, maybe?'

'No, it can't be,' another piped with surety. 'My Alexandra just returned from her Grand Tour and she *assured* me that *I* dressed in the latest style.'

'But who on earth is she? I've never seen her before. Or him, for that matter, wherever he's gone off to . . .' The woman stood on tiptoe, trying to catch sight of Zaccheus, unaware that he was passing right next to her, manoeuvring his way around the women.

'I don't know, dear, but if you ask me,' a buxom woman with her massive back turned to Zaccheus replied musically, 'it's scandalous! Quite cheap, baring those arms and showing that neckline like some –'

The woman who had been trying to catch a glimpse of Zaccheus suddenly found herself face-to-face with him. Blushing with embarrassment, she desperately tapped the big woman's arm to cut off her tirade. The woman turned, and saw Zaccheus. Her jaws snapped shut and she pronounced an indignant 'Oh!' from deep within her stately bosom with such vehemence, and flashed him such a dark, wrathful look, that he guiltily felt like the eavesdropper she suspected him to be.

298

'You sure took your time!' Phoebe whined crossly in a low voice. Her lips were still carefully curved in a smile for all to see. 'I felt stupid standing here all by myself!'

'Couldn't help it.' Zaccheus shrugged and handed her a glass. 'I was scouting around.'

'And?' She leaned close to him, sipping her champagne.

He didn't have a chance to reply, for behind him, he heard the sharp click of smartly snapped heels. Phoebe twisted around, her eyes flicking past Zaccheus as he turned slowly. A darkly handsome young man with amber eyes and continental manners, accompanied by a honey-blonde with a spoiled face, had come up to them. 'Please forgive the intrusion, but Clara here was dying to meet you,' the man said to Phoebe with a friendly smile. 'She's itching to know where you got your gown.' Clara bobbed her head eagerly and he turned to Zaccheus and clicked his heels again. 'May I introduce my fiancée, Miss Clara Anglejan? I'm Hezekiah Beaty. Welcome to New Orleans.' He and Clara Anglejan were also drinking champagne, and he raised his glass in salutation.

'How nice!' Phoebe simpered brightly. 'I love talking to people, and we don't know a *soul* here.' She paused, her features puzzled. 'How did you know we're from out of town?'

Beaty laughed with easy familiarity, showing even white teeth. 'New Orleans is a small town, really,' he explained. 'Between Miss Anglejan and myself, we know practically everyone worth knowing. Both our families settled here over a hundred and fifty years ago. In fact, we're distantly related. Over the last century and a half, quite a few Beatys and Anglejans married each other. Happily we're very, very distant cousins. Clara?'

'That's right, Hezekiah,' she replied in a low, honey-laden voice which matched her honey-blonde hair and honey-coloured lace gown.

Zaccheus held out his hand. 'This is my little sister, Phoebe, and I'm Zaccheus Howe.'

'Where're you two from?' Beaty asked.

'Tennessee,' Zaccheus lied smoothly. Since accents were easy to place and you couldn't fool many people with them, he always stuck to hailing from near the Missouri border. 'Right now we're staying in a suite at the Hotel Dixie. I'm here on business, and my sister doesn't get to travel a lot. She's never been to New Orleans before.' He gave a little laugh. 'So here we are!'

'What kind of business are you in?' Beaty asked with polite interest.

'Investments. My pappy left us quite a bit of money, and we decided to play with it and make it grow.'

'I was admiring your gown,' Clara told Phoebe. 'Where *did* you get it?'

'I found this marvellous little dressmaker in Memphis.' Phoebe looked down at herself. 'It's a copy of a gown I saw in a magazine.' She looked up at Zaccheus and knit her brows. 'Who was that lady in the engraving who wore one just like it?'

'Josephine,' he said. 'Napoleon Bonaparte's wife.'

'That's right!' Phoebe unsnapped her fan and vibrated it delicately back and forth. 'Isn't it silly? I keep forgetting her name.' She laughed a contrived little laugh.

'It's a very flattering gown,' Beaty said solemnly, 'though I take it that anything would look flattering on you.'

'Why, thank you, kind sir,' Phoebe said flirtatiously. She brought the fan up to her face so that it hid everything except her eyes. They appeared larger, more excited, and more expressive than ever. She was putting on quite a show for Mr Hezekiah Beaty, and Zaccheus

300

felt a sharp stab of jealousy cutting into his heart. She'd never flirted like that with him. Ever.

'How do you like New Orleans?' Beaty asked Zaccheus.

'Fine, I like it just fine.'

Beaty turned his attention back to Phoebe. 'And you, Miss Howe?' he asked in a peculiarly soft voice. 'Do *you* like it here?'

Phoebe gazed at him over the rim of her raised fan. Her eyes were serious, unsmiling. 'I like it a lot,' she said huskily, fuelling her charm even further. 'And I'm getting to like it more and more, Mr Beaty.' There was no mistaking the sudden smouldering heat beneath her voice, or the intent, steady glassiness gleaming in her eyes. It was as if someone had switched on a furnace.

Zaccheus exchanged glances with Clara Anglejan. They were both aware of the sparks which seemed to fly from Beaty to Phoebe and back like highly charged lightning bolts.

Clara Anglejan made a frustrated face. From her expression, it was clear that she wished she'd never had any curiosity about Phoebe's gown.

Zaccheus couldn't blame her. He was annoyed, too. It was high time, he thought, to steer the subject back to safer waters – profitable waters which would do him and Phoebe some good.

'Ladies certainly wear more jewels around here than they do in Tennessee,' he said in an offhanded voice. 'Like that lady over there, for instance.' He pointed with his chin.

Clara half-turned and frowned. 'You mean the old one, with all the wrinkles?'

And the necklaces, bracelets, rings, earrings, and tiara, he thought.

'Hmmm.' He feigned mild disinterest, as if the subject was merely polite small talk.

'Oh, *her*!' Clara waved a hand dismissively and

laughed too lightly – obviously grateful for the shift in conversation. 'Of course men wouldn't know of such things, but those jewels are all paste, Mr Howe. Every last necklace and bracelet. The tiara, too. You see, the Fourcades lost everything in the panic two years ago, and Mignonne's simply had paste copies made. Wears them everywhere, too, and pretends they're the real McCoy, and we all pretend we're impressed. That way she hasn't lost any dignity.'

He lifted his glass and swallowed some of the champagne. 'You're kind and sensitive,' he said, meaning it. 'I like that.'

Clara shrugged. 'The Fourcades are an old family, and very proud. It doesn't do anyone any harm.' Then she sighed. 'We just wish she wouldn't insist on wearing everything at once. She never did that before, with the real jewels. It sort of . . .' She frowned, trying to think of the right phrase.

' "Defeats the purpose"?' Zaccheus suggested.

'Exactly.' Clara Anglejan pronounced it eggs-actly.

Zaccheus stared across the lobby at Mignonne Fourcade. His eyes registered sore disappointment, but they registered something else, too. Relief. He felt warmly towards Clara Anglejan. Unwittingly, she had saved him a lot of trouble and embarrassment. He could just imagine staging an elaborate burglary, taking wing in the night, and then sending the fence a shipment of phoney jewels.

Clara's voice dropped to a confidential whisper. 'But over there? By that pillar?'

Zaccheus' eyes followed in the direction she was nodding. The large, buxom woman was the very one he had overheard gossiping, who had thought he was trying to eavesdrop on her and had turned to him and said, 'Oh!'

'Yes,' he said carefully.

'That's Eleonore Alice Qualey. Her family owns half of New Orleans . . . at least the half that counts.'

He continued to feign disinterest.

'Well, her jewels aren't exactly the biggest, and she's not exactly dripping with them, but they're the best, believe me. Everyone says she's got the finest taste in town. She should. She can afford it, with all that money. But she's a fool. Imagine keeping all those diamonds and a whole lot more all in her bedroom drawers! She even opens her jewellery boxes and shows all her friends and visitors everything whenever they come over to visit. Me, I'd lock them in the bank vault.'

He raised his eyebrows. 'Isn't she afraid of being robbed?'

Clara shook her head. 'I asked her that once. And do you know what she said?'

He shook his head.

'She said – get this, and I quote – ' She rolled her eyes as she tried to remember the exact words, and when she spoke it was slowly, from memory. ' "No one would dare rob me, my dear. With my connections, they'd never get out of the state!" What do you think of that?'

Zaccheus felt a chill settle over him. 'What did she mean, exactly?'

'She simply means, Mr Howe, that the Qualeys have every local – and national – law enforcement agency in their pockets.'

He whistled quietly, wondering what to say next when he was saved by the ushers who were starting to shake their little hand-held bells. Intermission was over. People quickly finished their champagne and began to drift back upstairs for the next act.

Hezekiah Beaty was holding Phoebe's gaze. 'If you're still in town three evenings from now, why don't you pay us a call? We're having a few people over at my family's for a quiet supper. The Qualeys, the Doughertys and the Laphams. We'd be delighted if you would join us. Your brother too, of course.'

Clara's eyes were bleak with hurt, and Zaccheus' heart

303

went out to her. 'I'm afraid we won't be here then, Mr Beaty,' he said with quick dignity. 'We have to leave before then.'

'Oh,' Beaty said blandly.

'But *I* don't have to leave! I'm delighted to accept for myself!' Phoebe did not look at Zaccheus, but he could imagine her cold, calculating smile.

'I'm afraid my sister is mistaken,' Zaccheus said swiftly. 'She regrets that she won't be able to make your supper, Mr Beaty.' He touched Phoebe's arm, but she recoiled.

Phoebe's eyes flashed with childish venom. 'Don't treat me like a child, Zaccheus,' she warned in a trembling voice. 'I'm your sister, not your wife.' She raised her chin and added pointedly: 'It would behove you to remember that.'

He was unable to keep himself from flinching. The threat was more than implied. It hung directly overhead, too close for comfort, suspended on too fragile a string.

He felt seized by a sudden, icy fear. The wrong words from Phoebe, and she would bring everything tumbling down on him.

'I stand corrected.' He smiled bleakly. 'It's just that you're too high spirited sometimes. I worry about you.'

'Then I suggest you worry a little less,' Phoebe snapped.

He caught Clara's sympathetic eye and turned to Beaty. 'I've changed my mind. I'd be delighted to extend our stay in order to attend your supper.'

He ignored Phoebe's wary look.

'Sorry about making such a fuss, Mr Beaty, but you know how little sisters are. Big brothers feel it's their God-given duty to watch over them.'

Beaty smiled. 'No harm meant, I'm sure. My intentions are honourable.'

'I'm certain they are.' Zaccheus shook hands with Clara and then with Beaty.

When the curtain rose on the second act, Zaccheus was not paying any attention to the farce onstage. His mind was elsewhere. On a buxom society lady named Eleonore Alice Qualey, who kept all her jewels in an unlocked drawer in her bedroom.

19

'You are *not* going to rob that Qualey woman!' Phoebe hissed venomously. She waved the vellum invitation Hezekiah Beaty had personally hand-delivered under Zaccheus' nose. 'I'm not going to let you! In fact, you are not going to rob anybody here in New Orleans.' She was pacing the living room of the Royal Suite in the Hotel Dixie with angry, hurried little steps. After she crossed the room several more times, she stopped, glared at Zaccheus, and tossed her white-blonde hair virtuously. 'I don't want *my* name besmirched here. I want it kept clean.'

Zaccheus stared at her. 'For whom?' he asked in a tight voice. 'Hezekiah Beaty?'

Phoebe let the invitation drop to the carpet. One moment she was standing perfectly still; the next she pounced into action. Letting out a shrill scream, she rushed towards him, hands waving, fingernails slashing.

He tossed his head back to avoid her slashing nails, managed to grab her by the wrists, and flung her angrily down onto a settee. She bounced a few times, and glared up at him balefully.

'I refuse to discuss this any further,' Zaccheus said with quiet dignity. He wiped his hands on his trousers, as if trying to cleanse them of some invisible dirt.

She sat there, seething.

Slowly, Zaccheus lowered himself into an armchair. He exchanged glances with Demps. The big Negro shrugged from across the room, sighed helplessly, and turned sadly away.

'Demps,' Zaccheus said softly, 'why don't you run down to the Western Union office. See if our money's arrived for the Jackson job yet.'

A silent signal seemed to pass between the two men. Demps nodded solemnly. 'I was just about to suggest that myself.'

Phoebe, unexpectedly, rose also. 'Wait for me, Demps,' she said haughtily. 'I'm coming with you.'

Zaccheus caught her by the arm. 'You're not going anywhere,' he told her quietly. 'You are going to stay here with me. It's time we had a good long talk.'

'Talk!' she scoffed, and threw off his hand and narrowed her eyes. 'You and I have *nothing* to talk about!' she snapped derisively. She glanced imperiously at Demps. 'Like I said, Demps,' she purred, 'you wait for me. I've just got to take a quick bath and change. Don't you listen to him, hear? He isn't himself today.' She glanced back at Zaccheus. 'Are you, *darling*?'

Secure in the knowledge that they would both do as she said, she raised her chin scornfully and crossed over to the corner where the tasselled bellpull, which summoned the maid, hung from the ceiling. She paraded slowly past Zaccheus as she walked to her room. Her stately exit was ruined when she slammed her door.

Demps looked questioningly at Zaccheus.

Zaccheus clapped his arm affectionately. 'Go on. I'll settle this.'

Demps nodded and left. Zaccheus sighed and waited half a minute. Then a petite mulatto maid knocked, entered, curtsied, and hurried through the living room to Phoebe's door to run the bath. Another knock, and Phoebe's door opened, closed, opened again. After the

306

maid finally left, Zaccheus crossed the room to Phoebe's, the thick carpet swallowing up the sound of his footsteps. For a moment, he stood perfectly still with his hand poised on the doorknob. He could hear water lapping in the tub. He shook his head. No matter where they were, it seemed that Phoebe spent half her time in the bathrooms, washing and scrubbing and perfuming herself, and the other half trying on her clothes and preening in front of a mirror.

Without further hesitation, he opened the door.

Phoebe's bedroom was dim and warm and feminine, fragrant with that same familiar, pleasantly heady scent he had smelled in her bedroom at the Flattses. The furniture was French, all delicate and curlicued. The heavy silk draperies were drawn across the French doors and the bedside lamps glowed dimly. On the bed, Phoebe's underthings were spread out on the silk covers. Just seeing the delicate, mysterious things Phoebe wore so close to her flesh brought an exquisite, unbearable ache into his groin.

He leaned over and with one index finger scooped up a creamy satin petticoat. He regarded it sadly. He and Phoebe had been together six months now, and these garments were all still a mystery to him. As was the woman they adorned.

He glanced at the other garments, each one as mysterious as the first. Lacy drawers. Soft slips. Phoebe's girdle, dripping with cords, with which she cinched her wasp-waist so tightly that it appeared even more wasplike. Her pale, embroidered camisoles, decorated with myriads of pale satin ribbons.

Each one of these undergarments touched her more intimately, and far more regularly, than he.

Abruptly he let the petticoat drop to the bed. It landed languidly, with barely a whisper, crumpling in upon itself in sensual folds. He stared at it a moment. Then he stepped slowly towards the bathroom door. It was half open, and clouds of steam seeped out into the bedroom. He could hear the high-pitched, musical drips of the taps. Then a few little splashes and a soft humming.

He recognized the tune. *Clementine.* Mouthing the melancholic words to himself, he wondered if he, like the sad troubador, had lost his Clementine, too:

> *Oh my darling, oh my darling,*
> *Oh my darling Clementine.*
> *You are lost and gone forever,*
> *Oh my darling Clementine.*

He pushed the door further open with his fingertips. The air in the bathroom was hot and humid, and he could feel himself breaking out in a sweat. But the sight which greeted him made him forget his discomfort. A single well-defined leg, foot arched, curved from a tub of soapy, pine-fragrant water. As he drew closer, he could see Phoebe through the ghostly screen of rising steam, her body low in the water, the back of her head resting on a pillow propped up against the rim of the tub, her loosened hair fanning out behind her.

As he watched, she lazily lifted a sea sponge high above her, squeezed it dry, and let the water dribble slowly down into the cleft between her breasts. She moaned contentedly and repeated the manoeuvre. After a while, she opened her eyes and reached for a bar of sherbet-coloured soap from the shallow silver dish.

The instant she saw Zaccheus her eyes widened and she crossed her soapy arms over her breasts. 'Get out!' she hissed, hurling the words at him. 'Get out, damn it!'

'Phoebe, what is wrong with you?'

'What is wrong with *me*?' She trembled with rage.

'Yes, you. Lately you've been acting as though you despise me.'

She laughed softly and shook her head. 'You're never going to learn, are you?'

'I didn't know there was anything to learn.'

She clutched the rim of the tub and rose to her feet, soapy water sluicing off her naked pink body. She no longer seemed to care whether she covered herself or not. She lifted her head challengingly. 'Now that you've seen me naked in the light, are you satisfied?' Her breasts heaved, and she narrowed her eyes. 'Take a good hard look at me, Zaccheus Howe – because this is the last look you're ever going to get!'

'Phoebe . . . why do you treat me like this?' he asked softly.

She didn't reply.

'We've got to talk, you and I,' he said.

'We have nothing to discuss.'

He remained standing there. 'Don't I do everything I can for you? Don't Demps and I go out and rob just to keep you in your damn luxuries?'

'I don't have to listen to this. *Otha!*' she screamed.

'Otha won't come,' he said softly.

She tossed her head. 'She comes whenever I bloody-well call her.'

'Not this time she won't.'

Phoebe narrowed her eyes to little slits, and then screamed again: '*Demps!*'

'Demps went to the Western Union office without you. We're alone.'

'You bastard!' she spat between her teeth. Then she reached for a big white towel and wrapped it around herself. She stepped out of the tub, water dripping on the floor.

'Phoebe, why do you behave this way? Demps and I arrange our whole lives around you, and you treat us both like dirt.'

'Arrange? What's this "arrange"? I can tell you what you arranged! You sneaked into my bedroom and made up all sorts of wonderful stories so I would get up and leave Muddy Lake with you. *That's* what you arranged!'

His mouth dropped open. 'Phoebe?' He looked stricken. 'You *wanted* to come. You *insisted*. Don't you remember?'

'Get out of my way. I have to get dressed. And stop staring at me like that!' With one hand she pushed him aside.

In a fit of anger, he lifted the silver soap plate as if to hit her.

She looked up at it in fear. Then she glanced at him.

His eyes had clouded over and slowly, he brought the plate down and stared at it. He turned it over and over, his frown of disbelief deepening. 'Where did you get this?' he demanded softly.

'It's the hotel's,' she said quickly. 'Comes with all the little luxuries.' She raised her head and smiled mockingly. 'Like the curtains and the towels and – '

His hand suddenly flashed. She cried out shrilly in pain, her own hand flying up to her cheek where his handprint glowed whitely against her soft, pink skin.

'I'm going to ask you one last time.' He held up the plate threateningly. 'Where . . . did . . . you . . . get . . . this?' He came slowly towards her and she backed into the bedroom, feeling her way with her hands. 'I told you, Zaccheus,' she said, her voice whiny with potent fear. 'It's the hotel's.'

'And the engraving? "LJB"? I suppose *those* are the hotel's initials?' His voice rose to a roar.

She steepled her hands together in front of her, as if in prayer. Her eyes were pleading. 'Zaccheus, it's just one little plate. Come *on*, Zaccheus.' She tried to laugh, but it came out sounding ugly and hollow.

'Damn you!' he screamed, and tossed the plate across the room with full force. It flew in an unwavering curve. The instant it slammed into the dressing table mirror, the silvered glass exploded into a cobweb, the shards

310

crashing down to the bottles of perfumes and toilet waters.

She clapped her hands flat against her cheeks and held them there, her eyes shiny.

'My God, Phoebe!' he whispered. 'Don't you realize what you've done? If someone had caught us with it we'd all be in jail? We've had a rule, damn it!'

She stared at him wordlessly.

'We agreed to ship everything off to Charleston immediately. *Everything!* You know we can't afford to be caught with a single stolen item! Not the tiniest, most worthless little thing!'

'Please, Zaccheus,' she whined. 'It was so pretty. I didn't think it'd do any harm. While you and Demps were packing the last barrel I sneaked it into my purse. It's small and pretty, and I like the way the fluted edges become little roses. *Please*, Zaccheus!' Her voice had grown tiny.

'Oh sweet baby Jesus. What kind of stupid idiot are you?' He glared at her and then his frown deepened. 'What else have you been sneaking aside all these past months?' he asked quickly.

She swallowed noisily. 'N-nothing, Zaccheus. Really. This plate is it. I *swear!*'

He gave an ugly snort of a laugh. *'You swear!'* Determinedly, he marched over towards the dresser.

She got there first, blocking his way. She faced him and the towel slipped to the floor, but she made no move to pick it up. Her face was pale. 'I . . . I think you'd better leave now,' she stammered.

His eyes bore right through hers. He realized suddenly that she was mustering all the courage she could lay her hands on. She was afraid. Terribly afraid. *Why?*

'I'll tell you once, and I won't say it again, Phoebe,' he warned quietly. 'Move aside.'

She stood her ground, her body quivering from fear. His hand blurred swiftly again. The sound of his open

311

palm making contact with her cheek was like a pistol crack. Her head jerked sideways and she tightened her lips, but otherwise she didn't move or make a sound.

'Now will you kindly move aside?' he asked softly.

She stood perfectly still, her eyes dark and challenging, and that made him all the angrier. He hit her again and again. Tears streamed down her cheeks, but she didn't utter a sound. Finally, he grasped her by the shoulders and flung her aside. She fell across the bed and lay there, face down.

Quickly, he pulled open one drawer after another and rummaged through them, tossing clothes, jewellery and underwear out on the floor behind him.

Suddenly he sucked in his breath. Rolled up in clothing, tucked into boxes, hidden inside shoes and scarves, pockets and hats – were the incriminating items he was looking for.

He couldn't believe how quick and light-fingered she had been, or how many of the stolen items which had been destined for the fence in Charleston were here in this very room. Had he and Demps been blind? Phoebe had been tucking away a good share of everything for her own little nest egg. And a 24-carat egg at that.

Sensing his fury, she raised her tear-streaked face from the bed. 'I-I just couldn't bear to see you sending all those pretty things off,' she whispered.

'And I suppose you didn't give any thought to how traceable these things are? Good God Almighty! If anyone had been suspicious of us and gone through our stuff, we'd be behind bars!'

'But they weren't suspicious,' she said truculently. 'Were they?'

'No thanks to you.'

'I'm sorry!' she snapped. 'What more do you want?'

He closed his eyes. He was tempted to say 'you', but he wasn't even sure of that anymore.

312

They sat quietly in the room, careful to avoid looking at each other. They didn't speak another word until Demps came in. 'What's the matter?' he asked. 'Somebody hold a funeral while I gone?'

Zaccheus shook his head. 'Did the money arrive?'

Demps nodded and handed it over. Zaccheus thumbed through the stack of bills and then stared at his friend. 'This is *all*?' His voice was an incredulous whisper.

Demps nodded. 'That it,' he said angrily. 'That son-bitch in Charleston, he screw us good. Next time I see him, I'm gonna get my hands round that scrawny, cheap-assed throat of his an' *squeeze*.'

'I think the problem's a little closer to home,' Zaccheus said obliquely.

'What you talkin' about?'

'Take a look around.' Zaccheus gestured.

Demps frowned and poked at Phoebe's clothes on the floor with the tip of his boot. 'So that why the money's so little! All the good stuff is here! Laws! Just lookit this diamond!' He bent down to retrieve it and held it up to the light.

'Someone,' Zaccheus said solemnly, 'has been keeping all the best stuff for herself.'

Demps turned to Phoebe, who hung her head and sniffled.

Zaccheus got wearily to his feet, went over to Phoebe, and stood there looking down at her. 'You'd better get ready. We've got Beaty's party to go to. Or have you forgotten?'

'How can I go?' she mumbled thickly through swollen lips, then looked up at him. One of her eyes was swelling up, too. She was going to have quite a shiner.

'You can and you will,' he said coldly.

'And if someone asks what happened to me?'

'I'm sure you'll be able to think of something.'

313

She gave a low, impersonal laugh. 'How do you know I won't tell the truth?'

'Because it'll be easier for you to lie,' he said grimly. 'It always is.'

'You . . . you *bastard*.'

He ignored her. 'Just make damn sure you keep that Qualey woman occupied, so she doesn't go home too soon. The same goes for her husband, if she has one.' He turned to Demps. 'Collect all of Miss Moneybag's hidden treasures and pack them up. Then send them off to Charleston at once. We can't afford to be caught with any of that loot. Then get another empty barrel ready. We're hitting the Qualeys' tonight.'

'Tonight!' Demps looked shocked. 'But you ain't ever been in that house! We don't even know what there is in there.' He paused and added softly: 'Or who.'

'I don't care,' Zaccheus said grimly. 'We're doing it tonight and then we're taking off from here. Somehow this town has lost its magic for me.' He stared at Phoebe. 'And God help us,' he added slowly, 'if everyone doesn't pull their fair share.'

'You makin' a mistake.' Demps shook his head ominously. 'A big mistake.'

Zaccheus' eyes were steady and unwavering. 'It'll work,' he said softly. 'It's always worked so far. Why shouldn't it work tonight?'

''Cause we ain't prepared.'

Zaccheus smiled humourlessly. 'We're prepared.'

They weren't prepared. It was the first time they had ever gone into a house blindly, and as a result, they had blood on their hands.

Zaccheus would never be able to forgive himself for what happened that night. Not for as long as he lived.

Things had gone wrong right from the start. The moment Phoebe arrived at Beaty's party, she overheard Hezekiah telling somebody that the Qualeys had declined his invitation. She'd waited a few minutes, pleaded ill, and rushed back to the hotel to warn Demps and Zaccheus. She was too late. They were already on their way to the Qualeys.'

The big house had been silent and dark, but it hadn't been empty. Snyder N. Qualey surprised them right after they'd broken in: the barrel of a pear-handled revolver greeted Demps in the chest. But Qualey made a fatal mistake. He didn't anticipate the big negro's strength or speed. In the brief struggle that followed, the gun went off. The old man's eyes widened and then he slipped slowly to the floor.

Demps grabbed Zaccheus by the arm. 'Come on!' he hissed urgently. 'Let's get us outta here!'

'Wait for me outside,' Zaccheus whispered. He turned on a lamp and bent over the crumpled old man to examine him. If he wasn't dead, hospitalization might yet save him.

He took one look, felt for the man's pulse, and promptly threw up. The old man was dead. Blood and guts were spattered all over the Savonnerie rug on which he lay.

It was then that he heard the shrill, reverberating scream. At first, he thought it came from within him. Then he whirled around, the slimy bile dripping from the corners of his mouth. An all-too-familiar woman was standing in the doorway, her massive bosom heaving, her plump hands covering her mouth.

'You've killed him!' she screamed over and over. 'You've killed him! You've killed my Snyder!'

Zaccheus flung up one elbow to hide his face, but he knew it was too late. Eleonore Alice Qualey had already taken a good long look at him. Within minutes, she would remember just where she had seen him before. In the lobby of the Comédie de la Quartier.

Something dark within him whispered urgently: *Kill her! Kill her before she can put you behind bars!*

315

But Zaccheus had no stomach for murder. He sprang to his feet. And ran.

20

Slowly he trudged through the murky Louisiana marshland, every now and then throwing furtive glances over his shoulder. He wrinkled his nose in disgust. A foul, putrid odour rose from the swamp, and the going was tough. The reeds were thick and head-high, and cut at his face. With every step he took, his feet sank deep into the shifting mud. It sucked and gripped at him, loathe to let him go. Insects droned angrily, and he kept slapping at his face and neck with his free hand. In his other he held the fishing line and the three whiskered catfish he'd caught.

He stopped for a moment and squinted up at the sky. The weather was as tense as he was. It couldn't seem to make up its mind whether to rain or not. Intermittent showers would drum down, then stop, then start up again, rustling the reeds and slashing sharp, painful needlepricks against his skin.

Ahead, he could make out the abandoned little hut on tall stilts rising up out of the marshlands. For the last few days, it had been home to him, Demps, and Phoebe. He figured that it was located about halfway between New Orleans and Baton Rouge, but he wasn't quite sure where.

He shivered as a sudden chill took hold of him. Never in his life had he felt quite so ill or helpless. Half of Louisiana was probably out searching for him.

When he reached the hut, Zaccheus climbed up the rickety ladder, crossed the narrow porch, and pushed the door open. And, just as quickly, closed it again. But too late. The sight which greeted him was one he would never forget. Phoebe, pale and pink and naked, was stretched out on her back, and Demps, black and muscular and naked, was atop her, growling fiercely as he thrust himself in and out of her, his dark buttocks gleaming while she gripped him urgently, forcing him ever further inside, her mouth gasping obscenities.

Numbly, Zaccheus let the fish drop down into the swamp below. Salt tears burned in his eyes. His whole world was collapsing.

Demps came out on the porch a minute later, buckling his grey trousers. His skin was sheathed in perspiration, a blush reddened his shiny black face, and his breath was still coming in short, laboured gasps. He hung his head in shame. 'I'm sorry,' he said with simple dignity, his hands hanging limply at his sides. 'It been comin'. It ain't her fault. It mine.'

Zaccheus took a deep breath. For an instant, he had felt the overwhelming urge to jump up and attack Demps, but the feeling dissipated as soon as it had come. It wasn't Demps' fault. He knew that now. Nor was Phoebe worth fighting over. He swallowed and turned around, smiling bleakly, his face a cracked mask of agony. 'No, Demps. The fault's mine,' he said in a trembling whisper. 'It's me who's been blind all this time. I saw the way she eyed you when she thought I wasn't looking, and the way she'd brush her leg up against yours when she was sitting beside you. I . . . I was a fool. I thought it was all innocent, you know? Friendly like.' He sighed painfully, leaned his forearm against a porch post, and buried his head in the crook of his arm. 'I put her way up on a pedestal. That was the main problem. She just didn't deserve it. She belongs down there.' He pushed himself away from the post and gestured at the murky, fetid swamp below.

Demps' voice was choked. 'I'm sorry. Really I am.' His eyes shone moistly. 'We're friends. I didn't wanna ruin our friendship. 'Specially not like this. I try to fight it. Really I did.'

Zaccheus clapped Demps on the arm. 'She's beautiful and desirable. There isn't a normal man alive who could have resisted her.'

Demps shook his head. 'I should'a.' His voice dropped to a self-flagellating whisper. ' 'Sides, I'm a nigger. Niggers don't touch white women. Not 'less they wants to be lynched.'

Zaccheus eyed him sadly. 'She was forbidden fruit, is all. That's part of what made her so irresistible.'

'Mebbe. Mebbe not.'

Zaccheus sighed and tightened his lips. 'Well, I guess I'd better go in and have a talk with her now.'

Demps shifted uncomfortably. 'Don't be too hard on her,' he said softly. 'She just a child still.'

'Yeah.' Zaccheus gave a short, mocking laugh. 'And she plays just like children, too. Eh?'

Demps averted his gaze.

Slowly, Zaccheus went inside, the screen door banging shut behind him. He couldn't keep from staring. Phoebe was over by the window, slowly getting dressed. She was bent forward, one foot resting on a crate, the strings of her corset in her hands, her hair falling down over her face. If she noticed him, she didn't let on.

He shook his head sadly. Any other time, he would have felt an ache well up inside his loins, but now he felt nothing. Absolutely nothing.

Strange, he thought, how suddenly everything had turned topsy-turvy. Even his emotions. He didn't feel the least inclination to reach out and touch her. For the first time, he could see her dispassionately, as if he were watching her eating or drinking instead of dressing. There was no mysterious sensuousness about her any longer. He had completely lost his appetite for her.

'You know,' he said softly, 'once, not so very long ago, you really had me fooled.'

She turned to face him, a tawny leopard's gleam in her eyes. 'Fooled!' she hissed. She tugged furiously on her corset strings and then straightened up, arching her back like a cat. 'I tell you who's been fooled! Not you.

Me! Because I thought you were something. But you know what? You *aren't!*'

He stared at her.

'Which is why I like Demps.' She curled a lock of hair around her index finger and toyed with it. 'And you know why? Because he's not holier-than-thou, Mr Almost-Preacher Man! Because he's a *man!* Because he knows how to make a woman feel like a woman! But mainly – because he likes *this* – ' She reached into her bodice, grabbed one of her breasts, and pulled it free.

Zaccheus turned away. Her nipples were still erect and moist and swollen from lovemaking.

He fought to keep his voice in control. 'I thought you were sweeter,' he said quietly. 'Less conniving. More caring. And I was under the impression you didn't like . . . to do . . . you know, physical things . . .'

'– Can't you say it?' she spat bitterly. 'Screwing! Copulating! *Fucking!*'

'Phoebe,' he pleaded in embarrassment, 'please don't use language like that. And tuck . . . tuck your – '

She looked down at herself. 'My tit?' She howled with laughter, spraying spittle all around, but a burning hatred smouldered deep within her eyes. Hands on her hips, she strutted tauntingly back and forth in front of him, one breast exposed, the other hidden, in a parody of a dance hall girl. The sterling chain was around her throat, the pansy charm hanging into the cleft of her bosom, and he clenched his fists, so great was the urge to tear it off her. To him, that charm symbolized everything that was good and pure. He had not stolen it. He had bought it with the precious little money that was his before his life had soured. He had bought it for his mother. *Oh God!* he moaned inwardly. How he wished he had given it to her instead of Phoebe. He had never given his mother anything.

'You think you're so good, you goddamn thief!' Phoebe spat out derisively, tossing her head and curling

319

her lip. 'Do you think I ever wanted you? You were convenient, that's all! I had to run off. And do you want to know why? Do you . . . *you* who always seeks the truth?'

He sank into a corner, his head in his hands.

'Well, I'll tell you why!' she shrieked shrilly. 'Because I met a man!' She held herself very erect and peered forwards, as if into a dream she had conjured up. 'Oh, he was a rich, handsome man. A man I did *everything* for. But he left me pregnant. And you, Zaccheus Howe, were mighty convenient! I ran off with you so that I wouldn't be burdened with shame. And you never even knew it, did you!' When he didn't reply she repeated, a little louder: '*Did you?*'

'Lies,' he whispered dully. 'All lies.'

'Lies!' she mocked him. 'Ask your precious friend Demps. When the carriage had the accident, and I couldn't travel – ask him what the doctor *really* said! Well? Do you want to go outside and *ask* him?' She stared at him through narrowed eyes. Then she threw back her head and laughed. 'You men are such fools! What did you think you were? God's gift to women?'

He lowered his hands and stared up at her. 'All I know,' he said in a whisper, 'is that you're not God's gift to man.' He couldn't help the ugly chuckle in his throat. 'Well, maybe I'm wrong after all. After what you just told me, maybe you *are* God's gift to man. To a lot of men!'

Her red face contorted with rage and her voice climbed to an even more hysterical range. 'You bastard! And to think I let you touch me!'

'Touch you!' he yelled. '*Once!*' He staggered to his feet, his face burning with rage. 'You went to bed with me *once*! And I suppose I can thank you for that because you were pregnant – because you wanted to pawn the baby off as mine!'

'You know why you're so upset?' she shrieked.

'Because you can't get it up like you should, that's why! When you take a woman to bed it's like some sort of slow, fumbling ritual. Christ! Did you ever hear of passion? Anyway, that one time was enough for *me*. You were nothing in bed! Do you hear me? *Nothing!* No wonder I wanted Demps to fuck me. His cock's a lot bigger than yours!'

For an instant, a blind fury tore through him. The little room reeled and clouded, and he lunged at her, wrapping his hands tightly around her neck.

She stared at him in sudden terror as his fingers began to squeeze into her throat.

'I'm going to kill you, you bitch!' he hissed. He shook her head, and it wobbled limply. 'Do you hear me?'

She opened her mouth to form a scream, but her face was frozen, the porcelain skin pulled taut by terror. It took all her strength merely to gasp for air. From her throat came strange loud clucking noises.

Suddenly Zaccheus heard a the screen door bang. Then he felt Demps behind him, and large black hands loosened his stranglehold.

Phoebe took a faltering step backwards, held onto the edge of the windowsill with one hand, and with the other clutched her throat as she took deep, rasping lungfuls of air.

Zaccheus began to weep uncontrollably.

'Cover your breasts and finish gettin' dressed,' Demps told Phoebe soberly. 'I think it's time we moved on and split up.'

She nodded, still hunched over. Angry blue bruises were already swelling up on her neck.

'And wear you scarf. Your neck doesn't look none too purdy.' Demps shook his head sadly. 'Not purdy at all.'

Phoebe eyed him strangely. 'If we split up, I want to go with you, Demps,' she rasped grotesquely. 'I don't want to go with him.'

'All right.'

For a moment she stood there stiffly, staring at Zaccheus. He gazed back at her through wet eyes. The pansy charm gleamed in the obscene cleft of her bosom.

'To think,' he sobbed quietly, his voice mournful with misery. 'To think that I put you in front of my Ma. I bought that necklace for her, you know. Not for you.'

'In that case,' she rasped, 'here! Have it back.' Her lips curled sourly. 'I don't want it, anyway. I don't want anything of yours. Demps is going to buy me another one. A prettier one.' She looked at Demps significantly. 'Aren't you, Demps?'

The big negro nodded wordlessly.

Slowly, she reached behind her neck, loosened the clasp on the sterling chain, and tossed the necklace at Zaccheus' feet.

'Gather your things up,' Demps told her. 'We'll wait for you outside. And take one of the diamonds out of your shoes. Leave it on the windowsill.'

Phoebe picked up one slipper, obediently took out one of the large diamonds hidden in the toe, and placed it on the sill. Its facets caught the dull light and glittered with a steely fire.

After the fiasco at the Qualeys' they hadn't dared return to the Hotel Dixie for their things. Phoebe's low-heeled, white satin slippers, now ruined with mud, were all they had left. Zaccheus' foresight had at least paid off. The two flawless diamonds, pried from their settings and secreted in the toes of her slippers, were all they had to show for their spree of robberies.

Demps took Zaccheus by the arm, pulled him to his feet, and led him outside. 'That diamond yours. As we agreed a few months ago, the other one is Phoebe's.'

'What about you?'

Demps shrugged philosophically. 'What would I do with a diamond? All it would do is cause me no end of trouble. It could even kill me. A nigger ain't supposed to be caught with a rock like that on 'im. I'd get lynched for sure.'

Zaccheus nodded. He could see Demps' point.

'I'm sorry I had to get rough with you in there,' Demps said sadly, 'but if I hadn't, you'da killed her.'

Zaccheus sighed heavily. 'Maybe it would have been for the best. Now one of us is still stuck with her.'

'Don't worry none. I can control her.'

Zaccheus nodded. 'I'm sorry things had to turn out this way. No hard feelings?'

Demps shook his head. 'No. No hard feelin's whatsoever.'

'What are you going to do now?'

'Dunno. Probably head up North.'

'And what are you going to do there?'

Demps shrugged. 'The same thing you're going to do, wherever you end up.'

Zaccheus looked puzzled.

'I'm going straight. And up North I'll be useful, at least. It ain't as backward as it is down here. Things are taking shape up there.'

'And Phoebe?' Zaccheus asked softly. 'How do you think she's going to take to this?'

'She won't, for long. And she won't be faithful,' Demps said thoughtfully. 'As soon as she's tired o' me, she'll waltz off and find herself a rich white husband. But right now, I'm the best she can hope for. And I'm something different for her.' He paused painfully. 'Like an artichoke, I suppose.'

'And you, Demps?' Zaccheus asked softly. 'You're too good for her. Why do you even consider being around her?'

'Because, right now she needs somebody. Anybody.' Demps grinned hugely. ' 'Sides, it works both ways, you know. Like you said earlier, she forbidden fruit. But so am I, as far as she's concerned. You see, I may be her artichoke, but she's *my* artichoke, too.'

323

'You think you'll make it up North all right? I mean, you were with me down in New Orleans. All they have to do is ask around at the hotel, and they have your description as well as mine.'

'I'll be okay,' Demps said definitely. 'They'll never recognize me. To them, all niggers look alike.'

Zaccheus winced.

'It's true.'

Phoebe came quietly out onto the porch. Zaccheus and Demps both looked at her.

'I'm ready,' she croaked hoarsely.

'You forgot you scarf,' Demps pointed out.

'Oh.' She touched her throat gingerly with her fingertips. 'I'll go in and get it.'

She went back inside. A moment later, she came out again, knotting the scarf around her throat.

Zaccheus and Demps shook hands. 'Good-bye, friend,' Demps said softly. 'God bless.'

'Take care,' Zaccheus said quietly. 'And good luck.' He turned to Phoebe, but she pointedly turned her back on him.

For a long time, he stood on the porch of the hut, watching Demps and Phoebe pushing their way through the swamp in a northeasterly direction. Then he went slowly into the hut. He picked the pansy charm up off the floor, stared at it, and put it in his pocket. Then he went over to the windowsill.

The diamond was gone. Phoebe had taken it with her.

He shook his head. So that was why she had 'forgotten' her scarf. To have an excuse to go back in and get the diamond. He smiled grimly to himself. The saying was old and trite, but true. How true. No matter what anybody tried to tell you, there is no honour among thieves.

Well, it didn't matter anyway, he told himself. Without the diamond, at least he would be able to start all over again. With a clean slate.

Slowly, he began to climb down the ladder into the swamp. Then he headed southwest, in the exact opposite direction from the one that Phoebe and Demps had taken. A route which would, eventually, take him to Quebeck, Texas.

BOOK THREE

1911

Elizabeth-Anne and Zaccheus

QUEBECK, TEXAS

1

It was high noon when the train from Brownsville pulled into Quebeck. Zaccheus swung his suitcase down onto the platform and hopped off. As the train hissed and chugged laboriously away, he glanced around the tiny station. He was the only passenger who'd got off, and nobody had got on. It all added up to a sleepy little town.

He picked up his heavy suitcase packed with Bibles and ambled over to the stationmaster's window. Summoning up his friendliest smile, he said, 'Howdy, friend.'

The grizzled old stationmaster, who was ticket salesman and Western Union operator both, pulled aside the glass window and squinted up at him. 'No more trains leavin' today. Next one's tomorrow mornin'.'

'That's fine with me,' Zaccheus said cheerfully. 'Could you direct me to the local hotel?'

'Ain't none 'round here, sonny. But there's a nice roomin' house in town, run by a Miz Clowney and her two nieces. She only rents rooms by the week, but if there's a vacancy, she's been known to make an exception.' The stationmaster squinted at him. 'If'n she thinks yer respectable enough, that is. She don't like no messin' around. Proper woman, Miz Clowney is. The nieces too.'

'How do I get there?'

'Go round front and take the traction into town. It'll get here in 'bout twenty minutes. The trip'll take another fifteen. Get off on Main Street when you see a big pink house. That's the place. But you'd best go across the street from the roomin' house, place called The Good Eats Café. You kin get honest wholesome home cookin' there, and that's where Miz Clowney usually is all day. Owns both establishments.' He nodded for emphasis.

'I'm mighty grateful.' Zaccheus placed his hands far apart on the sill, leaned close to the window, and assumed his most solemnly profound expression. 'You look like a fine, upright Christian man to me, my friend.'

'I ain't yer friend. I don't even know you.' The stationmaster squinted at him suspiciously.

Aware of the scrutiny, Zaccheus pulled his shoulders back and smiled disarmingly. He had finally topped out to his full height, and, at twenty-one, was a towering young man, though not one to instil fright. There was something friendly and open about him. His eyes were bright blue, he sported a thin, blond moustache, and his blond hair curled naturally. He stood dapper in his cream-coloured slacks, striped jacket, bright polka-dot bow tie, and straw boater. There was something almost elegant about him. The only thing which gave away the hardships and toil of his early years were his large, capable hands and thick wrists.

The stationmaster chuckled. 'From yer city clothes and the heft of that suitcase of yers, I can tell you're a salesman. Can spot 'em a mile away. I ain't buyin' nothin'.'

Zaccheus grinned. 'Who says I'm selling anything?'

'I do,' the stationmaster said crisply. 'Now scram.'

Zaccheus held both hands up, palms out. 'Will do, my friend. God bless you.'

'Need no blessin's an' no Bibles, neither. Last year, clown by the name o' Osgood suckered my wife into buyin' one.' The stationmaster shook his head. 'Tole

330

her I'd kill her if'n she as much as looked at another thing any travellin' salesman offered. Don't you know it, I came home last week and what'dyo think greeted my eyes? Slippers. There was a salesman through, and she'd bought mules for me an' the kids. Red ones, with big black dots all over 'em. Looked like giant ladybugs. Ugliest things I ever seen.' He shook his head sadly.

Zaccheus was not listening. He had caught the name Osgood, and that brought on a surge of anger. The people at the Wisdom Bible Publishing Company could have forewarned him that Roger Osgood had worked this territory already. Everywhere he went, it seemed that Wisdom Bibles had already been sold there. He smiled sheepishly. 'What time you say the first train leaves in the morning?'

'Nine-thirty for Laredo.' The stationmaster eyed him shrewdly. 'Bibles, eh?'

Zaccheus smiled and turned away. It was high time he stopped trying to sell the Lord. It was time he changed his merchandise. To polka-dotted mules, maybe. Anything but Bibles. Conning people into buying Wisdom Bibles was more difficult than he'd ever imagined it would be. It seemed that all he ever did was lug that heavy suitcase around. He was weary of doors being slammed in his face, countless people staring vacantly at him, mumbling, 'If we ain't got money for food, what makes you think we got money for books?' How was he to answer that? Growing up, food had been scarce, and he'd much rather have had a full stomach than a Bible any day.

It was a mean little living he was managing to eke out, and it barely brought in enough money to stay on the road. Still, it was a lot better than what he had done in the past. Ever since fleeing New Orleans, he had been determined to be honest and not to slip. He sighed to himself. Perhaps he should try some ruse. Maybe he was just *too* honest for this business. Perhaps that was why, in well over a week, after knocking on hundreds of doors, he'd only managed to sell five Bibles.

He left the platform and lugged his suitcase around to the front of the station. Setting it down, he mopped his forehead with a handkerchief. He was aching for a cool drink. It was ungodly hot out.

He gazed down the long, straight dusty road which led towards the town. Along the centre of the road ran two narrow railroad tracks, the ties buried somewhere beneath the packed dust and dirt. He judged the town to be at least a quarter of a mile distant. It shimmered in the unbearable Texas heat.

For a moment, he was tempted to walk into town, but then he decided against it. He might as well splurge and wait for the Quebeck Traction, the tram which made a loop through the town. He took off his jacket and swung it over his shoulder, he untied his bow tie, and unbuttoned the collar of his shirt. After fifteen minutes of sitting in the shade, he heard the slow, distant plodding of a horse. He looked to his left. The traction was arriving.

The solitary, antiquated, small-gauge railroad car was painted bright blue and was pulled by a sweating, plodding, old grey mare. The small, flat-top wagon had been converted into a passenger coach. There were four narrow slatted benches facing frontwards, open on both sides, so that passengers could just step up and slip into a seat or hop off wherever they desired. Steel posts held up the metal canopy which shaded the passengers.

Zaccheus paid the driver the nickel fare, swung the suitcase aboard, and hopped up. He took a seat right behind the driver's, and settled back on the bench. The wooden slats were hard and uncomfortable, but the shade was pleasant and welcome. It was a lot better than lugging the suitcase on foot.

There was the snapping of reins and slowly the horse began to move and the tram wheels began to turn.

Main Street, Quebeck, was like a lot of other Main Streets he had seen, only it wasn't as green a most. Water was scarce, and for things to grow they had to be carefully nurtured. Old houses with gingerbread-fretted front porches were set back in dusty little front yards, interspersed with flat-roofed buildings in need of paint and repair. A lot of ground floors held shops and businesses. There was a hardware store. A variety store. A grocery store. A post office. A nickelodeon. Dogs barked at the traction and made half-hearted attempts to chase it, but it was too hot, and after a few barks they slumped back down. A few dour women got on in front of the post office, their dusty pastel dresses long and prim, their hats shading them from the sun. Zaccheus doffed his boater politely and they smiled tightly. It was too hot to exchange meaningless pleasantries. Then, just ahead, Zaccheus saw a three-storey, pink gingerbread house.

He leaned forward. 'That Miz Clowney's Rooming House?' he asked the driver.

'Sure is,' the driver replied without looking back, and the traction slid to a smooth halt.

'Much obliged,' Zaccheus said and he hopped down, light and agile, to the dusty, sun-baked street. He stood clutching the suitcase as the tram pulled off again. He stared up at the house. It had obviously seen better days, yet there was nothing remotely neglected about it. Honeysuckle curled bravely around the porch posts, and other robust specimen plants abounded, some the likes of which he had never seen. But the *pièce de résistance* was a mighty, blooming wisteria, luxuriantly foliaged, that seemed to climb straight up into the air until it found purchase on the shingled porch roof up which it crept. It continued to climb around windows and flower boxes filled to bursting with blooms, until the fragile ends of it clutched a great brick chimney which rose majestically into the cloudless sky. The rooming house was an oasis against the blazing summer noon, a welcoming, cooling sight for tired eyes and parched skin. Only a discreet sign, half tucked away among the thickly leafed wisteria, hinted that this house was indeed a business establishment. The sign was oval, painted pink like the house, and was lettered with neat, florid green script, half of which was obscured by the wisteria leaves:

Clowney's Ro
Rooms by the Wee

Zaccheus turned around and looked at the opposite side of the street. A simple, two-storeyed flat-topped house, as plainly utilitarian a structure as the rooming house was decorative, squatted squarely, a hitching post running along the long, narrow porch. A large, black and white sign hanging above the screen door read:

THE GOOD EATS CAFÉ

He crossed the street, climbed the porch, and went inside, the screen door banging shut behind him. He found himself in an intimate, noisy little dining room, obviously very respectable, scrubbed, and clean. Checkered tablecloths draped the square tables which were surrounded on all sides by bentwood chairs. The wine-dark wallpaper was homely and faded, and Victorian pictures were framed in dark heavy moulding. Despite the dark colours, there was a brightly welcoming, cheery atmosphere to the room, perhaps due to the luncheon crowd, or the tiny bottles on each table which held small, freshly cut bouquets, or the newspaper rack in the corner from which hung several copies of the *Quebeck Weekly Gazette*.

'May I help you?' a soft female voice asked with forced politeness.

Automatically Zaccheus took off his boater and held it against his chest. He turned around.

The woman who had spoken was young and very pretty in a pert sort of way, with a heart-shaped face framed by two lustrous, dark pigtails tied with robin's-egg blue ribbon which matched the colour of her eyes. She was wearing a calf-length, smock-like dress with a high collar, loose long sleeves, and a huge waist pocket which hung heavily, full of jingling change.

'I'm looking for Miz Clowney,' Zaccheus said. 'They tell me she owns the rooming house across the street.'

Jenny bit down on her lower lip, nodded, and glanced towards the kitchen doors. 'You'll have to wait a while. Auntie's in the kitchen. She won't be out until the lunch rush is over. Sit down if you like . . . there's an empty table over there by the kitchen doors. Do you want something to eat?'

He shook his head.

'You can leave your suitcase by the front door. Nobody will take it.'

He smiled, gazing into her cracked-porcelain eyes, but it was impossible to look past the surface. The irises were glazed veneer, at once clear, and yet opaque.

She eyed him intently and tilted her head. He was aware of the faint sprinkling of freckles on her nose. 'Well, I'd better be off and clear some of the tables,' she said. 'I'll have Auntie come out soon as she can.'

'Thank you.' He took a seat and waited patiently, watching her hurry back and forth, carrying steaming plates of delicious smelling beef stew from the kitchen and returning weighed down by stacks of dirty dishes. From what he could see, the place was doing a thriving business, especially considering the size of the town. Each time the swinging doors behind him thumped open and closed, an almost visible, delicious aroma of cooking hit him squarely, and the cacophonous clatter of pots and pans seemed more pronounced. Occasionally, he caught the sounds of a woman's voice, firm but cultured, and the machine-gun staccato of a second woman speaking laborious English mixed with rapid-fire Spanish. He watched diners leave the money for their meals on the tables and get up.

It was nearly twenty minutes before Elender Hannah Clowney finally pushed her way briskly out through the kitchen doors, wiping her hands on a towel. Her piercing gaze made a sweep of the dining room. She wore a high-necked, cream-coloured blouse with long tight sleeves and a cameo brooch pinned to the collar. Her skirt was grey, with cotton dust ruffles which swept the floorboards. She was thin and elegant with chestnut hair streaked liberally with strands of silver. Finally her eyes came to rest on Zaccheus. She looked down at him with consternation. 'Oh! You weren't served –'

'No, ma'am, that's quite all right,' Zaccheus said hastily. He got quickly to his feet. 'You're Miz Clowney?'

Elender inclined her head.

'I didn't come here for lunch, ma'am. They told me to see you about a room.'

'I see.' Elender paused. 'How long do you intend to stay?'

'Overnight, ma'am.'

'Hmmm.' She pressed her lips together. 'As a rule, I make it a point to rent out rooms to regular roomers only. On a weekly basis.'

Zaccheus looked stricken. 'Please, ma'am. This town doesn't have a hotel, and I'm very tired. The train doesn't leave until tomorrow morning. The station-master said you sometimes made exceptions.'

She nodded. 'Very well. One night it is.'

But as it turned out, he would stay a lot, lot longer than that.

336

2

After she was satisfied that Jenny had everything under control, Elender escorted Zaccheus to the rooming house. 'It's a beautiful house,' he said as they crossed over to the other side of Main Street.

She stopped and gazed up at it, a faint smile on her lips. 'Yes it is, isn't it? Few people really "see" it, if you know what I mean, it's been here so long. They all take it for granted, myself included. Even I tend to forget that it has a kind of unofficial honourific name.'

'Oh?' He looked sideways at her. 'And what's that?'

She smiled. ' "McMean's Folly." That's what we call it around here.'

'Why? Because of all the plants?'

She laughed. 'I see what you mean. But no. It's the house's history. You see, after Neeland McMean went through all the pains of having it built in Missouri, and having it dismantled and shipped here and put back up, only to make his bride less homesick —'

'She left him!' he blurted out vehemently.

She looked startled. 'Why, yes. How did you know?'

He blushed suddenly. 'I–I didn't,' he stammered. Then he looked quickly away. 'I guessed it.'

'I understand,' Elender said softly. She touched his arm gently. 'Women . . . have been known to be unkind.' Her eyes clouded over as she remembered her own tragic youth. 'And so have men,' she added painfully. Then she clapped her hands briskly together, signalling a change of subject. 'Let's go in, shall we? You're fortunate, you know. There's only one empty room. It's quite a climb, though, and really very small, I'm afraid . . .'

It was on the third floor, in a narrow, circular turret.

337

Elender stood in the doorway, hands clasped in front of her, as Zaccheus inspected the room.

It surprised her, because none of her roomers had ever done that before, not in the way he did. Generally, they poked the mattress and peered into the wardrobe. He did none of that. Instead, he stood back and noted the architectural details, obviously fascinated by the elaborate plaster moulding which encircled the ceiling, and the three oriel windows which looked out onto the street.

'I like it,' he exclaimed.

Elender, ever the practical businesswoman, responded by saying, 'That'll be two dollars, in advance.'

He nodded, reached into his pocket, and counted it out.

She pocketed the money and smiled. 'Supper at the Good Eats Café is served from five o'clock on.'

'I'm not hungry,' he said quickly, stifling the growling of his stomach. There was no money to squander on sit-down restaurant meals. The room cost enough as it was, but given its comfort, he felt it well worth the price.

'Of course you're hungry.' Elender permitted herself a smile. 'The price of the room includes board over at the café. Breakfast, lunch, and supper.

He grinned sheepishly. 'Would it be all right if I took my lunch today instead of tomorrow, since the train leaves in the morning?'

'Then come across the street right now. After lunch, you still have supper and tomorrow's breakfast coming to you. You can unpack later.'

The Good Eats Café was empty. The lunch crowd was gone. He took a seat facing one of the windows so that he could look out across the street at the pink house. From the kitchen, he could hear the sounds of dishes being washed.

'Can I help you?' a soft voice behind him asked.

Zaccheus turned around. This time a different girl served as waitress, and in one glance he could tell that she was the antithesis of the other. He thought her to be about two years younger, about sixteen, he guessed; and whereas the other one had been coldly pretty, with hard, opaque eyes, this one was the exact opposite. She radiated a kind of fragile softness coupled with deeply-rooted strength and purpose. Her hair was the colour of golden wheat, pulled back in a fuzzy, thick ponytail, and her eyes were translucent aquamarine – so translucent that he could feel himself tumbling into their depths. She was dressed in a smock identical to the other girl's, with the same huge waist pocket, only hers was pale aquamarine to match her eyes. Despite the heat she wore spotless white gloves.

'Miss Clowney said I might have a late lunch,' he said.

Elizabeth-Anne nodded. 'I'll have Rosa heat up the stew. If that is all right with you?'

Zaccheus smiled. 'Right now, anything would suit me just fine.' He eyed her hesitatingly.

'Will there be something else?'

He fixed his gaze on the tablecloth, two fingers running in place. 'I was just wondering . . .' He glanced up at her and blushed. 'You're Miss Clowney's other niece, aren't you?'

Elizabeth-Anne felt the force of his brilliant blue eyes and lowered her own eyes demurely. Her voice was soft. 'In a manner of speaking, yes. Auntie adopted me unofficially many years ago, after my parents were killed in . . . in an accident.'

'I'm sorry to hear that.'

She smiled ruefully. 'That's quite all right.' Then her quivering smile broadened as she paused hesitantly. Almost furtively, she extended a gloved hand. 'My name is Elizabeth-Anne.'

He got to his feet and they shook hands, and her strong, firm grip surprised him. 'That's a very pretty name,' he said softly, staring deep into the limpid, shifting shoals of her eyes. 'Mine is Zaccheus . . . How–Hale.' For an instant, and he didn't really know why, he had been tempted to blurt out his real name to her. Just in time, he covered his blunder. Ever since New Orleans, he had gone by the name Zaccheus Hale.

'You're a new roomer?' she asked with quickening interest as he sat back down.

He nodded. 'Only for the night, I'm afraid.'

The corners of her lips seemed to tighten. 'Oh. I see,' she said, with visible disappointment. For a long moment they locked eyes. There was something very attractive about him, she thought; that, and something else which she had difficulty putting her finger on. After a moment she realized what it was. A kind of reckless excitement that he seemed to have suppressed smouldered deeply within him. He was unlike any of the young men she knew around here. Somehow, he seemed special.

'Well, I'll have your lunch ready in a moment,' she said quickly, suddenly afraid of her own runaway emotions. She made a nervous gesture of running her gloved fingers down along her sides; then she pirouetted swiftly and retreated into the kitchen.

As he watched her being swallowed up by the swinging doors at the back of the café, Zaccheus couldn't help thinking that Miss Clowney was blessed with two of the most attractive nieces a woman could ever hope to have.

A peculiar kind of longing started up within him. What a strange place Quebeck, Texas was turning out to be! The two young nieces . . . each attractive in a different sort of way, as unalike as night and day, each as unique as the hard, glittering coldness of a diamond and the shimmering red warmth of a ruby. The pink house . . . a fairy-tale dream come true, which had curdled into the symbol of a nightmare for some long-dead man named Neeland McMean. The turret room he was renting for the night . . . a charming, comfortable, cosy little room which he wished he could call his own forever. Miss Clowney . . . efficient, yet strangely and elegantly attractive, a friendly woman whose brisk, businesslike veneer could not quite mask the warmth of her heart. And, finally, there was Quebeck itself . . . this improbable, quiet, slumbering little town far off the beaten track, a town which was in the United States only by virtue of the side of the nearby wide river bank on which it had been built, a town where there was no danger of anyone ever discovering the truth about his sordid past. Combined, all these things suddenly made Quebeck extraordinarily attractive. It was the kind of place where, for the first time in years, Zaccheus felt certain he would be content to settle down and grow roots, a place where he believed he wouldn't mind forging a new life for himself.

In the stifling hot kitchen of the Good Eats Café, Elizabeth-Anne hummed softly to herself as she watched Rosa, the Mexican cook, dunk a ladle into a pot of water. Rosa shook off most of the water and then packed the ladle firmly with rice. The porcelain chimed clearly as the big, brown-skinned woman with her flat face flipped the ladle expertly upside-down in the exact centre of the plate so that the rice came out as if from a mould, in a perfect, steaming ball. Nodding to herself, Rosa then deftly ladled a generous portion of the chunky rich beef stew around the orb of rice, careful not to drip any on the pristine whiteness of the rice itself.

Rosa held the plate out to Elizabeth-Anne and grunted.

Elizabeth-Anne took it and looked down at it. For a moment, her face broke into an uncharacteristic scowl. There was no doubt in her mind but that the dish both looked and smelled delicious, but she felt the sudden urge to make it even more special . . . to add that extra,

341

artistic woman's touch which it lacked. She had a sudden inspiration. Quickly, she set the plate down on the table and hurriedly chose a perfect ripe beefsteak tomato out of the basket on the floor. She washed it and sliced it in half in a zig zag pattern, and placed one of the halves on a corner of the plate. She then sprinkled the tomato with parsley leaves, cracked a hard-boiled egg, and sliced it perfectly. She laid the centre portions with their rich yellow circles of yoke around the orb of rice, so that they overlapped slightly.

Rosa watched her from a distance with hooded, wise brown eyes, but her flat face was devoid of expression. When Elizabeth-Anne pushed her way back out through the swinging doors, the Mexican woman quietly padded over to the doors, pushed one of the flaps open a crack, and looked out at the handsome stranger. She nodded knowingly to herself. Only this morning, Elizabeth-Anne had been a child. But this afternoon . . . ah, this afternoon . . . she had turned into a woman.

When morning came, Rosa was not at all surprised to learn that the handsome stranger had decided to stay on a while longer.

3

The arrival of Zaccheus was a time point for both Jenny and Elizabeth-Anne.

It was like a fight to the death. Abruptly the rivalry which had always existed between the two of them deepened. They had both fallen head-over-heels for the stranger who called himself Zaccheus Hale, and for once Elizabeth-Anne was not content to simply withdraw and let Jenny walk all over her. For years, they had both lived under the same roof, two sticks of dynamite lacking only the fuse.

And now the fuse was not only in place; it had been lit.

Suddenly, both girls fought to outdo the other. In the past, they had taken turns serving lunches and suppers at the Good Eats Café, Elizabeth-Anne liking her job and taking it seriously, while Jenny, who obviously hated it, counted the hours and minutes until her shift was over. Now, overnight, they were both in the café at the same time, working the lunch and supper shifts, each one in her own way vying for the opportunity to serve Zaccheus in order to get his full attention. Jenny was more blatantly forward, relying on her pert prettiness and feminine wiles, while Elizabeth-Anne was subdued and quietly efficient, counting on her shy charm and all the little ways she could think of to make everyday things more special for him. But there was one thing both girls had in common. Each seemed suddenly more vibrantly alive. Each walked around with her face flushed, her eyes intense, her skin glowing. One smile from Zaccheus and they melted, their legs weak and trembling.

Elender could not help but become aware of the sudden tension. Yet some feminine intuition told her to stand back and let things take their natural course. She realized that this was one time when meddling would only confuse the issue, making things worse and stretching everything even more out of proportion.

Nor was Zaccheus unaware of the girls' attention. He would have had to be blind and unfeeling to miss it. But much as their flurry of activity pleased him, it unsettled him just as much. The last time he had been attracted to a woman had been to Phoebe Flatts – and only too late had he realized that Phoebe had wanted him only to suit her own purposes. Now, like lightning bolts out of the clear blue, here were *two* attractive young ladies

343

vying for his undivided attention. He hardly knew what to make of them, and for the first time since Phoebe Flatts' cruelty, he found himself flattered and . . . *yes*, actually wanting and *needing* feminine company.

Jenny aroused in him a kind of strutting, bantam pride. She was the more physically attractive of the two, the one who seemed so sure of herself; her facial expressions and her body language seemed to whisper unspoken promises.

Elizabeth-Anne, on the other hand, touched a sensitive nerve in his heart. Here, he knew, was someone who had been beaten down and had suffered; yet despite her shyness, she held herself with a kind of fierce, aloof dignity — there was a strength coursing through her which was so well hidden that hardly anyone even knew it was there. But he did. Something told him that she was special. She needed, he felt, only to be given a dose of kindness in order to have her dormant confidence restored.

When he sat down to supper the next night, Elizabeth-Anne and Jenny collided as they hurried to his table. Jenny turned her back to him so that he would not see her bared teeth as she hissed 'Scram!' to Elizabeth-Anne. Then she turned around, a sweet smile on her lips as she approached his table. 'We have a Texas-style chilli,' she said in a throaty voice, adding quickly in a whisper, 'and anything else you might want?'

He glanced up at her, his eyes unfocused as he gazed past her across the dining room. He could see Elizabeth-Anne gnawing on a clenched knuckle; then, when she became aware of his gaze, she swiftly whirled around and scurried into the kitchen.

Zaccheus withdrew his gaze and his bright blue eyes looked up at Jenny. 'What I want is to find out where I can hire a car.'

'Oh.' Jenny's face fell for an instant. 'There aren't any. But you could hire a horse and buggy at the livery stable. It's two blocks down Main Street. Next to Pitcock's Hardware Store.'

'Do you happen to know what time they open in the morning?'

'Six, I think.' Jenny hesitated. 'Will there be anything else?'

'The chilli, please.'

She tightened her lips and hurried to fetch it.

The next morning, Zaccheus hired a horse and buggy and started on his Bible-selling rounds.

It was late Sunday morning, five days later when the church service finished and the congregation came spilling from inside the blistered wood building. The white-hot sun was baking the rutted dust of Main Street with a furnace-like heat, but a slight breeze pushed the stifling air around, creating the momentary illusion that it was getting cooler, which it wasn't.

Jenny blinked in the sudden light, shielded her eyes with a cupped hand, and glanced around. Everyone was milling about as usual, catching up on the latest gossip. Beside her were Elender, who wore a severe, long black dress with a matching bonnet, only a touch of lace at her throat softening the funereal look, and Elizabeth-Anne in the hand-me-down flowered dress which had been Jenny's favourite until she'd outgrown it. While Elender and Elizabeth-Anne stopped to talk to the Byrd sisters, Jenny murmured her excuses and withdrew to the sagging white picket fence which surrounded the little church. She leaned against it, watching Zaccheus intently. He was standing on the top step of the church, conversing with Reverend Drummond.

'Jenny!' a voice hissed from the side of the building.

Jenny turned her head slowly as Laurenda Pitcock hurried over to her. Laurenda had grown up to be big-boned, with a heavy reddish face, the beginnings of a moustache, and tiny pursed lips. She was a full year

345

younger than Jenny, but her body had already filled out. Her hips were large and her bosom full and ripe.

'What do you say we pack a picnic lunch this afternoon?' Laurenda suggested hopefully. 'You, me and Red Brearer, we could all ride out to the bluff together.'

'Oh, I don't know,' Jenny said lazily, her eyes once again resting on Zaccheus.

Laurenda looked disappointed. 'We didn't see you for nearly a week now,' she whined reproachfully. 'You're no fun anymore.'

'Things will liven up, Laurenda.'

'Maybe we can go to my place? I stole some tobacco and rolling papers from my Pa. We can go out behind the shed and light up.'

Jenny shook her head. 'Not today, Laurenda. Maybe tomorrow.'

Laurenda made a sound like she was blowing a shred of tobacco off her lip. 'What have you been doing with yourself?'

'Working,' Jenny said truthfully.

Laurenda laughed. 'I thought you hated work.'

'I do,' Jenny said slowly, 'but sometimes there are distinct benefits.'

'Like the new roomer?' Laurenda said in a sly voice.

Jenny glared at her. 'How would you know?'

Laurenda shrugged. 'Word gets around is all.'

Jenny's voice was bitter. 'It sure seems to. But it better get no further than you. You open your big mouth, Laurenda Pitcock, and I'll open mine.'

'What about?'

Jenny smiled crookedly.

Laurenda tossed her head virtuously. 'Nobody will believe it.'

'Red likes to brag.'

'So? Everybody knows he's always lying.'

'So they do. But I don't lie. And everybody knows that, too.'

'All right, all right,' Laurenda conceded gruffly.

Jenny smiled at her. 'Get lost, Laurenda. I'm busy.'

'I didn't mean –'

'I'm busy, Laurenda.' Jenny's voice softened. 'I'll see you tomorrow. I promise.'

'Yeah. Sure.' Laurenda backed off, glumly studying the ground.

Jenny pursed her lips thoughtfully, as her best friend wandered off. Suddenly she pushed herself away from the fence, left the churchyard, and hurried back to the Good Eats Café. She took the steep stairs two at a time up to the second-floor apartment she, Elender and Elizabeth-Anne had shared ever since Elender had bought the building. Quickly, she changed out of her Sunday outfit to a cooler, less formal, and more flattering dress. It was printed with a tiny pattern of bluebells and suited her well. She studied her reflection closely in the mirror, then pushed her fingers through her hair, contemplating a new hairdo. Frowning, she let it fall back in place.

She smiled slowly. Today, she wasn't going to serve lunch or supper at the café. She would let Elizabeth-Anne do that. Laurenda had unwittingly given her a marvellous idea. Although he didn't know it yet, today, she was going on a picnic – with Zaccheus Hale.

Zaccheus heard the tentative knock on the door. He crossed the little turret room in four strides and opened it. His face registered surprise. Jenny was standing there, both hands gripping a large, cloth-covered wicker basket she held in front of her.

'Hello,' he said.

Jenny smiled flirtatiously up at him. 'Auntie's letting me borrow the horse and buggy, and I have a picnic lunch all packed. You see, my friend Laurenda Pitcock was supposed to come with me, but she's taken ill and everything's already prepared and . . . would you? I mean . . .' She tilted her head and lowered her eyes demurely. 'It's so quiet here and I hate to have to picnic alone.'

'Well . . .' Zaccheus compressed his lips and glanced behind him. 'Actually, I was just –'

'It would mean so much to me,' Jenny said quickly, her eyes searching his face. 'Please? Just this once? Auntie said it was all right with her, if it was with you.'

He smiled. 'All right. Wait for me downstairs. I'll be right down.'

They drove out through Geron's Fields and headed north along the enormous, meandering riverbed, passing newly planted citrus groves and endless expanses of cotton fields. Jenny did the driving and didn't stop the buggy until they came to a small bluff. Far out, they could see the mirror-like shine of pools of water. The water did not seem to be moving.

'Let's picnic here,' Jenny said softly. 'This is one of my favourite spots. See?' She pointed. 'You can see way into Mexico from here.'

'I've always expected more from the Rio Grande,' he said slowly. 'I always thought it was a real river.'

'Like the Mississippi?'

'Something like that.'

Jenny nodded. 'I know. But it does get a lot bigger. Especially in spring, when the snows melt up north. A few years ago it flooded and washed away half of Mexican Town.'

'It seems impossible.'

'I know. If I hadn't seen it myself, I wouldn't have believed it, either.' Jenny got the blanket out of the buggy and flapped it out over the ground. 'Are you hungry yet?' she called over her shoulder as she set the picnic basket down.

'I can wait.'

348

'Good. I can too.' She got down on her knees and smoothed the blanket out.

They sat down, hugged their knees, and looked over into Mexico. The afternoon was hot and lazy, and after a while they lay back, absorbing the sun. Jenny sighed contentedly. She crossed her arms behind her head. 'Where are you from originally?' she asked in an off-hand voice.

He opened one eye. 'Oh, all over,' he replied vaguely. 'I travel a lot.'

'That's what I've always wanted to do,' she said wistfully. 'But I've never been further than Brownsville.' She shifted and he turned slowly towards her as he felt a finger tracing a line down his chest. Then she suddenly rolled towards him, knelt over him, and clutched him tightly, her fingers digging into his forearms. 'I think I'm in love with you,' she whispered throatily.

He sat up straight. 'But . . . but you hardly know me!' he sputtered.

She flung her arms around his neck. 'That doesn't matter. Oh, Zaccheus, Zaccheus! I just *know* we're made for each other!'

He studied her face in the sunlight. She wasn't half as pretty out in the stark, unforgiving sunshine as she was indoors, he realized suddenly. Her skin wasn't as smooth and her eyes had a harder, more calculating glint. Still, she was pretty enough, but something about her frightened him. Perhaps it was because she was so brazenly forward.

He could feel her drawing closer towards him until her body was pressed against his. Gently, he took her by the wrists and pushed her away from him. He got to his feet. 'I think,' he said slowly, 'it's time we headed back.'

Her narrowed eyes blazed for an instant. Then she shrugged. 'All right,' she said simply. 'If that's what you want.'

'That's what I want,' he said softly.

She got up and watched expressionlessly as he gathered up the unopened picnic basket and blanket and tossed them into the buggy. After he helped her up on to the seat, he went around to untie the horse. Just as he was about to hop up beside her, she suddenly smacked the reins as hard as she could and yelled: 'Giddy-yap!'

Zaccheus jumped back as the horse took off. For a long moment he just stood there, puzzled, one hand resting on his hip, the other scratching his head thoughtfully. He stared after the cloud of dust being kicked up by the receding horse and buggy. "*Hell hath no fury like a woman scorned*,' he quoted aloud to himself. Then, resigning himself to the three-hour walk back into town, he took of his suit jacket and flung it over his shoulder.

He shook his head sorrowfully. No matter which way he turned, women always seemed to do him dirty. What was it with him? Why did he only seem to attract the virulent and spiteful ones?

Jenny hesitated outside the door of Elender's bedroom and took a deep breath to fortify herself. The dim hallway sconces cast shadows across her face. The generous pink slash that was her mouth drew back over her teeth as she smiled. Then she rapped decisively.

'Come in,' Elender called out clearly. She was sitting in front of her dressing table mirror, brushing out her hair in the glow of two lamps.

The door opened silently and Jenny slipped into the room. 'Auntie . . .' she said tentatively.

'Yes, dear. Did you have a nice picnic?'

'I . . . I have a confession to make, Auntie,' Jenny blurted out in a thin, reedy voice.

Elender stopped brushing her hair and peered at Jenny's reflection in the mirror. 'Yes . . .'

Jenny clenched her hands at her sides. 'Mr Hale went with me on the picnic this afternoon.'

'Oh? I thought you specifically told me you were going with Laurenda.'

Jenny bit down on her lip. 'I was, really I was. But she couldn't go at the last minute.'

'I see. And you asked Mr Hale, instead,' Elender guessed shrewdly, 'after I told you over and over again that you are not to see any man unescorted unless you have my express permission to do so.'

'Oh no, Auntie!' Jenny cried quickly. 'It was nothing like that! Honestly! He asked me to go for a walk with him, and since the picnic basket was already all packed, I thought . . . well . . .' Her voice trailed off.

'Well, what?' Elender prodded.

'Auntie,' Jenny began in a tiny voice, then trembled and hugged herself with her arms. 'It was horrible! *Horrible!* He . . . he tried to kiss me! He . . . he put his arms around me and felt –'

Elender dropped the hairbrush and it fell on the dressing table with a clatter. She spun around on the stool and faced Jenny, her eyes glittering darkly. 'If – and I use that word very judiciously, Jennifer Sue Clowney – *if* indeed Mr Hale tried to kiss you, well . . . in that case he's not to blame. *You* are. As far as I can see, he's a gentleman. You did not have my permission to go on a picnic with him. And worse yet, you've been throwing yourself at him in the most disgusting, unlady-like manner I've ever seen. I don't know what's come over you, but let me warn you, young lady.' She wagged a severe finger. 'I am not blind!'

Jenny's face reddened until it burned scarlet.

'I suggest,' Elender continued quietly, 'that you cease trying to throw yourself at Mr Hale . . . and that goes for any other man who happens by. One more problem like this and I'll see to it that you never leave this house again!'

'I'm not a child anymore!' Jenny retaliated in a truculent voice. 'I'm eighteen years old. You can't lock me up!'

'We'll see.'

'I'll run away! You'll never find me!'

'*Stop it*!' Elender yelled suddenly. Then her voice dropped. 'Don't be so *childish*.'

'Maybe I wouldn't be so childish if you stopped treating me like one.'

Elender sighed wearily. 'We'll talk about that some other time, Jenny, when we aren't so hot under the collar. For the time being, off you go to bed. You've a long day ahead of you tomorrow.'

Jenny looked at her quizzically. 'I do?'

'You do.' Elender tightened her lips. 'Since you blatantly disobeyed me, you'll serve both the lunch and supper shifts tomorrow. And every day for the next fourteen days, I might add.'

Jenny's jaw dropped. 'But Auntie!'

'This way,' Elender said in a chill voice, 'you'll have no choice but to stay out of trouble. Good-night.'

There was no doubt but that Jenny was dismissed. She mumbled something under her breath.

'What's that?' Elender said sharply.

'I said, "Good-night, Auntie".' Jenny slipped glumly out of the room.

When she was gone, Elender turned back towards the mirror and picked up the hairbrush. Slowly she resumed brushing her hair, staring at her reflection but not seeing it.

The girls have changed, she caught herself thinking sadly, and then frowned as she forced herself to change that line of thinking. No, they were not girls any longer. They were women. Jenny was eighteen and Elizabeth-Anne was two years younger, but they both stood on the very same threshold. How much longer would either of them – especially Jenny – listen to the voices of those who were older and, presumably, wiser? Not, when it came down to it, she thought bleakly, that she was any wiser than Jenny. Her own past, indeed Jenny herself – her flesh and blood which she dared not embrace publicly or even privately – proved that. She could not be, for much longer, the arbiter of Jenny's and Elizabeth-Anne's social lives, hearts, and futures. She could try to guide them a little longer, nudging them in the direction she thought was best, but she knew full and well that that time was very finite, and that the end of her influence was fast drawing to a close. A young woman's heart was, after all, a very delicate thing: no rhyme or reason could sway it. But it was time to face reality. Soon now, since Jenny had already entered womanhood, one other crisis was liable to rear its ugly head, and it was the one which Elender Hannah Clowney was not prepared to face.

For generally, with womanhood came love, and love was often followed by marriage. And with that on the horizon, wouldn't it only be a matter of time before Jenny came to her and demanded her birth certificate – the one which accused Elender Hannah Clowney of being not her aunt, but her mother?

Too soon now, Elender feared, the truth would have to come out.

'Oh, God,' she moaned to herself. She laid down the hairbrush, placed her elbows on the dressing table, and rubbed her eyes fitfully with the tips of her fingers.

It was then that she heard other knocks, this time on the parlour door down the hall. Slowly, she lifted her head, then got up, pulled on her embroidered robe, and went out into the parlour. She opened the door. 'Mr Hale!' she said with surprise.

Zaccheus held his boater against his chest. 'I'm sorry to bother you, Miss Clowney,' he said in embarrassment. 'Especially at this late hour. But I was hoping we might talk for a moment?'

'You're no bother at all. Do come on in.' She led the way into the small parlour. 'Have a seat, Mr Hale.' She watched as he sat down on the settee; she took a seat on one of the tufted chairs. 'Now,' she said. 'What can I do for you?'

Zaccheus cleared his throat. 'It's about your niece, ma'am. Miss Jennifer.'

A veil seemed to drop down over Elender's eyes. 'Yes?'

'She asked me to go on a picnic with her this afternoon.'

'I know that.'

He nodded. 'Miss Clowney, I don't know if it's my place to say this, but . . .' He tightened his lips and studied his folded hands.

'She tried to make advances at you?'

It was his turn to look surprised. 'How did you know?'

'I could see it coming. Jenny is very brazen. You see, for her, life here is very dull. You must excuse her, Mr Hale. I assume you behaved as a gentleman.'

He nodded and smiled bleakly.

'Thank you for telling me,' she said warmly. 'Now I think we'd better forget this unfortunate incident.'

'Miss Clowney?'

'Yes?'

'There's . . . something else.'

'And that would be . . .'

'Your other niece, Miss Clowney. I was wondering if I could have your permission to take her to see a picture show at the nickelodeon?'

'Elizabeth-Anne? Why, how wonderful!' Elender clapped her hands together and beamed with pleasure. 'You don't know what a world of good that would do her! She's had such an unfortunate, painful life, you know.'

'I guessed that.' He paused. 'I was also wondering why she . . . why she wears gloves all the time.'

354

'You must keep this between you and me, Mr Hale.'

'I won't tell a soul,' he promised solemnly.

'I'm sure you won't. You see, Mr Hale, when she was very, very young and impressionable, she saw her parents burned to death in a tragic fire. Her own hands were terribly scarred. Even now that they are healed, she still cannot bear looking at them.'

He eyed her sadly. 'I will never let on that you told me.'

'I appreciate that.' Elender got up from the chair and he rose also. 'Good-night, Mr Hale,' she said.

'Good-night, Miss Clowney,' he said.

4

Elizabeth-Anne gazed at herself critically in the mirror and stood there frowning while she adjusted her dress.

Her body was rigid and she held her hands stiffly at her sides. What she saw in the mirror did nothing to inspire her. She let out a painful, high-pitched little moan.

He's going to laugh at me, she thought miserably over and over. *Or worse yet, he's not going to show up at all. Oh God, why didn't I just turn him down? And to think of all the trouble Auntie's gone through to try and make this perfect for me. She's done my hair, and took in this dress so that it would fit to perfection. But it's all wasted. Nothing is enough. I don't look good and I don't feel good. Perhaps I'm forever doomed to spinsterhood.*

She scowled at her reflection. The white cotton dress with its twin rows of white, fabric-covered buttons tracing two lines from her collar down to her calves; the long puffy sleeves, buttoned tightly at the wrists; her tiny waist, accentuated by the cut of the dress; the wide-brimmed straw hat on her head, its crown wrapped in voluminous white tulle which flowed down her back; the white boots Auntie had lent her and which pinched her toes only slightly ('Thank goodness we've the same size feet,' Elender had said.) – to Elizabeth-Anne it seemed like a costume. She just wasn't used to dressing up so fancy. Nor was she used to the new hair-do; her wheat-gold hair was fluffed up and pinned in place and made her head look so much larger. Somehow it gave her an air of maturity which she found frightening.

When she heard the muted knocks on the door down the hall, a band of fear suddenly constricted her chest. *He was here already! Oh, God*! Quickly, she snapped the bedroom door shut and glanced around desperately, as if contemplating escape as she heard Elender's brisk footsteps passing her door. But there was no escape other than ducking out the window, sliding down the slanting porch roof, and then jumping down to the street below. Escape was impossible; she had never been a tomboy.

She was trapped.

Hearing muffled voices, she took a deep breath and held it in her lungs as she heard the footsteps passing her door. Then she slowly let out her breath again. She could hear more conversation, then Elender's musical laughter and the clinking of a glass.

I can't even move! she moaned desperately to herself. *My feet feel like they're encased in lead. Oh God, why can't the floor just open and swallow me up? Why can't I be dead?*

She heard Elender's footsteps again, and then a soft knock came on her door. As Elender pushed it open, she exclaimed: 'You look lovely!'

'No, I don't!' Elizabeth-Anne countered fretfully.

Elender frowned suddenly. 'Oh!' she exclaimed. 'What is it?'

Quickly Elender slipped into the room and shut the door behind her. Deftly, she began unbuttoning the front of Elizabeth-Anne's dress.

356

Elizabeth-Anne looked down at herself. In her nervousness, she hadn't even noticed the collar buckling; she'd missed a buttonhole, and all twenty buttons down to her calves were buttoned wrong. 'I'm so nervous, Auntie! Can't I just call it off?'

'Keep still, please.'

'Can't I plead ill or something?' Elizabeth-Anne added quickly: 'I *am* ill, you know. My stomach is all tied up in knots, and I've been running to the bathroom –'

'It's only your nerves,' Elender whispered gently. Then she smiled reassuringly as she stood back to study Elizabeth-Anne. She nodded to herself with satisfaction. 'Don't worry so much. Mr Hale is a very nice young gentleman, and he doesn't bite. Now, take off your hat and come out into the parlour. I've made a nice bowl of punch.'

'Oh, Auntie!' Hesitantly, Elizabeth-Anne took off her hat and held it in both hands.

Elender wagged a finger at her. 'Don't you "oh, Auntie" me,' she warned. 'It's a little too late for that. You're not a silly, tongue-tied schoolgirl any longer. You're a young lady, and you must act like one.' She tucked a stray hair back into Elizabeth-Anne's coiffure. 'There, you look perfect.' On an impulse, she kissed Elizabeth-Anne's cheek; then she took her firmly by the arm.

Reluctantly Elizabeth-Anne allowed herself to be led out into the dim hall.

'Don't be so stiff!' Elender hissed over her shoulder. 'Relax!' Then she smiled with amusement. 'I do declare. You're as nervous as he is!'

'He's nervous too?' Elizabeth-Anne looked surprised.

'He is. Now in you float. Like a princess!' Elender stepped aside, placed both hands in the small of Elizabeth-Anne's back, and gave her a little push. Elizabeth-Anne stumbled into the little parlour.

The scene which greeted her would be forever ingrained in her mind. In the time it had taken her to get dressed, Elender had transformed the dark, brooding parlour into a cheery, bright room. It was neat and comfortable as always, but the lace curtains were drawn aside so that the sunlight flooded in. The faded paintings, the dark wallpaper and rugs, and the heavy pieces of mahogany furniture seemed somehow airier, both lighter and brighter. A white lace tablecloth covered the dining room table, and she noticed that Elender had even run across the street to the rooming house to pluck flowers: they were arranged in cut-glass vases and seemed to be everywhere. The entire room was a riot of fragrant colours. On the sideboard stood the cut-glass punch bowl and a chocolate cake.

And there was Zaccheus.

The instant she came into the room, he hopped to his feet, a bouquet of daisies in his hand. His Adam's apple seemed to bob nervously, and somehow, that, more than anything else, made her feel instantly at ease. She put down her hat, gracefully crossed the carpet, and held out one gloved hand. 'Mr Hale,' she said formally. 'I'm . . . I'm honoured by your visit.'

'I thank you for allowing me to come.' He took her hand formally and held it. They both seemed startled by the invisible spark which ricocheted back and forth between them. After a moment, Elizabeth-Anne withdrew her hand. 'Please, won't you take a seat?' she offered.

He held out the bouquet. 'These are for you.'

'Thank you,' she said softly, her cheeks flushing pink. 'They're lovely.' For a moment she gazed down at the flowers. Then she gazed back up at him. 'Would you please excuse me while I put these in water? Please . . . do sit.'

He sat down and she hurried out into the hall, nearly colliding with Elender, who winked conspiratorially – she already had a vase filled with water in her hand. Elizabeth-Anne quickly arranged the daisies, took the vase, and hurried back into the parlour. She placed the vase on top of the spinet piano and stepped back to study the effect.

'I'm afraid bringing you flowers is like bringing coals to Newcastle,' Zaccheus said, looking around.

Elizabeth-Anne laughed. 'Not at all. One can never have enough flowers. And I treasure these the most.'

As she took a seat opposite him, he started to rise politely.

'If I might be so bold,' he said softly, 'you look very lovely.'

'Thank you,' she murmured graciously. 'Would you like some punch?'

He gestured to the marble-topped mahogany end-table beside him. 'Miss Clowney already served me some.'

'So I see.' She smiled and clasped her hands. 'A slice of cake, then?'

'Perhaps a little later.'

Out in the hall, Elender permitted herself a small smile. It was going even better than she had hoped. She smoothed her long grey skirt with the flat of her hands and went out into the parlour. 'I've taught Elizabeth-Anne to play the piano,' she said as she took a seat, 'and she plays beautifully. Since the show at the nickelodeon doesn't start for another hour, perhaps you would like her to play a few selections for us?' She gazed inquiringly at Zaccheus.

'I'm sure Mr Hale doesn't want to hear me play,' Elizabeth-Anne begged off demurely.

'But I do!' Zaccheus protested enthusiastically. 'Please! I'd be honoured!'

'Well, if you insist,' Elizabeth-Anne murmured.

'I do,' he said quickly.

Elizabeth-Anne rose and slowly went behind the piano. Scraping the stool forwards, she sat down and began playing a Chopin sonata.

The afternoon fled by so quickly that it seemed it was over before it had even begun. The hour in the parlour seemed mere minutes. After the Chopin rendition, Zaccheus begged her to play more, and she played the piano with a surety she had never known before. Then she and Zaccheus went to the nickelodeon and saw the fifth instalment of a continuing serial – one reel a week was shown. Afterwards, they walked up Main Street, and he bought them both an ice cream cone at the general store.

'It's good.' Elizabeth-Anne licked her strawberry ice cream carefully so it wouldn't drip down and soil her gloves.

He smiled.

'Auntie doesn't allow us to have ice cream often. She says it's so we won't get too spoiled.'

'She's very wise, I'm sure.'

'Probably.' Elizabeth-Anne frowned. 'But sometimes we wish we were more spoiled. Especially Jenny.' She looked sideways at him. 'She doesn't like me at all, you know.'

'Oh?' He kept his face impassive.

Elizabeth-Anne shook her head. 'It goes way back to when we were children and Auntie took me in. Jenny thought I was trying to usurp her place.'

'She still holds that against you?' he asked in surprise.

'I'm afraid so.' Elizabeth-Anne sighed and frowned. 'What she doesn't seem to realize is that I'm *not* a threat to her, not in any way. But it's difficult for her to accept that.'

They walked in silence for a while. After they'd gone a block, he spoke hesitantly. 'You know, it's curious.'

'What is?'

'Somehow, although I've just met you, it's as if I've known you for a long time.'

She smiled slightly.

'I mean . . . I'm not trying to embarrass you, but I

feel . . . what I mean to say is, you make me feel . . . comfortable. I think you're very nice.'

She tightened her lips bitterly. 'So does everyone else. "*Nice*".' She scowled. 'Everyone always thinks I'm so "*nice*". "Nice" describes any number of things. It's a greedy word, a safe word. The plainest thing in the world can be "nice".'

'That's not how I meant it,' he said quickly, nonplussed by her sudden vehemence. 'What I meant to say was that – you're special. That's what I meant.'

'Thank you,' she said stiffly.

There was another prolonged silence, during which he searched his mind for something to say. 'Do you like it here in Quebeck?' he asked finally.

She frowned. 'Well enough, I suppose. But sometimes . . .' She stopped walking and turned to him swiftly, a flush colouring her face. 'I know this sounds silly, but eventually, what I'd *really* like to do is move to a big city.'

'Any in particular?'

'No, not really. But I'll never forget Auntie telling me about this hotel she once stayed at in Brownsville. I made her tell me that story over and over. Other children like fairy tales, I suppose, but somehow, that hotel was my castle.' She gave a little laugh.

'Maybe you'll get a chance to see it someday.'

'Oh no! I wouldn't want to ever see it.'

'But why not?'

'Because I've built it up so much in my mind that by now I know it doesn't at all resemble what Auntie had described. I've let it grow completely out of proportion. The real hotel would be a vast disappointment to me.' Elizabeth-Anne's eyes focused on something invisible in the distance. 'The Hotel Garber,' she said slowly. 'That was the name of it.' She shook her head as if to clear it and gazed up at him. 'Have you ever stayed there?'

He shook his head. 'Can't say I have.'

'Well, anyway, Auntie and Jenny stayed there right before I met them. And ever since, it's been Auntie's dream to own a grand hotel. But it'll never happen, and she knows it. Still, she insists that having a dream is very healthy.'

'I couldn't agree more. And you . . . you'd like to own a grand hotel?'

'Oh yes!' Elizabeth-Anne's eyes sparkled with excitement and her words came in such a quick rush that they tripped over one another. 'I really like the rooming house and the Good Eats Café, you know. I like meeting people and making them feel at home. But from what Auntie's told me about the Hotel Garber . . . well, that's what I'd really like.' She smiled and added soberly: 'Of course, it'll never happen.'

'Don't ever say that!' he said sharply.

She glanced at him queerly. 'Why?'

'Because,' he said earnestly, 'nothing in the world is impossible. Dreams are . . . well, doorways to reality, actually. I've had dreams before, and . . . and they started to become reality, but . . .' His voice trailed off.

'But what?' She gazed at him intently.

He looked away. 'I messed them up. I didn't keep them in focus. I let other influences veer me off course and change them.' He sighed deeply for a moment. Then he brightened. 'I've stayed at lots of hotels, you know.'

'Really!' Her face lit up.

He nodded.

'Tell me about them!' she said urgently. 'Please, everything you can remember!'

He laughed. 'That would take days. Weeks, probably.'

'In that case,' she said softly, 'I suppose I'll have to listen to you for weeks.'

'I'm afraid you'd get bored.'

'Oh, no!' she vowed. 'Never! And you?' she asked. 'All

362

you've done so far is ask me questions and make me talk about myself. What about you? What do you want to do?'

'I'm not sure. I think . . . I think I'd like to stay on here. If I can find a job.'

She looked at him soberly. 'I'm afraid there aren't many jobs available around here.'

'I know that. But I'll try to find one.'

'I heard you sell Bibles.'

He grinned. 'Word sure gets around fast.'

'It's a small town . . . and *everyone* already has Bibles.'

'I know that. So I'll have to find something else. Something where I don't have to travel. Where I can stay put for a while.'

She looked surprised. 'You don't like to travel?'

'I do, but I've been on the road for too long now. It's time I settled down.'

'I'll ask Auntie about any available jobs,' she promised. 'If anyone knows of any, it's her. The Good Eats Café is the best grapevine in town. You wouldn't believe how people talk while they eat. I'll keep my ears open, too.'

'I'd be grateful.'

They walked in silence for a while, and when they reached the end of Main Street, they turned around and slowly retraced their way back in the direction from which they had come.

Zaccheus' heart was light. It was just as he had thought. Elizabeth-Anne was not at all like Phoebe or Jenny. She was shy but warm, and underneath all the benign surface traits she was brimming with dreams and ambitions. He barely knew her, but he felt extremely lucky. Somehow he knew she was just right for him. Maybe he hadn't lost his own dreams entirely . . . perhaps together, they could forge them into reality.

On sudden impulse, he reached out and boldly took

her hand in his. As his fingers closed over hers, she tensed, and when she looked up at him, her eyes held a peculiarly pale, faraway look. Then she seemed to relax and smiled shyly.

But there was nothing shy about the emotions which the touch of his hand aroused within her. She felt in the midst of an upheaval. Her stomach was trembling, aflutter with a thousand invisible butterfly wings, yet she felt an intense, physical awakening, a soaring such as she had never before experienced.

But she kept these powerful emotions well in check. She hoped that, to the casual observer, she seemed as quietly withdrawn as ever.

'Seems like you lost the new roomer,' Laurenda Pitcock said in a dry voice. She nodded with her chin.

She and Jenny were standing in the purple shadows of the alley beside the Good Eats Café. It was break time for Jenny, the halfway point between serving lunch and dinner, and Laurenda had dropped by for a visit.

Jenny watched through narrowed eyes as Zaccheus and Elizabeth-Anne walked slowly towards them, holding hands while engrossed in conversation.

They're *sure being friendly*, she thought bitterly. *And that expression on Elizabeth-Anne's face . . . it's one I've never seen before. There's a glowing intensity and vitality about her which is entirely foreign . . .*

Laurenda grinned. 'Looks like you played your cards all wrong, Jen. He seems to like the quiet types.'

Jenny whirled around. 'Shut up, Pie Face!' she hissed fiercely. 'I didn't want him anyway! I sent him packing!'

'Sure you did. First you fell all over him, and now you suddenly can't stand him.' There was a note of mocking laughter in Laurenda's voice. 'Face it, Jen. You lost him.'

'So?' Jenny clenched her fists and stood there stiffly. 'Who said I ever wanted him?'

'It's okay, Jenny. There'll be other men. Rich men,

364

not just some two-bit Bible salesman. He'll be here a while and then he'll be gone. You mark my words. You'll forget all about him.'

'Sure,' Jenny said absently.

'Besides,' Laurenda said cagily, 'look at it this way. If you can't have him, why should anybody else?'

Jenny stared at her. 'What do you mean?' she asked slowly.

'Oh, just give me some time to think about it,' Laurenda said loftily. 'With our brains, we'll be able to cook up something to break those two up. Right?'

Jenny looked at her for a long moment. Then her lips spread into a wide, devious grin. 'Yeah. We'll be able to cook up something good.'

5

Jenny pursed her lips as the four of them came out of the drugstore. 'What do we do now?' she grumbled in a bored voice.

Red Brearer kicked at a pebble and watched it bounce across Main Street, stirring up little clouds of dust. He was short and stocky, with a perpetually surly expression. His name was derived from his shock of orange-red hair which stuck out from under his cloth cap. 'I dunno. Wanna go over to the nickelodeon and see the show again?'

Jenny glanced up the street at the pink rooming house and shook her head. 'Auntie doesn't let us see the show more than once, and we've already been this week. Besides, I already spent my week's allowance. Auntie only gave me the money for the soda if I let Elizabeth-Anne come along.' She jerked her head sideways in Elizabeth-Anne's direction.

Red looked at her out of the corners of his eyes. 'You

work in the café. Why don't you keep some of the money? You know, just a little bit here, and a little bit there?'

'Are you kidding?' Jenny shook her head. 'Auntie's too sharp. She always knows exactly how much there should be. Even if I come out a nickel short she knows it. I don't know how she keeps track of it, but she does.'

A look of disappointment came over his face. 'There must be something we can do,' he mumbled.

Jenny suddenly snatched Red's cloth cap off his head and tossed it high into the air. He jumped up, caught it, and scowled at her as he placed it back on his head and pulled the visor down over his eyes.

'It still doesn't cover your carrot head,' Jenny said laughingly. 'I don't know why you even bother wearing it. Especially in this heat.'

Laurenda put a hand on Jenny's arm. 'I know what we can do!'

'Whoa!' Jenny cut her off and turned to Elizabeth-Anne, who was standing a few feet away. 'You've had your soda, 'Lisbeth-Anne,' she said succinctly. 'That's all Auntie required of me. Now scram. We want to be left alone.'

Elizabeth-Anne looked at each of them in turn. Only Red seemed slightly embarrassed. Then she shrugged and slowly walked off, hands in her pockets, chin tucked down into her chest. Behind her, she heard Jenny's stage whispers and then three loud shrieks of forced laughter.

Her face burned with embarrassment. Then, for some strange reason – an instinct or intuition – she suddenly felt a force drawing her eyes up to the pink rooming house. She could see a shadow in the third-floor window. And that, for some reason, made her shrug off her embarrassment. Lifting her head with pride, she headed for the Good Eats Café, every inch of her suddenly brimming with confidence and dignity.

Zaccheus stood at the oriel window, one hand parting the curtains, the other tucked into the small of his back. Down the street, he could see the young man and two young ladies obviously ostracizing Elizabeth-Anne from their activities. The way she walked along so dejectedly, hands in her pockets, tugged at his heart strings. She seemed so lonely, like a lovely vulnerable flower deprived of water. She positively drooped.

A sympathetic look came into his eyes, turning them startling blue, warm and liquid. He wanted nothing more than to rush downstairs, throw the haven of his arms around her, and offer comfort and succour.

Forget about them, he wanted to say to her. *You've got me*.

But at the moment, time was their enemy. He had things he had to do, and he couldn't procrastinate.

He consulted his pocketwatch, then snapped it decisively shut. If he didn't hurry, he would be late. And that was unthinkable, especially after Miss Clowney had gone through such pains to get him this job interview. Besides, he consoled himself, he would see Elizabeth-Anne later, after he got back. They'd agreed to meet at the tiny dusty park, with its dried-out shrubs and bandstand, at the south end of Main Street. Right now, he had time for a quick bath, and that was it. He was expected out at the Sexton ranch, and it wouldn't do to be late. Jobs for a young man who was good at figures and writing were not easy to come by, especially here in southwest Texas.

Twenty minutes later, as he headed out into the country in the buggy Elender had lent him, he noticed Jenny and her friends heading in the opposite direction on foot, towards a dilapidated shack at the far side of the railroad tracks. A half hour after that, he arrived at the sprawling Sexton ranch house with five minutes to spare.

He tethered the horse, slapped the dust off his

367

clothes, hopped up on the porch, and knocked confidently on the big double doors. A Mexican maid answered and led him down an endless series of cool corridors to Tex Sexton's office. Opening the carved, dark-stained door, she stepped aside to let Zaccheus enter and said: 'Meester Sexton be weeth you shortly. He out hunting.' Then she closed the heavy door quietly and he was alone.

The first thing which hit Zaccheus was the room's smells. The air was redolent with a mixture of expensive masculine fragrances: leather and wood, Cuban cigars, oils, and saddle wax. He walked over to one of the windows and gazed out at the ranchland at the back of the house. Cattle were grazing peacefully beyond the sheds and barns. He heard the heavy trampling of hooves, and several horses galloped into view and slid to a halt. Their riders, shotguns in hand, hopped limberly down off their saddles. One horse was riderless, but dragged a litter behind it. On it lay a slain deer.

Zaccheus nodded to himself. So the stories he had heard were true: Tex Sexton had indeed stocked a portion of his land with game.

As he watched, several ranch hands untied the deer from the litter and dragged it into a shed.

Behind him, he heard the oak door opening. He turned around slowly.

'Be with you in a minute,' Tex Sexton said abruptly, waving aside any greetings with a large, callused hand. Obviously, there were going to be no handshakes and no hellos. Zaccheus remained standing and watched as Sexton poured himself a glass of bourbon from the sideboard. Then he drained the glass, sighed deeply, banged it down, and went over to one of the deep, tufted black leather couches studded with gleaming brass nailheads. He threw himself down on it, hooking a leg over one of the arms, and studied Zaccheus quietly.

Though his body was relaxed, Tex's squinting eyes were wary.

Zaccheus studied him right back. Sexton didn't dress the part of the powerful gentleman rancher, and that surprised him. He dressed, in fact, like one of the ranch hands: he wore baggy whipcord trousers, a mended red-plaid shirt with flaps over the pockets, and worn, dusty boots.

Tex Sexton was close to fifty, but there was an astonishing, youthful vitality about him. His hair was thick and black, combed back and barely touched with grey at the temples. He was a large man, both in height and girth, but he was light-footed and carried his weight well. His face was long and brown and narrow, an outdoor face, the skin drawn taut across the bones and weathered with a network of tiny, shallow wrinkles. His mouth was large and thin-lipped, and held an expression Zaccheus could only interpret as sardonic, with a small, humourless smile twisting up the corners. His ears were large and stuck out at an odd angle, giving him a deceptively countrified look. Above all, he was impressive. The imperious self-assurance with which he held himself, and the steady gaze of his large, hooded, predatory black eyes belonged to a man who could take care of himself. Who instantly felt at home in any surroundings, no matter how far away from home he happened to wander. And that, Zaccheus thought for the first time in his life, all added up to one thing. Power.

Finally Sexton spoke. 'So you're the young man it was recommended to me I hire,' he drawled in a lazy voice. 'Your name?'

'Zaccheus Hale, sir.'

'Your accent puts you up north a ways. Kentucky?'

Zaccheus couldn't hide his surprise. 'Tennessee,' he lied.

'Yep, Tennessee. I can see that now. Usually I can place accents within a state or two. Mighty handy little

369

talent to have, if I say so myself. But your accent's bastardized. Sounds like you've been moving around.'

Zaccheus felt a clutch of tenseness pull at his stomach. *So Tex Sexton isn't as countrified as he appears*, he thought to himself. *He's obviously a shrewd man. I'll have to be on my guard, and watch every word.*

'Let me tell you something, son. Usually I don't hire people if they ain't from 'round here, 'less they're migrant Mexes. But you come highly recommended by Jesse Atkinson. Jesse's not only a good friend of mine but the president of Quebeck Savings and Loan, which I happen to own. Seems he heard of you from the lady runs the rooming house in town –'

'Miss Clowney.'

'Guess that's her.' Sexton nodded. 'Usually I'm not curious about outsiders, but seeing as to how you've been so highly recommended, and being a Bible salesman – well, a man that honest is rare.' He narrowed his dark eyes. 'Know figgers?'

'I can add, subtract, multiply, and divide, and work out percentages, if that's what you mean, sir.'

'And you can read and write?'

Zaccheus nodded.

'Good. Tell you what I need, and you tell me if that's what you got. Brains are a rare commodity 'round here, and they tell me you got one. What I already got are smart accountants and lawyers and managers and all that, but I've got a lot of businesses need seeing to. What I want is a loyal, sharp young man with a brain that goes clickety-click all of the time. Somebody who's got a nose for trouble, who can keep his eye on the overall picture without personal things or other people getting in the way. Somebody who can keep me informed. I don't want the nitty-gritty details. Just the overall picture. Get what I mean?'

'In other words, sir, you want a liaison between yourself and all the people heading the other businesses you own.'

'Liaison.' Sexton tested the word on his tongue. 'Good word, that.' He nodded. 'Yep, that's exactly what it amounts to. But more'n that. You gotta be a trouble-shooter, too. Keep your eyes on everything, and if something seems fishy, investigate. Keep your pulse on the hired people and keep your ears open in case anybody tries to make trouble for me.' The sardonic smile widened. 'Seeing as how bright and honest you're supposed to be, I thought maybe I'd give you a chance. Think you cut out for it?

'I don't want to be a spy, Mr Sexton,' Zaccheus said in a level voice.

Sexton threw back his head and roared. 'I don't want a spy, son! I got plenty of those already. What I want is a . . . what did you call it?' He squinted craftily. 'Liaison. Somebody to keep me abreast of the overall picture so I don't have to listen to two dozen people when one can do the same. Every week, I'll expect a written report on everything important going on. Everything in a nut-shell. Know what I mean?'

Zaccheus looked at him curiously. He didn't know whether he should be flattered or insulted. 'Why don't you get someone from around here? Someone you know you can trust?'

'Because,' Sexton explained patiently, 'the ones I do trust got jobs with me already. See, a lot of people around here don't like me, son. They're out to hammer me down. Seems they got a lot of preconceived notions about me. That's why I want you. You're fresh blood. Untainted and unbiased. You don't have any reason to hate me.'

'But I intend to stay here. How do you know you can trust me after I've lived here for a while?'

'Shit, son, I don't want some hobo who'll catch the

next train out. I want somebody who'll stick around. Permanent like.'

'And you trust me? Even if you don't know anything about me?'

'I go by instinct.'

Zaccheus was silent.

'Son, instinct is a talent you use to sniff out other talent with. And I sniff you out as honest.'

'I suppose I'll be spied on, too?'

'There you go already, throwing around ugly words.' Sexton sighed and smiled hugely. 'Sure, I'll keep my eye on you. What do you say? Want the job?'

Zaccheus hesitated for a moment. Then he held out his hand. 'I'm willing to give it a try, Mr Sexton,' he said slowly. 'Besides, what's the worst that can happen? I can always quit.'

'Now that sounds more like it.' Sexton jumped nimbly to his feet and slapped Zaccheus on the back. 'Tell you what, son. You come by at six in the morning and we'll get you started. From that minute on, you're on my payroll.'

'Yes, sir.'

'And one more thing, son.'

'Sir?' Zaccheus looked at him.

''Round here, I'm not "sir" or "Mr Sexton". We ain't that formal. Everyone calls me plain "Tex". Got that?'

An answering smile broadened Zaccheus' lips. 'Yes sir, Tex.'

'That's a little better, son,' Sexton said. 'Now you run on home and report back here tomorrow. Damned if I don't think you'll work out just fine.'

6

The town crazy of Quebeck, Willy Campbell, commonly called 'Mutt' by the children who taunted him mercilessly, lived in the shack way out next to the railroad tracks. Sometimes he lived alone, and sometimes he shared the shack with his wife and daughter. His wife, Sadie, and their daughter, nicknamed 'Railroad Yellow', both after her blonde hair and her habit of disappearing for weeks on end by jumping on railroad cars and riding off with the hobos – well, people tended to stay well clear of them. Mothers, trying to instil fear in their children, would warn, 'Now don't you wander off, or else Mutt Campbell's gonna get you, and if he don't, Sadie or Railroad Yellow will!'

Mutt and his family were not nearly as dangerous as everyone liked to believe. They were merely different – and unfortunately suffered from brain damage. It was that which set them apart, nothing more. The truth was, the Campbells were really rather benign if people left them alone. The problem was, no one did.

Jenny approached the shack in a crouch so that she wouldn't be visible to Mutt or the two women. When she reached it, she slowly straightened, keeping her back to the wall, and then inched sideways and glanced through the filthy, cracked, glass window. She nodded to herself with satisfaction. She could see Mutt rocking back and forth in an old rocker, singing to himself. Neither Sadie nor Railroad Yellow were within sight, and she was glad. Her plan depended on finding Mutt alone.

She moved her head away from the window and motioned for Red and Laurenda to join her. They ran through the high weeds in a crouch to join her. 'Who's in there?' Laurenda whispered.

'Just Mutt.'

'You sure?'

'Sure, I'm sure.' Jenny looked at her in disgust. 'Are you going to chicken out?'

Laurenda glared at her and Red glanced up at the darkening sky. 'It's gonna rain, I think,' he said worriedly.

Jenny looked at him. 'Afraid of getting wet?' she taunted in a whisper.

'Hell, no.'

'What do we do now?' Laurenda asked.

'We lure Mutt out of the shack, that's what.'

Laurenda tightened her lips worriedly. 'I don't want him to come after *me*.' She shivered visibly at the thought.

'He won't.' Jenny was very sure of herself. 'If he comes after any of us, the others will distract him. Got that?'

Red and Laurenda nodded reluctantly.

'And not a word out of either one of you,' she warned. 'Got that?'

Red nodded again, but Laurenda whined: 'I don't want to get into trouble. My Pa warned me that if –'

'Laurenda, just shut up and get over there, behind that pile of wood.' Jenny moved her hand in a wide, sweeping circle. 'When I holler, come running towards the house. Red, you stay right here and keep looking in the window. If things get out of hand in there, I'm counting on you to come in and rescue me.'

'You ain't goin' in there!' Red looked shocked.

Jenny smiled suddenly. 'Why not? It was your idea that we have a little fun with Mutt, remember? So let's have it.'

'But ain't you scared of him?' There was awe in his voice.

'No, I'm just going to excite him a little, that's all. And don't worry about me. You just both do your parts, okay?'

374

'And then?' Red pressed.

Then, Jenny said to herself craftily, although she did not dare say it aloud, lest it scare off Red and Laurenda, *then I'll promise Mutt Campbell the sun and the moon. I'll tell him to meet me at the bandstand once it gets dark. Only I won't be there waiting for him. Elizabeth-Anne will.*

When Zaccheus arrived back in town from the Sexton ranch, he had been whistling cheerfully. Only when he saw the envelope which had been slipped under his door did the whistle fade in his throat. Perplexed, he picked it up, tore it open, and frowned. He read and reread the short, floridly penned message with increasing disappointment.

> *Zaccheus,*
> *I hope you will forgive me, but I cannot meet you at the bandstand this evening like we'd planned as I am feeling somewhat unwell.*
>
> *Elizabeth-Anne*

He tapped the paper against his thigh, sighed painfully to himself, and gazed out the oriel window. Across the street, the windows above the Good Eats Café were glowing yellow. Behind one of them was Elizabeth-Anne.

For a moment, he considered crossing the street and calling on her. Then he shook his head. If she was feeling sick, then she surely did not want to entertain a visitor.

He flopped down on the bed, crossed his arms behind his head, and gazed morosely up at the ceiling. Suddenly he felt very much alone.

It was strange how her company – or the lack of it – influenced how he felt.

Once it got dark, Elizabeth-Anne hurried to meet

Zaccheus at the bandstand. Although daylight was gone, she had dressed with special care, and since it looked like rain, she carried an umbrella.

She glanced up at the rooming house. A light glowed softly in the third-floor oriel window, but she could not see Zaccheus' shadow moving about. She frowned to herself. Surely he would have switched the lamps off if he had already left?

For a moment she hesitated. Perhaps he had been in such a hurry to meet her at the bandstand that he had forgotten to turn off the lights? He might well already be waiting for her.

She glanced down Main Street. Five blocks away, enveloped in the darkness, was the bandstand. And Zaccheus.

She hurried more swiftly now. Her heart was light, her footsteps springy. Yet she felt terribly nervous. She couldn't bear to wait much longer to find out how his interview with Tex Sexton had gone. She knew that her future and his hung from that delicate thread.

She had nearly reached her destination when the first big splatters of raindrops plopped down to the dusty street. She started to run and jumped up under the sheltering roof of the bandstand. The raindrops sounded extraordinarily loud as they drummed on the tin overhead. She glanced around. She could see him leaning against the railing, a black shadow against a dark background. She had to smile. His back was turned and he was pretending he hadn't seen her. Propping her umbrella quietly against the railing, she tiptoed over towards him. 'When I saw you'd left the lights on, I was afraid you were still at the rooming house,' she said softly. She reached out, touched his back, and frowned. His shirt felt peculiarly coarse and stiff. Quickly she withdrew her hand.

Before she knew what was happening, she felt rough

hands scrabbling over her arms and shoulders. Clumsy fingers clutched her breasts cruelly.

'Owww!' she screamed. Fighting to tear herself from his grasp, she shoved the splayed fingers of one hand into his face. With her other, she tried to pull herself loose. When she somehow managed to push him away from her, she staggered backwards and stared at him in shock.

Hard animal eyes glittered back at her out of the darkness.

She felt hot tears streaking down her cheeks. Her mind was panicked with confusion. What was the matter? He had always been so gentle with her! He had always treated her so lovingly, so *sensitively*. He had never grabbed her like this, had never caused her the slightest pain, had never even eyed her breasts – let alone touched them! What could have come over him? *What?*

A sudden flash of lightning illuminated the sky and froze the figure facing her in a silver tableau. She sucked in her breath as the wave of shock hit her squarely in the face. Her mind reeled, and, unbidden, the screaming, taunting chant of the children's ditty about Mutt swelled to a crescendo in her mind:

> *'Who's gonna get ya?*
> *Who's gonna grab ya?*
> *Crazy Mutt,*
> *Mutt and his slut,*
> *and Railroad Yeller,*
> *They'll lock you in their cellar!'*

In those split-second flashes of lightning, she caught sight of the mad gleam flashing in Mutt's eyes, the saliva drooling from his open mouth, the swollen penis protruding angrily from his fly.

'*You tole me! You tole me you wanted me!*' he bawled in a whining voice. '*You promised me!*'

A wave of stifling nausea swept over her. For a moment, she was afraid she was going to pass out.

Mustn't, she hissed savagely to herself. *Whatever you do, you mustn't faint. If you do, you can't run. And you've got to get away from him!*

Weakly, she forced her legs to move. She took a faltering step backwards, then another, and another. The lightning flashed and then, once again, the nightmare scene was plunged into blackness. But even in the darkness she could sense him closing in on her, could hear the heavy hollow tread of his boots on the creaking boards of the bandstand. *Closer. He was coming closer* . . .

She jumped backwards and a scream died in her throat as she felt something hard pressing against the small of her back. It was only the bandstand railing, only a length of slats and banisters . . .

Then she smelled his fetid breath as he lunged at her. His unshaven face scratched against hers, and his powerful hands grasped her, pinching and groping, squeezing and ripping. She struggled to fight him off, but he was far too strong for her. From somewhere in the back of her mind, the thought flashed through her that the unbalanced are possessed of an unspeakable strength.

If you can't fight him, then don't even try, she cautioned herself. *Pretend to faint. Let him loosen his grip so you can escape.*

She forced herself to go limp and she could hear his gasp of surprise as she slumped, but his hands would not let go. She took a deep breath, summoned all her strength, and somersaulted backward. He was carried along by her momentum, and together they crashed in a heels-over-head somersault over the railing, down to the wet ground below.

Wooosh! She could hear the breath being knocked out of her.

She lay there, dazed, taking deep lungfulls of air. After a moment, she sat up slowly and shook the cobwebs out of her head. She was aching all over, but she was safe. That was all that mattered. Beneath her, Mutt Campbell had been knocked unconscious. She crawled off from on top of him.

And then, just when she thought she was safe, she felt arms encircling her from behind. She recoiled and let out a cry. 'No!' she sobbed. 'Don't touch me! Please don't touch me! *Please* don't.' She drew back towards the bandstand platform on all fours, her body trembling, like a tortured animal shrinking from the world.

But the touch, when it came again, was kind and gentle.

Zaccheus pulled her gently to her feet.

'What happened?' he asked her softly.

She attacked him suddenly, her wet, dirty gloved fists pummelling fiercely against his chest. 'Let me go!' she cried. '*Let me go let me go let me go!*'

He grabbed her by the wrists to restrain her and pinned her arms to her sides. She hung her head and sobbed uncontrollably.

'It's me! Zaccheus!' he whispered urgently, giving her a shake. 'It's *me*, Elizabeth-Anne! You're safe now.'

'Let me go let me go –'

He tightened his lips, realizing at once that she was in a state of shock. His hand flashed as he slapped her resoundingly across her face.

One moment she was still blubbering incoherently, and the next she raised her head and stared at him in surprise. 'Zaccheus?' she sobbed in a tiny voice. 'Oh, Zaccheus!' Then she threw her arms around him and clung to him desperately, sobbing and crying with relief. 'Thank God it's you! Oh, God, it was terrible!'

379

'Sssssh!' He patted her on the back. 'Tell me about it later. Come on.'

She turned her face up to his. 'Where . . . are we going?'

'Back to where it's safe and warm . . . where you'll be all right. Thank God I couldn't bear to be alone tonight. I had to get out of my room . . . and it's funny, you know? I felt like I'd be closer to you here than anywhere else. That's why I decided to come down here. Because we were going to meet here, it somehow seemed like it's *our* place.'

'Not anymore, it isn't.'

'No, perhaps not,' he said quietly. 'Let's go.'

'But what . . . what about him?' She gestured to the ground beside her.

Another bolt of lightning lit up the sky and Zaccheus followed her gaze. Mutt Campbell was groaning, his body flickering in the lightning as he suddenly sat up straight. He looked accusingly at Elizabeth-Anne, his face so contorted, his features stretched so out of shape that they looked like they belonged on a rubber mask. 'You tole me it was all right!' he cried. 'You promised! You came to the shack and you promised!' He shook his head and started crying like a baby. It was a plaintive wail, a cry of hunger and disappointment and hurt and fury. Then he got up on all fours and scuttled off into the darkness, his hurt-filled, high-pitched voice receding: 'I knowed it was too good to be true! I knowed it! I knowed it had to be 'nother trick . . .'

Elizabeth-Anne let Zaccheus lead her slowly up Main Street. Although she moved numbly, with listless obedience, she was already trembling less. The rain was heavy and cold, but neither of them seemed to notice. The lights in the windows of the houses lining the street were a salty scrim in front of their eyes.

But when Zaccheus took her to the rooming house instead of the Good Eats Café, she stopped and tensed, a cold fear growing in her eyes 'But . . . but this isn't home.' She stared at him in the light of the porch lamp.

'Sssssh,' he said softly. 'Just listen to me. I know what I'm doing.' He squeezed her hand and smiled reassuringly. 'Trust me.'

She bit down on her lip. Then she nodded without speaking.

'You mustn't loose your trust in me, no matter what happened back there.'

'What . . . what did happen? I . . . I don't understand. I thought you . . .' she stared at him.

'Someone,' he said, his voice bitter and angry, 'pulled a loathesome trick on us. And I think I know who it was.'

'A trick,' she repeated dully.

He nodded. 'When I came home, I found a note under my door. It was signed with your name and said that you weren't well and wouldn't be able to meet me at the bandstand.'

She stared at him. 'Jenny!' she whispered.

'Probably,' he sighed.

She shook her head. 'But why? *Why*?'

'Jenny's obviously jealous of us. But don't worry. It's all over now.'

Elizabeth-Anne shook her head. 'Nooo . . .' she said softly. 'I'm afraid it's not. It may be over for *now*, but it's not over. Not by a long shot.' She sighed and shuddered. 'It-it was horrible, Zaccheus!' Her voice was choked. 'Horrible!' she repeated.

'But it's over now. Come. Let's go upstairs.'

She stared at him with dawning comprehension. 'First he wanted to . . . and now you want to –' Words suddenly failed her.

'Yes, darling,' he said with gentle wisdom, and she realized suddenly that this was the first time he had ever addressed her so intimately. 'Yes, I want to. But for different reasons. I want to make love to you because I

381

love you, because I don't want this terrible incident to scare you away from something beautiful for the rest of your life. Because now is the time for you to realize that what happened back there had nothing to do with love.'

'But . . . we aren't even married!' she stuttered weakly.

He placed his hands on the sides of her face and kissed her lips. 'We will be. I'll speak to your aunt and the Reverend tomorrow. Meanwhile, now's the time to love away your hurt.'

A sudden knowledge glowed deep in her eyes and together they climbed the steps up to the porch, and then quietly tiptoed upstairs.

7

It was a night of revelations.

Once in his room, he took her wet, gloved hands in his, held them, and did not take his eyes off her. Then he leaned forwards and kissed the tip of her nose.

She felt her shoulders tightening and a prickling of chill fear, featherlike and ethereal, raced up and down her spine. Time seemed to slow, then crawl, then come to a stop altogether. It seemed to her that every tiny intake of breath, even the slightest movement, was magnified in sound and sight and meaning. Everything was at once dream-like, and yet heightened in crystal-clear clarity. She knew, instinctively, that the mating dance had begun, and she was both grateful and relieved that it was not a frenzied, primitive celebration, but a slow and tender waltz, a graceful, gentle waltz to which she did not know the steps, but through which he was guiding her so carefully.

Their eyes were locked, two distinct shades of blue, one bright and one aquamarine, communicating without speaking. She stared at him, her irises flaring, her face taking on an anxious expression.

'I love you,' he said so softly that for a moment she did not realize he had spoken it aloud. She gazed back at him, her lips trembling faintly. Then he let go of her left hand and held her right in both of his.

She let out a sharp cry of dismay as he began to peel off her glove. 'No!' she whispered in panic. 'Oh please, God, *no!*' She snatched her hand back, but he took it again, even more gently, and raised the gloved hand to his lips. She watched him warily as he kissed it. Her body trembled, and she was filled with a mixture of pleasure from the touch of his lips and agony of what would happen when he saw the mutilation which the glove sheathed.

He kept his hand on hers, head tilted downwards, and gazed solemnly at her.

'Don't be afraid,' he whispered. 'I love you. I love every part of you.'

Her lips trembled as she tried to smile.

Slowly, he peeled the glove off her hand, as if doing it faster would have caused her severe pain. She jerked her head sideways and shut her eyes to avoid looking at the ugly sight.

He kissed each finger, one by one, then touched his lips to her palm and, finally, the back of her hand. Slowly, she turned her head and opened her eyes. 'I want to be perfect for you,' she said thickly, her voice choked with misery. 'But these . . . these hands . . .' She held them up.

'I love you the way you are, darling.' He smiled, reached out, and touched her hair with his fingertips. 'I love your hair.' He traced his index finger down her nose. 'I love your nose.' He bent down over her hand again and kissed it once more. 'I love your hands. These hands are your hands, therefore I love them. Do you understand?'

She nodded hesitantly. 'But I can't . . . I can't bear to show them to anyone,' she whispered thickly.

'But why?'

'Because . . . because they're so ugly! They're so terribly disfigured!'

'*What*?' He stared at her. 'What in hell are you talking about?'

She frowned, then forced herself to hold up her ungloved hand in front of her eyes and study it closely. She was astonished. 'Why, it's . . . it's *healed*! she breathed in amazement. 'Zaccheus! There's nothing wrong with this hand!'

'I should say not.'

'But . . . for how long . . .'

'I don't know. When's the last time you looked at it?'

Tears suddenly rolled down her cheeks. 'Years and years ago. Oh, God. If I'd only known . . .'

'But you know now, and that's all that matters.'

'All those years, those painful years of hiding my hands.' She shook her head in despair. 'If only I'd known.' Suddenly she was racked with sobs.

'Hey,' he said gently. 'What's the matter? Aren't you glad about your hands?'

She nodded and sniffed.

'Then why are you crying?'

'Because, darling, I love you so very, very much! And for the first time in my life, I'm so terribly, terribly happy!' And she thought: *I'll never wear gloves again, never ever, no matter how cold it gets.*

And that thought brought on new tears. They overflowed from her eyes and spilled down her cheeks in moist rivulets.

He leaned his face close into hers, and with slow flicks of his tongue he licked her tears away, one by one. Then his lips barely brushed the soft downy hairs of her neck and she took deep startled breaths, as the tingle

384

of his lips roused the millions of fragile nerve endings to excruciating tremors which rippled in musical waves up and down her spine like nimble angel fingers across a harp. She parted her lips and moaned softly, whispering ecstasy in the night.

He placed his hands on her shoulders, leaned into her neck, and inhaled the fragrant sweetness of her body. She shut her eyes and clutched him fiercely. She felt his hands roaming over her shoulders, down her arms, a rhythm of nimble fingers, and she felt the humming vibration flowing through her. These were deep, vibrant chords, more like the rippling chords of a piano than the light fairy tingles of the harp.

He's playing me, she thought incredibly. *He's playing me as if I were an exquisitely rare musical instrument, lithely luring a melody out of me.*

His fingers flicked at the buttons at the back of her dress, but his lips remained at her neck. She remained standing, arching her back at the thrill of his touch. He genuflected on one knee, pressing his face sideways into her clothed groin until the dress hung loose. Then he raised the hem of the dress as he slowly rose to his feet and lifted it carefully over her head.

He helped her out of her underclothes, and then she shook her hair loose. Now she stood naked. He stepped back to look at her. He felt the breath catch in his throat. She was standing awkwardly, her hands at her sides, at once proud, and yet at the same time, unsure of her nudity. Her eyes sparkled like the jewels that they were. He thought her the most desirable woman in the world. With the pins out of her hair, it fell loosely to her shoulders, thick and golden and lustrous. Her skin was pale, radiant and porcelain-like in the dim glow of the single candle flickering on the table. Hers was soft skin, incredibly smooth and flawless, yet pulled tautly over a firm flat belly, rounded hips, and perfectly formed breasts which rode high and proud above the curving tautness of her ribcage. Her nipples were erect, a dark, wine-coloured red, and her pubis was golden and soft, a glowing, downy thatch of wheat.

He tore his eyes away from her and slowly stepped out of his clothes. She watched him without speaking. When he was naked, he went over to the bedside cabinet and opened a drawer. She watched him curiously, strangely disappointed that he did not immediately slide his own muscular, satiny skin against the porcelain smoothness of hers. But then he turned around; a thin thread of silver was pulled taut between his hands, and dangling from the centre of it was a pansy encased in crystal.

She stepped towards him and without being told, turned around, her back to him. She raised her chin and felt the soft touch of his fingers around her neck. The chain and charm were cool against her collarbone. Then she turned to him.

He smiled at her, watching her with an intense, transfixed expression. For the first time, the pansy charm, the symbol of his love, graced the neck it deserved. It had never looked more beautiful. He nodded happily as she raised one hand to the charm and felt it with her fingertips. It was a curious sensation, she thought, actually feeling something with her fingers instead of her gloves. 'Thank you,' she whispered huskily.

'It is I who must thank you,' he replied, and then his strong arms encircled her while his lips pressed against hers with a demanding urgency. She felt herself drowning in his little nibbles, the flicks of his tongue, and she responded in kind, groping him with equal urgency until her legs moistened with a peculiar wetness she had never experienced before.

He knew at once that she was ready. He took her by the hand and led her to the bed.

'Don't . . . hurt me?' she asked in a tiny, quivering voice. 'I've never before . . .'

386

'I'll be gentle,' he promised. He kissed first one porcelain shoulder, then the other. 'The first time, it nearly always hurts,' he explained softly, 'but after that, there's no more pain. Only the most beautiful, most driving sensation in the entire world.' He paused and smiled. 'You don't have to worry. I'll go slow and easy. I don't want to hurt you. Never, for as long as we live.'

She reached up and stroked his cheek with her fingers. 'If there has to be any pain at all,' she said solemnly, 'then do it quickly so that it is not drawn out. Let's get it over with. Because . . . because I want to be able to enjoy you, my love. I want to give everything a woman can possibly give, and more.'

The night became alive with the moist, sweetly succulent sounds of love. It was a splendid night, a night filled with passion and urgency, purposeful grunts and groans, nibbles and sweet little sucking sounds and tender words of love.

It was a night to remember. Slowly, inch by inch, they began to learn each other's physical geography by heart, he discovering a hidden freckle on her thigh, she a peculiar downy spot in the small of his back and the peculiarly sensuous way his sinewy muscles moved when he lifted his arm in a certain way. Every minute, it seemed, they discovered something new about each other. And then he filled her being entirely, driving her to passionate heights, easing off to restful valleys, and then pushing her to ever higher plateaus.

And, when she was no longer a virgin, his thrusts became powerful and demanding as he filled her entirely with himself. She moaned and cried as she felt herself heating up even more, and her body responded by clasping him tightly, urgently, and she felt the most exquisite, tingling passion welling up inside her.

The world became a whirling dervish. She closed her eyes and saw a rose blooming and then bursting and it threw its shattered petals to the wind.

'My love, my love!' Her voice floated about the room, up the walls, swirled around the ceiling.

His voice strained with urgency and melded into hers as he felt the world around him contract and expand, and he plunged into her as deeply as he could, until the most exquisite pain rushed over him and his seed burst forth.

Unknown to them, their first child was conceived sometime during that magical, very first night.

8

Since he had only begun his job at the Sexton ranch, and had no money saved, Elizabeth-Anne knew that Zaccheus could ill afford to buy both an engagement ring and two wedding bands. When he eagerly presented her with the pretty, quarter-carat diamond engagement ring he had arranged to buy on credit, she shook her head sensibly and closed the box. 'I like it,' she said. 'In fact, I love it. But we can't afford it.'

'But I bought it on credit!' he protested. 'I've spread the payments out over the next twenty-four months! We'll never even miss the money.'

'Credit is fine,' Elizabeth-Anne said with what would become her trademark, practicality. 'I'm not against it. But let's save it for something really important. We'll need to get plenty of things as time goes on.'

He looked patently disappointed.

'Why do I need an engagement ring, anyway? I have the pansy charm.' She smiled as she reached up to her neck to touch it. 'This means more to me than any engagement ring, ever.'

'But brides are supposed to have one.'

'But this one doesn't need it,' Elizabeth-Anne said

with finality. She smiled gently, kissed him, and handed him the tiny box back.

They settled for the two gold wedding bands, his thick and plain, hers narrow and decorated with a delicate border. She was delighted with it; it was a very pretty ring and she couldn't wait for the moment it would adorn her finger forever.

Meanwhile, the engagement ring went back to the shop. It was ironic, Zaccheus thought sadly, that after all the jewels which had passed through his hands, his bride would not have a diamond engagement ring gracing her finger.

Elender was happily making elaborate plans for the wedding. Following the ceremony at the Quebeck church, she wanted the reception to be held at the Good Eats Café. 'The parlour is much too small for all the guests,' she explained. For years, she had been secretly planning huge wedding ceremonies for both Jenny and Elizabeth-Anne; since she had never been married herself, she wanted both young ladies to experience the lavish send-off into married life she herself had never had.

'But, Auntie!' Elizabeth-Anne wailed in distress. 'I don't *want* a big wedding, and neither does Zaccheus.' She paced the parlour nervously, fidgeting with her fingers. 'We want it nice and small and intimate. Besides, neither of us has any really close friends we want to invite.'

Elender looked hurt. 'But there are neighbours and acquaintances. A woman only gets married once in her life –'

'I know that. But *please*, Auntie, respect our wishes?' Elizabeth-Anne sat down next to her. 'Let's keep it as small and intimate as possible. And we'd really prefer a tiny reception held here in the parlour to a big one downstairs. I talked it over with Zaccheus, and he's of the same opinion.'

389

Elender looked slightly miffed. 'You seem to lack,' she said specifically, 'any romantic notions. However, if that's what you want, how can I refuse you?' She sighed heavily. 'Now off we go to buy some fabric at the Byrd sisters'. Then we're going to see Mrs Velasquez in Mexican Town. They say she makes the finest wedding gowns in town.'

'Oh, Auntie! I don't *want* a wedding gown!'

'What!' Elender looked at Elizabeth-Anne in shock.

'Really, Auntie. What I'd like is a new Sunday dress, instead. I can wear it for the ceremony and every Sunday thereafter. That's much more practical than having something made to only wear once, and then to get moth-eaten. With a nice new dress, and hat and shoes, I'll be more than satisfied.'

Elender fanned herself bleakly with a piece of folded newspaper. Her dreams of a lavish ceremony were completely shattered. 'If that's what you want, then I have no choice but to indulge you – even if you don't indulge me.' She compressed her lips. 'Very well. A simple ceremony it is. Now, who do you think we should invite?'

'You and Jenny.'

'And?'

Elizabeth-Anne gazed at her levelly. 'That's it.'

'But . . . but Zaccheus will need a best man!' Elender sputtered.

'He doesn't know anyone around here well enough. Won't a witness do?'

'I think so. Now, about the honeymoon . . .'

'Zaccheus just started work, Auntie,' Elizabeth-Anne reminded her gently. 'He can't take time off yet. We've decided to delay the honeymoon until next year. He'll have two weeks of vacation coming then.'

Elender shook her head and clucked her tongue. 'Dear, dear. It won't be much of a wedding, will it?'

'It's plenty for us.' Elizabeth-Anne noticed Auntie's morose expression. 'Now what's the matter?'

'Nothing. But you're so . . . so practical.'

Elizabeth-Anne grinned. 'If I am, I only learned it from you.'

'I stand corrected. But you will let me do one thing, won't you, dear?'

'What's that?'

'Have your picture taken and put an announcement in the social page of the *Gazette*?'

Elizabeth-Anne smiled. 'That would be very nice.' Suddenly she leaned sideways and embraced Elender warmly. Then she drew back in alarm. 'Now what's the matter? You're crying!'

Elender sniffed, smiled through her tears, and produced a lace-edged handkerchief. She dabbed her eyes dry. 'It's only that I'm so very happy! And so terribly sad.'

'Sad? But why?'

'I didn't think I was going to lose you so soon.'

'Lose me? Auntie!' Elizabeth-Anne cried. 'Shame on you! You're not losing me! You're gaining a son-in-law. And think of all the children we'll have! You'll have gained a whole family!'

And the next morning, after Elizabeth-Anne had her picture taken, Elender marched happily into the office of the *Quebeck Weekly Gazette*. The next issue would announce the engagement. Elizabeth-Anne and Zaccheus were to be married the following Sunday.

'After the reception tomorrow,' Zaccheus said offhandedly at dinner, 'we'll immediately go home to our house.'

'You found us a house!' Elizabeth-Anne's mouth fell open. She stopped eating, put down her fork, and forgot the rest of her sliced pork roast. 'Well? Where is it?'

Zaccheus and Elender exchanged conspiratorial smiles across the table.

Elizabeth-Anne tapped her glass impatiently with the fork. 'Well?' she demanded. 'Out with it!'

'I think,' Jenny mumbled, pushing her plate aside, 'I don't feel well.'

Elender looked at her narrowly. 'Is something wrong?'

'No,' Jenny said glumly. 'It's nothing. Just a stomach ache, is all. May I be excused?'

Elender nodded and Jenny scraped back her chair and quickly left the room. When she shut the parlour door behind her, she leaned against the wall, shut her eyes, and inhaled a long, deep breath. She was shaking with fury. She had finally had enough! Her hatred towards Elizabeth-Anne and Zaccheus had reached the boiling point. She had had to leave the room – it was either that or she would have erupted on the spot. She was sick and tired of having to listen to their plans and having to see the way they ogled each other. It was sickening, really.

She tightened her lips angrily. She had been so *certain*. So absolutely certain her plan to separate them would work. But something had gone very wrong. All her plan had accomplished was to throw Elizabeth-Anne and Zaccheus even further into each other's arms. Worse, neither of them as much as mentioned what had transpired at the bandstand – as if nothing had happened at all! But surely they were aware of what she had done. If so, why, then, hadn't they mentioned it to her? Or to Elender?

Jenny's hands were trembling so badly that she clenched them in order to steady herself. Oh! It was all so much more than she could bear! But what really enraged her . . . what drove her straight up the wall was that Elizabeth-Anne, who was two years younger than she (and far less pretty, she told herself), had snared herself a husband first. Despite all the emotional and physical problems she was beset with, the circus freak was hearing wedding bells – and with her own unwitting help!

It was enough to make her *sick*!

Through the closed door, Jenny could hear the conversation inside the room continuing excitedly. *Such a happy couple*! she thought disgustedly. She didn't think she could bear to hear any more.

But something made her decide to stay put, press her ear against the door, and eavesdrop. And before long, she was very glad she did.

'Darling, I know it's not much of a house,' Zaccheus was saying, pushing away his unfinished plate.

'Well, isn't it time someone told me just what house it is?' Elizabeth-Anne demanded with mock petulance.

'Well, it's right here in town,' Zaccheus replied evasively. 'And from what Miss Clow – excuse me, *Auntie* told me, I think you'll be crazy about it.'

'It's not – not the Byrd cottage!' Elizabeth-Anne guessed delightedly.

'It is,' Zaccheus said.

Jenny pressed her ear closer. The Byrd sisters were eccentric spinsters. Identical twins, it was difficult to tell them apart since they dressed and sounded alike. They owned Byrd's Fabric Shoppe on Main Street, and worked together. Rumour had it that long ago they had both been in love with the same man and rather than one of them hurting the other, neither had married him. Up until now, Samantha Byrd had been living in the cottage while her twin, Susannah, lived above the fabric shop.

'I knew how much you've always admired it, my dear,' Elender said in a pleased voice. 'Since Samantha's arthritis has become worse, Susannah wants her to move in with her above the shop so she can take care of her. Samantha is not willing to sell that cottage, since it holds emotional ties for her – they were both born in that cottage, you know – but she is willing to rent it.'

'I still can't believe it!' Elizabeth-Anne cried. 'I've always loved that cottage.'

'Best of all,' Zaccheus said excitedly, 'it comes furnished. Miss Byrd is even leaving pots and pans and bed linen behind for our use.'

'And,' Elender pointed out dryly, 'that should appeal to your well-honed sense of thrift.'

'Oh, but it does! Oh, Auntie! I'm so excited I could burst!'

Outside in the hall, Jenny contorted her face as she mimed silently: 'Oh, Auntie! I'm so excited I could burst!' She narrowed her smouldering eyes dangerously.

'And, since you insisted you didn't want a lavish wedding,' Auntie continued, 'I used the money I'd saved up for it to increase your wedding present.' She paused dramatically. 'Your rent is prepaid for a year.'

'Auntie! You shouldn't have!'

Jenny contorted her face again. 'Auntie!' she mimicked soundlessly. 'You shouldn't have!'

Zaccheus cleared his throat. It was a loud, startling, significant sound, and it was not lost on Jenny.

Elender looked at him, then studied the floral pattern of the tablecloth. 'Dear?' she began tentatively, her index finger following the trail of the embroidered roses.

Elizabeth-Anne looked across the table at her. 'Yes?'

'This morning . . .' Elender's voice seemed to fail her, and she cleared her throat nervously. She raised her head and smiled sadly. 'This morning, Zaccheus and I had a heart-to-heart talk. He told me some things about himself . . . well, actually he was wondering whether he should tell you something or not, and he came to me for advice. My advice was to leave well enough alone, but he . . . he decided he wanted to tell you. Since he insisted . . .'

'What *is* it?' Elizabeth-Anne looked from one of them

394

to the other, her expression one of alarm. 'Is something wrong?'

'I don't believe a husband and wife should keep any secrets from each other,' Zaccheus said in a low voice. 'I want our marriage to have a foundation of honesty, even if it means calling it off.'

'Calling it off!'

'You see, there are some things I think you should know about me. Before the wedding takes place.'

Elizabeth-Anne stared at him in surprise. 'Like what?' she asked with forced flippancy. 'You snore? You don't like broccoli? You don't wash behind your ears —'

'Serious things,' he said quietly. 'Things about my past.'

Outside the closed door, Jenny's lips slowly widened in a cold smile. She could feel the beginnings of an exquisite excitement growing inside her.

'Your past?' Elizabeth-Anne repeated. 'Why, Zaccheus Hale! You're suddenly so serious. Don't make it sound so ominous. *Please*. Don't frighten me.' She gave a hollow, contrived laugh. 'Don't tell me you're a polygamist with wives hidden away in half the states of the Union? Well, I don't care! I love you anyway!'

'Perhaps it would be best if I left you two alone,' Elender suggested delicately.

Elizabeth-Anne nodded soberly, then changed her mind and reached across the table. She clutched Elender's hand tightly. 'No. Don't go. Since you've already heard it, what harm could it do?' Her voice suddenly cracked and she looked away. 'I-I don't want to be alone if it's something which will break my heart.'

Elender sighed: it came out a thin, reedy and painful sound. 'You won't be alone; Zaccheus is here. Anyway, all I can pray for is that what he has to tell you won't make any difference in your relationship. It didn't make me feel any differently towards him, because of his honesty. Remember, he didn't have to tell me anything. And I think that, more than anything else, indicates that he is a man of character.' She paused and added pointedly: 'We all make mistakes in our lives that we're sorry for later. God knows, I have made more than my fair share myself.'

'You?' Elizabeth-Anne asked in astonishment. 'I don't believe it.'

Elender gave a short laugh. 'I have.' She paused again. 'Now, before we get started, let me get up and turn on some lamps.' She smiled faintly. 'It's getting dark in here.'

Jenny heard Elender moving about the room. Quickly she left her listening post, tiptoed to the adjacent door, and flattened herself in the doorway. She waited a few minutes. When Elender didn't come out into the hall, she retraced her steps and kept on listening.

'Before we get onto this serious subject,' Elender suggested after she sat back down again, 'I should bring up another equally serious matter.' She faced Elizabeth-Anne squarely. 'It concerns you, dear.'

'Me?' Elizabeth-Anne looked puzzled.

'Yes, you. And now's the time to face it. Zaccheus must be made aware of it. And perhaps he is right. It is best if everything about both of you is brought out into the open. This way, your marriage won't begin with any hidden problems. You'll both start out with a clean slate, so to speak.'

'Yeesss . . .' Elizabeth-Anne said slowly, though she didn't know if she could bear to listen to anything. Her euphoric spirits were beginning to ebb dangerously fast. She had the sinking feeling that perhaps their love was no longer picture perfect.

Elender folded her hands on the table. For a moment, she seemed intent on studying her fingertips. 'I spoke to Dr Purris this morning,' she said softly.

Elizabeth-Anne stared at her. 'There's . . . there's

nothing wrong with you, is there?' she asked in a faltering voice.

Elender raised her head and shook it. 'No, no. Not with me. But since you and Zaccheus are planning to build a family, I thought it best to consult Dr Purris and ask his medical advice.'

'But what about?' Elizabeth-Anne asked anxiously. 'I've always been healthy –'

Elender lifted her glass of water, then put it back down. 'Elizabeth-Anne, dear, you are like my own daughter,' she said. 'Naturally, I want what's best for you. I don't need to tell you that, do I?'

Elizabeth-Anne shook her head.

Elender met her gaze directly.

'Ever since that tragic incident you witnessed when you were a child, you had trouble going to sleep. Remember? You used to wake up constantly in cold sweats after having the most hideous nightmares.'

Elizabeth-Anne felt an involuntary shiver spiralling through her body.

'So I gave you a little laudanum at bedtime,' Elender said, 'and I thought it was harmless enough. And after a while, we had to keep increasing the dosage. It helped you sleep and seemed to chase your terrible nightmares away.'

'It did help,' Elizabeth-Anne said softly. 'It still does.'

Elender hesitated. 'Dr Purris tells me that, after all these years, you are surely addicted to laudanum.'

'But I don't see –' Elizabeth-Anne began.

'Elizabeth-Anne. Zaccheus.' Elender reached across the table and held both their hands. 'Giving you that laudanum, Elizabeth-Anne, was probably the single worst mistake I ever made in my life. Dr Purris says that any addiction is terribly dangerous. Doubly so when a woman carries a child. Therefore, if you decide to have children, you must stop taking it, Elizabeth-Anne. Immediately.'

Elizabeth-Anne stared at her.

'I know, I know,' Elender said miserably. She held up her hand. 'It will be terribly difficult. Your body will rebel. Withdrawal can make you very ill. And . . .'

'And what?'

Elender stared intently at her. 'The nightmares may return.'

Elizabeth-Anne's face wore a fearful expression as she stared at Elender. Then, slowly, she turned to Zaccheus.

He smiled reassuringly, coiled an arm around her shoulders, and hugged her warmly. 'I'll help you, darling,' he said quietly. 'Together, we can conquer this. Together, we can do anything we set our hearts on. As long as we're together, only the sky's the limit.'

'Yes,' Elizabeth-Anne said sincerely. 'Together, we *can* do it. I *know* we can. Oh, I want us to have healthy children, Zaccheus! I-I think I can face my nightmares now.'

'Dr Purris said to tell you he will be only too happy to help you in any way he can. His door is open to both of you, at any hour of the day or night.' Elender sighed. 'That is the first serious problem which will confront you both.'

'And the second one?' Elizabeth-Anne asked fearfully.

Elender nodded at Zaccheus, and slowly, in a painful voice, he told Elizabeth-Anne everything. He talked half the night long and left nothing out – not his mother's illness, nor his robbing Bensey's Jewellers. And he told her everything about Phoebe and Demps, and Eleonore Alice Qualey and her tragically murdered husband.

As she listened outside the door, Jenny's face took on a rapturous expression. Her heart pounded excitedly. *Zaccheus – a thief? Zaccheus – wanted for murder? Even if he didn't commit it, he was wanted for it,* she thought with dizzying joy. *Oh, how precious! How very, very precious! She could just see it. The moment the Reverend would ask if there was any just reason why these two people should not be united as man and wife, she could blurt out: 'Because he's wanted for murder!'*

But she would not do that. That was far too easy. For once, she would guard her precious secret. She wasn't going to do a thing, not yet. She would bide her time and wait patiently – for years, if she had to. And then, when least expected, when Zaccheus and Elizabeth-Anne had the most to lose, just when they felt the safest – then, and only then – would she spring the trap.

After a while, only silence came from the parlour. Then Zaccheus spoke again. 'Does this mean you no longer want me, Elizabeth-Anne?' he asked hesitantly.

Elizabeth-Anne gazed at him for what seemed an eternity. 'No, it doesn't mean that at all.' She took his hand, held it tightly, and kissed it. 'I love you,' she said huskily, 'just as you told me you love me. I can never hold your honesty against you. Not for as long as I live. If you hadn't told me about it and I'd found out, well, that would have been different. But I love your honesty. I love *you*.' She paused and added softly: 'Your past changes nothing.'

'Then you *will* marry me?' he asked excitedly.

She clutched him fiercely. 'Yes, darling!' she cried. 'Yes, yes, *yes*!'

And outside the door, Jenny raised her head, smiled wickedly, and tiptoed off to her room.

9

It was the time they spent at the Byrd cottage that Elizabeth-Anne would remember as the happiest and most fulfilled years of her life. And what a beautiful, charming, idyllic place it was! Home, honeymoon cottage, hideaway, birthplace of her children — no matter how far she would roam to the ends of the earth, or how high up the social ladder she would soar, or with how many countless multimillions her bank accounts would eventually swell — somehow, everything which was ever truly important to her could be encapsuled, could somehow be condensed down to its beginnings, to the Byrd cottage. It was where her life truly started and where it was lived to the fullest — where life began, where life continued and thrived. If walls could tell tales, then it was the tales these very walls contained which she wanted told most, for they were stories of love gained and love lost, of happiness and sorrow, of illness and health, of triumph and defeat, of endurance and strength, and laughter, and tears.

She had always been charmed by the cosiness of the cottage, but the moment that Zaccheus swooped her up off the ground and carried her, giggling and squirming along the flagstone path which led to the cottage, past the white picket fence and through the creaking gate — that was when the magic began. And the instant he carried her over the threshold, the cottage took on a quality she had never known a house to possess. It was a haven. A sanctuary.

Above all, it was home.

'Zaccheus! I still can't believe it!' Elizabeth-Anne squealed as he carefully set her down in the small front hall. She flung her arms around his neck and kissed him fiercely. 'Elizabeth-Anne Hale. How does it sound?'

'Sounds great to me.'

'I'll never let go of you!' she promised, trapping his neck in the extended scissor-like pose of her arms. 'Never ever! Not for as long as I live!'

'You'd better,' he suggested laughingly, his blue eyes dancing, 'or else you'll never see our new home.'

She let go of him instantly, stood still, and gazed in

silence around the front hall. The breath caught in her throat. It was too beautiful for words.

I'm not going to change a thing, Elizabeth-Anne decided instantly. *It would be a sacrilege to spoil this beauty.*

Suddenly she tugged at Zaccheus' hand and led him around the cottage, chattering excitedly as she pulled him from room to room, studying the layout and decor, poking her nose into every last niche and cranny. 'I love it!' she said.

'I do, too,' he said, smiling, loving the excited gleam in her eyes, the rosy flush brought on by her excitement. She had never, he decided, looked more beautiful.

Elizabeth-Anne took a deep breath. 'Zaccheus! Just close your eyes and smell it!' She closed her own eyes and breathed deeply. The cottage had its own particular fragrance, a fruity fragrance with floral overtones, with the sweet scents of nuts and honey and the spicy smells of herbs.

The small living room was entirely panelled, and the walls were hung with Audubon bird prints. A larger, needlepoint rug covered the floorboards, and all the upholstery was cabbage rose chintz. It was an English country look, not at all stuffy, prim Victorian or spindly, masculine frontier: everything was plush, overstuffed, and eminently comfortable. A woman would be at home here, but it was no less comfortable for a man. The small, mullioned windows were swagged with the same chintz which covered the chairs and couch, and lace curtains diluted the sharp, intense Texas sun. A japanned table, one tiny Queen Anne tray table, and a butler's table in rich, glowing mahogany served the conversation grouping which faced the large fireplace. Cut crystal boxes, hand-painted Bavarian china plates, cobalt-blue glass, Chinese cachepots, and intricate needlepoint cushions, obviously crafted by Samantha Byrd herself, abounded. Yet strangely enough, the room did not look at all cluttered. It was comfortable and cheery, eminently cosy and inviting. Everywhere, vases held assorted bouquets of giant pink peonies and fragrant roses.

'The flowers are a gift from Auntie,' Zaccheus said. 'It's her housewarming present. She told me, quote, "I knew there was a good reason why I've been watering those plants around the rooming house for all these years", unquote.'

'I must not forget to thank her,' Elizabeth-Anne said. 'What's this?' She pointed to the couch. On it rested a large package wrapped in pale violet tulle and tied with a flamboyant violet ribbon delicately edged in white lace.

'I don't know.' Slowly Zaccheus picked it up. It felt surprisingly light. He squeezed it gently. It was soft, too. He noticed a small envelope pinned to the tulle. He handed the envelope to Elizabeth-Anne.

She tore it open and slid out the card. Painted in the left-hand corner was a lovely watercolour of a sprig of violet, and the message was inscribed in florid peacock blue ink:

> *A small something for your happiness forever.*
> *The Byrd Sisters*

'It's a gift!' Elizabeth-Anne cried. Carefully, she unwrapped the package. Then she let out a cry of delight. It was a needlepoint cushion depicting the facade of the cottage, and the embroidered words read:

> *May all who live here,*
> *No matter how far they roam,*
> *Return to this place,*
> *Which will always be home.*

'It's lovely!' Elizabeth-Anne cried softly, the tears moist in her eyes. 'I'll treasure it always.'

'There's more to see.' Zaccheus could barely contain his excitement. 'Come on.'

She hugged the pillow against her breast and followed him back out into the hallway and through a doorway to the sunny little dining nook. The tiny room was entirely white and the walls consisted of French doors set into a wooden framework. Two more French doors, set at an angle, made up the skylight roof. And everywhere she looked, there were pots of ferns. They were of all sizes and species, from luxurious grey-green staghorns to tiny, chartreuse forest ferns.

'Miss Byrd said they need misting three times a day,' Zaccheus said.

'And I shall not mind it one bit,' Elizabeth-Anne declared.

Between the living room and the dining nook was the kitchen. It was enormous and splendid and took up most of the ground floor. The ceiling was made of rough, smoke-blackened beams and the floor was laid with Mexican terracotta tiles waxed to a high gloss. Black iron skillets, copper pots and pans, wooden mixing bowls, earthenware crocks, and enamel colanders hung in profusion. A long refectory table, scarred and battered, with six rush-seated chairs, stood in the centre of the room. Along one wall was the wood-burning stove and two large, galvanized washbowls set flush in a wooden counter: water would have to be fetched from the pump behind the cottage. One entire wall consisted entirely of shelves displaying a conglomeration of plates and saucers, cups and, incredibly, an antique birdcage fashioned of wood and wire in the shape of a castle. It was purely decorative; no songbird inhabited the splendid premises.

'I'll buy us a canary the next time there's a fiesta in Mexican Town,' Zaccheus promised. 'That way, while I'm at work and you're at home, you'll have company.' He drew her close. 'Until our firstborn arrives, that is,' he said softly. 'Then, I'm sure, you'll have more company than you know what to do with.'

But it was the upstairs of the cottage that Elizabeth-Anne fell in love with the most. One bedroom was entirely devoid of furnishings. 'The nursery!' she cried.

And she knew by the way Zaccheus squeezed her hand that he had thought exactly the same.

The master bedroom, small as it was, tucked under a slanting eave, was pure heaven as far as Elizabeth-Anne was concerned. Pale green walls, built up with translucent layers of watery paint, gave the room the merest hint of colour. The moulding was constructed of rough, stained saplings and the bed was of thin steel, with a swirling headboard and a squared footboard, and was strewn with lacy pillows. The crocheted spread was bordered with tassels which swept the floor. Above the headboard hung a portrait; to either side of it were four framed flower prints, one hung directly over the other. A small writing desk, pushed against the wall in lieu of a bedside cabinet, its tooled-leather writing surface folded out, held writing implements and a lamp. The lace curtains, an ethereal pattern of delicate flowers drawn across the dormer window, let in the softest, most muted, romantic northern light possible.

Elizabeth-Anne charged breathlessly into the room, pulling Zaccheus along by sheer momentum. They tripped and fell backwards, startled and laughing, and bounced onto the cushiony softness of the bed, which creaked in protest. 'While we're here –' Elizabeth-Anne whispered solemnly.

Zaccheus finished the sentence: '– Let's take advantage of it and not waste a minute.' He enfolded her lithe body in his strong arms, and she sighed happily as he began to unbutton the front of her dress. She gazed dreamily up at the ceiling. Suddenly her breath caught in her throat.

'What's the matter?' he asked with sudden concern, tenderly brushing her cheek with his fingertips.

She struggled to sit up and stole another glance at the ceiling. He twisted around and followed her eyes.

Centred on the ceiling directly over the bed was a large red valentine. A copy of their wedding picture was glued to the heart. But this valentine was no symbol of love. It had been torn, rent right down the middle, tearing Elizabeth-Anne and Zaccheus away from each other.

There was something so shocking, so sick, so cruelly chilling about it, that neither of them was able to speak. Zaccheus tightened his lips and shook his head angrily. He did not need to hazard a guess as to whose handicraft it was. He hugged Elizabeth-Anne tightly, trying to shield her from the chill dread which he knew engulfed her. 'Try to forget this,' he said softly. 'It will never happen again.'

'But . . .' She stared up at him, her aquamarine eyes dulled with hurt. It was at once a plaintive and fearful look, a prognostication of more suffering to come. For too long now, she had been victimized by Jenny's vindictive plots and ploys. The message behind the torn valentine was only too clear. 'You don't know Jenny,' Elizabeth-Anne whispered, 'or the lengths she will go to, to break us up. This . . . this proves it.' She gazed up at the ceiling and shuddered.

He reached up and tore the ugly valentine off the ceiling. A portion of the pale paint tore off along with it, leaving a white comma-shaped streak. He crumpled the torn heart into a ball and tossed it to the floor. 'Jenny will eventually come around,' he said, hoping to sound confident. 'And if that doesn't happen, I'm sure she'll at least stay out of our lives.'

'But what if she doesn't?'

'She'll have her own life to live. She'll find a husband, have children, occupy herself with more important things than you and me. Honey, trust me. Please?'

Elizabeth-Anne gazed at him and nodded solemnly.

'Ours is going to be the perfect marriage.' He was silent for a moment while he traced an invisible line with his fingertip from her forehead, down to her nose, and to her lips. 'You'll see. Nothing will come between us. Ever. Not Jenny. Not anybody or anything. Our marriage is a marriage made in heaven.'

And it was.

Perhaps it was because it was Zaccheus' child she was carrying; perhaps it was the mother instinct with which she thought all women are born. Through sheer willpower and with Zaccheus' help, Elizabeth-Anne never touched laudanum again. And nine months later, she received her reward: a beautiful, lively, healthy baby girl.

She was named Regina Emaline Hale.

10

For Elizabeth-Anne and Zaccheus, their fifth wedding anniversary was a time to look back upon five fruitful years.

Life had been good. Nearly thirteen months to the day after she gave birth to Regina, Elizabeth-Anne delivered a second child, Charlotte-Anne. And nearly three years after Charlotte-Anne made her entrance into the world, she was followed by Rebecca Elender Hale.

Zaccheus' job had worked out far better than they had dared hope. Now, at twenty-seven, he had already been promoted three times and, by Quebeck standards, earned a princely salary. When he had first begun working for Tex Sexton, the townspeople had regarded him with suspicion and dread: they had long learned the hard way that anyone of importance in the Sexton empire was not to be trusted. But somehow, Zaccheus had managed not only to gain people's trust and keep it, but to keep his integrity intact. For the first time, people felt they had a champion who had Tex's ear, and who they could petition with their problems regarding any of the Sexton monopolies. Zaccheus proved that he was not loathe to put in a good word for anyone, or to intervene on their behalf with Tex or Roy, his brother, who was as feared as Tex. He became an unofficial buffer zone between Quebeck's citizens and the Sextons. The initial suspicion of him quickly died. He proved over and over that he was not a Sexton spy and that he had everyone's best interests at heart. Nor had he let himself become self-important or autocratic. In fact, whenever he could, he fought against unfair treatment of Sexton employees and those who depended upon the Sexton-owned businesses for survival. Tex Sexton tolerated Zaccheus' involvements because he was as scrupulously honest with him as he was with anyone else, and having him as a troubleshooter kept people from getting too restless and too angry. Too, Tex was fascinated by Zaccheus because he was the only person he had ever met who was not intimidated by his money or his power. And he was as hardworking and dedicated as he himself.

But it was to those in need that Zaccheus became a local hero.

When Abner Mason's irrigation water was about to be terminated because he couldn't keep up with the payments, Zaccheus interceded successfully to have the sluice gates kept open. 'Abner's got the best lemon crop for miles around this year,' he argued with Tex. 'You mark my word, it will be well worth it. Besides, this way his crop won't be ruined and he'll have to use your packing plant for which he'll have to pay, and your transportation system to ship out the crop, for which he'll have to pay too. If his water is shut off, you'll miss out on his packing and shipping. But with letting him buy time, everyone comes out ahead. Abner's reliable. He'll pay up as soon as he can. I personally guarantee it.'

When the entire Palacios family was fired from picking cotton – a meagre livelihood under any circumstances – because Luis Palacios was trying to organize the cotton pickers into a union, Zaccheus found himself powerless to do anything for Luis, but he did manage to get the rest of the family rehired.

When Tom Reubin, a farmer who leased his land from the Sextons lost his three sons in a tragic accident, Zaccheus organized an emergency detail which kept the farm working and saved the crops until a permanent solution was found.

When Roy Sexton complained bitterly about the amount of cotton being picked, Zaccheus tried to talk him into raising the pickers' wages to see if the added incentive would help. Roy reluctantly gave him his word that, if in a week the cotton picked by each worker would be a bushel more each day, a raise would be forthcoming. Zaccheus spoke to the pickers and told them what had transpired – and offered a bonus to whomever picked the most cotton in one day as well. That week, a record amount was picked, and Roy grudgingly approved the raises. The daily cotton quota remained high, thanks to the prospect of a bonus.

On the Hale homefront, the children were a constant source of joy and surprise. Regina and Charlotte-Anne were already talking up a storm and always seemed to be getting into mischief. Regina was the wildest of them, but it was Charlotte-Anne who both delighted and exasperated Elizabeth-Anne and Zaccheus the most. When she turned three, she began to wake up her parents constantly in the middle of the night in order to recount her dreams. Rebecca, the newborn, would surely be as much a joy. As much as she hated to, Elizabeth-Anne arranged for Concepcíon Sendano, a reliable, warm-hearted Mexican widow, to take care of the children during the day so that she could continue helping Elender out at the Good Eats Café.

Each minute of Elizabeth-Anne's life was filled, and it seemed that there never were enough hours in her day to go around. Wife. Mother. Housewife. Working woman. She had yet to celebrate her twenty-first birthday, but shouldered the burden of these responsibilities gladly. Somehow, she managed to juggle the limited hours of each day with a relaxed, cool insouciance. Besides, as she saw it, she had little choice but to continue working. She knew how heavily Elender relied on her help.

Elender was getting older, and if anything made the passing years less than perfect it was because Elender, at nearly forty-three, was no longer as healthy as she used to be. Elizabeth-Anne had always regarded her with love and respect, but now another emotion had crept in as well: sadness. It was getting more and more difficult for Elender to bend and do the chores she had always whisked through so effortlessly. She was suffering from acute rheumatism, and her joints and muscles were constantly inflamed and stiff, yet she refused to allow her illness to keep her from her work; she went about her business as usual despite her pain, putting in extra hours for any she lost by having to slow down. She was full of dignity and took her suffering in uncomplaining silence.

It tore Elizabeth-Anne's heart apart to see how much Auntie hurt. Yet Elizabeth-Anne never suggested to her that she retire or take it easy – she knew only too well that the rooming house and the café were Auntie's true lifeblood. The two businesses were more than just a way to make a living. They gave Auntie a sense of purpose and belonging, an importance in the community. For her, to stop working completely would have been to stop living entirely; to take it easy would have been to die a little bit at a time. And, though she had a little money tucked away, Auntie needed the steady income her work produced; retirement was out of the question.

Elender Hannah Clowney considered herself lucky on many counts. She had the two businesses, she had help, Elizabeth-Anne had grown into a fine woman, and she loved Zaccheus dearly. The children were an endless source of joy to her, and she delighted in spoiling them. She never tired of having them around her. Only Jenny made her less than happy. The older Jenny got, the more moody she seemed to become, and she was less use around the rooming house and the café than ever. It disappointed her no end – but Elizabeth-Anne took it as a mixed blessing. On the one hand, with Jenny refusing to work, there was twice as much that had to be done; on the other, at least Jenny stayed well out of the way.

The horrible valentine incident had been the last vicious prank that Jenny had played and Elizabeth-Anne was grateful for that. Zaccheus had been right, she thought. Jenny had found other things to occupy herself with, but what they were, she did not know. She was far too busy to squander time with what Jenny was doing, and the truth was, she really couldn't care less what she did, as long as it didn't involve her. But the best thing of all which the past five years had brought was dreams of the future. Elizabeth-Anne and Zaccheus saved money scrupulously, living frugally and banking the lion's share. 'Sometime, somewhere, an opportunity will come knocking,' Elizabeth-Anne said with sureness. 'We'll build a business of our own, and when that happens, we'll need the money.'

Life had slipped into a tranquil, comfortable pattern.

And then May of 1918 brought Jenny and Tex Sexton together.

Jenny had been marking time. Her dissatisfaction with all things ran far deeper, and was much more dangerous than anyone could imagine. She disliked Quebeck, which she considered a provincial backwater, she hated the people she knew, who she thought were nobodies, and she despised working at the café and the rooming house, which she thought made her a common labourer. She considered herself above all that. She felt the same way about the men she dated – she was too good to waste herself on them, even though at twenty-five going on twenty-six she was headed for spinsterhood. She quietly hungered for money, luxuries, and beautiful objects, but most of all she was ravenous for *power*. As she saw it, real power was a conglomeration of many things, information most of all, so she kept her eyes peeled for unusual goings-on and collected treasured tidbits of gossip. Without letting anyone know what she was up to, she started gathering dirt on people and collating it carefully in her mind, filing it away and storing it for future use. Just like she had done with Zaccheus. His sordid past, which she had overheard him telling Auntie and Elizabeth-Anne so long ago, was the pearl of her collection, but she knew better than to use it just yet. Power needed to be wielded discriminatingly, at precisely the moment it could do the most damage.

Power. The very thought of it made the adrenalin flow madly through Jenny's veins. But in order to satisfy her appetite for it, she knew that she had to first become someone other than Jennifer Sue Clowney. She needed a husband who already wielded immense power. Then, what she already knew, and the ever more delicious tidbits she would continue to discover, combined with his power, would make her stand alone – reigning supreme and invincible among all the women she knew. But to fulfil that vision, she knew that there were only two options left open to her. She would either have to leave Quebeck for Dallas or, preferably, some other major city, or else she could conspire to meet someone around here who fit her exacting requirements.

There were only two such men around.

Tex Sexton and his younger brother, Roy. And as Tex was not only the elder, but the more powerful of the two, that narrowed it down to only one choice.

Tex.

11

It was a little after eight in the morning when Jenny loaded her mare down with the artists' materials she'd ordered from the general store and which had had to be sent for from Brownsville. She mounted the horse with her usual proficiency. Elender had come out onto the porch of the Good Eats Café to watch. 'I still think you'd be better off with the buggy,' she called out. 'Are you sure you don't want to take it?'

Pretending she hadn't heard, Jenny snapped the reins, gave the mare a kick, and was off in a cloud of dust.

'I just don't understand her,' Elender said to Elizabeth-Anne, who had come out on the porch to join her. 'Jenny's never liked sketching or painting. I wonder why she's started now.'

None the wiser, they watched until Jenny disappeared from sight and then went back inside.

It was later. Jenny had ridden to within sight of the Sexton ranch house. It was built behind a manmade pond and atop a slight incline so that it dominated the surrounding white-fenced grazing lands and appeared to be forever on the lookout, watchful of anyone who might approach. Although it was a far from magnificent

412

building, the original white Greek Revival house had been repeatedly added onto at both ends so that it stretched out telescopically in both directions, each symmetrical wing decreasing in size.

She looked around in all directions. Her first order of business was to find as picturesque a location as was possible within sight of the house. Which was, she thought glumly, far more difficult than trying to find the proverbial needle in the haystack. There just was no picturesque view for miles around as far as she was concerned. Of course, there *was* the house itself, but using it as a subject would have been far too transparent.

She ended up choosing an unlikely spot where four fences dividing four separate grazing fields converged. The spot found, she dismounted, tethered the mare to the fence, and unpacked. She shook the blanket she'd brought out over the ground, set up the easel, pinned a sheet of watercolour paper to it, and licked her lips thoughtfully. Knitting her brow and concentrating carefully, she did her best to sketch the scene in front of her with a pencil. After a few minutes she stopped to survey her work.

She compressed her lips tightly. The subject matter was a skimpy setting to begin with – four whitewashed fences, irrigated grazing land, distant windmills, and herds of faraway cattle, but it wasn't half as bad as she had sketched it.

Don't make your lack of talent so visible! she warned herself. *And don't be impatient. Draw and paint to the best of your ability. If somebody sees this picture, especially Tex Sexton, he'll know something is up if it's so obvious that you can't even draw a straight line. If that happens, all your best-laid plans are sunk.*

Angrily, she snatched the paper off the easel, wadded it up, and started over again, this time more carefully.

Jenny knew she was no artist. She knew, too, that she

413

could never, under any circumstances, pass for one. She could only hope her lack of talent would be forgiven – and pray that Zaccheus, who of course she knew worked out here in the ranch house, was away on business somewhere. Elizabeth-Anne and Auntie had told her nothing, and she certainly couldn't ask. She feared that the single most real danger she faced was exposure by him. Should he somehow find out about what she hoped would transpire – even after the fact – and he voiced his suspicions, then all her careful planning would have been for nothing.

She sighed to herself. It seemed, suddenly, that everything she had planned was hanging by a slender thread indeed, a tenuous thread composed of one part careful planning and two parts chance.

The afternoon crawled by with interminable slowness. She hated sketching and painting. To her, it was tedious and boring, but she applied herself all the same. After all, she had set out to accomplish something, and accomplish it she would. She wasn't about to let tedium or boredom spoil her well-laid plans.

I'm getting closer towards my goal all the time, she kept reminding herself, *and that is all that matters*.

Still, she couldn't help but wonder how many hours – indeed, perhaps even days or weeks – it would be before she piqued Tex Sexton's interest.

She laughed softly to herself, for the first time seeing the ironic humour of the situation in which she found herself. It would be a not-so-poetic conclusion, she thought, if she never did get to meet Tex Sexton, but her painting improved remarkably.

Jenny needn't have feared. By the time one of the ranch hands brought word to Tex that a woman was ensconced in the western fields beyond the house painting a picture, his interest was definitely captured. He went out on the porch and looked over to where she

414

was at work. He could not see much; she was too far away.

He grinned to himself and shook his head. Ever since his wife, Yolanda, had died, women were beating a path to his door. Some of them were blatantly forward, others staged elaborate 'accidental' meetings. In one way or another they were all full of intrigue, and the thing they were after was always the same. But this was the first time a woman had ever come here under the pretence of finding something to paint.

'Original,' he murmured to himself. 'Very original.'

He glanced up at the sky. From the way the light was changing he could tell it was around three-thirty. In another three hours sunset would come. She wouldn't be able to paint at night; it would be interesting to see how she would handle that.

He sent for one of his ranch hands. 'Go see what she's up to,' he instructed, 'but don't tell her I'm here.'

'Should I send her away?' the young cowhand asked.

Tex looked at him in surprise. 'What for? She's here, isn't she? And since she's a woman I might as well make the best of it.'

And as the ranch hand walked off, Tex thought: *All women are the same. So stupid and transparent. They all want something from me, but none of them get anything, except for the* putas *from Mexican Town. They, at least, are honest.*

Does this one think she's any different? If she does, she's in for a vast surprise.

But it would be he who would be surprised, for he had no idea that he was dealing with someone as evilly clever as himself – someone on his very own level.

As time crept by, Jenny was not so sure she would ever come face-to-face with Tex Sexton. She was beginning to realize just how skimpy her plan of action really was, and how it depended on so many variables which she had absolutely no control over. For instance, any one of the ranch hands could have ordered her off the property. One came out to her, but she'd vaguely hinted something about having gotten permission. He grunted, looked at the sketch she was colouring in, scratched his head in bafflement, and had ambled back to the house. To get Tex Sexton, she hoped.

At a few minutes after five, Tex Sexton went back out on the porch and gazed out across the fields. She was still there painting.

He summoned one of his hands. 'Go over and invite her to dine with me,' he said. 'And before you go, have Carmen set another place for supper.'

The hand nodded and did as he was told. Fifteen minutes later he knocked on the door to Tex's study. 'She "declines",' he drawled.

Tex rose to his feet, clasped his hands in the small of his back, and paced his study thoughtfully.

An invitation to the house had always worked. Was it possible that she *was* different?

It was six o'clock and nightfall was fast approaching when Tex went back outside. He looked up at the sky and nodded to himself. The light had already changed significantly. The edges of the clouds were tinged in a pinkish glow, and the shadows the setting sun cast were long.

He glanced thoughtfully towards where Jenny was painting, his lips pursed in a soundless whistle. Initially, it had been his plan to wait until dark to see exactly what she was going to do, but suddenly he felt the restless urge for the company of a woman. Her declining the supper invitation had meant either of two things – she was playing hard to get, or else she really had no interest in meeting him, something he had trouble believing.

Curiously, somehow the thought of her out there brought an aching excitement to his loins. It had been

416

two whole weeks since he had last been with a woman. In fact, earlier in the day he had been contemplating on sending for one of the *putas* from Mexican Town, but when he'd heard that there was a woman practically outside his front door, he'd decided against it.

Only much later would Jenny learn just how accidentally well-timed her day turned out to be. This was the first time in weeks that Tex had been in the house all day long. Usually he spent his days outdoors, but every two weeks or so he had to catch up on paperwork; this was one such day. To add divine providence to accidental timing, Zaccheus was away on a business trip to Brownsville for two days and would not return until tomorrow. Fate was indeed smiling upon Jennifer Sue Clowney.

His hands in his pockets, Tex strode across the front yard, skirted the pond, and headed out to where she stood painting, her spine erect, one hand resting on her hip. Even from this distance, with her back turned to him, he could tell that she had a lithe body which even the plain, severe cut of her riding outfit could do little to disguise. The nearer he got to her, the more singularly attractive she seemed to become. Tex, conniver and schemer that he was, was for once unaware that she had dressed with scrupulous care, choosing this very outfit for just that effect, and that even her stance was studied. She had practised it in front of her bedroom mirror for hours.

Jenny had decided not to play the flirtatious female; she was certain that plenty of women had already tried that – and failed to win him. No, she was going to be feminine, but vigorous and proud, too. And she would keep her back turned to him, showing her face only at the last possible moment – to dramatic advantage.

When she heard someone approach her from behind, her heart skipped a beat. *Was it him? Or was it another of his flunkies?* She had rehearsed her lines a

417

thousand times, but now that she might need to recall them, they suddenly deserted her. She held her paintbrush between trembling fingers, quickly dabbed it in the jar of water, soaked the soft bristles in red paint, lifted it to the canvas and –

'You're trespassing,' a deep, deceptively lazy voice drawled behind her.

'*Oh!*' Jenny gave a squeal of surprise, as though she had not heard his approach; simultaneously, she artfully jerked her brush across the paper, leaving a thick blood-like streak across the pale wash. 'Oh no!' she wailed in dismay. She placed her hands on her hips and eyed her work morosely. 'Now look what you made me do! It's ruined! Don't you know better than to sneak up on people?'

'It's not very good anyway,' he said with a humorous chuckle.

Her cheeks blushed angrily and she whirled around, fighting to keep from showing her recognition. 'What do *you* know about art, anyway?' she snapped derisively with a toss of her head.

'I think I should be the one asking the questions,' he said, raising his eyebrows with mild amusement. His eyes swept her from head to foot. On his way over it had occurred to him that, unlikely though it may be, she just *might* be a plain, spinsterish young woman out for an afternoon of painting: from the cut of her outfit she had certainly tried to give that impression. But the face which now regarded him with flushed irritation was seen to its best advantage in the darkening, reddish light of the sunset, and her robin's-egg-blue eyes, framed by thick long lashes, had never looked more enticing. Her figure was slender, but there was nothing boyish about it. Nor did her clothes look quite so spinsterish when viewed from up front. Far from it. The riding skirt was pleated and dark, but fit snugly about her tiny waist. The collar of her plaid shirt, though

418

high-necked, was unbuttoned halfway down to her bosom, which would have looked obscene had she not tucked a lace handkerchief strategically inside.

His gaze lingered on her bosom. There was something decidedly feminine and overwhelmingly ripe about her, yet at the same time she managed to look young and vulnerable. But it had been her snappish outburst and taking the offensive which appealed to him mightily. That, coupled with her flashing eyes, had done it. It was so startlingly different from the fawning, sloe-eyed glances with which women constantly favoured him that he found himself instantly drawn to her like no woman he had ever met.

She turned away suddenly, too aware of his smouldering gaze. Tilting her head, she regarded her ruined picture. 'Maybe you're right,' she conceded grudgingly. 'It isn't very good.' She tore the paper off the easel and crumpled it. 'I'm afraid I just don't have the talent it takes.'

'Then why do you paint?'

She turned to him slowly. 'What else is there to do around here?'

He eyed her levelly. 'You'd be surprised.'

'Oh ho.' She laughed hoarsely. 'That isn't what I meant at all.' She tightened her lips. 'Well, if it'll make you feel any better, I'm sorry for having trespassed. Now, I think I'd better be leaving. It's getting late.' Quickly, she stooped over and began gathering up her things.

Suddenly she felt strong fingers clamping around her wrist like a vice. Then he pulled her up and turned her around to face him.

'Let me go!' she hissed, struggling fiercely.

He laughed, pulled her close, and kissed her. She pressed her lips tightly shut. When he let her go, she took a faltering step backwards. 'Animal!' she hissed,

419

wiping her mouth with the back of her hand. 'You're an *animal*!'

He chuckled with amusement. 'It's what you wanted, isn't it?'

She said coldly, 'How would you know what I want?'

'Simple. You came out here, didn't you?' He continued to regard her shrewdly. 'Don't tell me you didn't notice the sign warning off trespassers? I could have had you shot.'

She raised her chin boldly. 'You wouldn't dare!'

'I would dare. I happen to own this property. I'm Tex Sexton.'

'And I'm Martha Washington!' she countered nastily.

'Of course, I don't make a habit of going around shooting pretty young ladies. Especially not ladies with no apparent talents.'

Flushing even more deeply, she hurriedly picked up the easel and began loading the old mare.

'I reckon I'll see you around,' he said slowly. 'Once you've developed your talents, that is.'

She watched him turn and start to walk off. She licked her lips with apprehension.

Now was the moment, she knew. It was now or never. An opportunity like this would never present itself again. If Sexton didn't catch her in the act of contriving the accident, then everything would turn out fine. She had aroused him, she sensed, and in no small way.

Don't turn around, she willed him silently. *Whatever you do, Tex Sexton, just keep on walking and don't look back.*

Slowly, keeping her eyes on him, she reached into her pocket for the prickly burrs and slipped them under the saddle, and then mounted. The mare protested against the stabbing pain and kicked out with its hind legs. Then Jenny tightened her lips and viciously drove her steel spurs into the mare's sides.

The rest happened so quickly, Jenny completely lost control. Later she would realize the mare had reared up and bolted. But that was later. Right now, it was all she could do to hang on for dear life.

Everything happened in a blur. One moment she caught sight of Tex Sexton whirling around, and the next she was racing the devil to the far fence of the paddock, showers of earth and exploding tufts of grass flying up all around her.

The approaching fence seemed to grow in size before Jenny's frightened eyes. For an instant, she was frozen in genuine terror. Forgotten suddenly was her well-hatched plan. She only knew that somehow she had to stop the horse, and quickly.

But the mare had a mind of its own. The burrs tore into its flesh and Jenny's spurs had added even more ferocious pain: they had torn open its thick skin, and it was trying to run from the pain.

The fence loomed larger and larger, and then the horse leaped. The ground was left behind as they began to sail over the white-painted slats.

For a split-second, it looked as if they were going to make it.

But Jenny's mare was no jumper. She was a utilitarian work horse used to rutted roads and being harnessed to the buggy. As they flew through the air, its hind legs crashed into the fence and it lost its equilibrium. Jenny stifled her scream and tried to throw herself clear, but her left boot had become entangled with the stirrup and the horse hit the ground in a scrambling tangle. Jenny landed on her shoulders, was thrown free of the horse, and the breath whooshed out of her lungs. Her left leg was wrenched sideways and her entire body was shot through with pain.

But she didn't utter a sound.

The mare struggled to her feet, but collapsed again with sounds of anguish.

Tex had not wasted a moment. From the instant the mare had bolted, he had come chasing after them.

Within seconds he was squatting beside Jenny. He lifted her skirt, took one look at her leg, and gently moved her foot.

She averted her head and cringed as a thousand blinding arrows of pain shot through her, but she did not once cry out. She swallowed her moans.

Still silent, Jenny felt Tex slip one arm under her back and another under her buttocks. 'Where are you taking me?' she asked in a white-faced whisper.

'Damn fool woman. What were you trying to do, kill yourself?'

She shut her eyes.

'That horse needs to be shot. Both its hind legs are broke.' He paused, not mentioning the bloodied sides where her spurs had knifed into its flesh. He hadn't overlooked that. 'Least you don't have a broken leg.'

She opened her eyes. 'It's not broken?' she whispered.

He nodded and looked deep into her eyes. They were cloudy and fathomless, and try as he might, he was unable to read her thoughts. In fact, he could not even tell if she was frightened.

Somehow the fact that she hadn't once cried out appealed to him immensely.

He knew then that he had met his match.

12

It was a few weeks later. The scraping of cutlery against china rang out noisily in the dining room; from one corner came the scratchy music issuing forth from the Victrola Elender had set up. It was dinner hour at the Good Eats Café, and every table was occupied.

Elizabeth-Anne placed a plate in front of Sheriff Parker and looked up in surprise as Jenny came in

422

through the door. Jenny ignored her, looking around the café disdainfully.

Elizabeth-Anne walked up to her. 'Hello, Jenny,' she said quietly.

Jenny did not reply.

'Are you looking for someone?'

Jenny finally fixed her with a stolid look. 'Is Auntie here?'

'Yes.' Elizabeth-Anne nodded. 'She's in the kitchen.'

'Go get her for me, will you?' Jenny looked around again, folded her arms across her chest, and tapped one foot impatiently on the floor.

Elizabeth-Anne stared at her. Then she shrugged her shoulders and wiped her hands on her apron. 'Very well.' She turned and headed to the swinging doors which led into the kitchen. She pushed them open and they flapped shut behind her.

Rosa was standing in front of the big hot stove, ladling spicy hot chilli over plates of yellow saffron rice. Elender was stooped over the table, beating a bowl of egg whites with a whisk. 'How many more to serve?' she called over her shoulder when she heard Elizabeth-Anne come back in.

'Seven or eight.' Elizabeth-Anne paused. 'Auntie,' she said softly.

'Yes, dear?'

'Jenny's in the dining room.'

'Jenny's – ' Elender laid down the whisk and turned around. She smiled. 'Good. I've never seen this place quite so busy. We can use the extra help today.' She sighed, placed her hands in the small of her back, and stretched wearily.

Elizabeth-Anne looked at her expressionlessly. 'I don't think she came to help.'

'Oh.' Elender froze in the midst of arching her back.

'She says she wants to talk to you.'

'Well, here I am.'

'She wanted me to come and get you,' Elizabeth-Anne said pointedly.

Rosa turned around from the stove and rolled her dark eyes expressively. She set down the plate she was holding with a bang. 'As eef there eesn't enough to do 'round here weethout having to drop everyting when Her Highness say "jump"?'

Auntie ignored her. 'Very well,' she told Elizabeth-Anne, and smoothed her dress with her hands. 'Tell her I'll be right out.'

'Eef the young lady want to see you, why she don' come in here?' Rosa demanded, emphasizing each word with shakes of the ladle.

Elizabeth-Anne smiled timidly, reached past Rosa, and picked up three steaming plates. She balanced one on her forearm and carried one in each hand. With a sideways thrust of her hips, she pushed her way back out through the swinging doors.

'Well?' Jenny demanded.

'She'll be right out.'

'Good.' Jenny smiled. 'I would appreciate it if you joined us. I want you to hear what I have to say too.'

Elizabeth-Anne nodded absently and carried the plates across the room. She set one down in front of Mr McElwee, then turned and placed the others in front of the Byrd sisters. She glanced across the dining room: Elender was coming out of the kitchen.

Elizabeth-Anne felt a jolt of pain. She could sense that Auntie's rheumatism was exceptionally bad today, and it hurt her to see it. It worried her, too, that she was getting so thin. Elender's clothes, of which she had always been so proud, and which had always looked so elegant on her, were hanging off her as if from a scarecrow, and she walked painfully on flat slippers, taking careful little steps.

Elizabeth-Anne smiled automatically. 'Enjoy it,' she

told the Byrd sisters quickly, and then went over to join Elender and Jenny.

'Can we talk in private?' Jenny was saying.

Elender glanced around the dining room. 'We're really terribly busy right now, Jenny. Can't it keep until a little later?'

'It's important,' Jenny said emphatically. 'It'll only take a minute.'

'Very well.' Elender led the way out the side door into the hall. Jenny followed her and motioned for Elizabeth-Anne to tag along. Elizabeth-Anne fell into step behind them. It tugged her heart to see how slowly Elender had to climb the stairs.

When they got to the upstairs parlour, Elender closed the door softly and looked at Jenny questioningly.

Jenny's face was outwardly calm but an excited gleam danced deep in her eyes. Elender exchanged glances with Elizabeth-Anne, who gave a slight nod. She had noticed, too. Something was definitely up.

Jenny sensed their wariness. She reached out and took both Elender's hands in her own, something which she hadn't done for many years. Overcome, Elender looked at her with speechless surprise. Her lips trembled and tears gathered in her eyes as Jenny leaned close and blew a cold kiss past her cheek.

'Well?' Jenny asked finally. She disengaged her hands from Elender's. 'Isn't somebody going to congratulate me?' She turned to Elizabeth-Anne, unable to keep the triumph off her face.

Elizabeth-Anne stared at her, her hands in her apron pocket. 'What's the occasion?'

Jenny smiled crookedly. 'I'm getting married.'

'You're – ' Elender swallowed and looked at her queerly. 'But . . . but this is so sudden!' she sputtered. 'So – so out of the blue!'

'Aren't you happy for me?' Jenny asked, her voice suddenly turning bitter.

'Why yes, of course I'm happy,' Elender said quickly. She wrung her hands in agitation. 'Who – who is the lucky man?'

A triumphant gleam glinted in Jenny's eyes. 'I'll give you three guesses.'

'It's Tex Sexton, isn't it?' Elizabeth-Anne asked softly.

The triumph in Jenny's eyes faded instantly. 'How did you guess?' she demanded, and then laughed. 'Of course! How stupid of me! Your husband *would* have told you I was seeing Tex.'

Elender stared at Jenny. 'But . . . but you don't know him, do you? I mean, how did you meet him? I didn't even know you –' She turned to Elizabeth-Anne. 'What did Zaccheus tell you?'

'Only that Jenny and Mr Sexton were seeing quite a lot of each other. That's all.'

Elender's face was set in a wounded expression. 'And you didn't tell me? Neither of you?'

Elizabeth-Anne bit down on her lip. What could she have told Auntie? That Jenny was spending a lot of time out at the Sexton ranch? She wasn't Jenny's babysitter. If Jenny was carrying on an affair with Tex Sexton, it was no business of hers. Jenny was certainly old enough to lead her own life – without supervision.

Jenny raised her chin. 'We're getting married immediately. Tex wanted to wait and throw a big wedding here with all the trimmings, but we talked it over and decided to leave for Dallas in the morning instead. It'll be a very quiet ceremony, just the two of us and a witness, otherwise we would have invited you.'

Elender was stunned. 'In the morning?' she asked. '*Tomorrow* morning?'

Jenny nodded. 'We'll get married there and stay on a few days. I'll need to pack a few things, but not much. Tex is going to buy me a whole new wardrobe.' She sighed happily. 'Oh, and I'll need my birth certificate, Auntie.'

'You need your – ' Elender looked sudde.

'What's the matter? You do have it, don't y

'I . . . uh – yes . . . of course.'

'Well, don't be so damned mysterious about it!' snapped. 'I *need* it!'

Elender nodded, her face suddenly gone ashen. the time had finally come that Jenny would find out that she was her daughter and not her niece. She had always known that Jenny would eventually have to know, but she had always hoped she would have time to prepare her for it. But the opportunity had never arisen. Jenny had never given her the chance: she had always been so wild, so sour, so bitter.

Elender's mind swirled, turning back the years to those horrible nights in the big house on Beacon Hill in Boston so long, long ago. As year after year had passed, and she had built a new life for herself and Jenny, she had shoved those bleak memories aside.

Now the past had finally caught up with her.

Oh Lord, Elender prayed, *help Jenny understand that the indiscretion wasn't my fault entirely. I was a foolish young chambermaid with nowhere else to go and nothing to my name but guilt and shame. Times were different back then. I had no money. I had nothing. Not even my pride. All I did was listen to my employer's son and do as he demanded. Can I be faulted for that?*

Yes, you can, and should, her relentless conscience replied with agonizing candour.

'Wait here while I go get it,' Elender said stiffly.

Jenny nodded and watched, mystified, as she left the parlour and went down the hall to her bedroom. She looked at Elizabeth-Anne. 'I don't know what the big deal is. Do you?'

Elizabeth-Anne shook her head. She didn't know what was wrong, either, but something had shaken Elender terribly. She looked like a ghost.

After a few minutes passed, Jenny folded her arms

...her elbows with her index fingers. 'I don't
...s keeping her so long. I haven't got all day.'
...a while Elender returned, envelope in hand.
...alked with that peculiar kind of dignity, which
...beth-Anne realized she adopted whenever she
...eded armour.

'Sit down, Jenny darling, please,' Elender said in a
quivering voice. 'I think we need to have a long overdue
talk.'

Jenny stared at her. 'What about?'

'The birth certificate. Our past.'

Jenny narrowed her eyes. '*Our* past? What are you
talking about?'

'It's a long story,' Elender said wearily. 'Please, just
hear me out.'

'I don't have the time.' Jenny fished the envelope out
from between her fingers and Elender let out a strangled cry.

'Please listen, Jenny. Please!' she implored desperately. 'I don't care if you never listen to me again for as
long as I live. Just listen to me now, before you look at
that certificate!'

But Jenny was already sliding the certificate out of
the envelope. The paper was folded, and was old,
creased, and yellowed, worn almost transparently thin,
as if it had been handled a lot.

Jenny suddenly let out a keening howl and slapped
the paper against her thigh. 'You *bitch*!' Jenny
screamed. 'Oh, you fucking *bitch*!'

Elizabeth-Anne gasped. 'Jenny! You can't use language like that! Not with Auntie!'

Jenny whirled at Elizabeth-Anne, her eyes wet with
tears, yet blazing with a hellish fury. 'Oh, I *can't*, can't
I?' Hands on her hips, she looked Elizabeth-Anne up
and down. 'Who are *you* to tell me what I can or cannot
call that lying, two-faced bitch?' She thrust the birth
certificate at Elizabeth-Anne. 'Here! See for yourself!'

428

Her hands trembling, Elizabeth-Anne and read it, her eyes flaring in disbelief.

'Jenny, please,' Elender whispered hoarse darling – '

'Just listen to yourself!' Jenny spat. ' *"Jenny da* she mimicked, rocking her head from left to right. howled with hysterical laughter. 'Oh, this is *precious*! M, own mother treating me like a niece for all these years!' She threw her hands up in the air and stalked around the parlour, muttering curses under her breath. 'My own fucking *mother*! My MOTHER!'

'Jenny,' Elender begged. She looked as though she had suddenly aged twenty years. 'Jenny . . .'

'I'm leaving,' Jenny said suddenly. 'Do you hear me? I'm leaving for good. And I'll never come back! Ever! I never want to see you again for as long as I live!'

'Jenny, *please*.' Elender pleaded. 'You're my daughter. Don't treat me like this! You're breaking my heart!' She reached up to touch Jenny's cheek beseechingly, but Jenny recoiled. 'Jenny, you're my daughter!' Auntie appealed in a strained voice. 'Don't turn away from me!'

'Then why, pray tell, wasn't I your daughter all these goddamn years? Why did you lead me to believe that my mother was dead, and that you were taking care of me out of the goodness of your heart?'

'It was the times, Jenny. A woman alone – '

'Shit, shit, *shit*!' Jenny pounded her head with her clenched fists. 'SHIT! Will you just leave me alone?'

'You can't mean you won't ever come back, Jenny,' Auntie cried softly. 'You'll visit with me. You'll bring your husband and your children – '

'Like *hell* I will! I never want to see you again. Do I make myself perfectly clear? I don't want anything from you. Not your stinking love, nor your filthy lies. *Nothing*. And I don't want to inherit a goddamn thing of yours once you're dead, which for me can't be soon enough!'

beth-Anne cried. 'Oh, my God, Jenny!
an that! Tell her you don't mean it!'
u "*Jenny*" me, you freak!' Jenny whirled
e of them to the other.

're upset, darling, and that's understandable,'
der said in a civil, desperately soothing tone. 'Why
on't you sleep on it? Maybe you'll feel differently
tomorrow. We'll talk some more when you come –'

Jenny laughed. 'You're right about one thing. I *am*
upset. But I'm not about to sleep on anything. You don't
need me. You never even wanted me! This proves it.
You've got the daughter of your choice, anyway. Here!
Hold *her*! Hug *her*! Kiss *her*!' With that, Jenny grabbed
Elizabeth-Anne by the arm and, with the strength of a
madwoman, flung her across the room, straight into
Elender's arms.

'Just remember,' Jenny warned from the door, 'don't
try to come and see me. Because, if you're foolish
enough to try, I'll have you shot! For trespassing!' And
with that she tossed her head and stomped out, slamming the door with such force that the walls shook and
a picture came crashing down.

Elender clutched Elizabeth-Anne tightly and stared
up into her face. 'She can't mean it!' she whispered. 'She
can't!'

'Of course she doesn't!' Elizabeth-Anne humoured
softly. 'Of course she doesn't,' she repeated with her
lips, but as she stared out at the room over Elender's
head her eyes said differently.

'She'll make up with me,' Elender sobbed. She swallowed painfully and nodded emphatically. 'You'll see.
She was just angry, that's all.'

'Yes,' Elizabeth-Anne whispered, hugging her tightly.
'She was only angry. She'll come around, Auntie.'

'Yes, she will.'

430

But Jenny didn't come around. Nor was she a[...]
bing salt into wounds. When she gave birth to h[...]
born, the heir to the Sexton fortune, she made su[...]
news was plastered all over the front page of the *Qu[...]*
Weekly Gazette — which wasn't at all difficult to arrang[...]
since Tex owned the newspaper.

Elender bought several copies of that issue and read
each word religiously until she could quote the article
by heart. Carefully, she cut her grandson's picture out
of two of the copies and framed them. She placed one
on the bedside cabinet in her bedroom, and hung the
other one up in the kitchen of the café. Then she purchased a present, dressed with extreme care, and rode
out to the Sexton ranch.

She was turned away, but when she returned to town,
she told everyone what a lovely grandson she had, and
how much he adored her. The next day, she rode out
again, and once again she was turned away. The longer
she did not see him, the more she embellished the tales
of her grandson's activities. Every day for five straight
weeks she rode out to see him, and each time she was
turned away.

When Elender died at the end of that five weeks, only
Elizabeth-Anne knew that it was of a broken heart.

13

It was high noon, and the cortège slowly made its way
north up Main Street and out pas the cotton fields to
the cemetery beyond. Elizabeth-Anne looked down at
Charlotte-Anne and smiled bravely.

The child felt her gaze and looked up at her, the
large, blue eyes wide with cofusion. Charlotte-Anne
was only five and did not know what was going on,
and she was tired. Her legs ere aching from the long,

...ly slow walk, but her mother was holding her ...ghtly, so she couldn't lag behind. Regina was on ...eth-Anne's right, holding onto her other hand. ...ecca was dozing quietly in Zaccheus' arms.

Charlotte-Anne wished that her mother would let go of her. She wanted to walk alongside her daddy.

For a while, she occupied herself by concentrating on the way Elizabeth-Anne was walking. She had never seen this kind of walk before, and it fascinated her. She tightened her lips purposefully and tried to emulate it. It was a slow, dignified movement, almost like a dance. Charlotte-Anne finally gave up trying to walk that way, but she didn't like it when something proved imposs-ible.

They all wore black, and she didn't like that, either. In fact, she had cried unrelentingly when her mother had made her put on this dress. There was something unsettling and spooky about its sombre, colourless gloom. She wished her mother had let her wear her bright blue dress instead. Everybody said it matched her eyes.

Main Street was very quiet today, and she noticed that whenever they passed people, men would come to a halt, take off their hats, and hold them solemnly over their hearts. She twisted around and looked back over her shoulder. A few paces behind her walked the mayor and the sheriff. They were also dressed in black. And behind them she could see more townsfolk. It seemed that most everyone had turned out for the occasion.

Charlotte-Anne faced frontwards again. Just a few yards ahead of her was the car. It was a resplendent black car, with big, velvet-curtained windows all around. She could look in through the rear window and see the black polished coffin. Her mother had said that Auntie was sleeping inside it, but Charlotte-Anne couldn't see how she could be comfortable. The box looked awfully narrow.

She turned sideways, looked up at Elizabeth-[Anne] and gave her hand a shake. 'Auntie should have a b[ig] bed,' she announced in a clear, distinct voice. 'How [can] she sleep comfortably in a little one like that?'

Elizabeth-Anne's step faltered. Then she turned slowly and stared down at Charlotte-Anne. 'Your Auntie is comfortable,' she said in a thick voice.

'You're sure?'

Elizabeth-Anne nodded and gave her daughter's hand a reassuring squeeze. 'I'm sure,' she said gently, but looked quickly away. She felt that at any moment she would give in to the tears that threatened to choke her insides.

Charlotte-Anne craned her neck sideways. They were approaching the edge of the fields. Ahead was the cemetery with its crooked gravestones and crosses sticking up out of the ground. She gave her mother's hand another shake. 'Mama?'

Elizabeth-Anne looked down at her.

'D'ya think I can come and visit Auntie everyday? Maybe even sleep with her inside her bed?'

Elizabeth-Anne's wet eyes were warm with sympathy. It was a moment before she could trust herself to speak. 'Do you think it's nice to wake someone up when they're asleep?'

Charlotte-Anne frowned thoughtfully for a moment. She hadn't thought of that. 'Nooo,' she said finally. 'I don't think that's very nice. I hate to be woked up.'

Elizabeth-Anne smiled gratefully. 'You're a very nice young lady, Charlotte-Anne,' she said proudly. 'It isn't everyone who understands that.'

For a moment, Charlotte-Anne was warmed by the compliment. She had given the right answer.

But later, as Auntie's [casket] was lowered into the ground and the earth was being dumped in on top of it, she felt a sudden ter[ror and] buried her face in her mother's skirt. She wa[s af]raid to look, but she could

433

ne clumps of dirt pounding down against the top
e box. There was something terribly final about the
and. Then time itself seemed to stand still as a blood-
urdling wail, the likes of which she'd never heard,
drowned out all other sounds.

Charlotte-Anne peered timidly from around her
mother's skirt. Rosa, the cook, had collapsed in a gigantic
heap at the edge of the grave and was screaming, 'Santa
Maria! Santa Maria!' Her moon face glistened with a
mixture of sweat and tears, and her breasts rose and
fell as she beat herself with her knuckles. Finally, her
energies exhausted, Rosa's litany of despair settled into
a pitiful drone.

Elizabeth-Anne pulled her daughter closer to her in
a vain effort to shield her from Rosa's grief. But
Charlotte-Anne's terror was only reinforced. She had
never seen Rosa like this. Rosa was strong and brave and
not afraid of anything. Maybe she was upset because
Auntie had to sleep under the ground in such a narrow
box. Then she remembered something that had happened a few weeks ago.

She had taken a little duck carved out of soap and
buried it in the yard outside the cottage so no one could
find it but her. A few days later she wanted to play with
it, but she'd forgotten exactly where she'd buried it, and
she'd dug desperately for two days. But she never did
find it.

And now Auntie was going to disappear just like her
duck.

They walked home slowly, leaving Auntie at the place
with all the crosses, and for a long time the terror
wouldn't leave Charlotte-Anne. And then things got
even more confusing, because her mother suddenly
noticed a long, shiny car parked some distance away. It
was the biggest car she had ever seen, with a mirror-like
finish and white-walled tyres with shiny chrome spokes.

4.

There was even another tyre between the fender and the running board.

Her mother looked at her father.

'How dare she!' Elizabeth-Anne exploded quietly, her face red with blotches of rage. 'First she killed her, and now she's come to gloat over her burial. But she couldn't come to the funeral, could she?'

And her father put his arms around her mother and said firmly, 'Don't be upset. Eventually, she'll get what she deserves!'

Charlotte-Anne tugged at her mother's hand for one last time. 'What are you talking about?' she asked in her clear, tiny voice.

'Nothing, darling,' Elizabeth-Anne said huskily. 'Nothing. Only grown-up talk.'

But it wasn't nothing, and Charlotte-Anne knew it. Why else would her mother turn around and stare back over her shoulder at the Sextons' new car with such loathing?

Inside the car, Jenny, staring silently out through the windshield, watched the funeral break up. 'That's it,' she said aloud.

Tex leaned forward. He grasped hold of the steering wheel, eased off on the clutch, and pressed gently down on the accelerator. As the big car began to roll smoothly forwards, Jenny saw Elizabeth-Anne turning to Zaccheus, who was saying something, and then Elizabeth-Anne twisted around again, staring malevolently back at the car.

Jenny smiled tightly. Even from this distance she could tell that Elizabeth-Anne was angry – and a wild, violent satisfaction surged through her, a mad kind of joy. She felt truly happy for the first time in weeks. She sensed that the opening salvo of a battle which would last a long time had been fired, and that made her feel good.

435

'Let's go home,' she said to Tex. 'I've seen enough.'

Tex nodded but did not speak. For a while they drove in silence. Jenny rested her elbow on the leather armrest and her chin on her fist. She stared out the window and watched the fields and groves gliding slowly past. She was grateful for Tex's silence. Somehow he always seemed to know when to speak and when to remain silent. It was one of the things she liked about him. They understood each other.

It was she who finally broke the silence. 'Tex?' she said.

He turned to her.

She reached out to him with her left hand and traced her fingertips lightly down his thigh. 'Remember,' she reminded him, 'when you asked me what I wanted as a gift for giving birth to Ross?'

He nodded and turned towards the road again. 'I remember.'

'You told me I could have anything I wanted, and I told you I would think about it.' She took a deep breath. 'Well, I have. I know what I want.'

'And?' He licked his lips and forced himself to concentrate on the driving. He felt both a relaxed contentment and the beginnings of an immense excitement tingling inside him as her fingers cleverly explored his crotch.

She gazed down at his groin. 'I don't want anything material,' she said, frowning, and then looked back up at him. 'This won't cost you a thing.'

He turned to her again, his eyes filled with suspicion. He knew only too well how much material possessions meant to Jenny – and how much that facet of her personality was costing him. Her latest project was sprucing up the house both inside and out. She was planting a lavish garden around the pond in the front of the house with the help of the three full-time gardeners she'd hired. Simultaneously, she was redecorating the inside of the mansion, and she'd already spent a small fortune on antique furnishings and cracked old paintings. And on top of all that was her greatest love – clothes. She spent a fortune on outfits she never had time to wear and had already accumulated so many that one of the carpenters had to transform an entire bedroom into a walk-in closet. 'Well?' he said.

'I decided that instead of wanting some*thing*, I want someone.' She paused. 'Someone who works for you. I want to know exactly what he's up to at all times. And I'd like to have the last say in any decisions affecting him.'

'You're asking for a lot. You want power.'

'Only over two people,' she said quickly.

'Who's the first?'

'Zaccheus Hale.'

'And who's the second? Me?'

'Don't make jokes like that,' she snapped irritably. 'You should know better than that.' She shook her head. 'The second one's Hale's wife.'

He looked thoughtful and drove on in silence for a while. It was true, he reminded himself: after she'd borne him a son, he had felt so magnanimous that he had offered her anything she wanted, and he wasn't a man known to go back on his word. Still, Zaccheus Hale was a valued employee. The man he trusted most.

'Hale's important to me,' he said finally. 'He's got things under control like they've never been before. I depend on him.' His eyes flicked sideways at her. 'What do you want with him?'

'I want to destroy him.' Her voice was a low, intense whisper.

He looked at her sharply.

'Watch out!' she cried.

He turned forwards and swerved just in time to avoid a head-on collision with the daily Brownsville to Laredo bus coming from the other direction.

437

Horns blared angrily and the bus roared past with just inches to spare.

Jenny sighed with relief and rubbed her forehead with her fingertips. Her head was pounding and her heart was palpitating from the sudden surge of adrenalin. Slowly it receded and she felt herself settling back down.

'You want me to fire Hale?' Tex asked suddenly.

She swung around to face him. 'No!' she hissed sharply, her eyes blazing. 'I want to destroy him.'

'How?'

'I don't know,' she lied, knowing full well that she had already planned every last, intricate step towards Zaccheus' destruction. The only thing she did not yet know was when. She only knew it had to be when the time was absolutely perfect. She would wait years if need be — an inescapable web of iron needed time to construct. And besides, why should she ruin her own perverse joy by being too hasty? The sword had to descend at precisely the moment when it would hurt Zaccheus and Elizabeth-Anne the most. When that happened, her own pleasure would be unbearable.

'You're positive that this is what you want?'

She nodded. 'Another thing,' she said, fighting to keep the excitement out of her voice. 'I'll give you plenty of warning before I strike. This way, you'll have time to find and train a replacement for him.'

'I don't know,' he said slowly. 'I need Zaccheus. What'll I do without him?'

'Wasn't it you who told me only a few days ago that everyone is expendable?'

He grunted.

'Well then, isn't Zaccheus Hale expendable, too?'

He sighed. 'I suppose so.'

'In fact,' she said slowly, 'it would be poetic justice, would it not, if you let *him* find himself an assistant? If you had him choose his own successor without his even knowing what he's doing? If he's as smart and valuable as you think he is, I'm sure he'll come up with a most likely candidate.'

Tex grinned suddenly. 'Know what? You're a regular Machiavelli.'

She shrugged.

'No, I take that back. You're not a Machiavelli after all.'

'Then what am I?'

'Salome.'

She laughed. 'And I suppose Zaccheus Hale will be my John the Baptist?'

'If I let you have his head on a platter, yes,' he replied pointedly.

'It's important to me, Tex,' she said slowly. 'Very important.' She resumed toying with his crotch.

'Mind at least telling me why you've got it out for him?'

'Not at all.' Her hand slid further down into his crotch, her nimble fingers feeling for the length of his penis, which she knew lay against his left trouser leg, trapped there by his underwear. Already she could feel it was semi-erect. She smiled to herself and began to massage it in gentle, slow circles. 'I've got it in for Zaccheus Hale,' she said softly, 'because I don't like him. And because I despise that wife of his.'

'But you grew up together,' Tex said, trying to concentrate on the road, a feat which was becoming increasingly difficult. He licked his lips, a third of his mind on the sexual tension building up within him, sweet and unbearable, another third on the road, and the rest on the conversation. 'Weren't you two at one time like . . .' He sighed as a quiver rippled through him. '. . . Sisters?'

For an instant her hand was still. 'Sisters!' she spat, then continued to stroke him. 'God, no.' She laughed bitterly. 'I couldn't stand her. We got off on the wrong foot right from the start. She wormed her way into my life, stole Auntie's affection, and now she's waltzing off with what should be my house and home.'

'I thought you told me you didn't want it.'

'I don't. But I can't stand to see her getting it, either.' She sighed. 'It's too late now, I suppose. I'm sure she's been left the rooming house and the café. By next week, I suspect, she and that family of hers will have finished moving out of the cottage and into Auntie's apartment up above the café.'

'How do you know?'

'Oh, I know all right. Some things aren't that difficult to figure out.' She quickened her stroke now, and he growled in frustration as he felt his penis straining painfully against the double layers of restraining fabric.

'I want it, Tex,' she whispered. 'Let's do it right here. In the car.' Her eyes glowed with excitement.

'Are you crazy?' he growled, but she could feel the ever-more stiffening penis under her touch. If was rock hard now, trying to tent his whipcord trousers. Abruptly she changed her circular strokes and strummed her fingernails lightly across it.

'Damn it, Jenny!' He slammed on the brakes and pulled over to the side of the road. He stopped the car with a jerk, glanced in the rearview mirror, and scanned the road up ahead. There was no traffic coming in either direction.

He scooted sideways, towards her. 'All right,' he said quietly. 'You've got it. Against my better judgment.'

'Got what?' she asked in a trembling voice, afraid to anticipate, afraid to hear his verdict.

'Him later. Me now.'

Suddenly she flung her arms around his neck and pulled him close.

'Thanks, Tex,' she whispered in his ear, her breath warm and sweet and fragrant.

He gazed deep into her eyes, trying, futilely as always, to pierce through their cloudy armour. 'Why thank me?' he replied. 'You're Mrs Tex Sexton. And we're very much alike, aren't we, Jenny? We both want the same thing.'

She nodded and sought his lips, nibbling and gnawing at them with her teeth. Then she thrust her tongue urgently between them. She was filled with a lust such as she had never experienced before and felt a moistness dribbling down the hot flesh of her thighs. There was nothing, she thought, to intensify the pleasure of sex like getting absolute control over someone's destiny. Sex and power. Combined . . . combined they made her feel suddenly invincible.

Slowly she pushed him away, her fingers expertly undoing his fly. She reached inside and pulled out his phallus.

It leapt in her hand, trembling and rigid, the veins standing out in bold relief. She stared at it, her eyes gleaming hungrily, and then she slid back the foreskin. The purplish-red tip was shiny and moist.

With startling swiftness, she plunged her head down and swallowed him deeper than she had ever swallowed him before. Her head bobbed up and down, her mouth making urgent suction sounds, and all the while her mind was aswirl with thoughts of power. Before long, she could feel his phallus getting ready to burst. Then she heard the strangled cry coming up in Tex's throat, and in a fit of exquisite passion she plunged down, eating him as deeply as she could while burrowing her nose in the curly nest of his pubic hair.

The semen spouted forth powerfully, and she swallowed it greedily, wave after bursting wave, the thick, salty semen tasting all the more delicious because she knew it came from the wellspring of her newly acquired power.

441

14

Only once Elender was buried and Elizabeth-Anne found herself the sole beneficiary of her last will and testament did the finality of death truly sink in.

Up until then, there had been a dreamlike air of unreality about it all. There had been altogether too many things to arrange – the burial, the service, the flowers. As Jenny had divorced herself completely from Elender, it was Elizabeth-Anne upon whom the duties of the daughter had fallen. She received all the friends and acquaintances, each of whom offered her their sincerest condolences and, strangely enough, whom she ended up comforting as much as they comforted her. It helped her vent her immediate shock and grief, enough, at least, to help carry her through the first few unbearable days.

The sheer number of mourners staggered her. She had never stopped to realize just how popular Auntie had been; it had taken death to make her take notice of that, and Elizabeth-Anne sensed that these were not mere displays of sadness and grief . . . these were authentic emotions. Elender Hannah Clowney had been genuinely liked. She had been a pillar of the community, and even if she hadn't earned the abiding love of everyone, she had certainly gained their unanimous admiration and respect, a feat which was rare indeed.

Then there had been the reading of the will, and that suddenly hammered home her grief. After the flurried hurricane of activity she suddenly found herself in a vacuum, with time on her hands to think. It was then that the pain and the profound sense of loss set in. She knew she was helpless to fight against it, so she let it come. And what a terribly cruel pain it was! Auntie had been a mother to her, as well as her confidante, mentor, 'aunt', and best friend. She found herself grieving for all these individuals separately, realizing just how many people she had lost with the death of one unique individual.

In order to draw strength for herself, Elizabeth-Anne drew her family around her and hugged them close, seeking solace and comfort from them, and that helped reduce the pain a little more. But she discovered, to her amazement, that it was Auntie's legacy which alleviated her grief most of all. Although she had been helping Auntie for years, working in both the café and the rooming house, suddenly finding herself the owner of these businesses was quite a different matter from simply working in them. Far more time and dedication were now required of her, and for that she was grateful. Just when she was afraid that she had too much time on her hands in which to conjure up painful memories and mourn forever, she had no choice but to throw herself into the businesses with all the energetic slavishness and zealous stamina she could muster.

And energy it drained out of her, which was precisely what she wanted. The more fiendishly she pushed herself, and the more ragged she ran herself, the less time she had in which to be confronted by her loss.

Zaccheus offered to quit his job working for Tex Sexton in order to help her with the two businesses, and he was both disappointed and pleased that she did not want his help. 'At least not yet, Zaccheus,' she tried to explain. 'It's good for me to keep every minute of the day filled.'

But the thing which surprised them both the most was that, just as he was considering quitting his job in order to help out, Tex offered him a handsome raise no one in his right mind could refuse.

'It's destined, you see?' Elizabeth-Anne flashed Zaccheus her first strained, fleeting smile in weeks. 'You have your work, just as I have mine. Besides, if we worked together, who would be in charge? You? Me?' Her lips held another ghost of a smile and she took his hands and held them. 'We'd only begin to squabble and end up hating each other. And I don't want that to happen . . . not ever.' She shook her head. 'It just isn't *healthy* for a young married couple to be around each other twenty-four hours every day. Besides, I prefer you to be gone all day. That way, each time you come home I feel like a newlywed.'

He looked down at her, his face serious but his lips and eyes smiling. 'Mama,' he said softly, using that endearment for the first time ever, 'you're something else. You know that?'

She laughed suddenly, and after the dark, quiet weeks of solemnity the sound of happiness was music to his ears. His own happy laughter merged with hers. Then he hugged her fiercely, a pleased, grateful expression on his face.

'Now off you go,' she said, slapping his buttocks affectionately. 'Your day may be over, Zaccheus Hale, but mine isn't. Not by a long shot.'

And as he grinned and walked off, she regarded him fondly, thinking to herself: *Why shouldn't he look pleased? And why shouldn't I be? It is high time to take stock of our blessings. We've both come through a great deal together, some things which many marriages couldn't have survived. The three girls are turning out exceptionally beautiful and intelligent. Regina is already — seven?* She frowned. *Is that possible? Has time flown by that quickly?*

With death had come reflections of blessings which up to now had been taken for granted.

They all enjoyed good health. They were happy. Overall, despite the tensions and naturally competitive circumstances of each workday, Zaccheus' job was going exceptionally well; his raise proved that. Most important, he genuinely liked what he was doing. Working for the Sextons was by no means a piece of cake, but somehow he alone of all their employees was left unharrassed. There was a popular saying in Quebeck: 'The Sextons get richer while the rest of us get poorer', but that didn't apply to the Hales. And although Zaccheus worked for Tex and spent a lot of his time out at the ranch, he rarely ran into Jenny. Both of them made a point of avoiding each other. Those unavoidable times when their paths did cross, she would pointedly ignore him, sailing past like a duchess, her head held high as if he did not count, and that suited him just fine.

Yes, other than Auntie's death, which had come as a staggering blow to all of them, things *were* on a wonderfully even keel. Sometimes, Elizabeth-Anne feared that things seemed to be going almost *too* smoothly.

Life was good and abundant.

There were the two houses they had inherited from Auntie, and considerable savings, too. No fortune, but no piddling amount, either; added to their own savings it came to a tidy nest egg. They were far from rich, but they were comfortably well-off and had financial security. They were unburdened by bills. Nor was there need to worry about bad times on the horizon. There was plenty saved up to tide them over these, should they, God forbid, ever visit. Nor did they need to pay rent anymore, although the cottage had been inexpensive by any standard. As Jenny had predicted, they had moved into Elender's apartment above the café.

Every passing year was better than the previous.

And then the highway was planned. It would stretch northwards from Brownsville to Laredo, bypassing Quebeck two miles out across the fields, and connect with another new highway which swung from Laredo over to Corpus Christi on the Gulf.

Nothing sates the hungry wheels of commerce more fully than routes of transportation, and the excitement in Quebeck was intoxicating. Even the old die-hards who had originally been opposed to a new highway had become converts. Every day, it seemed, someone in Quebeck was buying a new car. Those who owned horses and buggies, like Elizabeth-Anne and Zaccheus, were fast becoming the minority – soon horse-drawn transportation would disappear forever. The highway would see to that.

15

Zaccheus looked around from his high perch atop the buggy seat. The early evening sunset was spectacular, striating the sky in the west with the deep rich tones of oranges, yellows, and reds and streaking the wisps of high cirrus clouds above him with the paler, more delicate pastel shades of lavenders and pinks. For once, he was immune to the splendours of the setting sun.

He sat looking around with little interest. The field at which Elizabeth-Anne had asked him to stop the buggy was large and uninspiring. Scrub brush and waist-high dry weeds inhabited it, but little else, Zaccheus thought grimly, except bugs and, possibly, snakes.

'Well?' Elizabeth-Anne asked with the subdued excitement of a schoolgirl showing off.

'Well, what?' he demanded. He turned slowly to face her. 'I was under the impression we were going to a *special* place,' he said. 'But *this*!' He indicated the insignificance of the field with an indifferent gesture and barked a short laugh. 'Elizabeth-Anne, it's nothing but a field badly in need of irrigation!'

'No, Zaccheus,' she said with such solemn intensity that he dared say no more. 'It's *not* just another field. This is a *special* field.' She got down off the buggy and stood there in the waist-high weeds, hands on her hips, and looked up at him. He was sitting stiffly erect, his face creased in a frown of confusion.

'Close your eyes,' she said suddenly.

'What?' He stared down at her to see if she was serious.

'Just close them, Zaccheus. Please?'

'Oh, all right.' He smiled indulgently and did as he was told. 'Well?' he asked.

'Now, just imagine in your mind everything I'm about to describe to you.'

He vent a sigh and nodded.

'In front of you, about fifteen yards away, is the new asphalt highway. Wide and sleek, with lots and lots of cars zooming past.' She paused. 'Can you hear them?'

He frowned and shook his head. 'No, I can't honestly say I do.'

She made an impatient sound and raised her eyes heavenwards. 'Well, *imagine* you're hearing them, then.' She waited a moment. 'Now do you hear them?'

He nodded to humour her. 'Can I open my eyes now?'

'Not yet. Now, the cars are whisking back and forth in both directions. But not only cars. There are trucks and buses too.' She had turned around; he could tell that from the way her voice changed. 'Can you see them?'

He nodded doubtfully.

'The field all around you has been mown down . . . the weeds are gone and there's short grass everywhere . . . right behind you is a huge building facing the highway . . . one storey, but very long . . . a series of buildings, actually.' Her voice came from a different direction now; she was walking around. 'Now, each building consists of an individual room with a bathroom and a covered parking place for a car. And in the centre of it all is the office. In fact, the very spot where you're sitting right now is a large curving driveway. To your left, facing the road, is a huge sign that's lit up at night. It reads: "Tourist Court".'

447

His eyes opened.

'Do you like the idea?' she asked hopefully, coming back over to the buggy. She looked up at him, her eyes shining.

'It might be a good idea,' he conceded, nodding.

'Imagine the business this place will do!' She looked at him closely. 'Don't you think it would make a good spot for a tourist court?'

'It makes sense,' he said carefully.

'Just think! There won't be another one for a hundred miles around! It'll do a booming business. But before it's begun I still have to convince one of the parties involved.'

He frowned and said slowly, 'And who is this other party?'

'Guess.'

He made a face. 'I'm afraid to.'

She smiled. 'You know I'm never one to be frivolous with money. But this isn't throwing it out the window. It's an investment, Zaccheus! It's the opportunity I've been waiting for. Really, darling, this is the chance of a lifetime!'

'It's the chance to go broke, too. What you're proposing would cost a fortune!'

'We've got money,' she said quietly.

'I don't know . . .' he mused slowly, and rubbed his chin thoughtfully. 'We'll really have to think it over well. We can't go rushing into something like this blindly. There are a lot of things to consider. Building costs, financing, purchasing the property . . .'

'The property's already taken care of,' she said softly.

'Take that by me again?'

'It's ours, Zaccheus. I . . . I already bought it.'

He stared at her. 'I thought that whatever we do, we'd always decide to do it *together*. That's what we always agreed upon.'

'Yes, but I – ' She whirled suddenly and threw her

hands in the air. 'Damn it!' she cried. 'I wanted to surprise you.'

'You did surprise me,' he pointed out quietly, hopping down off the buggy.

She glared at him. 'Well, you're suddenly acting as though I stabbed you in the back or something. As though I cheated you.'

He tightened his lips across his teeth. 'I suppose you've made up your mind?'

She nodded.

His jaw trembled, but somehow he managed to keep his voice from quivering. 'I only hope to God it works out.'

'Why shouldn't it?'

'It just seems – so quick.' He sought her hands and held them desperately. 'Elizabeth-Anne, it isn't that I don't want us to do it. Believe me, that's not it at all. It's just . . . well, like you're rushing into it.'

'You've got to take advantage of opportunities when they arise,' she said stubbornly. 'God knows, they don't crop up often around here.'

He pursed his lips with disapproval and then sighed. *Well, what is done is done,* he thought stolidly, his cheeks ticking. *He might as well yield to the inevitable and make the best of it. Otherwise, a battle between them could rage, causing irreparable harm to their relationship. Nothing was worth that. Not all the money in the world.*

He took a deep breath and asked, 'Who owned this property before us?'

'Who owned it? Why, Tex Sexton, of course.' She laughed shortly. 'Who else owns any land around here?'

'Did the highway commission buy the land for the highway yet?'

She shook her head. 'They're in the process of doing that right now.'

'How far does our property reach?'

She pointed.

'And the highway?' He looked at her hopefully. 'Is it going to run through our property?'

'If you're asking is the commission going to have to buy the land from us, the answer is no. Everything surrounding us is Sexton's property, and it's coming through his.' She laughed shortly. 'You don't think he'd throw that in, too, and give us an easy profit as a present, do you? The commission's paying top dollar for highway land. Tex Sexton has got his own little thing going.'

Like fleecing the highway commission, he thought.

'May I ask,' he said slowly, 'how much you paid for this property?'

'A hundred and fifty dollars.'

'A hundred and fifty!' Zaccheus stared at her incredulously.

'What's the matter? Why are you looking at me like that? It's dirt cheap.'

'That's exactly what I mean,' he said drily. He looked at her closely. 'Don't you think it was a little *too* cheap?'

And a pessimistic voice inside his head said: *Why would Tex Sexton have sold it this cheaply now when it would surely be worth so much more once the highway was built? Besides, Sextons didn't sell land. Not ever. Somehow, their selling Elizabeth-Anne this property didn't add up.*

'You've got a bill of sale and a deed, of course?'

Elizabeth-Anne laughed. 'What do you take me for? A fool? Everything's in order. I consulted Eblin Keyes and he's drawing up the papers.'

A Sexton lawyer, he thought, and sighed. There was small choice in rotten apples. How far did you have to travel to make sure your lawyer wasn't a Sexton lawyer? Then he put a screeching stop to his wandering imagination. Perhaps he was making a mountain out of a mole hill. After all, wasn't he getting along just fine with Tex Sexton? Didn't his raises come as regularly as clockwork? Didn't Jenny carefully steer clear of him and

Elizabeth-Anne? So what was there to worry about? Paranoia didn't do anyone a bit of good.

Zaccheus swallowed the frog clogging his throat. 'All right, darling,' he said hoarsely, 'if it means that much to you, and if you're sure everything's in order, go ahead and build it. I'll help in any way I can.'

'You mean that?'

He nodded and she threw her arms around him.

'It'll work out, darling!' she cried excitedly. 'You'll see! And you won't be sorry, either! This is going to be the biggest, most successful tourist court in all Texas!'

The long refectory table was draped with a priceless Kashan rug. The sterling Edwardian candelabra bristled with glowing white candles, the china was English cobalt blue rimmed in gold, the napkins were thick, creamy Irish linen monogrammed with the ubiquitous 'S', and the cutlery was sterling, each heavy piece intricately carved from a single length of silver. The food was as splendid as the setting. There were giant shrimp, trucked in that very morning from the Gulf, and three-inch-thick rib-eye steaks which had been aged right out back of the ranch house.

Jenny moved slightly sideways as the Mexican serving girl wordlessly placed the bowl of crushed ice, crowned with four giant pink shrimp, in front of her. She ignored the food, leaned her bare elbows on the table, and steepled her fingers. She tapped her index fingers against her lips as she stared across the table at Tex.

He felt her gaze as he speared a shrimp, his lean, taut face and usually predatory eyes carefully impassive. Without even looking over at her, he could feel the intense excitement emanating from her face. It seemed to hit him in radiant waves.

'Well? Have you set things up?' she asked finally, unable to contain her impatience any longer.

He chewed his shrimp reflectively and didn't reply.

'Did you talk to Jesse about the loan?'

He finished his shrimp in his own sweet time and reached for the massive crystal goblet of white wine, letting her wait and making the tension within her grow unbearably. It was amazing, he thought, how when she wanted something badly enough, she managed to swallow all remnants of her pride and revulsion and barter for it.

He was waiting for that now. When she'd initially brought up the subject of his telling Jesse to let Elizabeth-Anne and Zaccheus have a big loan, he'd let her wait and stew in her own juices before consenting to do so. Only after she had promised to take him – not from the front as man and wife, but from behind, like an animal – had he agreed to talk to Jesse. If nothing else, he had to admit that Jenny at least kept her end of the bargain. Despite her obvious pain and discomfiture, she hadn't cried out once. She had, in fact, pretended to relish it so much that afterwards he wasn't quite so sure she really hadn't enjoyed it.

She was like no other woman he had ever known. And yet, after nearly four years of marriage, he often felt as though he did not know her at all. In many ways, they were very much alike; in many others, they were still strangers. They had sex frequently, but he knew that it was not love-making by any means. It was grim and exciting. Fierce and energetic. It was coupling, but it was not love – and he knew it.

He looked across the table, eyes intent, studying her. She was wearing a thin, low-cut blue dress, her shoulders bare, the rows of diagonal silver fringe which trimmed it flickering in the candlelight. He wasn't quite so sure he liked this new 'Roaring Twenties' style she had picked up on her travels. The flapper fashion was too boyish to really suit her.

She was waiting with barely controlled expectancy.

452

Somehow he imagined her to be a panther, poised to pounce at a scrap of meat.

'Well, did you talk to Jesse yet?' she asked again. 'And what about Roy? Did you ask him about jacking up prices and delaying the deliveries?'

'Not so quick.' He smiled benignly at her. 'What's it worth to you?'

She rubbed her lips together, as though she had just applied a layer of lipstick. 'What do you want, Tex?' she asked finally.

He dabbed his lips with his napkin. 'Show me your tongue.' He gestured with his hand.

She glanced quickly behind her to see if any of the servants were looking, or if Ross had finished eating in the breakfast room and the nanny was bringing him in to say good-night. Other than the serving girl, whose eyes were studiously averted, the coast was clear.

She glanced significantly in the girl's direction.

Tex shrugged. 'Let's see your tongue,' he said again.

Jenny tightened her lips. Then slowly, she opened her mouth and showed him her tongue. It was pink and moist.

'You know where that tongue hasn't been yet?' he asked with deliberate cruelty.

Her tongue slid back between her lips and she clamped her mouth shut.

'Well?'

Wearily she sighed.

'Are you gonna do it?'

She stared at him in sudden loathing, then nodded.

'But you've got to *like* doing it,' he said softly. 'You've got to promise me you'll *enjoy* it.'

Her smile was sickly. 'I'll enjoy it,' she whispered in a strained voice.

But later, when he lowered his bared buttocks down

into her face, she had to struggle to keep from being sick. Even then, as soon as he was through, she jumped from the bed and barely made it to the bathroom.

As she vomited, Jenny realized for the first time just how much she had come to despise her husband.

16

They applied for a loan of ten thousand dollars at the Quebeck Savings and Loan, the Sexton-owned bank.

'Hell,' Tex Sexton had magnanimously told Zaccheus, 'tell old Jesse to make it twelve thousand. There are always unforeseen expenses when you're building something. Won't do to be on too tight a budget. I've seen too many good businesses never take off because they were underfinanced.'

'Twelve thousand dollars is – well, a *fortune*!' Elizabeth-Anne told Zaccheus anxiously as they left the bank. 'Maybe we should have borrowed less? After all, we have nine thousand saved up.'

He shook his head. 'Tex is right, I think,' he said levelly. 'Besides, we can always return what we don't need.'

'But I still don't understand about the collateral! Why the café?' she asked. 'Why not the rooming house? As a piece of property, it's worth a lot more. It would only stand to reason they'd want to protect their interests.'

Zaccheus shrugged. 'Beats me.' Suddenly he laid a hand on her arm. 'Don't worry so much, Mama,' he said softly. 'Maybe they're trying to give us a break. Have you ever considered that?'

No, I haven't, she thought uneasily. *Sextons* never *give anyone a break*.

Out at the Sexton ranch, Jenny celebrated the news of

454

Elizabeth-Anne's bank loan with a glass of bootleg French champagne.

'I still don't understand why you wanted them to put up the café as collateral instead of the rooming house,' Tex said. 'It's the far less valuable property.'

'It's simple, really,' Jenny said. 'You see, the rooming house doesn't mean half as much to her. It's the café where she spends most of her time. And they live right upstairs. Besides, the café brings in a lot more money than the rooming house.' She smiled. 'It'll hurt them worse to lose it.'

In due course the highway surveyors were done and the blueprints of the tourist court were drawn up. Elizabeth-Anne and Zaccheus finally broke ground and work began in earnest.

Each morning thereafter, the two Hales rode out to the site long before daylight made its appearance in order to be there by sunrise to inspect the progress of the previous day. Sometimes the girls went along with them, and although they were invariably sleepy on the drive out, by the time they reached the site they were wide awake and ready to have a ball. There was no playground quite like a construction site, Elizabeth-Anne thought drily as she watched them get dusty and dirty and scrape their shins. When she voiced her worries that they were all growing up to become tomboys, Zaccheus laughed. 'They'll outgrow it soon enough. You'll see. In a few years you'll have wished they hadn't.'

Neither Elizabeth-Anne nor Zaccheus could quite explain how they managed to juggle their time. There were only twenty-four hours in each day, but somehow they managed to pack each minute full of fruitful achievements. They all had to pitch in and help, the girls included. Yet they all thrived, and dead tired as they were at the end of each day, those months were the most exhilarating of their lives – and none of them

would have had it any other way, especially not Elizabeth-Anne. With the added work came more and more
responsibilities, which she shouldered cheerfully.

There was so much to do it was mind-boggling. Every
phase of construction had to be overseen. Zaccheus suggested that the Sexton Construction Company build the
tourist court, but Elizabeth Anne had other ideas.
Wisely, she made it seem that they were his.

During one of their planning discussions before
ground was broken, she looked sideways at him. 'It's
wonderful how well things are going, don't you think?
And you know, we're really very lucky. The girls are
pitching in, and I didn't even have to ask Rosa to come
to work early. Imagine! She knows how busy we are,
and suddenly she starts showing up two hours early.'

'She is a jewel,' Zaccheus agreed. Then he laughed.
'A big two-hundred-pound jewel, at that.'

Elizabeth-Anne poked him in the ribs with a sharp
jab of her elbow. 'Now that's not nice, and you know it.
There's no one as devoted to us as she is. I thank God
we have her.'

'Sorry, Mama,' he said, pulling a straight face. 'I stand
corrected. She *is* worth her weight in gold. A lot of the
Mexicans are, you know. It's a pity they don't have more
opportunities. Everyone likes to say they're lazy, but
they're not. The problem is, nobody wants to give them
any responsibility. Everyone's afraid they'll take away
the higher paying jobs of the whites.'

'Why, Zaccheus!' Elizabeth-Anne exclaimed. 'What a
good idea!' She clapped her hands together in delight
and rested her head against his shoulder.

He frowned. 'What's a good idea?'

'What you just said. Hiring Mexicans and giving them
a chance. I should have thought of that myself! Rosa's
nephew, Carlos Cortez, is an engineer, and he's never
had the opportunity he needs. I hear he's very talented.
He can be in charge of building the tourist court, and

he'll see about hiring everyone we need. His people will work hard. It's like you said, they have to, just to prove how capable they are.' She sighed happily. 'Sometimes you make me so happy. I'm *proud* of you!'

And after that, he thought ruefully, what choice did he have but to follow through with 'his' suggestion? He couldn't help but feel that he'd been very cleverly railroaded.

He thought to himself: *She's a clever cookie, that wife of mine.*

Despite all there was to do, life was comfortable; week after week brought new plateaus of happiness and peaks of surprises.

Six-year-old Rebecca found her first boyfriend, a schoolmate named Gentry Olivant. '*Yech!*' her sisters teased her mercilessly. 'Nobody's named Gentry *Olivant*. At least nobody *human*. Besides, he's got elephant ears and chipped front teeth.'

'*I* think he's handsome!' Rebecca cried loyally every time they teased her and called him 'Gentry Elephant'.

Regina celebrated her eleventh birthday and Elizabeth-Anne took the time out to plan a surprise party for her and invited all her school friends over to the café that afternoon.

Elizabeth-Anne and Zaccheus contemplated purchasing a car, but frugality won out. Eventually they would buy one, they decided, but not just yet. They would wait until the tourist court was completed and bringing in money.

Elizabeth-Anne would never forget that spring of 1923. Her joy knew no bounds. She was pregnant again. 'This time it'll be a boy!' she promised an exultant Zaccheus. 'I *know* it will!'

'I don't care what it is!' he declared joyfully. 'Son, daughter, twins – I'll love him or her or them all the same!'

457

'I'm worried though,' Elizabeth-Anne confided to him. 'It's bad timing. Having the baby now will slow me down. And there's so *much* to do!'

He laughed. 'Mama,' he told her, 'in the twelve years since we've been together, I've never seen you let anything slow you down yet.'

How wonderful those months seemed as they raced through them. The stormy clouds on the horizon had yet to come and nothing gave them an inkling of the web Jenny had spun.

They were at the construction site, Elizabeth-Anne and Zaccheus, with the girls playing tag in the fields.

'It's really coming along,' Elizabeth-Anne said. 'Look, part of the concrete foundations have already been poured!'

'By next week sometime, the timber framework will start to go up. It *is* amazing, isn't it?'

They both turned to look at the horizon. Beyond it somewhere, slowly but surely, yard by yard and mile by mile, the highway coming north from Brownsville was approaching ever closer.

Summer came, and with it the first indication that treacherous waters lay ahead.

Doing paperwork and accounting, paying the bills and making financial projections was Zaccheus' responsibility, so he was the first to see the storm clouds gathering. He waited a while before mentioning anything to Elizabeth-Anne. He didn't want to scare her unduly. And besides, he wanted to have absolute proof before confronting the issue.

It was but a matter of time. After several weeks of suspecting inconsistencies, he could keep quiet no longer.

For Elizabeth-Anne, the day dawned with the usual everyday anxieties, but she could see no major danger looming on her horizon. She awoke feeling safe and secure, certain that all was well in her snug little world. The morning was crystal clear and the stars seemed brighter and closer to earth than ever.

As usual, Carlos Cortez was waiting for her and Zaccheus at the construction site. Cortez was always the first to arrive in the morning and the last to leave at night. She knew that hiring him had been a good choice. No one could ask for more dedication from anybody.

'I don't believe it!' Elizabeth-Anne marvelled as she stared around at the dark, ghostly shapes. 'Half the framework is already completed!'

Carlos Cortez nodded. 'My men work fast.'

'Indeed they do!' Elizabeth-Anne hooked her arm through Zaccheus'. 'Come on, darling!' she said excitedly as the dawn began to pale the night sky. 'Let's poke around!' She shook her head in wonderment. 'I didn't realize the tourist court was so big! Now that the timber frames are half up, it looks – well, *monstrous*!'

'And expensive,' Zaccheus added quietly.

She caught the undercurrent in his voice and glanced at him sharply. This was the first time he had voiced concern over the budget. 'What's wrong?' she asked gently.

'Nothing's wrong, exactly. But since I drew up the original estimates, costs have been spiralling steadily upwards. I hadn't taken that into account.'

'You mean it won't come in within the budget?' She smiled. 'Well, don't worry. I didn't really expect to repay the extra two thousand early.' She paused. 'How far overbudget do you think it's going to run?'

He shook his head. 'I don't know, exactly,' he said cautiously, 'but it looks as though it might go well over the extra two thousand. We may have to dip into our savings.'

Her fingers clasped his arm tightly, but she did not say a word. She didn't have to: the pressure she applied on his arm said it all.

'These units are expensive,' he explained. 'Especially the plumbing and the wiring. It would have been a lot cheaper putting up a single large building, but . . . well, that would have been a *hotel*, and not a tourist court. That's what's costing us . . . that, plus the fact that nothing's getting any cheaper.'

'At least we have money in the bank,' Elizabeth-Anne said.

'I hope it's enough.'

'You hope what?' She stared at him.

'I'll have to go over the figures with Carlos this weekend, but I only think it fair to warn you . . .' He hesitated uncomfortably, and looked out over the fields in the direction from which the highway was coming. 'I would have told you earlier,' he said softly, 'but I didn't want to worry you. Not until I was sure.'

'And now you are?'

He nodded. 'Now I am.'

Summer dragged on, and then events overtook them.

17

It was the beginning of August; they had been married thirteen years. And their time together was running out. The happiness they shared and the dreams they pursued would soon be no more. Such great happiness could not last. The fickle wheel of fortune and the plot Jenny had hatched were too potent to withstand.

The strong noonday sun baked the fields remorselessly and the Mexican labourers were hidden, enjoying their siesta in the shade behind stacks of lumber and building materials as Zaccheus pulled up in the Sexton Model T Ford he had use of. The construction site seemed deserted.

He killed the engine and the silence was almost eerie. But from the shadows, he could feel the small army of Mexican workers eyeing him curiously.

'El Jefe.'

The boss. That was how he was known by them.

He saw Carlos Cortez striding towards him from the patch of shade. 'You sent a message that it's urgent you see me immediately?' he asked as he climbed out of the car.

Cortez nodded. 'Sí, Señor Hale. It is very, very important.' He gestured to the far end of the site. 'Let us talk over there. Some of the men understand English and I do not wish for them to hear.'

Zaccheus nodded. 'All right,' he said, his voice sounding unnaturally loud in the silence.

He had been in his little office next to Tex Sexton's large study, going over the ledgers of the various Sexton-owned businesses, which he did for two weeks of each month, when Carlos Cortez's messenger had brought the note summoning him at once. It was a cryptic message, but nonetheless one he couldn't ignore. Carlos Cortez was never one to get unnecessarily worked up or to cry wolf.

They took the wide path that had been trampled down over the past weeks towards the foundation of the last building, at the far end of the tourist court. When they reached it they sat down on the raised concrete porch. Carlos Cortez produced an open pack of cigarettes and offered it delicately to Zaccheus, who shook his head. Cortez took one for himself, lit it, and took a deep drag. 'Things are not right,' he said softly.

Zaccheus stared at him. 'What's wrong?'

Cortez laughed mirthlessly. 'What is not wrong, señor? Coyote Building Suppliers, they always raise their prices. Nothing arrives at the time it is promised. For some things we have waited for weeks now.' He paused, and added softly: 'You work for Señor Sexton. Can you not appeal to him?'

'I already did. He says there is nothing he can do. He says the building supply company is his brother Roy's.'

Something flickered deep within the Mexican's dark, liquid eyes.

Wearily Zaccheus looked out across the fields.

Cortez smoked in silence for half a minute. 'There is something else. It worries me even more.'

Zaccheus turned to him.

Cortez ground the cigarette out under his heel. 'We are always short of supplies. What is delivered is carefully inventoried, but then . . .' He shrugged. 'When we use the supplies, much is missing.'

Zaccheus' voice was hushed. 'You mean someone is stealing from us?'

The Mexican's expression did not change. 'The last night, I spent it here, Señor Hale,' he said in a hushed voice. 'I wanted to see for myself.'

'And someone came? To steal?' It was more a statement than a suggestion.

'Sí.' Cortez nodded. 'It was after midnight when they arrive. There were two trucks and five men. I did not try to stop them. There were too many of them, and only one of me.'

'It would have been stupid to try anything,' Zaccheus agreed. 'Did they see you?'

'No, señor. But I recognized two of them . . . and the trucks.'

Zaccheus stared intently at him.

Cortez did not speak.

Zaccheus' voice was a bare whisper. 'Who were they?'

Cortez remained silent.

'They were Sexton men, weren't they?' Zaccheus said tightly. His bright-blue eyes turned dark and stone-like with anger. 'It had to have been.'

Cortez nodded. 'And the trucks, they were Coyote Building Suppliers trucks. I am sorry, señor.'

'I should have known,' Zaccheus said bitterly. 'First they sell us the materials, and then they steal them back to sell them all over again.'

'They are not good people, señor.'

'I know.' Zaccheus sighed. 'And I am one of them.'

'Señor?'

'I work for Sexton. Or, I should say, I *worked* for him. I am resigning today.'

Cortez looked at him and nodded. 'That is good.' He paused. 'About the thefts, señor. What are you going to do?'

Zaccheus' voice was thoughtful. 'When is the next big shipment coming in?'

'Tomorrow afternoon is when it is scheduled.'

Zaccheus rose from the porch. 'Then they are likely to come again tomorrow night. I will spend it here; I will have to,' he said.

Cortez looked at him. 'Then I shall spend the night here with you, Señor Hale,' he said softly. 'Better that there are two of us. Those men, they look dangerous.'

'No.' Zaccheus shook his head. 'This I must do myself.'

'Then be careful, señor. If you change your mind . . .'

Zaccheus smiled. 'I won't, but thank you. You're a brave man, Señor Cortez. There are not many men in this state who would dare put themselves in that position.'

'*De nada.*' Cortez shrugged. 'It is nothing. They are thieves and must be stopped.'

'I will stop them.'

Cortez stood there, smiling sadly. 'You, too, are a brave man, Señor Hale,' he said softly. 'I only hope you are not a foolish one, as well.'

'No!' Elizabeth-Anne gasped. It was approaching dusk and they were standing on the porch of the café. 'No, Zaccheus. I forbid it! You can't. If you go out there tonight, I think you ought to get Sheriff Parker to go with you.'

He smiled. 'Don't worry so much, Mama. I'm just going to hide on the site to see what happens.'

'I'm scared, Zaccheus.'

He smiled. 'Don't worry so much. I'm not going to play the hero. But we've got to find out exactly who's behind the thefts. How else can we stop them?'

She stared at him. 'Still. I wish you wouldn't go.'

'I have to. You know that.'

She nodded and came into his arms. He held her close, a feat which was becoming increasingly difficult with her pregnancy. He could feel her trembling.

He smiled down at her, his eyes tender. 'Let's stop worrying, and go upstairs. I've got an hour to kill and I intend to put it to good use.'

She laughed in spite of herself. 'The baby might kick you,' she warned teasingly.

'Then let it kick.'

She laid her head against his chest and gazed at the setting sun. It was huge and orange, poised above the roof of the rooming house across the street. For a moment it seemed to hang there hesitantly. Then suddenly, it slipped down, down, down until it was a mere thin horizontal line along the roof; then it was gone.

She felt his hand tugging at hers.

'But the girls!' she protested weakly. 'Really, Zaccheus!'

'Rosa will keep them busy. Come on. It's our last chance until tomorrow morning.'

She felt the warmth of him pressing against her body and her own answering warm tremor.

He kissed her deeply, urgently, then laughed softly as she turned away from him.

'Zaccheus,' she laughed. 'What will the neighbours think!'

'Who cares what they think?' he whispered softly, turning her face back around. 'Time's-a-wasting.'

She stared into his eyes. 'Yes,' she whispered in return. 'It is.'

18

It was after midnight and Zaccheus had been sitting cross-legged in the weeds for hours now, a bottle of cold, sugared black coffee beside him. Fifty feet in front of him, that morning's newly delivered pallets of lumber, piles of copper plumbing pipes, and giant rolls of electric wiring were black shadows against the dark sky.

The fields all around were eerie, moonless, and dark. Field mice scurried in the high dry weeds; in the distance, a coyote howled. Cicadas and crickets shrilled and trilled their night songs.

It was in the hour after midnight when he finally heard the distant, laboured rumbling of approaching trucks. As they neared, the insects and animals stilled a moment before continuing their nocturnal cacophony. Three sets of headlights dipped and rose on the dirt road.

Zaccheus crawled forwards to get a better view and squatted behind a thorny bush. He blinked his eyes at the sudden brightness and froze as the vehicles made the turn in the road and came straight towards him, momentarily blinding him. The front vehicle, he saw now, was a car – a brand new Cadillac, all chrome and shiny red paint. His heart beat like savage jungle drums. He knew that car. It was the only one like it in the entire county.

It was Roy Sexton's. Roy . . . Tex's younger brother. He should have known.

Then he heard the squeal of brakes and the slamming of doors. The vehicles' headlights were left on to bathe the construction site and men were moving about, unhooking the tailboards of the trucks. He saw Roy Sexton climbing out of the Cadillac and stretching, then hooking his thumb in his belt. Six men, all Sexton ranch hands, ambled up to him.

'I don't know,' one of the men drawled. 'What if they left somebody here to guard this stuff? They must be wise to us by now.'

'Don't be a chickenshit, Billy,' Roy said derisively. 'Them Hales is a bunch of shitheads. Wouldn't know it if their tits or peckers was missin'.'

The other men laughed.

' 'Sides,' Roy went on, 'the workers is all Mexes. Anybody steals, it's them gets blamed.' He chortled and let fly a wad of spit.

It was all Zaccheus could do to keep from jumping forwards. His eyes were like silvery pinpoints in his face and a killing anger and mortal outrage consumed him. So this was how they perceived the Hales, was it? Well, they would learn differently soon enough.

The theft was well-coordinated and efficient. Roy, obviously in charge, led the way to the stacks of that morning's delivery and gestured to what the men should take. From his vantage point Zaccheus watched as they formed pairs, and began carrying building supplies to the trucks.

It didn't take them more than half an hour. Then Roy shouted, 'That's enough,' and they hooked up the tailboards and climbed back into their trucks.

'You comin', Roy?' one of the men called out of the cab of a truck as he raced the engine.

Roy flapped a hand, signalling for them to drive off.

'I'll just poke around a few minutes. You all go on. I'll catch up with you later.'

The heavily-laden trucks roared off, their headlights rising and dipping back the way they had come, leaving behind air foul with the stench of exhaust.

Roy was alone, prowling around in the light of the Cadillac's big powerful bug-eye headlights.

Zaccheus hesitated, then rose from his hiding place and started walking towards him. He felt blinded by anger and it was as if his heart and pulse were trying to run away.

'Roy!' The name came out as a sharp bark.

Roy Sexton turned around in surprise and Zaccheus eyed him murderously in the glare of the headlight beams. He saw the lean, tanned face, the almost black, squinty mean little eyes, and the strong cleft jaw. He also sensed, not for the first time, the tense brute strength and animal cunning coursing through Roy's taut, wiry physique.

'You been stealing from us a long time, Roy?' he asked softly.

Roy had tensed for a moment when he'd heard his name called out. Now he relaxed slightly. 'You gonna do something about it, boy?' he grinned.

Zaccheus looked at him coldly. 'I want what's ours back, Roy.'

Roy looked at him with a bored expression and turned away.

The words tore venomously from Zaccheus' lips: 'You Sexton son of a bitch! You're thieves and liars and racketeers, the bunch of you! And you, you low-life son of a bitch, are the worst sneak thief of them all!'

Roy Sexton turned back around. 'I'd watch my mouth if I was you, Bible salesman,' he warned quietly. 'One more word outta you and you don't need to bother reporting to work tomorrow.' He gave a low, ugly laugh. 'You can peddle Bibles again.'

'Yeah? What're you going to do? Fire me?'

'Mebee.'

Zaccheus laughed softly. 'I quit yesterday, or hadn't you heard? Now get in your car and get off my property. I don't want no yellow-bellied thief despoiling it any longer.'

Roy came at him in a blur, fists flying, and Zaccheus quickly ducked. He tackled Roy around the chest and the two men went sprawling to the ground and rolled over a few times. Roy bucked and threw Zaccheus off and jumped nimbly to his feet. Spying a foot-long iron pipe on the ground, he grabbed it and wielded it threateningly at Zaccheus, a wild kind of joy burning in his mean little eyes.

Zaccheus was back on his feet now. Tempted though he was to watch the moving iron pipe, he kept his gaze on Roy's eyes – they, better than his weapon, would signal his attack when it came.

It came then. Zaccheus saw it coming and threw himself aside; the pipe thudded into the ground where he had been crouching a moment before. He walked cautious circles around Roy.

Roy, crouching, laughed confidently as he kept turning to face him. He feinted a few moves with the pipe, keeping Zaccheus back. Then he lifted it high and brought it whistling down.

Zaccheus barely leapt aside in time. Even so, the pipe came down on his shoulder and there was a sickening crack. Lightning bolts of pain shot through his arm and down his chest and back, and he stumbled.

Roy Sexton laughed and thrust forwards with the pipe, forcing Zaccheus to dance back against a four-foot-stack of lumber. Zaccheus' eyes darted about in panic. Now he could no longer spring backwards; he was cornered.

Gritting his teeth in pain against his shoulder, Zaccheus reached up and swung himself up to the top of the lumber stack. He leapt to his feet and stood there a moment, looking down at Roy. Then he turned and ran nimbly along the ten-foot length.

Behind him, Roy threw the pipe onto the stack of lumber and hoisted himself up. Grabbing the pipe, he ran after Zaccheus.

There was another, lower stack of lumber six feet away. Zaccheus took a leap and jumped down onto it, his sudden weight shifting the boards. He could feel them collapsing under his feet; he jumped down to the ground and leapt clear.

It was a moment later that Roy did the same, but the result was disastrous. The lumber had shifted precariously under Zaccheus' weight, and it was now unevenly distributed. The moment Roy's feet landed on it, the stack gave way under his weight and he found himself falling backwards, arms flailing.

'What the – ' he screamed, and those were the last words Roy Sexton ever uttered. Then the ground rose up to meet him and the back of his head hit an exposed pipe.

Suddenly there was silence.

With a racing heart, Zaccheus slowly approached him.

The headlight beams of the Cadillac still stabbed into the night, flood-lighting the eerie scene.

'Roy,' Zaccheus whispered.

There was no reply, and a cold sweat began to pour from his body.

'*Roy!*'

Roy Sexton stared up at him with unseeing eyes. Blood poured forth from a gaping hole in the back of his head.

Zaccheus' stomach began to churn convulsively and he jerked up and turned away, clapping a hand over his mouth to stifle the sickening bile rising up in his throat. After a few moments, he took deep lungfuls of air and then slowly looked at the body again. He felt for a heart-beat.

There was none. Roy Sexton, Tex's little brother, was very, very dead.

Finally he stood up wearily and walked in a daze over to Roy's car. He steadied himself against the car's open door. For several drawn-out moments he stood there, breathing deeply. Suddenly he was very tired. Sighing deeply, he closed his eyes.

He knew what he had to do. He might as well do it, and get it over with.

BOOK FOUR

1924

The Grass Widow

1

Elizabeth-Anne read the note for what must have been the thousandth time.

> *My Dearest Wife and Children,*
>
> *By the time you read this I will be gone from your lives forever. It was Roy Sexton and his men who have been stealing from us. When I confronted him, he tried to start a fight out at the construction site and fell, splitting his head open on a piece of pipe. He is dead.*
>
> *I did not kill him, but you know as well as I do that the courts around here are controlled by the Sextons, and that I would surely be sentenced to death for something I did not do.*
>
> *I am so sorry for this stupid fate which forces us apart, but I must leave, and alone. I cannot ruin your lives by taking you with me.*
>
> *Elizabeth-Anne — I plead with you to stay in Quebeck and finish the tourist court. You must nurture this dream of yours — this dream that we started fulfilling together.*
>
> *Regina, Charlotte-Anne, and Rebecca — I plead with you to help your mother and to remember your father as the good man that I hope you believe he was.*
>
> *Never doubt, my beloved, that I love all of you and always will, but that I must do what I am doing. Please forgive me.*
>
> *Your Loving Husband and Father,*
> *Zaccheus*

n a moan, Elizabeth-Anne let the note slip soundy through her fingers. Once again, the tears slid wn her cheeks and a lump rose up in her throat. The ouse seemed so empty . . . so unbearably empty. It was as if with Zaccheus gone, its very soul had departed.

In the days following Zaccheus' flight, she had been as brave as she knew how. Sheriff Parker had questioned her, and she had shown him the note, which he had kindly let her keep. Search parties had been sent out for Zaccheus, but they had found no trace of him whatsoever. It was as though he had disappeared into thin air.

But perhaps the most frightening aspect of the nightmare was the fact that she had heard not a single word from Tex and Jenny. She could only wonder what their ominous silence meant – but she felt she knew Jenny well enough . . . and knew Tex's reputation for retribution . . . that they must be planning some awful sabotage to get even.

She had tried to clear her mind of these dark, swirling thoughts and concentrate on her most difficult task – giving the girls comfort. They were heartbroken, as was she, but they proved themselves true Hales. Like herself, they were determined to put a brave face on their sorrow and help each other through this period of emptiness and misery. Each of them harboured the hope that someday Zaccheus would be able to return.

But deep down inside, Elizabeth-Anne knew better. He could never return to Quebeck. Ever. Not if he cherished his freedom. Not if he didn't want to hang.

That terrible truth was horrible to comprehend.

He could never return.

Not if he didn't want to hang.

Elizabeth-Anne's life had suddenly become living agony. One day Zaccheus had kissed her, had made love to her. Now she found herself alone. The girls were

fatherless. She was husbandless. They were all of th
alone.

Alone.

The terrible ache was enough to shatter her heart. If
it weren't for the girls and the child within her, she
would have tried to kill herself. She wouldn't even have
had to use a weapon, of that she was sure. She would
simply have died slowly, little by little, grieving herself
to death of a broken heart.

She shut her eyes painfully. There was a name for
women whose husbands, for whatever reason, had
upped and left them.

She shuddered as the name sprang into her mind.
Grass widows. That was what they were called. And that
was what she had now become.

A grass widow.

She knew how people pitied grass widows. Yet how,
at the same time, they eyed them with deeply rooted
suspicion, as they did divorcées. There was a stigma
attached to being a grass widow. Grass widows, it was
said, tended to prowl. They were after any available
man, even other women's husbands.

The tears blurred her vision. Then suddenly she
blinked them back and raised her head proudly, holding her chin erect. Right now, she couldn't afford to
cry. She couldn't afford the luxury of showing her
emotions. She had to be strong. Above all, she couldn't
show her misery – not when the girls needed comforting.

She placed her hand on her breast. Zaccheus was in
there, inside her heart. There he would live forever.
And he would live in his child which she was carrying
as well.

She reached up and felt the cool, crystal smoothness
of the pansy charm around her neck. He was there, too.
In fact, everywhere she looked, she could see evidence

im. And she would keep it that way. She would keep erything of his just as it was.

Zaccheus might be gone, but their love would live forever.

2

Elizabeth-Anne could see Regina waving to her from in front of the Good Eats Café. She waved back from atop the buggy seat and smiled for the first time in weeks.

Thank heaven for the girls and all my responsibilities, she thought. *During the hectic hours of each day there is little time to stop and consider just how much I miss Zaccheus.*

Although he was gone, her workday didn't change. She kept to her routine, getting up every morning as usual before dawn and riding out to the construction site – from which she was now returning. It was not the same without him. These morning inspections were when she missed him the most . . . and at bedtime. Her bed felt so terribly empty without him beside her.

She drew to a stop in front of the café and looked down at Regina. *Yes*, she thought again, *I've got so much to be grateful for.*

Her momentary reverie over, she started to ease her weight down off the buggy. Regina held out one hand to help and she took it. The moment her boots touched the ground, she rumpled Regina's hair and frowned. 'Why so sullen?' she asked. 'Charlotte-Anne been giving you trouble?'

'No.' Regina shrugged, looked down at her feet, and kicked at a pebble. Then she squinted back up at her. 'It's nothing I can't take care of. You know how Charlotte-Anne is. Pushy.'

Elizabeth-Anne couldn't help laughing; it felt good.

Regina drew herself up with hurt dignity. 'Besides,

she's learning. I won't let her step all over me, and I'm not going to put up with those airs of hers, either.'

'I'm sure you won't,' Elizabeth-Anne said with mock solemnity. 'Now how about giving your mother a kiss?' She held out her cheek.

Regina hopped up on tiptoe and pecked her awkwardly on the cheek, then fell into step beside her as they went inside. 'Guess what, Mama? We served twenty-seven breakfasts already.'

Elizabeth-Anne stopped in her tracks. 'Twenty-seven! But that's —' She let out an impressed whistle. '— That's our best showing yet!'

Regina nodded happily. 'Comes to a little less than seven dollars.' Suddenly she slapped the palm of her hand across her forehead. 'Yikes!'

Elizabeth-Anne stared at her. 'What is it?'

'Rosa sent me out to bring in some more wood.'

Elizabeth-Anne smiled as Regina hurried off. She was proud that her daughters were such bright, hardworking credits to her. She was certain that each one of them would go far in this world.

With that comforting thought, she went around the side, opened the screen door, and entered the sizzling kitchen of the Good Eats Café. A blast of hot, humid air hit her squarely in the face. She let the screen door bang shut and lifted her crisp, white apron down off the hook beside it. Quickly, she looped it around her neck and reached behind her, tying it in the small of her spine.

Rosa was standing in front of the big stove, frying eggs and bacon. The moment she heard the door banging shut, she glanced over her shoulder. *'Buenos días, señora.'*

'Buenos días, Rosa,' Elizabeth-Anne returned. 'Busy morning?'

'Beesy!' Rosa inflated her cheeks and let the air out slowly. 'Ees a real beesy day! I don't tink have no day

477

ke today. Never before. We serve so many breakfasts, you soon get tousans of dollars!'

Elizabeth-Anne laughed. 'Oh, Rosa. I only wish that were true.' She regarded the big Mexican woman with affection. Rosa was a jewel, and as hardworking as they came. She was short and heavy-set, with a cheerful, puffy face and gleaming black hair around which she wore flowered handkerchiefs tied like a turban. Tiny gold loops dangled from her pierced lobes. Due to the stifling heat of the kitchen, her embroidered, off-white blouse was unbuttoned as far down as decency would allow, and her sleeves were rolled up her thick, powerful arms . . . arms strengthened from a lifetime of lifting cast-iron pots and heavy skillets. Her tawny skin gleamed with perspiration.

Elizabeth-Anne started to clear the table as Rosa slid a spatula under the rashers of bacon and flipped them over. Suddenly the swinging doors leading to the dining room burst open and Elizabeth-Anne could hear the sound of voices and cutlery and china. She turned around. Rebecca had come flying in.

'Oh, *Ma*-ma!' Rebecca wailed dramatically. 'My feet are *killing* me!'

'Then take a break, darling, and let Charlotte-Anne take over.'

'Charlotte-Anne!' Rebecca narrowed her eyes. '*She's* still in bed. *Claims* she's ailing.'

Elizabeth-Anne raised her eyebrows. 'Did she say what's wrong with her?'

'Noooo . . . just that she's unwell.' Rebecca glanced in Rosa's direction and lowered her voice to a whisper. 'Rosa went up and took a look at her earlier. Says there's nothing wrong with her.'

Rosa's acute hearing had caught the whisper. 'No, there eesn't,' she scoffed. She turned around from the stove and waved her spatula angrily. 'She like us to tink she's deleecate, but she ees fine, you mark my words.

478

Meanwhile, Regina and Rebecca have been se.
everybody alone. *Again*.'

Elizabeth-Anne sighed. 'I'll go upstairs and check ◄
her in a little while.'

'Mama?' Rebecca said quietly.

'What is it, dear?'

'Maybe . . . maybe there really *is* something wrong
with Charlotte-Anne. I don't mind serving for her, too.
Really I don't.'

Elizabeth-Anne hugged her daughter. 'I know you
don't, dear.'

'Maybe Charlotte-Anne should see Dr Purris again?'

'Maybe she should,' Elizabeth-Anne mused aloud.
'She *has* been feeling unwell an awful lot lately.'

At the stove, Rosa rolled her eyes skyward.

'Well, I'd better go make my rounds of the dining
room before everyone's gone,' Elizabeth-Anne said. By
reflex, she smoothed her hands over her apron and
patted her hair. She considered greeting her customers
personally and getting their opinions on the food and
the service to be of paramount importance. A lot of
the café's success, she believed, was due to the personal
attention each and every guest received. People liked
being made to feel welcome and at home.

'I start lunch soon,' Rosa said. 'We weel have pork
chops, saffron rice, an' corn. We got a good deal on
pork. José breeng eet later. Deener weel be boiled beef,
red cabbage, corn muffeens, and persil potatoes.' She
looked at Elizabeth-Anne questioningly. 'Ees okay?'

Elizabeth-Anne clapped the woman on the shoulder.
'It all sounds wonderful, Rosa,' she said, then pushed
open the swinging doors that led into the dining room.
Smiling pleasantly, she started making her rounds.

At the table closest to her, she saw the thin, pinched face
of Hugh McElwee as he gingerly picked at his scrambled eggs with a fork. McElwee was the publisher of the

ck Weekly Gazette and he picked at his food like
picked at the words in the articles he published
. slowly, as if there was something distasteful about
hem. A confirmed bachelor, he lived across the street
in the Hale Rooming House. A victim of myopia,
he always seemed confused by what went on around
him.

'Good morning, Mr McElwee,' Elizabeth-Anne said
cheerfully. 'Is everything to your liking?'

He seemed startled to hear her and looked up
sharply. 'Oh, good morning, Mrs Hale,' he said in his
high-pitched voice. He smiled and nodded. 'Oh, yes,
yes. Everything's fine. Fine.'

Elizabeth-Anne leaned close into his ear and lowered
her voice confidentially. 'I'd like to speak with you alone
tomorrow, Mr McElwee, if that's all right with you. You
see, I've decided to change some things around here.
Starting next week, instead of serving only one entrée
for lunch or dinner, we'll have dishes for our guests to
choose from. Just like in big city restaurants.'

He nodded sombrely. 'My, yes . . . that *is* news. It will
make a good article.'

'Fine. We'll have lunch together tomorrow and I'll tell
you all about it. It will be my treat.'

'Oh!' He looked pleased. 'Thank you. Is twelve
o'clock all right?'

'Twelve o'clock it is.'

'Good morning, Mrs Hale!' a voice called out, and she
turned to face the Byrd sisters, whose cottage she and
Zaccheus had rented. They were seated in their favourite corner.

Elizabeth-Anne inclined her head. 'Good morning,
Miss Byrd.' She acknowledged the other sister by inclin-
ing her head again: 'Good morning, Miss Byrd.' For
some silly reason, she always felt she had to divide her
attention and conversation evenly between them. They
had that kind of effect on you.

480

The first sister set down her cup of tea. 'Samanth and I were wondering –'

'Don't take any heed, Mrs Hale,' the second sister said in quick apology. She glared accusingly across the table at her identical twin and wagged her spindly finger admonishingly. 'That's *not* nice, Samantha,' she said indignantly. 'You know very well that *you're* Samantha, and that *I'm* Susannah.'

'Don't listen to her, Mrs Hale,' the other sister said severely. 'Samantha is always trying to play practical jokes on people. It gets tiresome. Really it does.' The sigh of exasperation which followed sounded brittle.

Elizabeth-Anne shook her head and smiled. The dour-looking Byrd sisters were the town pranksters. Like children, they were always in good humour; unlike children, they cloaked their pranks with a veneer of righteous, tight-lipped severity. They seemingly never tired of trying to confuse people. Although Elizabeth-Anne had long learned to tell them apart, she still pretended she couldn't. 'If you don't both stop this foolishness,' she warned, 'one of these days you're going to get the wrong names on your tombstones.'

'You really think so?' they chorused in delight.

'I do.' Elizabeth-Anne nodded. Then she changed the subject smoothly. 'Is the food to your satisfaction?'

'The food?' A shocked expression of disbelief crossed one spinster's face. 'If we wanted to eat well, why, we'd cook at home! Right, Susannah?'

'Right, Samantha.'

'Aha! I caught you!' Elizabeth-Anne cried, wagging a finger. 'You've just changed identities again. A moment ago, *you* were Samantha, and *you* were Susannah.'

'Good heavens, no. *You're* the one who's confused. Isn't that right, Susannah?'

'Indeed it is, Samantha.'

Shaking her head in bemusement, Elizabeth-Anne moved on around the large room.

Dr Lusk. Dr Purris.' Elizabeth-Anne acknowledged the town's two medical men, the dentist and the doctor.

Both doctors gripped the edge of the table and started to rise, but Elizabeth-Anne quickly waved them back into their seats. 'I'm delighted to see you both here again this morning. Is everything to your satisfaction?'

'Yes, indeed,' Dr Purris said.

'Absolutely,' Dr Lusk added.

'Well, enjoy your breakfasts.' As she started to turn away, Elizabeth-Anne hesitated. *Perhaps I should ask Dr Purris to come upstairs after he finishes eating to examine Charlotte-Anne*, she thought. Then she decided against it. First, she would see for herself whether a doctor was indeed warranted. And, since Rosa believed her daughter's illness to be the result of hypochondria at best, or contrived at worst, she would sit down with Charlotte-Anne and explain to her that doctors' bills, unless absolutely necessary, were to be avoided at all costs.

'Can we be of any help, Mrs Hale?' Dr Purris asked curiously.

Elizabeth-Anne shook her head and smiled. 'Oh . . . excuse me. I was just thinking of something . . . no, everything's fine. But it's kind of you to ask . . .'

Everything was not fine, she discovered at that moment:

'Coyote Building Suppliers was sold yesterday afternoon,' someone behind her was saying. 'Tex and Jennifer dropped by the office without warning and had me draw up the papers. Didn't even send for me to come out to the ranch. Imagine.'

'Hmmm, yes. Quite out of character for them. Sold, you said?'

'Well, not really sold. The sale was just a legal formality. For some reason, Tex signed the whole kit and caboodle over to his wife. For a dollar.'

An icy dread froze Elizabeth-Anne to the spot as the words sank in. Jenny now owned Coyote Building Suppliers? Was it possible? Every muscle in her body suddenly seemed to ache. Without even looking behind her, she knew to whom the voices belonged. Eblin Keyes, the lawyer, and Jesse Atkinson, the president of Quebeck Savings and Loan. Both men were in Tex Sexton's employ.

Without moving her head she glanced numbly around the dining room. Besides Keyes and Atkinson, she still had three other people to greet. Mr Haggard, the impassive undertaker, a thin, brittle man in a black suit, and sharing a table over by the window, obviously engrossed in their conversation, Mayor Pitcock and Sheriff Parker. She knew she should go over and say a few polite, welcoming words, but she couldn't. After the bombshell she'd just overheard, her feet wouldn't move.

But they had to. It was imperative that she ride out to Coyote right away and find out what in the world was going on. At least she was now certain why Coyote continued to raise their prices so usuriously. Jenny – not Tex, but *Jenny* – was trying to drive her out of business. Knowing your enemy was supposed to be half the battle, she'd once heard said, but small comfort that knowledge brought her now. Jenny. Vindictive, vicious Jenny, whom she'd never tried to hurt, with whom she'd tried, unsuccessfully, to strike a thousand truces.

Once again, Jenny is out to get me. Will some things never change?

'Ah, good morning, Mrs Hale.' Eblin Keyes' greeting gave Elizabeth-Anne no choice but to turn around. She moved slowly, painfully drawing her face into an inscrutable mask.

No one would have believed what an effort it took. Her features were unyielding, as frozen as a starched shirt that had been left hanging out in the cold.

Her voice was faint and quivering, and sounded as if

it belonged to someone else. 'Good morning, Mr Keyes. Mr . . . Atkinson.'

Eblin Keyes smiled up at her. 'It's going to be a scorcher of a day,' he said.

'Why . . . yes,' Elizabeth-Anne said numbly. 'Err . . . excuse me . . .' She forced herself to turn back around and walk towards the hall door, her every step slow and weary.

3

By the time Elizabeth-Anne closed the dining room door quietly behind her, the initial shock was starting to wear off. Her mind slowly began to function again.

First I'll drop in on Charlotte-Anne, she decided. *Then, I'll freshen up and get changed. I've got to drive out to Coyote immediately. I can't let Jenny get the upper hand . . . not when the tourist court is at stake.*

The room Charlotte-Anne shared with her sisters was the largest bedroom on the top floor of the café building. The floor and walls were narrow vertical planking painted white. There were three iron bedsteads in the room, a large table, and three straight-backed chairs. There was enough space between the beds to have bedside cabinets between them, and against the opposite wall stood three wardrobes. In front of the windows, livened with red-checked curtains, was a dresser with an oval mirror and a low bookcase filled with second-hand volumes. Elizabeth-Anne was a great believer in education, self-education as well as what was taught in school: the books were nearly all non-fiction.

Charlotte-Anne, clad in her nightgown, was sitting up in her bed with several pillows propped behind her back. As soon as she heard Elizabeth-Anne's footsteps out in the hall, she snapped shut the copy of *Pride and Prejudice* which she'd borrowed from one of her school-mates, pushed it under the pillows, and laid back, pulling the sheet up over her.

She heard her mother knocking softly on the door.

'Is that you, Mama?' she called out weakly, clasping one hand into a fist and coughing delicately into it.

'Yes, it's me.' Elizabeth-Anne opened the door a crack and peered into the room.

Charlotte-Anne looked up and smiled bleakly. 'Morning, Mama,' she said between coughs.

'Morning, Charlotte-Anne.' Elizabeth-Anne marched briskly into the room and pulled aside the curtains. 'It's stuffy enough in here without cutting off the fresh air,' she said severely.

'Yes, Mama,' Charlotte-Anne replied in a weak voice.

Elizabeth-Anne sat down on the edge of the bed and looked at her daughter. Charlotte-Anne was the middle child, and of the three, had been the most difficult to deliver. Her hair was the typical Hale trademark, a rich, ripe shade of wheat, but incredibly fine and silky. She was tall for her age, and very slender, with pale flawless skin, pale pink lips, and another Hale trademark, aquamarine eyes, though this particular shade of aquamarine was so incredibly pale it both enchanted and made one feel ill at ease at the same time. They were eyes that seemed to pierce right through you, they were that startling. Yet the pale hair, pale complexion, and pale eyes gave Charlotte-Anne a peculiar beauty Elizabeth-Anne had never before seen in anyone.

She laid a hand flatly against Charlotte-Anne's forehead. It felt neither hot nor cold. She had no fever, that much was clear. 'Rebecca tells me you're not feeling well,' she said.

'No, Mama, I'm not.'

'Is there anything particular you think is wrong with you?'

485

Charlotte-Anne's face was bland. 'Nooo . . . it's just that I feel real weak.'

'Well, you don't have any fever.' Elizabeth-Anne sighed and clasped her hands in her lap. 'Perhaps we should take you to see Dr Purris?'

'Oh no, Mama. It's nothing serious. I'm positive.'

'But you're feeling under the weather so often. That's just not natural for a healthy young lady.'

Charlotte-Anne's eyes dropped. 'I know . . .' She bit down on her lip.

'Charlotte-Anne?'

Charlotte-Anne's pale eyes looked up.

Elizabeth-Anne took a deep breath. 'I don't think I need to tell you that these bouts of illness you're complaining about are cropping up quite often. It worries me. Also, we don't have money to throw away frivolously on doctor's bills. We're very strapped right now.'

Charlotte-Anne nodded. 'I know that.'

'Are you certain you're not feeling well?' Elizabeth-Anne watched Charlotte-Anne's reaction closely. 'I hate to think you're trying to shirk your chores.'

Charlotte-Anne turned away. 'You've been listening to Rosa!' she accused bitterly.

'Yes, I have,' Elizabeth-Anne nodded. 'I don't think I need to tell you we can't afford dillydallying around here. Everyone has to pull his own share. It hurts me to have to do this, but from today on, each morning you feel unwell, you shall stay in this room until the next morning. You shall not go to school, meet any of your friends, or go anywhere except to the toilet when you have to. I know it's severe, but if you're ill, you shall have to remain quietly in bed. Do I make myself clear?'

Charlotte-Anne nodded and broke out coughing. 'Yes, Mama,' she said glumly. 'I'm being punished for being ill.'

Elizabeth-Anne shook her head. 'No, you're not. But if you're indeed ill, you shall need all the rest you can get.' She paused. 'I really don't think it's fair to your sisters to have to pull their own weight *and* yours so often. Do you?'

'Does this mean I have to stay in this room all day?'

'It does.' Elizabeth-Anne got to her feet. 'Now, I have a lot of errands I must run today.' She bent down and kissed Charlotte-Anne on the forehead. 'Good-bye, dear.'

'Bye, Mama.'

Charlotte-Anne watched her mother leave. As soon as the door closed behind her, she sat forwards and stuck out her tongue. Then she dropped back on the pillows. She was seething with anger.

I'm being punished, she thought with fury. *That's the only word for it. And why? Because I'm ill. Well, it isn't far from the truth. Getting up before the crack of dawn and preparing things for other people's breakfasts, just like having to wash other people's filthy lunch and supper dishes, is disgusting. It's a dirty business, and I'm sick and tired of it.*

I'm not anybody's servant.

Now, confined to her room, she suddenly didn't even feel like reading any more. The day was ruined.

She reached under her pillow for the book and flung it across the room.

'*That blasted Rosa!*' she yelled.

4

The stifling, dry Texas heat sat broodingly atop the flat arid landscape. Even though she had put up the top of the buggy and sat in the shade, Elizabeth-Anne's clothes clung wetly to her body.

She did not like being caught outdoors in the daytime heat. As a rule, she tried her best to avoid it, but today a second, more pressing rule took precedence: never put off any urgent – *nasty* – business. Take care of it immediately, and get it out of the way.

Coyote Building Suppliers was situated about five miles southeast of Quebeck, right next to the completed stretch of new highway. Elizabeth-Anne's eyes clouded over. The new highway only served as more evidence of Tex Sexton's power. He would possess enough influence to have changed the course of the highway so that it passed directly in front of his thriving building supply business.

In front of the large warehouses was a huge parking lot, suspiciously newly paved with asphalt identical to the new highway, and facing the highway was a huge billboard painted to look like a coyote. Beneath the coyote was the legend:

COYOTE BUILDING SUPPLIERS

And under that:

General Contractors and Suppliers

Elizabeth-Anne turned the buggy into the parking lot and slowed down. Quite a lot of trucks and cars were parked there. Horse-drawn wagons and buggies like hers were getting rarer and rarer. She nodded to herself, noticing Ross Sullins' black Model T Ford parked in the shade. Ross Sullins was the manager of Coyote – another of Sexton's many minions.

Elizabeth-Anne pulled in on the reins, and as soon as Bessie came to a halt, carefully climbed down from the buggy. She reached into her pocket, produced a lump of sugar, and fed it to the mare. While it chewed contentedly, she flipped the reins expertly over a post. Then, compressing her lips, she glanced down and quickly smoothed her grey maternity dress with the palms of both hands. She adjusted her hat, inhaled another deep breath to stifle the chill trepidation that, despite the white-hot heat, she felt coursing through her whenever she had to deal with any of the Sexton-owned businesses, and without further ado strode briskly towards the office of Coyote Building Suppliers. From the sheds out back, the high-pitched screeches of saws set her teeth on edge.

She entered the office through the open door. It was dim inside and it took her eyes a moment to adjust. Although the windows were open, it was even hotter in here than it was outside. She could feel herself breaking out anew with perspiration and fanned herself briskly with the sheaf of thin yellow papers she carried. A large, angry horsefly dive-bombed circles around her. She spun around, waving it away; it found the door and buzzed back outside.

Ross Sullins was hunched over behind his scarred rolltop desk. He was a big unshaven man with shifty gimlet eyes, oily skin, and a large, pointed nose. Elizabeth-Anne had never seen him without a match stuck between his teeth.

When he heard the crinkle of her paper, he craned his neck and peered over the top of the desk.

She said, 'Mr Sullins, could I have a word with you, please?'

With a sigh, he reluctantly scraped back his chair, got to his feet and came slowly around from behind his desk. 'What you want?' He was looking hard at her, the match bobbing around in his mouth.

Without speaking, Elizabeth-Anne thrust out the sheaf of yellow invoices Carlos Cortez had given her this morning. He glanced at her, then took them and flipped negligently through them. He squinted and passed them right back to her. 'Ever'thing's in order, it seems to me.'

Elizabeth-Anne forced herself to keep her temper in check. 'Perhaps it does to you, Mr Sullins,' she said quietly, 'but it doesn't to me. Would you care to look at these invoices again and explain to me just why the

489

prices listed are what they are? It seems to me that they've skyrocketed again.'

'Overheads, ma'am. 'Sides, prices always go up. Lumber's gettin' more expensive ever' day. So's bricks and mortar. Wouldn't a happened if you'd ordered ever'-thing at once.'

She stared at him. 'If I need to jolt your memory, Mr Sullins, we *did* order everything at once. It was you yourself who kept telling me — repeatedly — that you were out of stock, and that I'd have to wait until you restocked. Each time I ordered a truckload, it was the same old story. Only a partial order would be delivered.'

Ross Sullins worked the match around from the left side of his mouth to the right. 'We do a lot of business,' he said vaguely.

'Certainly you do,' she said softly, 'but I'm no fool, Mr Sullins. My eyes don't deceive me. I can tell when your warehouses are fully stocked.'

'We always got lotsa stuff on hold for people,' he said evasively. 'You know, stuff they had on order, waitin' to be picked up or delivered.' He looked even harder at her. 'You're not tryin' to suggest we're out to cheat you?'

'I never said that, but it's interesting that you should bring it up.' Elizabeth-Anne paused. 'Don't get me wrong. I don't mind paying for what I buy. That's the way the world is run. By money — and supply and demand. What I do mind, however, is highway robbery. In all its ugly facets.'

He grinned. His two bottom front teeth were missing. 'Ever'thing's in order. Now, I got a lot of work to do —'

Without warning she brought her fist crashing down on the top of his desk. 'Do not dismiss me so lightly! I'm *not* one of your illiterate customers. I can read, write, and do arithmetic as well as you can . . . and probably better. When prices are raised by a hundred and fifty per cent in a little over nine months — that's *robbery*! Anybody knows that.'

'Maybe you'd best talk to Mr Sexton. All I do is take his orders. They all come from him.'

'And I suppose it was *he* who told you to raise the prices of everything I buy?'

'Hey, now look here –'

'No, *you* look here, *Mr* Sullins.' She pronounced each syllable distinctly. 'I am only too aware that your customers do not all pay the same prices for the same items. Coyote, it seems, bills their clients on a sliding scale.'

He shrugged. 'What gave you that idea?'

'Let's just say that a little bird whispered it in my ear.' She narrowed her eyes. 'I don't like being played for a fool, Mr Sullins.' Then she laughed softly. 'Well, I guess it was bound to happen to both of us.'

'Huh?' He eyed her suspiciously. 'What's happened to both of us?'

'Mr Sullins. Did you know that my Mexican labourers refuse to take orders from me?' she asked chidingly. 'For everything I want done, I first have to go through my foreman, Carlos Cortez.' She shook her head. 'Can you believe it? The men think it's unmanly for them to take orders from me, because I'm a woman.'

He chuckled. 'Well, I can't say I blame 'em. It ain't natural, somehow. Even for a Mex.'

'Mr Sullins.' The corners of Elizabeth-Anne's lips curled downwards in disdain. 'Your orders no longer come from Mr Sexton. Perhaps you weren't informed about it yet, but Mr Sexton sold Coyote Building Suppliers.'

Sullins couldn't help showing his surprise. 'He . . . did?'

'He did.' She nodded, folded the yellow invoices with slow deliberation, then ran her fingernail slowly along the crease. She eyed him significantly. 'How does it feel to be doing what every Mexican refuses to do?' she asked softly.

491

His eyes pinched nearly shut. 'What're you talkin' about?'

Elizabeth-Anne couldn't help feeling satisfaction at the look of annoyance which crossed his face. She said, 'Your boss, Mr Sullins, is now a woman.'

'What?' The match actually fell out of his mouth.

'Yes. You heard me correctly. This company was sold to *Mrs* Sexton. She's now your boss.' Elizabeth-Anne tucked the invoices into her purse. 'Well, it seems I've taken up enough of your time. Since we can't come to terms, I'm going to have to try and sort this out with your new employer. You see, Mr Sullins? You, too, have been played for a fool. I suppose it's between us women now.'

And with that she walked out of his office, leaving him standing there, stupefied, his mouth hanging open. She didn't look back, and it was just as well: Ross Sullins slowly bent over, retrieved his match from the dirty floor, and stuck it back in his mouth.

When she reached her buggy, she untied the reins and glanced up at the sky. The sun was rising steadily to its noonday height. It would soon be ten o'clock. The hottest part of the day was upon her. Yet she couldn't dawdle . . . couldn't take a siesta and wait for the cool, late afternoon.

She had an appointment with someone she didn't relish seeing.

She climbed heavily up on her buggy and snapped the reins. She had no choice . . . none at all. All along, she had been filled with the dread feeling that she'd have to head out to the Sexton ranch to have a talk with Tex. That would have been bad enough, but since this morning, things had changed. She could have reasoned with Tex much better than with his wife, of that she was certain.

Well, there was little comfort in it, but at least she now knew with certainty what was up.

Jennifer had decided to drive her out of business.

To ruin her once and for all.

Some things hadn't changed over the years, Elizabeth-Anne thought grimly. She'd tried to stay well out of Jenny's way. But Jenny had obviously just been biding her time.

Now she would have to come face-to-face with her.

It was something she could well do without.

5

The entrance to the Sexton Ranch was so conspicuous no one but a blind man could have missed it. The road leading into it was flanked by tall wooden poles, and a huge overhead sign arched across them. THE GOLDEN S RANCH, the huge letters burned into the wood proclaimed proudly, and to either side of them was hammered a king-size, gold-tone horseshoe intertwined with the letter S. Two other prominent signs, one on either side of the entrance, warned:

PRIVATE PROPERTY
NO TRESPASSING. NO HUNTING. NO
SOLICITING.
VIOLATORS WILL BE PROSECUTED TO
THE FULLEST EXTENT OF THE LAW

And smaller letters read:

CAUTION:
ARMED GUARDS
GUARD DOGS

IF MAKING DELIVERIES
DO NOT STRAY FROM ROAD

Elizabeth-Anne pulled on the reins and slowly turned Bessie into the private road.

She pressed her lips grimly together, vaguely wondering if she would be considered a tresspasser. It wouldn't surprise her in the least.

Flocks of blackbirds heard her approach and burst out of the scrub fields. Mockingbirds chattered obscenely from an occasional tree. Overhead, a lone hawk banked slowly, intent on small prey, and somewhere in the far distance, a mere speck in the powder blue sky, a vulture did its lazy, patient circling. Something wounded lay out there, something dying, and the vulture waited for its death throes to pounce on the unfortunate creature. Like the Sextons, who owned this land.

For the better part of a mile, the property was simply a monotonous terrain of flat, dusty scrubland. Then, suddenly on her left, was an endless expanse of surprisingly lush green ranchland, fenced off from the road by miles of barbed wire. The lushness was owed to the miriads of tall windmills on derricks which turned lazily in the hot breeze. Herds of grazing cattle – Brahman, Charolais, and Black Angus – roamed contentedly in the heat shimmer, swatting away flies with lazy flicks of their tails. To the right, the land had become slightly more hilly, and had been laid out in precise, geometrical citrus groves. The trees were startlingly green after the expanse of scrubland, and fruit hung on them in rich yellow and orange clusters. Mexican labourers were swarming through the groves, picking the fruit and emptying it into bushel baskets for ten cents an hour. The citrus scent was fragrant, strong, and clean.

Sexton country, Elizabeth-Anne thought to herself. She had never been here before, but she had heard enough to know what to expect. The ranch was comprised of sixty thousand sprawling acres. There was the gently rolling, fertile grassland, the lushly planted green citrus orchards, thanks to the complex irrigation network which directed water from the Rio Grande basin, and the hundreds of windmills and artesian wells which forced it up from deep beneath the ground. From what she could see, the Sextons had doubtlessly worked miracles. If they hadn't derived so much of their wealth through oppression and underhanded dealings, through stomping out the competition and driving smaller landowners out of business, through carefully planned, usurious loans made with the sole intent of repossession – if it weren't for the evil ways they had gained their wealth, Elizabeth-Anne would have allowed herself to be impressed.

Another two miles, and the barbed wire fence turned into miles of white wooden slat fences. Behind it, herds of horses galloped and roamed.

Horse breeding was another of the many profitable Sexton sidelines.

And then, finally, on a sloping rise, she could see the house.

It was huge and white and rambling, and gave the impression of being somewhat low because it was so long; it had obviously been added onto many times whenever more space was needed or desired. The central part of the building was two storeys high, a glistening, white wood structure with tall, simple square pillars supporting the verandah, and a cupola, with a weathervane on its peak, crowning the roof.

This central-most portion of the building was flanked on both ends by large, identical one-storeyed wings with steeply pitched black roofs sprouting dormers, and even lower, longer additions had been added onto those.

It was the most stunningly symmetrical house Elizabeth-Anne had ever laid eyes on. As she neared it, she could see that the windows were graced by wooden shutters painted green, which gave the house the impression that it was situated in a far more verdant setting than it actually was. But the shutters were not merely cosmetic; at the height of the noonday heat, they could be pulled closed to keep the insides of the house cool.

A few hundred yards from the house, the dirt road gave way to an elegant gravel driveway which completely encircled the most precious status symbol of them all – a manmade lake of approximately a square acre in size, with a small island, which boasted its own small dock for rowing boats, in the middle. The water was placid and green, and lent more than just a vision of coolness; Elizabeth-Anne swore that as she approached it, the air around the lake seemed decidedly more moist and humid than the normal dry, oven-like Texas furnace. And, as if this was not enough, the island boasted a single huge, luxuriant weeping willow which had been transported there and planted while nearly full-grown.

That most water-loving of trees was, ultimately, even more than the tens of thousands of acres, the rambling mansion, and the cooling lake, the single most potent and frightening symbol of Sexton power that Elizabeth-Anne had encountered to date. Whatever a Sexton wished for, it seemed to state emphatically, a Sexton got.

Other people dreamed, but Sexton dreams had a tendency to become reality.

As the driveway progressed towards the ranch house, Elizabeth-Anne noticed a profusion of shrubs and flowers. Wagging tongues had it that Jennifer Sue Sexton employed three full-time gardeners; now, Elizabeth-Anne understood the necessity for them.

Without warning, four madly baying dogs suddenly came running from somewhere around the corner of the distant house. Bessie immediately began to whinny and rear. Elizabeth-Anne, herself stiffening perceptibly, fought to remain calm and brought the mare under control.

She couldn't blame her horse for wanting to get out of there. For an instant, she was tempted to flee too. The dogs were big black-and-grey brutes, and they seemed to run as heavily as horses, their huge paws throwing up clumps of gravel. They raised their heads and lifted their black lips to show long, lethal fangs; rumbling growls resounded deeply from the depths of their broad chests. She relaxed somewhat when they fell in, two on each side of the buggy, and paced themselves, trotting along beside it.

The moment Elizabeth-Anne pulled the mare to a halt in front of the rambling, symmetrical house, a lanky ranch hand clad in blue jeans, Stetson, plaid shirt, and buffed brown boots, ambled along the verandah with a rolling, bowlegged walk. He leaned lazily against one of the dazzlingly white porch pillars, eyeing her through squinted, sun-crinkled eyes, his leathery face tilted sideways.

'Please step down off yer buggy slowly, ma'am,' he called laconically in a dry, gravelly voice, the thumbs of both hands tucked into his hand-tooled belt.

Elizabeth-Anne cast a worried glance down at the prowling dogs.

He said, 'They's all right, long as you don't make no sudden moves.'

'I'll try to bear that in mind,' she said tightly. She got very carefully down off the buggy and winced as the dogs moved in to sniff her. After a moment, the ranch hand placed two fingers between his lips and let out a long loud whistle.

Immediately, the dogs went galloping off, tails wagging.

Elizabeth-Anne breathed decidedly easier.

'Now they smelled you, they won't bother you none, ma'am,' the ranch hand said.

She nodded and began to tether Bessie to the porch railing.

497

'Ma'am?'

She looked up. 'Yes?'

'Deliveries is taken in the back.'

Elizabeth-Anne flipped the reins over the railing one last time and turned to him, her chin raised. 'I am not here to deliver anything.'

With a practised jerk of a thumb, he pushed his Stetson back on his head. 'What you here fer, then?'

'To see Mr Sexton on a business matter.'

He nodded, apparently satisfied. 'Wouldn't know nothin' 'bout that. He ain't here noways.' He turned his head and let fly a squirt of chewing tobacco. 'Reckon he won't be back fer a good hour or so.'

She smiled thinly. 'Then I suppose I'll have to wait.'

He shrugged. 'Suit yerself, ma'am. I'll have one of the hands go water yer mare, if you like.'

'I'd appreciate that.'

'Just go on in the house. Gal name of Rosita'll take care of you in the meantime. Tell her Jim Bob said it was okay.'

Elizabeth-Anne nodded and smiled her thanks. She reached into her pocket for a lump of sugar and fed it to Bessie. She patted her neck, and then turned and stepped up on the verandah. It was perceptibly cooler there than it had been out in the sun.

As soon as Elizabeth-Anne reached the big front door, it was opened from the inside. A Mexican maid dropped a polite little curtsy. She was in her twenties, with sparkling black eyes and dusky brown skin. She wore a plain black dress that reached midway to her calves; the collar was edged with tiny scallops of lace. She looked at Elizabeth-Anne questioningly.

'Are you Rosita?' Elizabeth-Anne asked.

The young woman nodded.

Elizabeth-Anne smiled. 'Jim Bob said I should see you about waiting for Mr Sexton.' And she offered up a quick, silent prayer: *Please, Lord, don't make it necessary for me to run into Jenny.*

'Mr Sexton be back later. You wait in his study, Miss,' Rosita said. 'This way, please.'

She was led from the front hall to the far end of one of the added-on wings. The walk seemed endless.

Finally, Rosita paused in front of a door. 'Wait in here, please, Miss,' she said, opening it. Then she dropped another quick curtsy and retreated.

Elizabeth-Anne was delighted with the unexpected opportunity of being able to roam alone around Tex Sexton's study. Nothing else gave away a man's character, both his weaknesses and his strengths, as the clues which could be found in the room he felt most comfortable in.

She walked around slowly, hands clasped behind her, as she inspected the study. It was beyond any shadow of a doubt a man's room; the air smelled faintly of leather and cigar smoke. The ceiling overhead was constructed of blackened wooden beams. The floor was crafted of gleaming vertical boards of dark-stained pine, and scattered casually about on it were geometric Mexican and Indian area rugs of intense colour and subtle beauty. Above the brick fireplace set in a herringbone pattern hung the only painting in the room. It was a large, splendid Remington oil painted in rich tones of golds, reds, and oranges. It depicted two mounted cowboys lassoing a steer which had crashed down onto its forelegs. It was at once a powerful, provocative, and beautiful picture, full of dazzling light and movement. Gazing at it, Elizabeth-Anne could almost hear the bellowing of the steer, the trampling thunder of the horses' hooves on the hard-packed ground, and the swishing sound of the lasso sailing through the air.

She looked around. Overall, everything about the room bespoke of a man to be reckoned with.

She was about to sink into a leather couch when she

noticed the silver-framed photograph on the desk. She reached past the big hand-tooled blotter and picked it up. She studied the photograph closely. It was Jenny, and she had one leg propped up on a fence rail, one hand on her hip, her cowgirl hat hanging from behind her neck. A cool smile was captured on her lips.

Pursing her lips, Elizabeth-Anne studied the picture thoughtfully. This wasn't the same Jenny she had known. Certainly, the basic features were the same. But Jennifer Sue Sexton was not the Jennifer Sue Clowney of her memory. *This* Jenny held herself with poised self-assurance . . . with the aloof confidence which only great wealth can provide. She had to admit to herself that, even if Jenny's features were rather hard, she *had* turned into a rather striking, coldly chiselled beauty.

She heard squeals of delight drifting in from outside. Quickly, she set the picture back down and drew close to the window. She stood there looking out, a ghost of a smile playing across her lips.

A little boy astride a pony was being walked around a paddock by a ranch hand, the child wearing an adult's Western hat; it came down to almost his nose.

Elizabeth-Anne watched for a while. She was almost certain that this was Ross, Tex and Jenny's child, the one which Auntie had tried so hard – and unsuccessfully – to see.

Suddenly the little boy wanted to ride faster, and the beautiful tableau was shattered. The ranch hand kept holding the pony back, and the boy yanked his hat off and began beating him with it. His lips were angry and his eyes flashed petulant, childlike hatred. 'Tom, you damn idiot!' he screeched. 'Can't you see I wanna go faster?'

The ranch hand leading the pony ignored him, but Elizabeth-Anne felt a chill settling over her; it was as if a dark cloud had suddenly obscured the sunshine. What she had just witnessed was a parody – both of expression and voice – of Jenny, right down to the protruding lips. Clearly, the child was taking after his mother. It was such a pity, for he was a lovely, angelic child to behold. Yet when he spewed forth his hatred, he was transformed into something spiteful and . . . yes, monstrous.

Quickly, Elizabeth-Anne turned away from the window.

And a sudden vice gripped hold of her ribs, applying so much tight pressure that she thought her bones would break. She had not heard the door opening. Nor did she know for how long she had been observed.

For standing in the doorway, in a wide-legged stance, her slender, tapered hands resting on her hips, and a brushed-suède ranch hat atop her head, was Jennifer Sue Sexton.

'Well, well, well,' Jenny said with a sardonic smile. 'Just look what the cat dragged in!'

6

Time seemed to slow, then stop entirely.

The unexpected sight of Jenny caused Elizabeth-Anne to experience that peculiar, prickly sensation of her hackles rising, that tingling whisper of a thousand tiny nerve ends bristling from the back of her neck to the top of her head. She had experienced that exact same reaction two weeks earlier at the construction site, when she'd nearly blundered into a rattlesnake.

For a long time the two women stood with their eyes locked, neither of them breaking the silence.

It was a silent test of wills.

Finally, Jenny ambled forwards with deliberate laziness, her fingers still casually poised on her hips. Her head was tilted at an oblique sideways angle, and her eyes, that peculiar colour of a robin's egg, made a slow, sweeping, head-to-toe inspection of Elizabeth-Anne.

Elizabeth-Anne stiffened, her arms held awkwardly at her sides, her fists tightly clenched. She kept her chin raised as she returned Jenny's stare, her own pale aqua-marine eyes making less of a production but inspecting the other woman cautiously, and with no less interest.

The photograph on the desk had been flattering to Jenny, Elizabeth-Anne could see that now. Over the years, Jenny's blue eyes and pale lips had hardened, and her skin was tanned and turning leathery from too much time spent out in the sun. But it would not be true to say that some things never changed. They did – and for the worse. The cruel, calculating glints which flashed in Jenny's eyes had become, if anything, only more pronounced than they had been when she was a child.

Complexion aside, the outdoors seemed to suit her. She held her back straight, her legs were lithe and shapely from exercise, and her waist was narrower than Elizabeth-Anne had remembered, its slimness accentu-ated by the silver Mexican conch belt which matched the silver-sheathed tips of her emerald-green string tie. She had on snug whipcord trousers which were tucked into hand-made, six-stitch boots. A plaid, pearl-but-toned workshirt. And the sand-coloured cowgirl hat which was far from ordinary: the hatband encircling the crown was made of pavé diamonds interspersed at intervals with square-cut emeralds the size of a thumb-nail.

Faced with all that expensive glamour and cool self-assurance, Elizabeth-Anne felt peculiarly homely. Sud-denly she was all too self-conscious of her grey maternity outfit and her sensible lace-up boots which needed new soles so badly.

It was Jenny who broke the silence. 'Do you remember that day we blindfolded you and tore your gloves off?' She regarded Elizabeth-Anne closely.

Elizabeth-Anne looked at her steadily, her eyes unwavering. 'It was a cruel, childish prank,' she said with stiff dignity.

'Was it?' Jenny laughed again, and her voice grew stridently penetrating. 'We all thought it was very funny.' She looked suddenly pleased. 'It was my idea, you know.'

'That thought had crossed my mind at the time.'

Jenny's eyes narrowed. 'You didn't accuse me of it when it happened.'

'Why should I have?' Elizabeth-Anne held up her hands. 'It wouldn't have done me any good. You would only have thought up ten more ways to get back at me. Early on, I discovered that it was far easier to keep quiet and stay out of your way than try to fight you on your own terms.'

'Is that what you've been doing by avoiding me all these years?'

Elizabeth-Anne did not reply. All she could think of was in what a ludicrous direction this conversation was headed, and how childish it all sounded now. How long could grudges be held? Other people embraced after such long absences. But not Jenny. Oh no. She honed in swiftly, her every word a sharp razor making another deep slash, opening one wound on top of another, slashing with frenzied indiscriminance until she drew as much blood as her victim had in him.

There was a subdued knock at the door and then it opened and Rosita scurried in, carrying a single tall, icy glass of lemonade on a silver salver. The maid flushed with embarrassment and studiously avoided looking at Elizabeth-Anne.

Jenny reached for the lemonade and sipped slowly, holding her little finger away from the glass and glancing at Elizabeth-Anne over the rim, her eyes registering juvenile satisfaction.

Elizabeth-Anne allowed no expression to show on her face. The drive out here to the ranch had been a long and hot one. Her throat felt parched – especially parched now that Jenny was pointedly drinking cool lemonade in front of her.

I won't let myself get angry, Elizabeth-Anne told herself firmly. *So what if my horse is watered and I thirst? The horse is a far more important priority; it has to pull the buggy and drive me back to Quebeck. There will be time enough to quench my thirst later.*

She took a deep breath. 'The reason I came here,' she began succinctly, 'is to –'

'Always to the point, aren't you?' Jenny interrupted irritably. 'Just like Auntie. Never wasting any time or mincing words.'

'I find it cuts down on problems. Besides, time is precious. I'm a busy woman.'

Jenny leered at her. 'I don't know how *busy* you are, but you certainly are a *quick* and *slippery* woman. Let me see . . .' She tapped her lips thoughtfully and paced the room slowly. 'Yes, you've been more than busy. Not one to waste time by any means. In the time you can say Jack Robinson, you ended up with Auntie's rooming house *and* the café. You stole Zaccheus away from me. But then, I should thank you for that, I suppose, seeing as how he's a murderer.'

'He is *not* a murderer! Roy's death was an accident!'

'Then why didn't he stay and face the music?' Jenny smirked.

'You know very well that Zaccheus would have been sentenced to death by a Sexton-controlled court if he had stayed here. Because of you, I'll never see him again. His children will grow up without a father.'

'How *too* sad for that litter of little bitches you've dropped!' Jenny smiled triumphantly and then pointedly looked Elizabeth-Anne up and down. 'Now I see you're going to drop another little bitch.'

'If you insist on referring to my children as a *litter*,' Elizabeth-Anne said haughtily, 'I might point out that you've *dropped*, as you put it, one of your own.'

'Oh, yes!' Jenny said. 'I have a child, a *beautiful* child. A boy of Tex Sexton's . . . a child with a brilliant future. He won't want for anything.'

'Mine do not want for anything, either,' Elizabeth-Anne countered with dignity. 'Perhaps we should both count ourselves lucky.'

'Ah.' Jenny smiled. 'But you're not lucky.'

'What do you mean?'

'Oh, I don't know.' Jenny shrugged vaguely and took another sip of lemonade. 'What do *you* think I mean?'

'To be truthful, I haven't the foggiest.'

'You should, Mrs Construction Engineer, owner of Quebeck's first tourist court. You think you're the only woman around here who does anything, don't you?'

'Nooo . . . I don't. In fact, I should welcome you to the small, exclusive ranks of America's businesswomen. Coyote is quite an impressive business, if I say so myself. Of course, even I would have been able to afford to buy it for a dollar. Even the poorest Mexican urchin could have come up with *that* amount of money. So I can't really say I'm impressed with the way you acquired it.'

Jenny leaned close towards her. 'How did you find out about it, anyway?'

Elizabeth-Anne smiled. 'Let's just say the walls have ears. Anyway, while we're on the subject of Coyote, that's exactly what I came here to discuss with you. I suppose it's you I should see about my invoice problems.'

'What's there to talk about?'

'What's there to talk about!'

'What are you? A parrot?'

505

'Jenny, those bills are all wrong, and I think you know it.'

Jenny tossed her head. 'I don't concern myself with the day-to-day operations of Coyote. We have hired people to do that. Speak to the manager.'

'I did.'

'Then the problem should be settled.'

'It isn't, Jenny.'

'First of all, let's get one thing straight. I'm not Jenny to you, despite the unfortunate fact that we grew up together in the same house. I'm Mrs Tex Sexton.'

Elizabeth-Anne tightened her lips. 'So be it, *Mrs* Tex Sexton.'

'That's better.' Jenny's eyes flashed with satisfaction. 'Now, *Mrs* Zaccheus Hale,' she said magnanimously. 'What favours have you come to petition me about?'

'I'm not petitioning you. I've come to discuss a business problem. These, in particular.' Elizabeth-Anne produced the sheaf of invoices from her purse and held them out, but Jenny refused to take them. 'You're not delivering according to orders, and you're constantly raising prices on me.'

'If you don't like it, take your business elsewhere.'

Elizabeth-Anne laughed bitterly. 'There isn't elsewhere, and you know it. You Sextons have bankrupted all the competition.'

'Business is business. It's not my fault if you go overboard and buy what you cannot afford. Perhaps you should take a simple course in economics.'

Elizabeth-Anne was silent.

'If I were you, *Mrs* Hale, do you know what I would do?'

'Tell me, please,' Elizabeth-Anne said with a sigh. 'I have the feeling you will anyway, whether I wish to know or not.'

'If I were you,' Jenny said slowly, 'I would be content with what I have. I wouldn't become so . . . ah . . .

visible. I would stop what I was doing, cut my losses, and be content with the way things are.'

Elizabeth-Anne frowned. 'I don't think I understand.'

Jenny's eyes flashed. 'It's simple, really. What I'm trying to tell you is . . . don't get too big for your britches. Don't get *too* ambitious. This isn't the time or the place.'

Elizabeth-Anne bristled suddenly. 'Are you threatening me?' she asked coldly. She stared at Jenny, her gaze level.

'Good heavens, no!' Jenny laughed artlessly. 'I just want to make sure you don't make a mistake, is all. It's so easy to get into a financial jam when you set your sights too high. Why, even I have to be careful!'

'You?' Elizabeth-Anne laughed shortly.

'Oh yes, indeed,' Jenny said smugly. 'You see, I've just begun a new business. I registered it at the courthouse only yesterday afternoon. Judge Hawk was *so* helpful. *Jennifer S. Mineral Excavations, Inc.* is what I'm calling it. Tex thinks I'm biting off more than I can chew, but I don't think so. My feeling is that you can never be too diversified.' She smiled. 'But enough about me. It's you I'm worried about. You see, the trick is that you've got to be able to *afford* what you're doing.'

Elizabeth-Anne wondered why Jenny was telling her all this. 'All I can do is wish you good luck,' she said stiffly, 'though I hardly think you'll need it. I'm sure you'll succeed.'

Jenny's face held a sphinx-like expression. 'You are my luck, so why shouldn't I succeed?' she asked, suddenly speaking in riddles.

Elizabeth-Anne looked at her quizzically. Obviously, it was high time she steered the conversation back on course. 'About these bills, Mrs Sexton.'

'Mrs *Tex* Sexton.'

'Mrs . . .' Elizabeth-Anne sighed heavily '. . . Tex Sexton.'

'Those bills are correct. I checked them out myself the day before yesterday.' Jenny took off her hat and twirled it on her index finger, watching the emeralds and diamonds flash as they spun around, a glittering whirling dervish. She kept the hat balanced so proficiently that it was obvious she had practiced that little act to perfection.

Elizabeth-Anne folded the invoices. 'I suppose,' she said, 'it's meaningless to say that if they're not corrected I may find it necessary to take you to court?'

'You'd be wasting your time and money. Judge Hawk has been in our pockets for years now.'

Elizabeth-Anne let out a deep breath. 'You wouldn't, by any chance, be trying to drive me out of business, would you?' She eyed Jenny narrowly.

'Who? *Me*?' The twirling hat came to a rest; Jenny's look of surprised innocence was patently faked.

'I can't think of anybody else who would try such underhanded dealings. Can you?'

'Watch yourself,' Jenny growled in a low warning voice. 'If I want, I can squash you as easily as a bug, anytime I please.' Her pert nose wrinkled disdainfully. 'I don't need to be insulted by you, you goddamn freak.'

'I'm sorry to have to say this, *Jennifer*,' Elizabeth-Anne said with pointed iciness, 'but Auntie was right.'

'Oh? In what way?'

'She confided in me once that she was afraid you were not quite right, if you know what I mean. You harbour grudges and slights which should long have been forgotten. And both Auntie and I knew full and well why you married your husband.'

'And pray tell, why?'

'To get back at us,' Elizabeth-Anne said with unruffled calm. 'At Auntie. At Zaccheus. And me. You don't love Tex. You never have. You're in love with his money and his power. I wonder if he knows that?'

Elizabeth-Anne paused. 'How does it feel to sell oneself?'

'Get out of here!' Jenny's voice was a low, rasping whisper. 'Get out of here and never darken my door again! Do you hear me?'

Elizabeth-Anne shrugged wordlessly.

'Well?' Jenny shrieked with ear-piercing shrillness. 'Do I have to throw you out?'

Slowly, Elizabeth-Anne walked to the door, her head held high. She grasped the wrought-iron handle and pulled it open. For a moment, she turned around and stared at Jenny.

Jenny's eyes were fiery with murderous hatred and her breasts were heaving.

'You may have won Tex,' Elizabeth-Anne said quietly, 'but you did not get Zaccheus. Nor will you always get what you want, no matter how hard you try. And I can promise you one thing. What you will get, Jennifer Sue Sexton, is everything your black heart deserves!'

Jenny let out a shriek, looked around madly with blazing eyes, and lunged at a Remington bronze. She grasped the sculpture in both hands and lifted it high.

Elizabeth-Anne shut the door just as Jenny flung it. The sculpture crashed heavily against it, splintering one of the oak panels.

Even on her way down the hall, Jenny's tirade followed Elizabeth-Anne. 'Those prices were *nothing*! *Nothing* compared with what you're going to pay, you bitch! I'll raise them five hundred per cent! A *thousand*! And that tourist court of yours? It'll rot, you freak! You wait and see! You'll never open the doors to that goddamn precious tourist court you and that bastard Zaccheus conceived! I'll see to it if it's the last thing I do!'

It doesn't matter, Elizabeth-Anne told herself over and

over as she drove off swiftly. Even if Jenny raised Coyote's prices astronomically, she could still make do . . . she would *have* to make do. She would order only what she needed. From outside, the tourist court would look complete, but she would only finish half the units on the inside, if it came to that. That would cover the usurious prices until money started to roll in from the finished units. And she could even go one better. She could buy everything else she needed in Browns-ville and have it transported up here if she had to.

There was more than one way to skin a mean cat.

But as much as she tried to calm herself, the adrenalin raced madly through her. Her heart was palpitating and her hands were shaking violently. She knew that Jenny's threat was not an idle one. And Sexton threats were not to be taken lightly. When Jenny had screamed that the tourist court would never open . . .

Elizabeth-Anne shivered suddenly, despite the heat. A deep fear gnawed in the pit of her stomach. *Don't you think about it!* she told herself over and over. *It'll be all right. Everything will turn out all right.*

She tightened her lips resolutely. She would not allow herself to be frightened. Not by Jenny. Nor by Tex. Not by *anybody*. She would show them! She would make herself an example and show everybody who ever cowered before the Sextons just how savagely one could fight back. She would not allow herself to be intimidated or defeated: she would fight tooth and nail. She would be a worthy opponent.

She would win.

She tightened her lips even more resolutely.

If Jenny thought she could take the tourist court away from her, well, then she had a major surprise coming.

But Elizabeth-Anne was the one in for a surprise. When she got back from the ranch, a visitor wearing expensively tailored city clothes and driving a brand new blue Chrysler was waiting for her at the café.

'Miss Elizabeth-Anne Gross?' he asked.

She stared at him. He was a big man, heavy-set and florid-faced. 'I . . . er . . . I'm Elizabeth-Anne Hale now,' she said. 'I haven't gone by the name Gross in . . . oh, well over thirteen years.'

'If we could, er, talk in private, ma'am?'

Her first panicked thought was: *Zaccheus! They've caught Zaccheus!*

'Are you . . . a . . . policeman?' she asked shakily.

'Good Lord, no.' The man chuckled. 'Godfrey Greenley at your service, ma'am.' He produced a calling card and handed it to her formally. 'As you can see, I'm an attorney in Brownsville.'

She looked at the engraved card. 'Then this isn't about Zaccheus?' Her relief was immense.

He frowned. 'Er . . . can't say that it is, ma'am. This concerns an . . . ahem . . . an inheritance.'

Godfrey Greenley coughed, *ahem*-ed, and *er*-ed a lot. His conversation was filled with *whereases*, *whereuntos*, and *insofar ases*.

Elizabeth-Anne had taken him upstairs to the second-floor parlour, and Rosa had brought up a pot of coffee.

Greenley sipped his and set it carefully down. He cleared his throat, rose to his feet, and paced around importantly, tucking his thumbs under the lapels of his waistcoated suit.

Elizabeth-Anne sat on the settee, feeling the baby inside her kicking as she watched him.

'I drove up in person to . . . er . . . investigate to my satisfaction that you, Miss Gross . . . er . . . Mrs Hale . . . are indeed the person I am looking for. Insofar as I have asked around, I am satisfied that you are.'

She looked up at him, her hands folded in her lap. 'You said this involves an inheritance?'

He nodded gravely. 'I did.'

'Then there must be some mistake.' She laughed softly. 'You see, Mr Greenley, there is nobody I could conceivably inherit from!'

'You *were* once known as Elizabeth-Anne Gross?'

'Yes, but there —'

'And your parents *did* die in a circus fire back in 1901?'

'Why, yes. But I don't see —'

He stopped pacing and smiled; his teeth were large and tobacco-browned. The front two were chipped. 'You're her, all right. Permit me to say, Mrs Hale, as a rule heiresses don't usually try to tell me they're not entitled to what is rightfully theirs.' He chuckled. 'If anything, once there's the smell of money, heirs, both real and fraudulent, tend to pop up all over the place!'

'But what . . .'

'It's all right here.' He took an envelope out of his breast pocket. 'Whereas I could explain it to you, this letter should clear up the . . . ah . . . mystery even quicker.'

'Yes, well, but who's it from?'

He passed it over to her. She looked at it. *Elizabeth-Anne Gross*, a laboured script read. She turned it over. It was sealed. She looked at him.

'Open it,' he said gently, producing a well-aged briar pipe and leather tobacco pouch, 'it's yours. Mind if I smoke?'

'No, no, go right ahead.' For a moment Elizabeth-Anne just held the envelope and stared at it. Godfrey Greenley busied himself pushing the shredded tobacco down into the pipe and eyed Elizabeth-Anne while he lit it. He frowned as he puffed. He couldn't imagine anyone not tearing into that envelope. From long experience, the smell of money usually turned people wild.

Sighing, she slowly tore the envelope open. The sheet

of paper inside was thin and yellowed. She unfolded it. The writing was simple and straightforward and filled with spelling errors.

Dear Elizabeth Anne Gross

By the time you read this I'll be dead and burried. You probably dont remember me or my late husband Bazzel Fritts. I'm not too proud of what we done, tryin' to pass ourselves off as your relatives all them years ago. We ain't related to you, and we got paid a tidy sum by Miz Clowney so we'd leave you with her. That woman sure did love you I could tell. Well, Bazzel and me moved on and invested that money and it's grown to a nice little nest egg. We lived quite comfortably and then Bazzel he up and died. Everything's mine now, and since I don't have no next of kin, I want you to have it. I know this is something of a surprise and all, but you was such a cute kid and I felt bad about our charging Miz Clowney to let her keep you.

God bless,
Amanda Fritts

Elizabeth-Anne's eyes were moist with tears. 'Auntie had to give them money!' she said softly. 'She never told me!'

Godfrey Greenley cleared his throat.

She looked up at him and sniffed.

'The woman who made out the will wrote that letter quite some years back,' he said. 'Does it explain everything?'

Elizabeth-Anne wiped her eyes with the back of her hand and nodded. 'Yes.' Then she cleared her throat and said, louder, 'Yes, Mr Greenley, it does.' She smiled sadly.

'Good. Then I'll just read you the will and drive back down to Brownsville and execute it.'

Elizabeth-Anne nodded absently. How strange things

513

had turned out! she thought. Money from heaven, that's what it was. And never had she needed it more.

So fate *could* dish out just as many good surprises as bad ones.

She raised her head. 'Mr Greenley? I was wondering if I could impose on you?'

'Ma'am?'

'Could I ride back to Brownsville with you? There's some . . . personal business there I'd like to take care of.'

'Of course. I'd be . . . er . . . delighted. If there's anything else you need . . .' He smiled magnanimously.

'Just the name of a good building supply company, that's all.'

'Consider it done. I'll take you there myself.'

And that was how the Hale Tourist Court was finished on time – and without any more of Coyote Building Suppliers materials. Thanks to Amanda Fritts, Elizabeth-Anne could now afford to bypass the Sextons and have everything transported from Brownsville – on the new highway. She liked to imagine that Jenny was angry as all hell. And she thought: *Well, let her be.* And couldn't help adding: *Maybe she's so mad she'll burst.*

8

It was the grand opening of the Hale Tourist Court – and a week before Elizabeth-Anne's baby was due.

As if to cooperate fully, the weather was crisp, bright, and blue. There wasn't a cloud to be seen.

On the podium, the singer wearing the black mantilla set high on the tortoiseshell comb was finishing the last, drawn-out notes of 'La Paloma'. The Mexicans hollered, clapped, and whistled, and even Quebeck's Anglos cheered and applauded enthusiastically.

The singer made a gracious sweeping bow, exchanged bows with the guitarist, blushed, and hurried down the steps to be swallowed up by a crowd of admirers. The six-man brass band sitting on the porch of the manager's cabin started up again and broke into a brassy John Philip Sousa march.

The festivities had been planned as a mixture of Anglo and Hispanic traditions. Elizabeth-Anne set great store by all men being created equal.

Everyone wore their Sunday finery, and even the completed Hale Tourist Court was dressed up for the occasion. Bright red, white, and blue bunting was draped from the little front porches of the individual cabins, and flags snapped in the breeze. In the distance, a big, rectangular billboard with a gold coronet jutting out over the top had just been unveiled. It faced the highway; HALE TOURIST COURT, the bright red block letters read, and under that, large black script letters announced: *Luxury Fit For A King — At Commoners' Prices.*

Elizabeth-Anne, dressed in a loose, brightly flowered cotton maternity dress, gazed around with a mixture of proprietary pride and aching bone-weariness. For the first time in months she seemed relaxed. Her eyes sparkled and she looked radiant.

At last — at long, long last, she thought — *it is* finished. *And it will be a success. I can feel that in my bones as surely as I can tell that this fiesta, celebrating its grand opening, is a huge success.*

Nothing succeeds like success.

She glanced towards the individual units stretching out from either side of the central manager's cabin. A long red ribbon stretched from the furthest unit on the extreme left all the way to the furthest one on the extreme right. Behind her, on the asphalt driveway which curved in from the blue-black twin lanes of the new highway, long trestle tables had been set up an were draped with white cloths. On them, platters were piled high with local delicacies. Beer and wine flowed freely for the adults, and for the young ones there were sweetened fruit juices and pinwheels and balloons. She smiled, watching children shriek and squeal as they dashed around holding aloft their twirling pinwheels, while the adults roamed between clusters of friends and neighbours. She was gratified to note that most of Quebeck and Mexican Town had turned out for the occasion. The only people who were conspicuous by their absence were the Sextons, and she was gratified to see that, too. Jenny had never wished her well. She had set up stumbling blocks every step of the way and had been at least partially responsible for Zaccheus' life being in ruins. Now that she had succeeded despite Jenny's attempts at sabotage, she was certain that Jenny was out at the ranch, seething. Which was just as well.

'Hold it, Mrs Hale!' a voice called from beside her.

She turned. Hugh McElwee from the *Quebeck Weekly Gazette* set down his tripod, ducked under the black cloth which draped the camera, and held up the flash. After it popped and a shower of sparks rained down to the ground, he ducked back out. 'Thank you, Mrs Hale. And congratulations.'

'Thank *you*, Mr McElwee,' she said, and joined the Reverend, who was standing off to one side having an earnest conversation with the young Catholic priest from Mexican Town.

'This is one of our town's finest hours,' the priest told her warmly. 'You've done more to lift the morale of Mexican Town than anyone, Mrs Hale.'

Elizabeth-Anne smiled. 'What can I say, Father? My workers were good workers. Without them, I hate to have to think where I would be.'

And she thought: *I know where I would be. I would have* The Sextons *would have triumphed again. Thank God*

I had the sense to use the Mexican labourers instead of the Sexton construction firm's.

The Sousa march came to a crescendo and Mayor Pitcock leaped up onto the podium clutching the sheet of paper on which he had written his speech. He held up his hands to silence the crowd.

Slowly everyone stopped talking and turned to face him. He smiled, adjusted his tie importantly, and twisted his neck as if his shirt collar were too tight. 'Ladies and gentlemen. Señoras and señors . . .' His voice was loud and uneven. 'I am proud to be here today, as I am sure all of you are, too.' He consulted the prepared speech he was holding. 'Nothing is as vital to a town as commerce, and with this new highway, this *artery*, if you will . . .' He rambled on a while, and people soon began to get restless. Finally he looked up from the paper. 'We have one person to thank for this, and I wish you would all join me in giving her a long, loud ovation. Ladies and gentlemen, señoras and señors. I give you – Mrs Elizabeth-Anne Hale!'

There was a thunderous roar of applause as Elizabeth-Anne strode as quickly through the crowd as her pregnancy would allow. She stepped up on the podium, tears sparkling in her eyes, and nodded several times. Finally she held up her hands. 'Señoras and señors,' she began in a clear, distinct voice, pointedly addressing the Spanish-speaking population first. She smiled and sought out the eyes of her workmen. 'Fellow amigos. Ladies and gentlemen. I feel at a loss for words to describe the way I feel today – the gratitude that I owe your overwhelming work and devotion on this project, and the belief you had in it to sustain it. It would never have been possible without the many, many long and arduous hours you have given – along with your blood, sweat, and tears – to see it through to completion. There were many times when we all thought that it would never happen, that the odds were too overwhelming.

But because we all believed, because we all gave it our very best, a dream has become a reality. And I think we've proved something else, too. That we *can* work together, all of us, regardless of which side of town we come from. I think it's time, since I've come to know so many of you, to stop having a Mexican Town and a Quebeck. It's *my* town. *Your* town. It's *our* town.'

Elizabeth-Anne's voice broke, and tears began to slide down her cheeks. 'I don't know what else to say except . . . I'll never forget what we've accomplished here. Never. Gracias,' she whispered. 'Thank you.'

She stepped heavily down off the podium to thunderous applause.

'Goddamn it, Harvey!' the mayor hissed to someone, 'If that wasn't a campaign speech, I don't know what it was. Next thing we know, she's going to be running for mayor —'

Suddenly Carlos Cortez was at Elizabeth-Anne's side. 'Señora, we have two little problems.'

She turned to him and wiped her eyes. 'What's wrong?'

'First of all, you forgot to cut the ribbon.' He held out the scissors.

She laughed. 'So I'll cut it. And the second problem?'

'Two carloads of travellers . . . well, they just pulled in looking for a room. And we're not even set up yet!'

Her eyes flashed. 'Like hell we aren't! Get them into units three and four right this minute!' she said crisply. Then they both threw back their heads and laughed uproariously. Finally she looked down at the scissors she was holding and thrust them back at him. 'Go run and cut the ribbon so that they can check in. I've got to go find Rosa and see where she had them put all the sheets and blankets!'

It was evening. Carlos Cortez drove them back into town in a borrowed Ford and dropped them off in front

518

of the café. Elizabeth-Anne smiled across the seat at him. 'Thank you for the ride, Señor Cortez,' she said. 'It was very kind of you to bring us back.'

He shrugged. '*De nada*. It is nothing. I'm glad, Mrs Hale –' He stopped suddenly, then smiled. 'This is the first time in years that anyone has taken on the Sextons and beat them in building any kind of business around here. And it is the first time I have ever had the opportunity to prove what I can do – besides yard work. I'm glad.'

'And so am I.' Elizabeth-Anne twisted around in her seat. 'Come on, girls.' She watched as Regina, Charlotte-Anne, and Rebecca piled out of the back of the car.

'Señora?' Carlos said softly.

Her legs half out of the car, Elizabeth-Anne turned around to face him. 'Yes?'

'There is one mystery I still have not solved. I know you ran out of money long ago. Where did you get the rest you needed in order to complete the tourist court?'

'I seem to have a guardian angel,' she said softly.

'It seems, señora, that you do indeed.'

She smiled. 'Well, the girls are waiting.' On an impulse she leaned over and kissed his cheek. '*Buenos noches*, Carlos,' she said using his first name for the first time. 'And thank you.'

'*Buenos noches*, señora,' he said politely.

She shook her head. 'Elizabeth-Anne.'

He grinned suddenly, showing strong white teeth. 'Good night, Elizabeth-Anne.'

She stood outside on Main Street watching him drive off. She took a deep breath and smiled. She felt good for the first time since Zaccheus had left. She felt totally alive. And tired. Absolutely dead tired.

'Off to bed,' she told the girls.

They groaned, but they came up to her, one by one, and kissed her goodnight. Then they dragged themselves reluctantly upstairs.

For a while, Elizabeth-Anne stood outside on the porch. She tilted her head back. The night was cool and clear, exactly the same kind of night as that last one she had spent with him. Even the moon was the same.

'I did all right, Zaccheus, wouldn't you say?' she whispered into the night. 'Wherever you are, I think you'd be proud of me today.'

Then slowly, wearily, she trudged upstairs. She was tired. She didn't ever remember having been this tired in all her life. It was as if all the sleep she had missed during the past several months was cumulatively catching up with her.

She looked in on the girls. They must have been worn out, too. They were already fast asleep.

She went to her room and lowered herself down on the stool in front of her dressing table. She took the pins out of her hair, one by one. Then she moved over to the bed and sat down on the edge of it. For once, she didn't even bother to get undressed. She didn't even take off her sturdy boots. Her eyelids closed even as she was sitting down, and by the time her head touched the pillow she was already sound asleep.

9

That night she dreamed the nightmare again. The same nightmare she had dreamed ever since she was six years old. It never varied. Always, it was the same.

Once again, she was leaping from trapeze to trapeze, but this time it was not Szabo who was chasing her through the burnt-out circus, leaping nimbly through the surprisingly smokeless air — it was Jenny. Jenny with skin hideously charred and blistered, like blackened, wrinkled paper partially smoothed back out. Where Jenny's skin had been burned through, she could see the baked, festering flesh beneath, rotting and crawling with maggots.

Music seemed to come at her from all sides — the madly

racing, insistent chime-like tune of a calliope, ever speeding up faster and faster until the tune was no longer recognizable.

As Elizabeth-Anne dived from one trapeze to another, swinging out over the flames, she caught sight of what lay below her, and she sucked in her breath. A forest of charred tent poles plunged down, down down—down to blazing infinity, to eternal roaring hell itself, and slowly swinging trapezes stretched for mile after endless mile. Sliding slowly and silently under some smooth, mysterious loco-motion, one-dimensional cut-outs of everyone she had ever known — Zaccheus, Szabo, Marikka, The Frittses, and Auntie — glided untouched through the flames. Overhead, from horizon to horizon, the sky was an inverted bowl of fire, oppressively low and red and blazing. The calliope seemed to fuel the flames. As the music gained speed, so too the flames gained power, crackling ever higher and faster.

She glanced behind her and opened her mouth to form a scream, but no sound was forthcoming. Jenny had been chasing her for an eternity, and was gaining on her.

'You stole Zaccheus and Auntie from me, 'Lisbeth-Anne!' Jenny shrieked over and over, her hideous, high-pitched voice echoing back and forth with resonant hollowness. 'You stole from me, and now I'll burn you, you freak!'

Elizabeth-Anne glanced back over her shoulder again. Jenny was gaining even more quickly on her now. Her legs were spread apart, each bare, charred foot balanced on a different trapeze, and the flaming torches she brandished in each hand sent chimeras of orange, wind-blown flames across her shriv-elled skin. Her blackened, wrinkled face was contorted into an evil mask, and bits of her nose and cheeks crumbled away, showing the decomposing skull underneath. ' 'Lisbeth-Annneeee . . .' Jenny's lips were curved in a wide satanic grin, but it was her eyes which were the most terrible thing of all to behold. They bulged and leered and burned deeply with a thousand ferocious fires and seemed to pierce right through Elizabeth-Anne's own.

Jenny arched her body and swung faster, leaping effortlessly ever closer. The crackling torches flared, sending showers of red sparks into the gusting wind. The stench of things burning was overbearing, and Elizabeth-Anne's throat felt raw and scratchy.

Suddenly she could no longer breathe. Her lungs felt as though they were going to burst and she fought for air, but there was none to be had. The fire was sucking up all the available oxygen, fuelling itself into an even greater fury, and she knew that if she did not fall from the trapeze down, down, down into burning, everlasting death, then she would surely suffocate at any moment.

She tried to breathe more deeply. More quickly. More desperately.

Air! Air! *AIR!*

Her body was screaming for air –

The nightmare seemed so real that she writhed and coughed in her sleep. Her head was throbbing violently, and she was racked with convulsions, her arms flailing, her head whipping from side to side on the pillow. She screamed and gasped in agony, her mouth moving furiously but emitting no more sound than pitiful little sobs.

Then suddenly she sat bold upright, at once wide awake.

It was like awakening in a blast furnace. Her bedroom seemed brighter than a thousand blinding suns, and was filled with a crackling roar. The walls pulsated and flickered with orange, white, and yellow, and the floor was a lively sea of flames. Greedy tongues of fire were lapping the walls, tasting the pink cabbage-rose wallpaper and devouring it hungrily.

I'm still dreaming! she thought as she looked around in puzzled confusion. *Why am I not waking up?*

And then she smelled the faint, unmistakable odour of kerosene on top of the stench of burning, and suddenly the terrible realization hit her.

'Oh, my God!' she mouthed in panic. 'I'm no longer dreaming! My bedroom really *is* on fire!'

She sat huddled there on the bed in bewildered fear. She knew she had to try and jump out of bed and make a run for the door, but she couldn't move. *She couldn't move!* She let out a high-pitched keening sound. What was it? Why couldn't she make a run for it through the flames? Why was she *frozen?*

The waves of intense heat were unbearable; everywhere she looked, things shimmered as though seen through rippled glass. She heard a sudden *Whoosh!* and spun her head to her right. She let out a drawn-out whimper. Dancing dervishes of flame were flicking at one of the curtains; then it caught fire, a pillar of flame shooting ferociously up the fabric, all the way to the ceiling.

'Oh, God!' She shielded her face with her arms against the heat. 'I'm going to die,' she whispered to herself, her teeth chattering noisily. 'Me and my baby both, we're gong to *die!*' As if to emphasize this fact, she felt a sharp, violent kick within her belly.

She buried her face in her hands, the tears streaming down her cheeks. 'Oh my God, my God, we're both going to die the horrible death of my nightmares!'

And then, above the hideous roaring and furious crackling she heard another sound. A high-pitched, staccato series of laughs.

'*Ha-ha-ha-ha-ha-ha!*'

It was a musical laugh, a well-modulated scale rippling up and down the register.

Slowly, she let her hands drop. Now even more terror seized her in its grip.

Jenny! That was *her* voice. *She* was somewhere close by.

She turned her face towards the door, forcing herself to look across the floor of fire. Behind the flames, out in the relative safety of the hallway stood Jennifer Sue Sexton. Her face and body shimmered in the radiant waves of heat like some terrible yellow-and-red mirage.

Elizabeth-Anne looked desperately around for an avenue of escape. Somehow she had to get out of this inferno . . . had to escape this terrible madness while there was still time.

"Lisbeth-Anne . . .' Jenny sing-songed in a clear, mellifluous voice. 'You're going to die!'

'Nooooo!' The scream burst forth from Elizabeth-Anne, the very cry of fear and terror which had been welling up inside her even while she had been asleep. Now it burst powerfully from within her, and with it she somehow gained the power of movement. Gone now was the paralysis of terror. She scrambled about the bed on her hands and knees like a caged animal, seeking escape.

The window! I have to get to the window! The porch roof slopes down outside it, and I can slide off it, jumping down to the safety of Main Street! Yes, the window —

— No, not the window! Not with the baby I'm carrying. The impact of the jump would surely kill or damage the unborn child as surely as if I remained trapped in this room and we both burned to death.

'Oh, sweet baby Jesus,' she prayed, 'I can't even jump out the window! I don't even know if . . . if I have the courage to cross that burning floor!'

Jenny smiled crookedly across the room at her. 'I've been waiting for this!' she sang. 'Oh, but how *badly* I've been waiting for this!'

'You're mad!' Elizabeth-Anne sobbed in a choked voice. 'You're a lunatic! Why didn't we all see it before? You're stark, raving *mad*!'

'So I'm mad, am I?' Jenny chortled gleefully, her eyes flashing. 'Well, I know what you're going to be shortly! A pile of ashes! You and that precious *baby* of yours!' Her hysterical peals of laughter reverberated above the roar of the flames . . . seemed to fan them . . . seemed to intensify the hideous devilishness of the nightmare Elizabeth-Anne was living.

'I've got to get out!' Elizabeth-Anne repeated over and

over to herself in a desperate murmur. '*Somehow I've got to get out of here!*'

'You were always afraid of fire, weren't you 'Lisbeth-Anne?' Jenny taunted. 'Oh, but it's a fitting end for you, isn't it? Poetic, I'd say.'

'Oh, God!' Elizabeth-Anne whimpered, thrusting one hand in her mouth. 'Oh, God!' Her eyes darted about wildly. Only the bed was not yet a sea of fire, but she knew it was only a matter of seconds before it, too, would erupt into flames. And then what? She scrabbled around the mattress, her hair falling down over her face, her eyes wild with fear. She couldn't jump out the window to safety; she couldn't even gather up the courage to jump off the bed, race to the door, and go rushing out. She couldn't! *Not through fire. Anything but fire.*

This can't be happening, she screamed silently to herself. *No! It can't be! I'm dreaming. It's an extension of my nightmares. That's all it is!*

At that very moment, the first tongues of flame shot up around the bed, gorging themselves on the sheets.

She squeezed her eyes shut and pounded her forehead with her fists. '*I've got to wake up! I've got to wake up!*'

''Lisbeth-Anne,' Jenny sang liltingly, 'it's not going to help you to shut your eyes. 'Lisbeth-Anne, you're going to *burn!*'

Elizabeth-Anne clapped her hands over her ears. 'Stop it!' she screamed, shaking her head furiously. 'Stop it *stop it* STOP IT!'

'How does it feel, 'Lisbeth-Anne? Is it *hot*? Is it *smoky*? Do you smell your burning flesh yet? *Is it like it was with the CIRCUS?*'

'*STOP IT!*'

'Oh, no, 'Lisbeth-Anne. This is far, far too precious. And look, you're not the only one who's going to burn. You're not going to be alone. Look here, 'Lisbeth-Anne! Look at what Jenny's got!'

Elizabeth-Anne slowly opened her eyes. They were stinging and gritty from all the smoke. She gazed at Jenny through the haze of tears.

'See what I got, 'Lisbeth-Anne?' Jenny held up a can. 'More *kerosene!*'

'Help me, Jenny!' Elizabeth-Anne pleaded, one hand clutching her belly, the other one reaching out in despair. 'Oh God, Jenny, please help me get out of here!'

Jenny laughed scornfully. 'Oh no, you're going to *burn!* You and that precious *baby* you're carrying! See you later, 'Lisbeth-Anne.' She gave a little wave of her fingertips. 'I've got to finish what I've started. I've got to go douse the bedroom of that sweet little litter of yours. Three of them, aren't there? All peacefully asleep, I noticed.'

Despite the roasting heat Elizabeth-Anne felt an icy, sickening panic shuddering through her bones. Jenny was not only going to kill her – she was after the girls too! Somehow, she had to protect them from this maddened, murderous creature.

The rushing of her blood and the pounding of her heart screamed through her body. Forgotten for the moment was the floor of fire and the flames roaring angrily up the walls. She knew what she had to do. The mother instinct in her was aroused, and more than blood now pumped through her veins. The adrenalin rushed potently through her too.

With a cry of rage, Elizabeth-Anne flung herself off the bed just as it went up in flames. She hurled herself towards the open door, snatching up the first weapon which caught her eye – Auntie's silver hairbrush lying on the dressing table. She was not even aware of how much heat the handle had absorbed. She only knew that somehow – by whatever means were at her disposal – she had to stop Jenny – and quickly. She had to protect her children. Nothing else mattered.

Jenny's mouth hung wide with surprise as Elizabeth-Anne leapt through the flames, the brush held high. Then it came arcing down with all the force and lightning speed Elizabeth-Anne could muster. Jenny saw it coming, but too late. She let out a shriek as the brush slammed down on her skull. Then her eyes rolled upwards in their sockets and she crumpled to the floor, her hands letting go of the big square tin of kerosene. It thumped down to the floor beside her.

Elizabeth-Anne raced down the hall to the children's room. 'Regina! 'Becca! Charlotte-Anne!' she screamed at the top of her lungs. And she told herself to hurry –

– To hurry before the fire spread even more, cutting off their escape –

– Before the can of kerosene Jenny dropped got so hot it would explode.

The girls were already awake, jolted from their sleep by her screams. They were sitting up in their beds, clutching the covers against their necks. The moment she flung open their door, they saw the orange, flickering hallway outside and stared at her with open-mouthed terror.

'Come *on*!' Elizabeth-Anne screamed at them. 'What are you waiting for!'

At once they scrambled obediently out of bed. She shepherded them quickly down the hall, past the blazing conflagration that was her bedroom, past Jenny, who was lying on the floor moaning, shaking her head fuzzily. Their footsteps drummed a rapid tattoo down the stairs.

From upstairs came a mighty crash, and the entire building shook. Chunks of plaster rained down on them. Rebecca glanced up with a terrified expression.

'Hurry!' Elizabeth-Anne screamed.

Suddenly, miraculously, they were outside on the porch. The night felt invigorating, fresh, and cool. Coughing and gasping, they stumbled into the middle of Main Street and skirted Jenny's big, new Cadillac, fire-engine red and gleaming, which was parked right outside the café. They bent over and breathed deep, noisy, grateful lungfuls of air.

Never before had fresh air tasted quite so rich and sweet.

Elizabeth-Anne coiled her arms around the girls and pulled them close. They stood huddled together, gazing up at the top floor of the café, their chins raised, their sweat-soaked faces flickering.

'Mama? Why doesn't the fire engine come?' Rebecca cried quietly.

'It will, darling, but I'm afraid it's too late,' Elizabeth-Anne whispered. She shook her head, overcome with an indescribable, inconsolable sadness.

The entire top floor was now a fiery pyre, an inferno of wind-whipped flames, and as she watched, a flaming timber beam crashed down to the ground floor with a massive shower of yellow sparks. The first floor started catching fire too, the old dry timbers of the house feeding the greedily roaring flames, bathing Main Street with the blinding, flickering glare of a noonday sun. Everything reflected the fire. The mirror-like finish of Jenny's car, the windows of the rooming house across the street. From everywhere, people came running out of doors, and a crowd swiftly began to gather, staring up at the blazing fire as if mesmerized. In the distance, the clanging of the fire engine could be heard, but the loudest noise was that of the raging fire itself.

Elizabeth-Anne shook her head wearily. In there, amidst the holocaust, were all her family belongings, every precious trifle and treasure, every photograph and bibelot, every love letter Zaccheus had ever given her – the fire was consuming it all with a marked disregard for financial and sentimental value. The sense of loss she felt was immeasurable, and a lone tear streaked down her cheek, the salt coolness making her scorched face smart as if it were on fire. She sniffed and then wrinkled her nose; she could smell the revolting odour of her own singed hair.

She tightened her lips, suddenly angry with herself. Her hair would grow back. Furniture and property could be replaced. Things which were destroyed were not really lost – she would forever treasure them in her memory. What mattered was that she and the girls were alive. That was *all* that mattered. Everything else was replaceable.

A sudden murmur swept through the crowd, and Elizabeth-Anne turned quickly to look. A long gleaming white Packard was pulling up on the other side of the street, its white headlights cutting a wide swath. She recognized the car instantly; so did everyone else. It was Tex Sexton's.

The car door slammed and Sexton got out. He glanced up at the inferno. Then he noticed his wife's Cadillac parked in front of the blazing café, and he craned his neck as if looking around for somebody. Then quickly he rushed at the crowd, pushing aside people, peering closely into the women's faces, shaking others by their clothes. Elizabeth-Anne could hear his voice rising: '*Jenny! Jenny!* Have you seen my wife? Have you? Where is my wife? *Jenny!*'

Elizabeth-Anne closed her eyes.

Suddenly a gasp swept through the crowd. Somebody began to scream; someone else pointed to the roof of the café. The first scream was followed by another, and yet another. Then a dead silence descended on the onlookers. Backlighted by the fire, a lone figure was silhouetted on the roof, dashing about madly, laughing hysterically.

'Oh my God!' Elizabeth-Anne whispered in agony, her lips trembling. 'Oh my *God*, it's *Jenny*!' She buried her face in her hands. 'Not again! Must I witness a horrible death by fire again!'

'*Jenny!*' Tex Sexton's voice boomed out resonantly. '*Jenny! Come down from there!*'

Jenny staggered about, arms outstretched, fingers splayed, as if she were trying to ward off the intense heat. 'If you want me to come down, you'll have to come and get me!' she sang out.

Sexton looked around desperately. 'Go in there, somebody!' he yelled. 'Go in and save her! I'll give a thousand dollars to the man who goes in and saves her!'

The crowd suddenly turned their heads away.

'You! I'll give you two thousand!' Sexton shook the man nearest him, but the man turned away wordlessly.

'Save her!' he implored someone else, but he, too, turned away.

'Isn't there a man here who wants to earn ten thousand dollars!'

Still no one spoke. Finally, Tex took a deep breath. Then he dashed to the house. There was a scream of agony and then he was through the flames, fighting his way inside.

It was at that very moment that the can of kerosene exploded and the house collapsed in upon itself. Everyone drew back as the boiling, flaming timbers came crashing down, one after the other, throwing showers of sparks hundreds of feet up in the air.

The last time anyone saw Jenny, she was standing on the roof, arms outstretched as the roof gave way under her. The next instant she was gone, swallowed up by the flames.

The last anyone heard of Jenny was her wild, shrill, madness-filled laughter reverberating from within the angrily crackling flames.

And then nothing more could be heard but the sounds of the fire.

The stranglehold the Sextons had held over the county was no more.

EPILOGUE

1928

QUEBECK, TEXAS

Elizabeth-Anne led the little boy along the edge of the newly-planted lemon groves, holding onto his tiny hand. Their faces were dappled by the early morning sun filtering through the shifting patterns of the leaves in the slight breeze. Insects buzzed about and blackbirds perched quietly on the power lines which ran along the other side of the highway. Across the asphalt lanes, barren brown fields stretched to the horizon, and there that startlingly clear, powder-blue sky began, filled with high puffball clouds.

She walked slowly so that her son had no trouble keeping up with her. She was dressed in a beige skirt and an elegant, high-necked lace blouse much like the ones Auntie used to favour, and the boy was wearing a navy blue sailor's suit trimmed in white. Occasionally a car would roar past on the highway, and the sudden rush of wind felt warm against their faces. Despite the early hour, it was already hot out.

Elizabeth-Anne turned around. A few yards behind them, the three girls were sitting in the back of the big black car, fanning themselves with newspapers. The top was down, and Carlos Cortez was sitting behind the wheel. He was driving them to the train station. The trunk was tied down to keep it from flying open; it was filled to overflowing with boxes and suitcases.

Elizabeth-Anne got down on one knee so that her face was level with her son's. She coiled one arm around his shoulders and pointed down the road. 'Take a good look at it, son,' she said quietly. 'That will one day be yours. That, and a whole lot more.'

Zaccheus Hale Junior looked at the complex of buildings and then up at her. 'It's the tourist court,' he said in his clear, tiny voice.

'The tourist court,' she repeated softly. She took a deep breath, shook her head, and squeezed his shoulder affectionately. 'Zaccheus, Zaccheus. It's not just a *tourist court*. It's the *Hale* Tourist Court! It's our *lives*!'

'Lookit all the shiny cars, Mama,' he marvelled. 'Have you ever seen so many?'

Elizabeth-Anne smiled. Her swift gaze had already counted eighteen cars, and she automatically calculated what eighteen occupied rooms added to her coffers overnight. She could barely subdue her excitement. 'That's nothing, darling,' she said. 'You just wait and see! Soon there'll be ten tourist courts and a hundred and eighty cars! And then a thousand tourist courts with –' Suddenly she laughed helplessly as her ambitions overcame her. As she got back up she lifted him up and held him high. She let out the same playful groan she always did lately when she picked him up. 'My, my, but you're getting big and heavy, young man,' she said in a mock bass voice.

Zaccheus giggled and flung his arms around her neck. Then, slowly at first, but with gathering momentum, she began a pirouette at the side of the road. Faster and faster she spun until both of them became a whirling dervish.

He squealed happily and she laughed with delight. Finally she slowed, dizzy and panting, and staggered to a stop.

Suddenly his face creased into a frown and he became solemn. 'Why are we leaving, Mama?'

She looked into his eyes for a long time. 'Because your Mama has a lot of work to do, darling,' she said slowly.

'Because she's going to build many more tourist courts like that one.'

'But why so many? Isn't one enough?'

'Because it's a dream I have, darling. It's something which I have to do. Something which I love doing. That's what dreams are for, you know – to make them into reality.'

Suddenly she felt his hands at her neck. 'What's this, Mama? You wear it all the time.'

She glanced down at herself. He was holding up the pansy charm Zaccheus had given her so long ago, and it caught the sunlight, the crystal flashing brightly, the pansy looking as fresh and velvety as the moment it had been pressed flat. She smiled as he rubbed the smooth crystal with his fingers. 'It's pretty, Mama.' He looked up at her. 'I want it.'

'Of course you do,' she said, laughing, 'but I'm afraid your Mama wants it too.'

'What is it?'

'A flower.'

'What kind of flower?'

For a moment her face grew strangely pensive. Then she smiled radiantly. 'It's called a love flower.'

'A love flower,' he repeated, and for a moment he digested that thoughtfully. 'I love your love flower,' he said finally. His face brightened. 'May I have it?'

'Not yet, darling.'

'Perhaps tomorrow?' he coaxed hopefully. 'Or next week?'

She shook her head. 'I don't think so, darling. It's for a girl. Maybe one of your sisters will eventually get it. But when you're old enough, you'll have that.' She nodded towards the tourist court.

'I love you, Mama.'

'And I love you too, young man.'

'Someday I'm going to marry you.'

'Oh ho! You are, are you?' She looked at him closely,

and the breath suddenly caught in her throat. She felt a stifling wave of heat, and a thousand pinpricks rippled up and down her arms and tingled at the nape of her neck. For an instant, the present merged with the past. For the first time, she noticed just how much like his father little Zaccheus looked. Her heart skipped a beat and then pounded on heavily. For a moment the most intense joy and the deepest sorrow she had ever felt washed over her and merged, bittersweet and painful, a feeling so tremendously powerful that she did not know if she could survive it. What was it that had made her aware of the resemblance? The sun? The shadows? Or was it simply an illusion?

She inspected him more closely, stroking the blond curls out of his eyes. No, it was not an illusion; she could see that now. He was Zaccheus' son – a miniature Zaccheus, right down to his ear lobes. His eyes, his lips, it was all there, an eerie reincarnation. Looking at him now, she realized, must be like looking at the mirror image of his father when he had been the same age.

Strange that she should only notice that now. Why hadn't she seen it before?

She smiled as she carried him back to the car. Carlos Cortez saw them coming and got out. He held the door open for her and she climbed in, putting Zaccheus on her lap. Cortez walked around the front of the car, got back in on the driver's side, and slammed the door shut. He looked over at her questioningly.

Elizabeth-Anne paused hesitantly for a moment. Dozens of conflicting emotions were bombarding her from all sides, now that she was set to leave Quebeck. Here she had lived through good times and bad, happy times and sad. Here she had had to fight against all odds to achieve her dream, and here she had triumphed in no small way.

'Well?' Carlos Cortez said finally. 'You want to leave or stay?'

She looked at him for a long intense moment. Then quickly, as though she was afraid she would change her mind at the last minute, she inclined her head in an affirmative nod.

'Which is it?'

'We leave,' she said firmly.

'Dallas?' he asked. 'As planned?'

She shook her head. 'Where's the single largest concentration of population in the country, as well as the finest network of highways?'

'The East Coast. New York.'

She nodded.

'Well?'

'New York,' she said. 'Of course.'

He eyed her strangely and then his lips broke into a wide grin. She heard the engine under the hood cough to life. The gears meshed, and the gravel crunched under the tyres as the big car slowly began to nose forward. Carlos twisted around to look back over his shoulder and he swung the car around in a circle. They headed in the opposite direction, surging past the Hale Tourist Court and then picking up speed.

Elizabeth-Anne did not once look back. She sat erect and proud as the tourist court was left behind.

Am I sad, now that I have truly decided to leave? she asked herself.

She frowned momentarily. No, strangely enough she did not feel saddened at all. She felt . . . yes! Liberated. It was simply a matter of knowing that the Quebeck chapter of her life had drawn to a close. Auntie was dead and buried. Zaccheus was gone. Jenny and Tex no longer stood in her way. The rooming house was sold, and so was the new café she had built on the ruins of the one which had burned down. There was nothing left here but the ghosts of the past. Good ghosts and bad ghosts, but ghosts all the same. Ghosts and the tourist court. She would have to come back here now and again to check up on it, but for the time being it was being run efficiently by trusted help, with Rosa in charge. Yes, it was indeed high time she moved on. She realized, finally, that she did not need to stay here in order to be close to what she and Zaccheus had once shared. She had those treasured precious years locked away in her mind, and she could recall them instantly at will, reliving them in her memory whenever she so pleased. Besides, she always had the children. Because of them, wherever she would go, no matter how far and wide she travelled, Zaccheus would always be beside her, invisible but alive in her heart.

Above all, she told herself, *I have the children.*

They mattered and the tourist courts she had planned on building mattered. The tourist court here was but the beginning. The beginning and, in a way, the end, too. The end of yet another portion of her life. Yet it was also the means to achieve yet another splendid chapter. That was what life was – an endless series of rich, adventurous chapters unfolding before her. No, Quebeck was no longer important. What *was* important was the future which loomed large and bright and glorious on her horizon. She could see that plainly now. Despite all the pain she had had to suffer in the past, she had been born, she decided suddenly, under the luckiest of lucky stars indeed.

Her eyes gleamed with aquamarine anticipation.

How many other people had so much waiting for them down the road?

SINS

Judith Gould

Helene Junot – young, lovely head of an international
magazine empire. Women envy her. Men desire her. But
behind her ravishing beauty and her brilliant brain lies the
memory of a nightmare. A nightmare Helene is
determined to avenge.

SINS is the story of a daring yet vulnerable woman with
the courage to use any weapon to achieve her burning
ambition.

A woman whose search for happiness and revenge
threatens to lead her to deadly sins.

FUTURA PUBLICATIONS
FICTION
0 7088 2400 5

THE LOVEMAKERS

Judith Gould

It was the world's most luxurious hotel empire – a monument to the ruthless determination of four powerful women, counting no cost in the drive of their ambition.

Elizabeth – fragile and vulnerable on the surface, diamond-hard beneath, whose struggle to bring up her children in New York never caused her to lose sight of her dream . . .

Charlotte – sensuality's slave, who deserted her family for an Italian prince, only to find her ecstasy turned to nightmare in war-torn Italy . . .

Anna – orphaned, anonymous, unaware of her noble heritage, who followed a path of gold from the ashes of World War II . . .

Dorothy – poor little rich girl, target of her father's bitterness, whose multi-million dollar legacy made her powerful, desirable, ultimately invincible . . .

Four stunning women; four passionate lives; four patterns of success.

FUTURA PUBLICATIONS
FICTION
0 7088 2917 1

FAME AND FORTUNE

Kate Coscarelli

In glamorous Beverly Hills, casual sex is taken for granted, driving ambition is commonplace – and true love is the rarest commodity of all.

In search of that elusive emotion are four women, close friends, and all facing major upheavals in their lives:

PEACH – blonde, beautiful, wealthy and newly widowed – shocks her set by taking her pleasure with a younger man – Hollywood's hottest glamour boy.

Within the walls of her exclusive beauty salon, GRACE shares the whispered secrets of the super-rich. Few suspect that Grace's glossy veneer hides a brutal past and dark secret of her own.

For years, MAGGIE has played second fiddle to her high-powered husband Kirk. Now she's the most sought-after designer in Beverly Hills. But is Kirk man enough to take his wife's success?

LAURA – perfect wife, perfect mother, perfect hostess. Surely that's enough to keep any man? So why is her handsome doctor husband seen around with sex-symbol Ghilly Jordan?

In the bestselling tradition of LACE and SCRUPLES, FAME AND FORTUNE has it all – exciting sex, horrifying violence, passionate struggles for power, security, survival – played against a glittering background of wealth, glamour and luxurious sensuality.

FUTURA PUBLICATIONS
FICTION
0 7088 2611 3